"Sarina's Archers"

formally published in ebook format as "Sarina's Bowman"
which has been totally revised for this edition.

Millfield
Publishing

Sarina's Archers

Spiderwize
Remus House
Coltsfoot Drive
Woodston
Peterborough
PE2 9BF

www.spiderwize.com

A CIP catalogue record for this book is available from the British Library.

ISBN: 978-1-912694-14-3

Dedication:

To Helen, for making it possible,
and to Tina for her expertise.

Thanks to Amanda Sinclair for her cover design.

Map of Fameral

(Not to Scale)

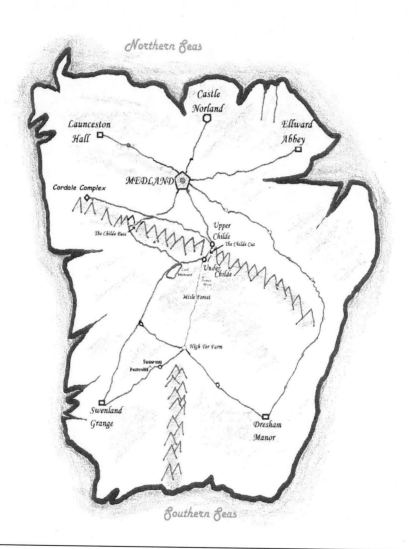

Introduction to the "Sarina" Series

While giving her name to this series, **Sarina**, a racing kertle, a horse like animal, is a major 'character' in the first book, "**Sarina's Challenge**," but only plays a supporting role in the books that follow.

The Sarina Saga tells the story of the island continent and people of Fameral as seen through the eyes of the main characters in each of the seven planned books.

"**Sarina's Archers**" follows on directly after **Sarina's Challenge** but should be read after the second book "**Sarina's Smith**," which is set mid-way through the time frame of "**Archers.**" While minor 'spoilers' for each other, these two books can be read independently but are best read in the order indicated.

The whole series comprises, so far: -

"Sarina's Challenge"

"Sarina's Smith"

"Sarina's Archers"

"Five days to the veld, five velds to the alphen, five alphens to the bathern and five batherns to the turn"

(Children's chanting song, taught to teach the Femeral calendar.)

~~~~~~~~~~~~~~~~~~~~

"Five hours to the phase, five phases to the day,

(therefore, twenty-five hours to the day - Femeral time basis)"

~~~~~~~~~~~~~~~~~~~~

"Five Stips to the Slend, five Slends to the Strand"

(Basic Femeral currency system.)

Chapter 1

Bryland was in a state of panic, his world had come crashing down and he was running from the humiliation that had suddenly overwhelmed him. Well, he was running as fast as one good and one gammy leg would allow him. Until a few hours ago he was proud to be known as Bryland Doltaary of The House of Swenland. Now that title screamed of shame and disgrace.

He had been a senior member of The House of Swenland's stable staff, responsible for the training of the top-flight racing kertles. Now his master, Neldon Swenland, had been proved to be a cheat and a liar of the worst kind and had been taken away from The Challenge field by the guardians in ignominy with his hands tied behind his back. Bryland had been involved in the young lord's schemes without realising that was what he was doing. But his innocence was of no consequence, the whole world would know that Bryland had trained the three kertles used in the deceit.

He had been a naive fool to trust the young Lord Swenland, the fact the he had been deluded into the plot was of no significance; it was he who had carefully trained the three racing kertles to be able to perform in different ways. Now he could see why Neldon had been so pleased when their top racing dam had laid a clutch from which three identical siblings had hatched; he must have been planning this scheme for several turns.

The best of the three had been trained to run the full five leagues of the Challenge course while the next had been restricted to racing just three leagues but much faster. The third kertle had received even more special and highly unusual training making her good at racing a league at top speed, resting and then racing another league. With the hindsight that the final day of the Challenge had brought, it was obvious what Neldon had tried to achieve; to use two kertles to run the full course, changing mount after the first league and then back again at the end. Why hadn't Bryland seen what had been going on?

'You're a fool Bryland Doltaary!' he berated himself as he fled the Challenge ground where even now he could hear the echoes of the cheers that rang out as the result was announced. He made his way back to the city, dragging his lame leg along as fast as he could back to the Swenland Mansion, right in the centre of Medland. As he entered the Pentangle he could see crowds starting to gather, eager to get good vantage points around the balcony where the award ceremony would take place. The last thing he wanted was to see a lot of people, someone might recognise him, so he slipped around the government building and made his way to the back of the Swenland Mansion.

He let himself in via the rear gate and, as he had expected, the central courtyard was completely deserted. All the stable staff, and probably the whole of the household entourage, was up at the Challenge finishing ground. He made his way to his own quarters and quickly stuffed a large bag with the things he thought he would need. Instinctively he only selected nondescript clothes; any garments that bore any colour or insignia of The House of Swenland were avoided. Already the outline of a plan was taking shape in his mind. The one problem was that he only had one good thick travelling cloak and that was in Swenland colours. It would have to do, now the turn was entering the Planting bathern he couldn't survive out in the wilds without its warmth and insulating properties for very long, but he would have to look to change it as soon as he could.

He then made his way to the kitchen and supplied himself with food that could be easily carried and easily eaten as he travelled. This was helped by the fact that great platters had been prepared for a buffet to feed the whole household when they returned from the Challenge. He created a rather large space on one plate that held roast kitchen fowl portions. His guilt at this vandalism was somewhat assuaged by the feeling that The House of Swenland owed him a great debt; his loyalty to the house had cost him his social standing, his future and worst of all, his self-respect.

From the kitchen he made his way to the stables and looking around the stalls, most of which stood empty, he selected a good two turn old dray and began to put saddle and tackle on him. The

Swenland stables was home to kertles of all types, not just the racing animals that had been Bryland's main focus of attention. The one he selected was of the type called drays, strong sturdy animals, used for everyday riding or haulage; the even heavier ones were used to pull ploughs out in the farms. The gelded animal responded well to the young trainer, for while Bryland had supposedly only been involved with the racers, he had never shirked the everyday tasks that the lesser kertles required to be done. Most of the Swenland animals knew and trusted him.

He thought through what he was about to do and realised that he needed to take a night shroud for his mount and waterproof bedding for himself. He raided the store room and soon had the dray well loaded with all his provisions and equipment. He felt guilty at taking all this equipment, let alone the kertle, but decided that it was the least The House of Swenland owed him; after all, he hadn't drawn any pay for two alphens.

Finally, he was prepared, and he made his way from the Swenland mansion, using the smaller side streets as much as possible. He wended his way through the outskirts of the town and into the Dreslah Park. The wide green spaces of this elite recreation area were a pleasant change from the cramped confines of the city streets. The Park was empty at this time of day, especially on the final day of the challenge. He took no pleasure in seeing the majestic sweep of this formal recreation area and very quickly he was out of the manicured grounds of the park and onto a road that he knew led up to the main road that would take him all the way to Upper Childe.

He had named the dray. 'Rufran' several alphens ago and the kertle seemed to respond to the name for he made little snickers whenever

Bryland addressed him. He was good honest working kertle with no real vices, other than a liking for small biscuit treats. They trotted along at a gentle pace although Bryland would have preferred to have travelled much faster; so anxious was he to put Medland behind him. He was desperate to leave a lot of things behind him; The House of Swenland and Neldon Swenland in particular. The worst thing was his feeling of disgrace and the humiliation at having been involved in such a reprehensible undertaking. The sooner he was clear of all that and could build a new life for himself the better.

Just what that new life would be he had no idea. No doubt it would have to involve kertle training or husbandry of some kind, that's where his expertise lay. But in that way lay problems; he was well known as a kertle trainer and he wanted to hide his previous existence, he would have to find something else to make a living. He didn't want to be just a common labourer but that might be all that was open to him now.

His route took him away from the metropolis and through some high class residential areas before he reached a more rural part of this former Norland countryside. In his haste and disturbed state, he barely noticed the subtle change of the countryside as he left the last of the residential areas and entered the more pastoral part of south Norland. The House of Norland may have been dissolved ten turns ago, but the legacy of the former Lord's House was a well-maintained country side with good roads and neat tidy, well-kept villages, so very different from the rough and ready nature of the House of Swenland domain in the South West of the continent.

He slept that night in a small copse where there was ample grazing for Rufran and he could use the saplings and dense vegetation around their base as a wind break. Not wanting to draw attention to himself he decided to not build a fire although his body ached for a hot drink. He satisfied his thirst from one of the flagons of wine that he had liberated. The alcohol did help him get to sleep but did nothing to help him keep warm and he awoke several times shivering with the cold, the nights could be quite chill this early in the planting bathern.

It was a miserable night and in the morning light as a thin mist covered the trees he struggled from his sleeping furs and decided that he would light a fire to make a hot drink. The activity and the warmth from the small blaze that he soon had going, cheered his despondent mood. Cradling a mug of kandrel to warm his hands he thought through things a bit more clearly in the fresh morning air. He would have to sort out this living rough business; it had been a terrible night. As he sat he rubbed his chin in contemplation and felt the stubble that had grown since he shaved the morning before. It was then that he realised he had forgotten to pick his razor and strop in his hurry to leave the Swenland Mansion.

He turned over his outer sleeping bag and discovered that the underside was wet from where it had lain on the ground. He could easily have put some of the bracken and ferns under his bedding to keep it off the ground; that would have been a more comfortable mattress to lie on anyway. He had learnt his first lesson in living out in the wilds. He pulled out the inner furs and threw them over a branch to let the air dry them off a bit.

He tended to Rufran and was pleased at how well the kertle had coped with this sudden change to a rustic existence; the animal was used to sleeping in a comfortable straw strewn stable but seemed to have survived the night in the open without a problem. In due course they continued on their way through the well-tended and well-maintained farmlands dotted with pleasant neat villages. Bry quickly made a better job of living rough as the days progressed. Half way through their third day on the road, in the late afternoon the buildings of Upper Childe were clearly in sight.

As they passed through the buildings at the edge of the town Bryland decided; he would take off his Swenland cloak to hide his identity and then seek lodgings for the night in a suitable inn. He passed one or two that didn't seem very welcoming and found himself at 'The Northern Star.' The name didn't encourage him much, but the timber framed, black and white inn was in good repair and the central courtyard, when he entered it was clean and tidy, which spoke volumes for the housekeeping standards of the establishment.

A groom appeared when he heard Rufran's claw sets rattling on the cobbles and came over to the new arrival. Bryland negotiated a stall for Rufran and once confident in the competence of the groom, left the kertle in his care. He took his personal bag and headed into the inn where he had been told he could get a hot meal and lodging for the night.

At first, he was quite happy with the price he was quoted for the accommodation of him and his kertle but with a jolt he realised that the money he had with him would not pay for too many such nights. He was no longer a man of means.

As he sat in a corner of the inn's main room he pondered over the options that lay before him; they were pitifully small. There were a few regulars in the bar and their conversation was all about the

Challenge that had taken place in far off Medland. The news of the result had obviously only just reached the town. This filled Bryland with some concern, he could do without people focussing on the disgrace that had befallen The House of Swenland.

'Seems we have a new Lord Norland,' the Landlord said to the company in general. Guardian Felshaw was in for his lunch earlier and he said that signals had just arrived. So, I was right, that was the son of the old lord who was here a couple of velds ago with Chamberlain Draxen! Seems he won the Challenge and claimed the reinstatement of The House of Norland as his prize. He's also marrying the young Lady Swenland, so there are big changes afoot.'

'Bout time too,' one of the old men sitting right up at the bar contributed to general agreement around the room. There then ensued a general discussion on how bad things had been since the dissolution and how much better they would be if The House of Norland was reinstated and the new Lord was as good as his late father. The main bone of contention seemed to be the wages that some fifth masters were prepared to pay the common farm labourers.

'Well maybe things might change with the new Lord Norland, his father was always a fair man,' one of the older regulars said to the assembled company.

'Yeah, and hogs might fly!' one of the younger men scoffed, 'there's only one way for us common working men to get a fair wage and that's to gang together, to unite and force the fifth masters and their farmers to pay us what they should.'

'And just how you going to do that then?' another man asked.

'By refusing to get ribbond at the hiring fairs unless they offer us a decent rate, that's how!'

'Now look here young Natheal,' the former speaker said, 'just how does refusing to take a job when it's offered help anyone. Just makes you worse off, as far as I can see.'

'But not if everyone says the same thing,' Natheal replied, getting on to his feet and grabbing everyone's attention. 'If all the workers at a hiring fair refuse to accept an unfair offer of work, the farmers have to improve what they offer. We did it down at Vale Farm last turn and made the old devil pay us twice what he was offering at the start of the fair.'

'Is that the Vale Farm where the farmer has had to sell up because he couldn't make a profit when he sold his crops?' a voice from the back of the room asked.

'If he can't manage his affair's that is not my problem,' Natheal replied dismissively, 'he'd been robbing his workers for years, his permanents as well as the fee earners. The point I'm trying to make is that if we workers gang together we can get a much better life for ourselves. Look at me, worked most of the past turn and the best I can afford to wear to come here tonight is this tatty old waistcoat,' and he held out the sides of the ragged leather garment to make his point.

'So how does this scheme of yours work then?' the landlord asked, not that he was really interested, he just liked it when a good discussion took place, it kept the coins trickling over his counter.

'If enough people get together the farmers soon learn that they can't get the workers they need at the paltry wages they're offering,' Natheal explained.

'But there are always some who are desperate for work and will take the first place they are offered, whatever the wage,' another person said.

'Yeah, well then, we just have to make it clear to them that they would be better off waiting for that better offer,' Natheal said with a sly grin.

'You mean you beat them up if they don't do as you tell them,' the same voice said from the rear of the room.

'Well sometimes some gentle persuasion is necessary,' Natheal replied, 'now let's have another round.' This was met with a general cheer and Natheal knew he had won another bar room argument. He'd been travelling all round North Fameral trying to get support for his radical ways of thinking and met with some resistance and some support. He'd been to Launceston and then to Norland and Ellward. Now he was on his way to the towns and villages south of the Childe Mountains. He expected to get more support for his ideas down in the Swenland Fifths where the farmers were notorious for the tight-fisted dealings with their workers. He'd not had much luck so far up north; the Launceston and Ellward fifths seemed to pay reasonable rates. He had, however, been able to get some women workers on his side. This was largely due to the efforts of his twin sister, Pardrea who had taken his revolutionary ideas very much to heart and had promised to do what she could to help the cause.

Little did anyone in that bar room realise that getting better wages for the workers was just the tip of what the Lathers hoped to achieve. Their parents had, unintentionally given their offspring a twisted view of the world. The parents own ineptitude had meant that times were always hard in the Lather household and the blame was always put on the ruling families and their fifths. The elder children, Natheal and Pardrea, were indoctrinated at a young age into thinking that all the troubles of the world stemmed from the four, formally five ruling dynasties. From there it was but a short step to their believing that by overthrowing the ruling families all Fameral's troubles would be solved. As they grew, the twins began to make plans to bring about a revolution. They soon realised that they needed to get the support of the common people and they hatched their plan to disrupt the hiring fairs. When Jedraah Balental at Vale Farm had gone bust, they were secretly delighted and blind to the hardship that ensued among the permanent farm workers who looked to Jedraah. They saw that episode as the start of their revolution to free Fameral.

All this animosity, that was rife in that bar room, was a total revelation to Bryland; living down in the south western part of Fameral he had been sheltered from the discontent that had been widespread in the central and northern regions and, living in the Swenland household, he had been unaware of the dealings out in the Swenland fifths. He would have liked to hear more of this different viewpoint, but the conversation was dragged back in an unwelcome direction by the landlord who regaled his audience with an account of how Lord Neldon Swenland had tried to win the challenge by cheating and had been taken into custody.

'That's all I know as yet,' the landlord replied to the questions that were thrown at him, 'you'll have to wait till Guardian Felshaw is back in here later. He may have found out more details by then, but I don't think he'll have heard any more than I've just told you.'

Bryland sat in a daze, the shock that he had suffered over the past few days was back with a vengeance. The opinions expressed and implied around the barroom had only helped to increase his state of panic. The underlying hatred of The House of Swenland was an unwelcome revelation. He felt very alone and isolated.

He finished the tankard of ale and made his way up to the room he had been allocated. As he undressed for bed he realised that he might as well make the most of the comparative luxury that the inn provided; he was headed into the wilder parts of the island continent and such niceties would be few and far between. As he snuggled into the clean sheets and feathered mattress the comfort they provided did little to lessen the loneliness of his situation. He was cutting himself off from a relatively comfortable and high-status life. Everything was about to change. Had already started to change! Lady Janilla was marrying this new Lord Norland. That raised some questions; what had happened to Lady Parina? As the eldest daughter she should be married before her younger sibling. But that had been a forlorn hope, the poor girl was extremely plain, not to say downright ugly.

Bryland had always thought the jokes and comments about Parina's looks were very cruel. She had been very kind to him and always was very grateful whenever he had brought out her riding kertle. He had noticed, from afar, that she had the sweetest nature and was always thinking of others. The other servants seemed to just see her looks and right her off, but Bryland had always seen through the exterior and knew she was a very caring and intelligent young woman. It was true that while Parina was very plain, her sister Janilla was a real beauty. Not that she ever made a big thing of it.

The Swenland girls, he knew, were very nice people and their brother had appeared to be so as well. The young Lord Swenland had befriended the young stable lad when he had first been appointed to The House and had helped him develop his skills with the kertles. As his prowess with the racing animals increased, Bryland had been admitted to Neldon's inner circle of friends. His status had risen, and he had enjoyed the privileges that his position had brought. Now that was all behind him, he would have to make his way in the real world.

The next morning, he luxuriated in washing in warm water from a jug brought by one of the serving wenches and as he dressed he looked at himself with a critical eye. He knew he was average sort of height and had a fairly athletic build, neither too slim nor too fat; the healthy exercise he got in his stable hand duties kept him in good shape. He looked critically at his face in the mirror on the dresser and decided that he was not bad looking although he hesitated to think of himself as handsome. He had nothing to be ashamed of, he decided. Except that was, for his twisted left leg.

Some birth defect had ensured that the limb had grown with an abnormal twist that gave him a permanent limp and he had always assumed would put females off wanting to get to know him. Ah well he couldn't do anything about the deformity; he would just have to accept the disadvantage he thought it gave him.

Chapter 2

In Medland the festivities seemed to go on forever; the end of Challenge ball had been a joyous event celebrating not only the outcome of this turn's Challenge but two impending weddings. Janilla Swenland had specifically invited the ladies Katrina Dresham and Maglen Launceston to be her bride's companions. Maglen had been a little surprised by the invitation; she knew that Katrinna and Janilla had formed a friendship during the eve of Challenge ball when the Dresham girl had managed to deflect an attempt by Lord Swenland to force a betrothal between Janilla and Maglen's brother Crelin.

When Maglen got a chance to talk with Katrinna as they met to meet with Janilla to discuss the wedding arrangements she discovered that there really was a nice person inside the haughty persona that Lady Dresham displayed to the world. By tacit agreement they arranged to dull down their own appearance's so that they would not detract from the brides.' The Swenland girls had decided that they would be married at the same ceremony so even Janilla played down her looks so that Parina's lack of them was not emphasised. Not that Janilla had much success; she was just too stunningly beautiful for that. She would look good in anything she wore.

All four girls formed a bond that might have surprised their parents. Fameral politics relied heavily on the family ties that could be strengthened by judicious marriages and the female offspring of the ruling families were simply pawns in that process. The disgraced

Lord Swenland had hoped to strengthen his ties with The House of Launceston and Lord Launceston had welcomed the potential link that would have been made if his son Crelin had married Janilla. Their marriage would have helped to ensure the supply of good grain that his people desperately needed. The northern houses of Launceston, Ellward and now Norland could grow a small tough type of brown grain, but it made terrible bread and was really only fit for kertle feed. In fact, it was an excellent feed for the kertles. The human population needed the good plump, white grain that was grown south of the Childe Mountains to feed themselves.

But Janilla was marrying the new Lord Norland so those ties were now not possible. In the aftermath of the Challenge and the ball that followed Lord Launceston was lost in thought as he considered what options were open to him. He desperately needed to secure his House's future food supply. The House of Launceston did produce a sufficient amount of wool to be able to trade but they were always the junior members at the trading table; he needed a family tie to give security.

His thoughts inevitably turned to the other southern house, Dresham. They had as good a grain production as Swenland and he would much prefer to deal with Galtaain Dresham rather than Simvasten Swenland; he'd never trusted the man from the south west. Well, if he couldn't marry his son to the Swenland girl, perhaps he could use his daughter to form a permanent link with The House of Dresham. Galtaain Dresham had a son, Sorjohn, of marriageable age. Having made that decision, at least in his own mind, he relaxed and began to enjoy the end of meet celebrations.

Maglen was not so relaxed about the decision her father had made, in fact she was furious.

'How could you father!' Maglen screamed at her sire, 'I've never spoken to the man; I've only seen him at a distance across the dance floor at the ball. I'll not do it.' They were sitting enjoying a late breakfast a few days after the end of Challenge ball. Lady Launceston and her son had things to do and had left the father and daughter to finish their meal.

'Now Maglen, get down from that high kertle,' her father chided her, 'I've not done anything yet. I'm simply telling you that I intend to talk to Lord Dresham.'

'Well you needn't bother,' Maglen shouted, totally un-mollified, 'I'll not marry anyone I haven't chosen for myself.'

'Now look here young lady, I suggest you get to know Sorjohn Dresham and decide that he's the man you want to marry because he is the man you will marry if Lord Dresham and I can reach an agreement.'

'You mean you'll make me marry him whether I want to or not, that's just not fair!' Maglen said as she buried her head in her hands and dissolved into tears. Her father had never been this unreasonable before.

'Maglen,' Lord Launceston said standing up and raising his voice, 'you are the daughter of one of the highest houses in the land and as such you have a duty to your house and family. You will do as I command, and you will be pleased to do so, it is your duty!' He had then stormed from the room leaving Maglen shocked and in tears.

Sometime later Crelin found his sister still crumpled in her chair sobbing her eyes out. The twins had always had an emotional link. Despite what many thought they were not telepathic, they could not read each other's thoughts, but they always sensed the other's moods and knew if the other needed them. As babies when one cried the other joined in in sympathy and their poor mother and her nursery staff were never sure which one needed attention. As they grew older, visitors would be amazed at how one would pass something to the other knowing that the other wanted whatever it was. They had never made much of the ability; it was private, something they shared to the exclusion of the rest of the world.

'Madge, whatever is the matter! I was over in the stables and I knew something was wrong,' Crelin said, using the pet name he had for his sister. He came around the table and put his arm round her shoulders. Maglen raised her head and buried her face in her twin's neck.

Between sobs she managed to tell him the details of her recent discussion with their father.

'But would it have been that bad, Madge?' Crelin asked.

'How can you ask that?' Maglen responded, 'you know I don't want to get married.'

'I know you don't want to just yet, but we both know we'll have to at some time.' Crelin said.

'But I want to decide when I get married and to whom.' Maglen replied a little disconcerted that Crelin didn't seem to understand her position, 'surely you don't think I should have agreed to father's demands!'

'Well no, I suppose not,' Crelin confessed, 'but would it have been so bad. He had me virtually betrothed to Janilla Swenland a bathern ago, before all this business with the new Lord Norland developed.'

'Yes, but you quite like Janilla,' Maglen replied, 'and she is probably the most beautiful woman in Fameral.'

'Yes, but that's all I knew about her, I'd only met her a few times, I may have danced at the last Challenge Meet,' Crelin told her, 'and any way you're a very attractive young woman, you know you are, I've told you often enough.'

'I think you're a bit biased in your assessment, Maglen replied, 'but I know nothing about Sorjohn Dresham, I know his sister Katrinna a bit but that's a lot better than I know him. Katrinna and I were able to talk a lot at the weddings, she's much nicer than she first appears but I've hardly spoken two words with her brother. He's very quiet so it's difficult to know what he's really like.'

'Can't help you there,' Crelin replied, 'he was at Jaxaal's bachelor party, but he just sat off to one side and hardly spoke at all.'

'Well that does nothing to promote him as the sort of person I would want to marry!' Maglen retorted.

'No, but it takes nothing away from him either,' their mother said as she entered the room. She had obviously been listening to the earlier interchange.

'Oh Mother! You can't really want me to marry someone that I've not got to know and love, can you?' Maglen beseeched her parent.

'Well your father has good reasons for wanting a union with one of the southern families.'

'Mother!' Maglen wailed as her hopes of maternal support withered.

'Maglen,' her mother replied, 'you are the daughter of one of the five ruling families in Fameral and as such have privileges and benefits way beyond those of other people. But with those come responsibilities. When you are married to Sorjohn Dresham, like me, you will be one of the highest ladies in the land. You will have wealth and influence. I think marrying someone your father has chosen for you is a small price to pay to have such benefits.

'Mother, you cannot be serious! You can't expect me to marry someone I haven't chosen for myself!' Maglen implored.

'Why not, I did. Your Grandfathers got together and arrange my marriage to your father without my knowledge. The first time I met your father was two days before our wedding. And we've been very happy ever since.'

'But mother, that was in olden times,' Maglen complained naively.

'It may have been in what you call 'olden times' young lady,' her mother admonished, 'but with the reinstatement of The House of Norland, those times are coming back, and it is even more important that your father can make good ties with the other houses. It is also important that you learn to do your duty and obey your father's wishes.'

It was a very sad Maglen Launceston that made her way to her room where she threw herself on her bed and wept bitter tears of despair.

Sometime later she stirred herself and rinsed her face at her wash stand and looked at her reflection in her dressing table mirror. As she stood patting herself dry, she looked critically at her face; Crelin was right, she was an attractive young woman, but then she knew she must be, he never lied to her, nor she to him, there was no point they both would know if there was any deceit in what the other said. She dried her lower face with the towel and could see the elegant cast of her jaw line, that was a feature both she and Crelin had inherited from their mother.

But of course, it was her looks that her father was relying on to make her an attractive part of the deal her hoped to negotiate with Lord Dresham. This put her right back in the desperation she had felt earlier, and she had thrown herself back on her bed where she sobbed bitter tears.

Chapter 3

The morning mist sent a shiver down Bryland's body as he stepped out into the inn yard. He hurried into the stables to get the benefit of the heat the animals generated. He had enjoyed a very good breakfast and had called for extra portions of the superb roast hogs meat that had been served. He knew he was digging deeply into his slim money reserves but to Alphos with the future, he'd just have to work out how to earn some more. He checked Rufran over and was pleased with the way he had been fed, watered and groomed. He gave the stable lad responsible a good-sized tip enjoying the bravado of the moment even though he knew he would regret it later

'Why thank-you kind sir,' the stable lad responded as he fingered the slend coin; the going rate was usually only a stip, 'it was a pleasure to look after him. A fine kertle from good stock.'

Bryland realised that a kertle from the stable of The House of Swenland, even a working dray like Rufran would be a rarity out here in the country; he would need to be careful, the kertle's obvious breeding might give his own identity or origins away. As he rode out of the town he pondered whether he should consider selling the kertle and buying a cheaper one from lesser stock. That would replenish his supply of money and help him blend into the places he was bound.

As he entered the wooded part of the trail above the town he realised that he was getting very cold; the morning mist was biting through his light clothing. He stopped and unpacked his travelling cloak and put it on, immediately feeling the benefit of its many warming layers. Sadly, it was not reversible, so he couldn't hide away The House of Swenland colours but just now he needed the warmth. Rufran appeared to be untouched by the chill in his travelling shroud and the exercise would be helping to keep him warm. It only took a short time, during which the sun had burnt off the morning mist before they reached the entrance to the Childe Cut. The Cut was a place Swenland men did not venture, it was a historically a Norland stronghold and there were lurid tales told about the fate of unwary travellers who ventured into the Cut and were never seen again.

But Bryland had no option, he needed to get to the lands beyond the Childe Mountains and the Cut was the only sensible route open to him. The Childe Pass, away to the east, was the usual way Swenland people crossed the mountains but he didn't want to run into anyone who might know him. He would have to brave it out. As he approached the actual entrance to the cut he took off his cloak and packed it in his saddle bag. He had been warned often enough that people wearing Swenland colours were not very welcome in the cut. Once in there, where the sun could not reach it was still cold but not as bad as it had been out on the trail in the mist.

He was amazed at what went on in the cut, a geological fault had cleft the mountains in two and a small land shift eons before had opened up a passage right through them. But then the path widened at some points due to rock falls and possibly man mad excavations. Here some enterprising traders had set up shop and it was with some relief that Bryland was able to buy a steaming cup of kandrel and a bun. The drink and the process of eating warmed his chilled body. Having finished his snack, he decided to put on a second shirt to help keep him warm and he felt a lot more comfortable as he continued into the cut. Sometime later he reached a water fall that fed the stream beside which he had been travelling and he allowed Rufran to quench his thirst. He had been warned by the stall holder where he had bought his drink that this was the last source of water in the Cut.

They progressed on their way and made very good time, but it was still early evening when they finally left the confines of the cut and emerged on the southern side of the mountains. The countryside was noticeably different on the southern side of the mountains compared to the north. Gone were the pleasant views of green fields and grasslands, normal in the north. Even this close to the mountains the land that lay ahead was predominantly browner sun burnt vegetation. But looking further into the distance there were clumps of green scattered around and away on the horizon, Bry could see the green tree tops of the Misle forest.

The primary moon, Alphos, had risen as soon as they emerged and her soul mate, Bathos, was just showing above the trees when they reached the village of Under Childe. The temperature here south of the mountains was noticeably warmer than it had been in the north. On the outskirts of the village he stopped and checked his supply of money. Hunger had forced him to buy a meal from a wayside vendor about mid-afternoon, despite the sizeable breakfast he had devoured back in Upper Childe and this had further diminished his slender stock of coins. He decided he could just about afford another night in an inn and then he would have to make decisions as to whether to sell Rufran or not.

He made his way into the centre of the village and found an inn called The Five Houses where he decided to stop for the night. He was warmly welcomed, he was the first traveller to come through the Cut since the end of the Challenge and everyone was anxious for news from north of the Mountains.

Bryland would have preferred to sit quietly on his own and eaten his meal in solitude but the landlord and the other regulars in the bar insisted on asking, 'had he been in Medland?' and 'had he seen the Challenge?' He told them that he had and immediately regretted doing so for he was then compelled to relate all that had happened. He was questioned about the new Lord Norland and though he tried to make light of what he actually knew he ended up giving a fairly full account of the five days of the Challenge. It was obvious from the reaction of his audience that The House of Swenland was not very highly thought of; everyone, it seemed, were delighted that The House of Norland was to be restored. Many in the bar expressed hopes that they might be affiliated into the new house.

'But surely only either the Houses of Swenland or Dresham can rule here, south of the Childe Mountains?' Bryland asked.

'Don't you believe it,' the landlord said, 'there's more unaffiliated land in this part of the continent than looks to any house. Lord Dresham is not too bad as a master, as I understand it, but I don't know of anyone who likes or admires Lord Swenland. He's never been popular around here. He got short shrift when he tried to assume some fifths down long meadow way a few turns back, terrible man.'

Bryland sat in a state of shock, deep inside he'd always been uneasy about Lord Swenland's morals and motives, but he'd never been exposed to this sort of antagonism towards his former house master.

He sat quiet for a while but then the two serving wenches came and pestered him for details of the new Lady Norland and he tried to tell them what he thought a stranger might know of Janilla. It was tempting to add a lot of detail about her and her family to which he was privy, having been part of the household, but he restrained himself. He was then told that Jaxaal Oostedd as he had purported to be, had stayed at The Five Houses on his way up to Medland.

'I actually served the new lord Norland,' one of the girls preened herself. The other then retorted that she had made up his room and taken him hot water in the morning.

'Your dray is stabled in the very stall where Sarina had lodged the night she had spent at the inn,' a stable lad volunteered not to be outdone.

The conversation continued for a while and Bryland was glad when the subject turned to a forth coming competition that was to be held in the village square. He gathered that this was based on a toy used in a childrens game that had developed in the Dresham region this involved a bent piece of wood with a cord tied between the two ends. When a slender shaft was notched onto the cord and pulled back, bending the wooden bow into an arch, and the shaft, when released, would fly off. The game was to see who could get a shaft nearest to the centre point on a greased surface . Bryland was enthralled by this and admitted that he had never heard of this game or of the equipment that had been described.

'The men taking part used to be called Bowmen,' the stable lad told him, 'but , because the bow makes an arch when the string is pulled back, they started calling it Archery and the people involved, Archers. I'll go and fetch my bow and some shafts,' the stable lad announced, 'down Dresham way they call the shafts, 'arrows' which seems a good name.' he added and rapidly disappeared.

He returned a short time later with his bow, several arrows that had half feathers stuck on the notched end and a large flat board. He proceeded to hang the board on the back of the door and Bryland saw that the surface was covered in a thick layer of breesh hen fat or something similar. This glutinous surface was then smoothed with a flat blade so that, he later discovered an arrow hitting the board would leave a mark where it hit. A white disc was then placed in the centre of the board and the stable lad took up a position at the opposite end of the bar.

'In the main competitions the targets are made of twisted straw and the arrows stick in so where they hit can be seen,' the stable lad explained. The drinkers who had been sitting near the door sensibly moved away from the proximity of the target as the stable lad took up his position.

He selected one of the arrows and notched it onto the bow string straightened the arm holding the bow and using his other hand pulled back the string and took aim. Releasing the string sent the arrow flying across the room and it hit the target with a satisfying thud before it fell to the floor. A man standing near the target peered at the mark it had made in the greased surface and announced that the shot had been low and to the left of the centre but only a hands breadth away. Another man then took over the bow and he fired an arrow which was also a hand breadth away from the target. The competition between the two then continued until the stable lad actually hit the white spot and was declared the winner. The loser then bought a round of drinks and everyone discussed how each man had done.

Bryland was fascinated by this whole process; he'd never seen anything like it.

'Oh, it's been played in Dresham for several turns,' he was told by a drover who had joined the party earlier in the evening. 'There they play it outside with bigger bows and targets a lot further away, fifty or a hundred paces, sometimes more. They play for big money prizes. The best Archers make a living out of their winnings.

'We're not so behind the times here,' the land lord told the drover, 'we have competitions in the village square with five targets every Alphen end. This inn, "The Five Houses," have a team entered each time.'

Bryland was invited to try his hand and after a few false starts was able to send the arrows unerringly towards the target. He was challenged to a competition by the stable lad and once they had agreed that it was just for fun, Bryland hadn't the funds to pay if he lost, they competed for the best of five shots. The stable hand won in the end, hitting the target twice to Bryland's once but everyone agreed that he had a natural talent for the game. As they sat enjoying the drinks that Bryland was felt obliged to buy despite the earlier decision, after the match he took the chance to study the equipment. He recognised the two different woods from which the bow and the arrows were made. The bowstring was a recognisable thread, carefully twisted to give a non-stretching cord and covered in a wax coating. He went to bed that night with his head full of ideas about this new game and the equipment it required.

The next morning, he again checked his money reserves and found that the previous evening's largesse had virtually wiped him out. He had just enough to cover his night's board and the stabling fee for Rufran. He had a quiet word with the Landlord to see if he could negotiate a way of getting a meal. Suddenly the genial host became a hard-faced business man and Bryland realised that any deal he made would be in the Landlord's favour. He fetched his travelling pack and took out a few items he would be willing to relinquish and displayed them for the landlord's inspection. The goods met with a few grunts and a lot of air sucked between the teeth.

In the end Bryland decided that the few stips that were offered were an insult and began to stow them back in his pack. The Landlord then turned his attention to Rufran and they went and inspected the kertle.

Again, the landlord tried to talk down the kertle's value but Bryland was having none of that, he was an expert when it came to kertle flesh. Every bad point that the Landlord tried to highlight, Bryland argued from a position of strength and the Landlord had to acknowledge that he had met his match when it came to assessing the animal. But he did know a good kertle when he saw one and eventually agreed a fair price.

Chapter 4

Bryland was very sad to have to say goodbye to Rufran; he'd been a good trustworthy companion on the journey from Medland and been a friend when Bryland had needed one. So, it was with a heavy heart but a reasonably full money bag that Bryland hoisted this pack up on his back and trudged out of the inn yard. As he turned his face to the south and headed towards his new life he stopped when he reached the corner. He was having second thoughts about the sale but immediately realised that it was too late, the decision had been made. He also realised that he needed to think about his footwear. The boots he had on were what he always wore but they were light weight, high quality leather boots as befitted a member of one of the high families. They would not last long on the rough roads that now lay ahead.

Bryland sought out a shoemaker and went into the man's shop. He was about to order to have a pair of boots made when he realised, with a jolt, that he was no longer a member of the class for which that was normal practice. Apart from which he couldn't afford the time to wait for them to be made. Instead he started looking through the stock of ready-mades that were piled against the wall. He eventually selected a pair of tough hard-wearing boots that would last him a very long time. He exchanged some of his newly gained coins for the boots and a large jar of protective wax which he could use to keep them, and all his other leather goods, waterproof. He fell into discussion with the shoemaker and discovered that he prepared all his own leathers in a small tannery out at the back of his shop.

The shoemaker/tanner considered himself to be foremost a leather dealer and was only too pleased to talk about this aspect of his expertise and treated Bryland to a tour of his premises. Some parts of the process were well known to Bryland; they had similar sheds for stripping and curing the skins back at Swenland Mansion. The shed that was devoted to the dying of the skins was something new and they spent a long-time in there as Bryland asked to be shown all the different process.

One particular vat was used, he was told, to treat and colour fine leathers and cloths. The evil smelling liquid that swirled around the tub was kept at a slightly raised temperature to increase its effectiveness. Bryland was about to put his hand in the liquid to test the temperature when the tanner stopped him.

'Will it scald me?' Bryland asked, 'it doesn't seem all that hot.'

'Oh no sir, it's barely lukewarm, just a comfortable bath temperature, but it's a very powerful dye. You get your hands in that and they'll be stained brown for a couple of batherns. It dyes cloth and hair as well. Makes a lovely job of waterproofing as well, it does sir, but it does stain something awful.'

This got Bryland thinking and as he was about to say good bye to the shoemaker when he had an idea. The leather man was a little bemused at the suggestion but agreed that Bryland could dunk his travelling cape in the tub. Bryland fetched the cloak having carefully turned it inside out so that most of the Swenland colours were hidden and proceeded to drop it into the evil liquid. They left it in there for several minutes and they pulled it out using a pair of wooden tongs whose discolouration showed that they had been used for this purpose many times.

The cloak was hung above the tub to drain while the two men shared a jug of steaming kandrel. Like the crowd in The Five Houses the night before, the shoemaker was desperate for news from Medland and Bryland regaled him with details of the Challenge and its outcome, managing to avoid any mention of his own involvement. Like the others in the inn last night, the shoemaker was clearly ill-disposed towards The House of Swenland. By the time their mugs were empty the liquid had stopped running from the cloak and there were now just a few occasional drips. The shoemaker carefully wrapped the cloak, now a nondescript brown colour all over, in greased waterproof cloth with instructions on how Bryland should unwrap it and let it air dry as soon as he could.

As Bryland crested the hill as he had climbed out of the village he looked back and saw the spread of the houses below him with the imposing backdrop of the Childe Mountains behind them. He wondered if he would be back this way again. He might have well enjoyed his last night of comfort for some time. He had replenished his supplies and knew he could feed himself for a few days from what he carried but he would need to think about his longer term needs very soon.

As he made his way off the hill, rapidly leaving Under Childe behind them, Bryland was overcome with a feeling of loneliness. He'd cut himself off from all the friends and the life he'd known before. Despite the uncomfortable nature of the general conversation regarding The House of Swenland he'd enjoyed his evening in the inn last night. The camaraderie and the banter had been fun, and he had to admit to himself, he had enjoyed the company of the two serving wenches.

He was twelve and a half turns old, two and a half beyond his majority, and most men his age would be married or planning to be so, very soon. He had never bothered 'chasing the girls' as most of his friends had done, his deformed leg was an impediment which he foolishly thought would put off any female from considering him as a partner, but he did realise that deep down he would need to think along those lines very soon. He walked on and by mid-afternoon was well into the Misle Forest. There was a well-trodden path through the forest he'd been told, and he enjoyed walking through the woodlands, but his pack was very heavy. He'd originally packed on the basis that he'd have a dray to carry him and his goods and the weight for a single, if very fit, although lame, young man was nearly too much. As it turned into late afternoon he turned off the path and fought his way into the trees, hoping to find a suitable place to make camp. He was climbing a slight rise and as he crested the top of the ridge he came across a small clearing. There was a small stream running down the valley on the other side of the glade and the gentle gurgle of the water was a pleasant, musical accompaniment. He took off his back pack and let it rest against a tree. He was very tired after his days walk and he needed to rest.

He took a drink from a small water flagon he carried and realised that despite his good-sized breakfast, he was hungry. Well this was as good a spot as he was likely to find, and he decided to make camp and spend the night here. The first thing he did was to unwrap the dyed travelling cloak and hang it from a tree. He was careful to use a pair of leather gloves when handling the still wet cloth but realised that in doing so he'd stained a very good pair of fine riding gloves.

'*Well, this is no time to worry about being fashion conscious,*' he told himself, but he did then rub the gloves all over in the staining liquid that still oozed from the cape. He was pleased with the result and saw that the new colour was ideal for hiding the bright colour they had been. This was an important factor in the new life he was already planning for himself. He unpacked his luggage and studied all the clothes he had with him. Some he carefully folded and stowed away at the bottom of the bag. These were the best things, the slightly 'dressy' clothes which he wanted to keep in their pristine condition. He looked at the rest and saw that he had a couple of pairs of britches and matching jerkins which were quite light in colour and would be easily seen against the greens and browns of the woodland.

He took the still sodden cape down from the tree and spread it out on the grass. He then laid the garments he wanted to dull down on the cape and folded it, so the garments were completely covered. He then rolled the cape tightly into a roll which he secured with cords. This he lay to one side, hoping that the dye would transfer to the garments and turn them into the dull brown that his cloak had become.

He then turned to and started to create a camp site for himself. He found he'd stumbled on an ideal place; he'd got water, a well-drained site with plenty of cover and suitable trees to make the basis of lean-to shelters. In a short space of time he'd got the basics set up with somewhere to sleep, a fire going and water coming to the boil. He'd cut some bushes, these he knew were called broom, and laid these as the mattress for his bed space. This was tucked in beneath a tree which would give him some shelter from rain and the bushes at its base gave some wind protection as well.

He stripped off and, naked, plunged into the stream. The water was cold and took his breath away, but it felt wonderful to get rid of the sweat and grime of his travels. He towelled himself down after his bath and sat by his fire enjoying a mug of kandrel. He got dressed in warm clothing; he'd already learned that living in the open was a cool affair once the sun went down even though this was supposedly not the coldest part of the turn. He had no choice but to wear the outer clothing that he had travelled in; the rest was either stowed away as 'best' or wrapped up in his cloak being dyed. He made a meal of half of the food he had left from what he had taken from the Swenland Mansion in Medland and sat sipping wine from a flagon, pondering his immediate future.

It was as he sat thinking through his pressing problems of food and shelter that he was joined in his little glade by a red cannis that trotted into the clearing up wind of Bryland's fire. The animal obviously didn't expect to find anyone or anything in this part of its territory for it progressed half way across the clearing before it saw Bryland sitting against a tree. Its first instinct was obviously to run but it stopped as soon as it had started and simply stared at the interloper to its domain; its bushy red tail held out behind it. Bryland sat transfixed by this visit. He then began talking very softly to his visitor.

'Well my fine friend, and a good evening to you,' Bryland began, 'I hope you don't mind this intrusion into your realm, but I didn't know you were in this area.' He hadn't seen any tracks or any sign of a burrow when he had first checked the clearing for such indications of occupancy. The Cannis was obviously bemused by this stranger into his world but his curiosity overcame his natural inclination to run and he lay down watching the stranger intently. Bryland was just about finishing a kitchen fowl leg when he thought that the smell of his food might be what was attracting the small wild dog.

Being careful to not move too quickly he tossed the leg bone towards the cannis using mostly his fingers and wrist top propel it rather than a big arm movement. The Cannis's first reaction was to run but either the fact that the projectile was in no danger of hitting him or he could smell the meat still on it he held his ground and then slinked towards the morsel. This he gathered up and removed it to a safer distance away from the human resting against the tree. So began a strange and wonderful friendship that was to develop during the coming velds.

That night Bryland slept a lot more comfortably than he had the first night of his flight from Medland. He had sorted out the bedding underneath him which held him off the hard ground and gave him some protection from the cold. The waterproof sheet that had wrapped his cloak served very well as wind break immediately behind his sleeping bag. It didn't rain that night and a gentle breeze dispersed any mist that might have formed as dawn broke.

He rose and refreshed himself in the stream before eating some of his remaining flat cakes. He had bought some more of the grain from which they were made in Under Childe, so he knew he could replenish that part of his larder. He had noticed that the hill beside him was covered in bushes and a shrub, the parlip, which had a very nutritious root system. He would be able to dig up some of them; roasted in the fire they were delicious. His only real problem was meat; he needed to establish a means of supplying himself with an adequate source.

As he sat drinking the single mug of kandrel he was allowing himself now he needed to budget his rations, he realised that there must be small animals that he could hunt; the red cannis obviously made a living out here therefore he could as well. He cleared away his breakfast and tidied his camp so that his occupation of the glade was not immediately obvious. He put all his food stuffs into a bag which he then hung at a good height in a tree to stop his red cannis friend or some other sneak thief from taking it. Just before he left his camp he decided to untie the bundle of clothes he was dying in his cloak and spread them out over suitable bushes. He chuckled to himself as he realised that putting the clothes out to dry made nonsense of his earlier attempts to disguise that he'd been there. He then went in search of suitable trees.

He was looking for the type of wood that would enable him to make a bow and some arrows of his own. He found what he was looking for within shouting distance of his camp and proceeded to cut suitable branches. He had a couple of small sharp knives with him as well as a good-sized dagger the length of his forearm. As he hacked away at branch the thickness of his wrist he bemoaned the fact that he had not thought to arm himself with a sword when he left Medland. But the dagger was a good weight and well made. He had bought it from the smith who made it at Cordale Complex when he was there last turn.

Eventually he was able to return to the glade with a good supply of material from which he thought he could fashion a bow and some arrows. His first attempt served as a good learning exercise, but he immediately realised that it was not an easy task to shape the wood as he wanted it. The branches natural taper towards the tip was ideal.

The trick was to get the other half shaped to match, cutting a tapering shape from the thickening wood. At his third attempt he managed to get roughly what he was after. He searched through his pack and found the ball of twine that he had thoughtfully packed and proceeded to fashion a bowstring. He'd notched the ends of the bow and was able to tie the cord that he had made onto one end but fixing the other was a problem.

At first, he had simply tied it to the bow leaving the string hanging loose but this didn't give enough tension to the bow when he pulled the string back. The bow he had used in the inn had been pre-tensioned so that the bow was already arched with the string pulled taut. Buy tying the string to the bow while already arched was a near impossibility and after a while he gave up. He pondered the problem over an illicit mug of kandrel. Then it came to him, he'd simply have to make a loop in the end of the string which would be easier to slip over the end of the bow. This worked, once he had modified the shape and depth of the notch that he'd cut in the end of the bow.

He was pleased with himself after his day's work and the off cuts and chippings that he had created went towards feeding his fire that evening. The new wood created some smoke which bothered him slightly, but he avoided putting too much on all at once. But this made him realise that he would have been better making his bow from seasoned wood. This led him to thinking that the bow he had made would probably be improved by drying so he hung it high in the branches over the fire where it would get a gentle drying heat without burning.

He was just finishing the last of his kitchen fowl portions when the red cannis returned. The animal trotted into the centre of the clearing and sat down staring intently at Bryland in expectation. He wasn't disappointed as with a chuckle Bryland tossed each bone to the animal as he was about to finish stripping the meat from it. By the end of this process the animal was laying just a couple of paces away gnawing on the last of the bones. He was obviously completely at ease being this close to the human and his fire. Bryland sat in bemused amazement.

When it became clear that there was going to be no further food offerings coming his way the Cannis rose, stretched and then trotted off the way it had come.

'Good bye my friend,' Bryland called as the cannis was about to disappear at which point the animal stopped, turned its head, looked at him before trotting out of sight.

The next morning Bryland set about testing his new bow. He quickly realised that the arrows were as important as the bow and he spent a long time fashioning acceptable pieces. He practiced incessantly, determined to improve his accuracy with the new toy. He then made the leap to thinking of it as a weapon instead of just a toy when he saw a breesh hen and fired at it. He missed but realised that he could easily have hit it and claimed his first 'kill.' He then adapted all the arrows he had made by making the end taper to a point. As his skill improved he realised that the shaping of that point was critical, a rough-cut end made the arrow veer in its flight. He also soon learned that it was easier to hit a vertical branch than it was to hit a horizontal one; the effect of gravity was very marked when you watched an arrow in flight from the Archer's perspective.

He made a point of practicing every day and his ability rapidly improved. At the end of an Alphos he knew he could hit a leaf at will at twenty paces or so, whenever he wanted.

Chapter 5

Maglen was a very contrite young woman as she and her brother reached their majority a bathern after the Challenge. Neither of her parents had mentioned an arranged marriage since the episode in Medland just after the Challenge Meet. She was petrified that they would make some announcement about something along those lines when the ball to mark their majorities was held. But nothing transpired and Maglen tried to enjoy the event; after all it was supposed to be her and Crelin's big day.

The ball was held at Launceston Hall and her mother had revelled in the preparations for the event. She was determined that it was to be the biggest social affair since the marriages of Janilla and Parina Swenland. Lord and Lady Norland were invited as were Lord and Lady Ellward. There had been a long discussion between Maglen's parents as to whether they should invite the southern family heads and, in the end, Feraard Launceston had won the argument and the houses of Dresham and Swenland were invited to attend.

Feraard undoubtedly intended to use the event to further his interactions with the other houses. He was still a little unsure of the regency rule of Darval Ellward and his wife Parina now they had charge of Swenland. He has never trusted the old Lord Swenland, now, by all accounts, rapidly descending into a crotchety old age in his small estate. Initial reports suggested that the blind Darval Ellward was a very competent estate manager and Swenland was already showing signs of renewed prosperity under his guardianship. Whether it was he or his new bride who were responsible for this transformation wasn't clear but he quite expected that it was the combination of the two. It was early days, but the success of their marriage was further justification for his belief in arranged marriages. The young Lord Neldon Swenland was undergoing guardian training and Feraard had heard no news of him. That might have been a possible match for his daughter Maglen but for the disgrace Neldon Swenland had brought upon himself. Lord Launceston was now convinced that the best deal he could achieve would be with The House of Dresham.

Lord Jaxaal and Lady Janilla Norland had arrived with a flourish in a glow that their love for each other seemed to exude. Feraard tried to use their happiness as another example of how arranged marriages could work but his argument was quickly dismissed by his daughter who understood the 'arrangement' had been contrived by Jaxaal himself. There were no indications that the Norland marriage was about to bear fruit but Parina Ellward came to see Maglen and apologise that fate had decided that her pregnancy would become common knowledge at the time of Maglen and Crelin's majority ball. Maglen was delighted for her and her husband and the two developed a friendship in the days leading up to the ball.

'Well I suppose you could say that ours was an arranged marriage,' Parina confided, and it has turned out really well, so far but Darval and I had fallen as much in love as Jaxaal and Janilla had. It was genius of Jaxaal to manipulate things, and my father, so that our marriages solved a great many problems.'

'That's what I thought had happened,' Maglen agreed, 'my father has rammed down my throat that your marriages were arranged but I told him that you were all very happy for those arrangements to be made. I'm not in love with Sorjohn Dresham, I hardly know the man, and certainly don't want to marry him.'

'And I don't think you should either,' Parina agreed, 'I was very lucky to meet Darval, he's not a bit bothered in the fact that I'm ugly,' and she held up a hand to silence Maglen who was about to argue the point.

'I am very well aware of my looks and my ungainly body,' Parina stated, 'and being sister to one of the most beautiful women in all Fameral has not been easy. Janilla, bless her, has never made comparisons or used her looks to hurt me and has always been a real supportive sister to me, but the fact remains that nature had decided to encumber me with this,' and she raised her hand towards her face. But don't think Darval doesn't know what he has lumbered himself with. He and his sister Felda, who is also blind, can see more with their hands than you or I ever will with our eyes. They worked out that Jaxaal was actually their first cousin simple by feeling his face.'

'Felda is an amazing little girl isn't she,' Maglen commented, 'and so talented, I don't think I'll ever forget the way she and her sister and brother, the three Ellwards entertained us at the Eve of Challenge Ball, just before. 'and she petered out realising what she had been about to say and to whom.

'Just before my father attacked Jaxaal in the Ellward's courtyard,' Parina finished for her, 'Don't be embarrassed by our family history. I'm not, it happened, we've just got to accept it and get on with life.'

They carried on their conversation as they walked arm in arm in the Launceston Hall gardens.

'Felda is the sweetest thing you know,' Parina told Maglen as they skirted a large water garden, 'she says she is only worried about what's in here and she taps me on the chest. She says she isn't bothered by what's here and then she wipes her hand down my face.'

'Are she and her brother really totally blind, I'm told they can do some amazing things despite their handicap?' Maglen asked.

'Oh yes, quite blind,' Parina confirmed, 'they've both developed their other senses to compensate and in doing so have gone way beyond normal sighted peoples' abilities. It can be quite unnerving at times. But as for this arranged marriage business,' Parina said, returning to the previous subject of conversation, 'I know Janilla will be as incensed as I am at the prospect and if there is anything we can do to help, just let us know.'

The arrival later that veld of the Dresham family a day before the ball was a traumatic affair for Maglen. Etiquette demanded that she be present to welcome her guests as they arrived, but she had told her brother she would rather be swabbing the kitchen floor with the scullery maids than meeting Sorjohn Dresham.

Despite her outward misgivings, Maglen was still intrigued to see what this Sorjohn Dresham was really like. She had met him occasionally over the turns and briefly at the last Challenge Balls of course but hadn't had an opportunity to get to know him. She was loathed to do so and was barely civil to him when he arrived with his parents at Launceston Hall. The lunch the families shared after the Dreshams' arrival was an upsetting affair for Maglen; her father kept trying to involve both her and Sorjohn in the conversation. Maglen had some awareness of the mischievous character of Sorjohn's sister Katrinna and knowing this was able to put up with some pointed jibes about getting her to know her brother a little better. The luncheon over the adults suggested that Maglen and Crelin show Sorjohn, Katrinna and their younger brother Prellard, around the grounds of Launceston Hall.

Once outside the house and away from their parent's attention, Katrinna came and grabbed Maglen by the arm and dragged her ahead of the three men so that she could talk privately to her young hostess.

'I'm sorry about all that talk over lunch,' Katrinna apologised, 'do you forgive me? I'm sorry, but I couldn't resist watching you and Sorjohn squirm.'

'You were doing that on purpose?' Maglen asked in surprise.

'Oh yes, my parents know I have a wicked sense of humour and they would be expecting me to do something along those lines. But I could see that you were very uncomfortable, I am truly sorry.'

'That's all right,' Maglen replied, thinking it was anything but that. 'But please don't egg my father on anymore in that direction.'

'I take it you don't wish to marry my brother any more than he wants to marry you?' Katrinna queried

'No, I don't,' Maglen said emphatically and then immediately apologised, 'I'm sorry I don't mean to be rude about your brother. I hardly know him, what little I do know of him he seems quite nice and if I got to know him better; I might decide I'd like to marry him. It's just that I can't stand the idea of being forced to marry someone I haven't chosen for myself.'

'Oh, I know just what you mean,' Katrinna replied, 'Sorjohn and I feel exactly the same way and our parents have promised us that they will never make us marry anyone we don't wish to.'

'But if our fathers agree to the match, won't yours insist that Sorjohn does marry me?' Maglen asked.

'I doubt it,' Katrinna replied to Maglen's relief, 'we had a long discussion about it on our journey here. Did you know that your father had written to mine?'

'No, I didn't know that,' Maglen replied a little disconcerted, 'he hasn't said anything to me about doing so.'

'Well he did, and he broached the subject of your marrying Sorjohn. If it's any comfort, father was a bit put out about it, he doesn't like the idea of being asked to make any of his children marry for political reasons. I don't know if you know but Dresham has a surplus of grain that we think Launceston needs. In return we could usefully use some of the wool that you produce but more than that, we need to be able to use your ports to trade with the rest of the world. Our coast line is subject to the most horrendous tides and fearful storms; seafaring from southern Fameral is quite impossible.'

'I was aware of some of that because Crelin has shared some of the things he's been taught.' Maglen replied.

'Oh, your parents work on the old-fashioned lines that mere girls don't need to know about politics and trade, I take it?' Katrinna asked.

'Yes, I suppose they do, I've never thought about it in that way,' Maglen replied.

'Well that's the only reason father didn't reject your father's approaches about an arranged marriage as soon as they arrived, but he has promised Sorjohn that he won't make him do anything that he doesn't want to do,' Katrinna told her.

'You mean if Sorjohn says he likes me, your father will agree to it and mine will force me to marry him!' Maglen exclaimed.

'Oh, I don't think it will come to that,' Katrinna reassured her, 'if the truth be known, Sorjohn has fallen in love with someone else. He won't say who, but I wouldn't be surprised if it wasn't one of the Ellward girls.'

'You can't mean Felda!' Maglen exclaim in surprise.

'Oh no, isn't it funny everyone thinks of Felda before they think of Geldren,' Katrinna replied.

'Geldren Ellward,' Maglen said, considering the implications, 'well that would forge links between your house and the Ellwards and they have as many wool beasts, sheep, as we have and almost as many good harbours.'

Exactly,' Katrinna replied triumphantly, 'but Sorjohn won't say or do anything until he's had a chance to get to know her better and anyway, she's a turn away from her majority so it's all academic at the moment.

Chapter 6

Far away from Launceston hall, Bryland was as apprehensive as Maglen was as the time for the ball approached but for a completely different reason. He had prospered after a tricky start to his woodland existence. He had gone hungry for a veld or two once his supplies of meat had been eaten by him and his red cannis friend. He had only survived by digging up some parlip roots and roasting them in the embers of his fire. Breakfasts and lunches had comprised of berries and the fruits that were just ripening on the trees. If nothing else this kept his digestive system on the move. He knew he had to get some meat and other things to balance his diet, but that was easier said than done.

His first attempts at setting snares were singularly unsuccessful and his early attempts at using his bow were failures, the arrows just wouldn't fly straight. During his second veld in the woods he did get a small amount of meat in the form of the remnants of one of the Cannis's hunts. He had been sitting by the fire in his camp when the cannis had appeared with a small breesh hen in its mouth. It had been several days since Bryland had been able to offer the cannis even a small morsel. And it seemed that, tired of waiting the animal had decided to bring his own contribution to the camp. It had squatted down in the centre of the clearing and proceeded to devour most of the fowl. It had then picked up the remnants and trotted up close to Bryland and dropped the carcass at his feet.

Inspecting what was left of the fowl, Bryland found that he was left with both thighs which gave him his first full meal for a veld or more. More importantly he was also left with a copious number of feathers and this gave him the means of putting flights on his arrows. With this improvement his hunting rapidly became more successful.

His first kill was a full grown brindle stag. The poor animal was on its last legs anyway and as he butchered the stag, Bryland realised that it was a very old animal and hadn't been feeding very well. Its flesh was thin and very tough and made poor eating, but it was his first kill and Bryland was elated. He was also able to boil down the animal's hooves to make very effective glue which improved the way he was able to fix the feathered flights to his arrows. From then on, his hunting became much more successful.

He had always understood the way animals behaved and he was able to put this understanding to good use in tracking and stalking his prey. He learnt a lot very quickly and he also improved his skill with the bow, becoming very accurate with his shots. He felt very pleased with himself to be able to offer his four-legged friend some significant contributions. This became routine and the cannis began accepting the offerings and disappearing with them. Bryland began to suspect that he might have a family to support; this was the time of turn when female cannis would be whelping their litters.

This was proved right when late one evening the whole family visited him. The male trotted into the clearing followed by three lively young cubs. Bryland welcomed his friend with an offering of scraps from his evening meal. The cubs quickly caught on and were soon fighting over the pieces of meat thrown their way. A few minutes later Bryland saw that another adult was peering at the scene from the vegetation. This was obviously a female as she was noticeably smaller than the male. Bryland tossed her a piece of meat as casually as possible so as not to scare her and after a while she ventured to join the rest of her family in the centre of the clearing.

Bryland was overjoyed at this development; he was really feeling at ease in his new world and was obviously being accepted by the inhabitants. He had noticed that several birds became regular visitors to his clearing and he welcomed the company they provided. He began roving further afield from his base in pursuit of suitable game. He learnt quickly how to clean and prepare the skins that were a by-product of his hunting for food. As his stock grew he realised he might be able to return to Under Childe and trade for things he needed. He still had a well-stocked money bag, he had nowhere to spend the money he had got from the sale of Rufran, so he was feeling quite expansive.

He had improved his living conditions by building some rudimentary walls of woven branches and withies. He planned to buy a good axe next time he was in Under Childe; this would greatly ease his house building progress. He thought through all the things he needed to get and now that he was on his way back to the village and he suddenly felt not so sure about his ability to get a good deal for the skins he carried. His apprehension did not dwindle as he entered the village and he kept his head down hidden within his subtly coloured cloak as he made his way back to the shoemaker's shop. The shop was closed when he arrived, but he went around the back of the building and found the owner busy in the tanning shed. He displayed the skins he had brought with him and soon fell to negotiating a price. His heart sunk as the familiar sound of breath being sucked in through the teeth as the shoemaker inspected each one carefully. Despite his misgivings, Bryland was pleasantly surprised at the sum of money that he was offered, and the deal was soon done. As they sealed the transaction with a few drams of distilled liquor, the shoemaker asked if Bryland was entering the bow competition that was being held that night. He told him he didn't know about it but an hour later Bryland was ensconced in the 'Five Houses' enjoying a good meal with his entrance for the competition signed and paid for.

He had been asked his name and had given it simply as 'Woodsman.' There were many men in the bar with bows over their backs that were also there for the competition; it was a much bigger affair than Bryland had first thought. He ate his meal and drank straight pump water; he wanted to keep his senses as sharp as possible. Not so many of the other competitors who were quaffing great volumes of foaming ale. The noise in the bar was getting louder and the inn keeper had trouble getting everybody's attention. When he did he announced that it was time he selected the men who would represent the 'Five Houses.' He wondered around the bar with coloured ribbons in his hand.

'There are five targets set up for this competition, so I want five Archers to represent the inn, one at each target. It had been explained to Bryland that each Archer would fire five arrows at his appointed target. The Archer who got closest to the centre would win a monetary prize and go through to the five-man final. In that final each man would have five arrows and the best shot of those would win the competition and a significant amount of money. It had cost him a whole strand to enter and looking around the bar he realised that he was up against stiff opposition in terms of numbers if not expertise. The quality of that he would find out later. The inn keeper had selected four of his champions and was still holding the final ribbon and looking around the bar. He looked at the table where Bryland was sitting and obviously made a decision for he came striding towards it. But Bryland's fears that he was about to be selected were relieved when the ribbon was handed to another Archer sitting in the group.

The time for the competition arrived and the inn emptied as everyone pushed through the doors and made their way into the village centre. The place was crowded; the small village square was jammed packed with Archer and spectators. Every house that bordered the square had its upstairs windows open and dozens of people were hanging out of the windows trying to get a good view of the proceedings. Each inn had put up teams and these individuals were allowed to select the targets at which they would shoot. The rest, Bryland included, had to queue to be issued a coloured disc denoting at which target they would compete.

Bryland made his way to his allotted target and waited in line to take his first shot. There would only be one winner from each target and the way it worked was that each man would shoot and the one nearest the centre would not have to shoot again unless someone got closer. Bryland selected his first arrow with care, making sure it was the best he had with him; straight and true with the feathered flights well set.

He had worked out during his learning period in the woods that setting the flights so that they made the arrow rotate in its flight improved the accuracy tremendously. Looking carefully at his competitors arrows he realised that none of them appeared to have done this to their projectiles. His turn came; he took careful aim, controlling his breathing to keep his body as steady as possible. The arrow flew straight and true but hit the target a couple of finger breadths away from the centre. But it was the best arrow on that target so far. The competition continued and there was a tremendous cheer when a competitor on one of the other targets managed to actually hit the white disc marking the centre.

Then disaster struck when Straaka, a Archer on Bryland's target also hit the white spot which meant that he was definitely through to the final. Straaka was an enormous giant of a man with a big chest and arms to match. Bryland thought that his chance had gone as several of the Archer on his target were packing up saying they couldn't hope to match the winners shot but the official in charge of his target asked if Bryland wanted to carry on. When Bryland queried the merit in doing so he was told that if he could also hit the white spot he also would go into the final as well. He recovered his best arrow, preened the flights and took careful aim, waiting until what breeze there was had died down. The arrow flew straight through the still air and hit the white spot right in the centre. A tremendous cheer went up and Bryland was roundly congratulated, not least by the Archer who had already booked his place in the final even though it meant he had to share the prize money for the target with Bryland. The landlord of the 'Five Houses' came and added his congratulations and suggested that he had been tempted to make Bryland one of his chosen representatives but had opted with one of his regulars, to keep the peace.

The final when it came was a tense affair. A new target was set up at twice the distance of the first round. There were six finalists and great cheers went up as each was announced. The acclamation when

Bryland was announced was somewhat muted; he was, after all, a comparative stranger. The rules remained the same as before but now that there were only the six competitors each man's turn came around that much quicker than in the first round where there had been up to a dozen men to a target.

The standard of marksmanship was noticeably higher, and no arrow was more than a hands breadth away from the centre. With his third shot Bryland was able to hit the white spot and a great cheer went up to honour his achievement. The competition continued until the final contestant was about to take his last shot. It was Straaka and Bryland wished him good luck. Whether because of his good wishes or despite them, Straaka also managed to hit the white spot and a tremendous cheer went up as the crowd realised that the competition would have to go into another round. They were loving this excitement.

The targets were again moved another ten paces back and the two Archers took their places. Straaka went first and got very close to the centre. Bryland was equally as close and they had both fired three arrows. With his fourth arrow Straaka managed to just clip the edge of the white disc and Bryland acknowledge it as a hit but was overruled by the official judge who deemed that the arrow must be completely inside the white disc to count as a full hit.

'But that does place Straaka in the lead young man,' the official told Bryland, 'you'll have to hit wholly in the white to beat him.' Bryland rose to the challenge and took very careful aim again waiting for the wind to drop. He fired and the cheer that went up told him that he had hit the white. But Straaka was not to be beaten that easily and his final arrow also hit the white fully inside the disc. The official then explained that while only hits on the white counted he told Bryland that, since Straaka's early arrow had grazed the white it counted and that Bryland would have to equal or better that shot to stay in the competition.

'No pressure then,' Bryland quipped as he stood to take his final shot. He could feel the tension in the crowd as he took his place on the firing line and a trickle of sweat rolled down his face as he pulled back the bowstring. But he wasn't going to allow himself to be distracted and the arrow flew at the target hitting the white virtually in the centre.

Straaka was the first to congratulate the winner and the big man hoisted Bryland up on his shoulder and paraded him round the square. In a brief ceremony the results of the competition were announced, and their winnings presented to all of the finalists and the winner. Bryland offered to share the winner's purse with Straaka since the result had been so close but the big man would hear none of it.

'You just buy me a drink and we'll call it quits,' Straaka told him, 'but be ready, I'll beat you in the competition next Alphern!' In fact, Bryland bought him several drinks and these were matched by those that Straaka bought and it was a very drunken pair of Archer who staggered out of the bar early the next morning trying to find somewhere to sleep.

After his success Bryland returned to his woodland hideaway and sat one evening taking stock of his situation. He had managed to accumulate a goodly sum of money relatively speaking and could easily afford to buy back the kertle he had taken from The House of Swenland; he knew Rufran was still kept by the landlord at the 'Five

Houses,' he had dropped into the stables every time he went back to Under Childe to sell his skins.

On one trip he had visited the village smithy and had bought several metal tools and appliances that made life a lot better. The best buy had been an axe; with this he had been able to fell a few larger trees and branches and had turned his rudimentary shelter into a two-roomed hut with a raised platform at the back of the rear room for his bed. He had lined the roof and walls with more of the greased oil cloth which made the structure wind and rain proof. He had even extended the roof over the area to one side to provide a roomy stable shelter should he decide to buy Rufran back.

All in all, life was pretty good he decided as he sat on his porch area after his evening meal. As usual the Red Cannis appeared and approached Bryland in hope of an evening meal. He was not disappointed. Bry Woodsman had secured himself in the woods, able to live off the land and had learned a new skill. His prowess with the bow had become known and he was always being challenge by some hopeful; he had yet to be beaten which also increased the weight of his money bag.

He was tempted to travel down to High Tor Farm and perhaps beyond to Dresham where he had heard there were regular bow contests with even bigger prize purses than Under Childe could provide. But part of him was loathed to leave his little woodland glade. It was home now. He had built a comfortable, if rustic, little habitat that would keep out the worst of the winter weather during the Planting and Dormant batherns. The water supply from the stream was good and clean but he had no idea if the stream would freeze during the Dormant bathern. Well, time would tell. He did, however begin collecting a store of firewood.

The next day he made up his mind and decided to return to Under Childe and purchase Rufran back from the landlord of The Five Houses. The landlord was delighted to see his inn champion; Bryland's feats with the bow ensured a good turnout at every contest and his coffers filled, quite nicely, every alphen. He was not so pleased when Bryland announced the purpose of his visit; the kertle was the best dray the landlord had in his stable and he was loathed to part with him. But more than that, Bryland's need for him suggested that the Archer would be travelling again, and the landlord would lose his main Archer attraction.

The figure the landlord suggested as they began the negotiation was a grossly inflated version of the sum he had paid for the kertle. Bryland protested but the landlord pointed out that he had to feed and keep the kertle all the time he had lived in his stables and he should be compensated for that. Bryland did some quick calculations and worked out what it would have cost him to pay for a bathern's stabling which put a different slant on the calculations, even if the landlord had got some good work out of the kertle, effectively for free.

In the end they did reach an agreement and it was a happy Bryland who rode Rufran out of the village, even if his money purse was now a lot lighter. He decided that he had enough in store at his camp to live off until the next competition and he hoped to replenish his money then.

Chapter 7

The turn rolled on and it was a bathern after their majority that Crelin and Maglen were talking about what the future might hold. Their father had been on several trips south of the Childe mountains. The weather had been ideal and bumper harvests were being forecast down in the grain growing regions of Dresham and Swenland. Feraard Launceston had been doing his best to secure good trading deals with both the southern families. Lord Dresham had proved very reserved when he had met with him and Feraard was unable to get any firm undertaking. He did little better when he dealt with Darval and Parina Ellward in their role as regents of The House of Swenland. Feraard Launceston realised that Darval would naturally be making beneficial deals with his father Lord Ellward. He had returned home with no guarantees for his house's future grain supplies. He even considered travelling over the northern seas to the lands there where they too could grow good white grain, but that ploy had been the downfall of the previous Lord Norland and he didn't want to go down that path, irrational as the fear night be.

Jaxaal Norland had, no doubt, assured his house's future with deals with his wife's former family and anyway, Jaxaal was so deeply involved in rebuilding his family's estates that he had little time to concern himself with his neighbour's problems. Lord Launceston was feeling very alone and isolated.

There was nothing for it he would have to forge stronger family ties with The House of Dresham; Maglen may not like it but she would have to marry Sorjohn Dresham, her house needed that union. He broached the subject that evening over dinner when the family were all together.

'Well Maglen,' he asked,' you've had a bathern or so to think over my proposal that you should marry Sorjohn Dresham; have you come to any decisions?'

'Well you'd better ask the young Lord Dresham if he wishes to marry me before you start making any plans along that line father,' Maglen replied. She had been dreading the raising of this subject again. She'd even hoped that with the passage of time it had gone away, but it obviously hadn't. She was glad she had thought through what she would say to her father if the matter re-arose.

'As I understand it his father won't make him marry me unless he wants to, and I believe his affections lie elsewhere.' She added triumphantly.

'He'll do what his father tells him to do,' Lord Launceston replied in a harsh dictatorial tone, 'as will you, young lady.'

'I'll not marry anyone just because you want me too!' Maglen exclaimed standing up and knocking her chair over.

'You'll do as you are told, young lady, make no mistake. While you are my daughter you are a member of The House of Launceston and you will do whatever is in the best interest of your house. As head of the house, I will decide what that should be. Do I make myself clear?' Feraard shouted.

'I'll not marry anyone I don't wish to,' Maglen shouted in reply.

'While you live under my roof you will do whatever I decide is the best thing for you to do,' he screamed, 'you're not the daughter of some farming yokel, able to pick and choose. You're the daughter of one of the highest families in the land and you have responsibilities as such, you don't have the option of choosing. The daughter of a minor family may have that luxury, you do not.

'I'm sorry father,' Maglen sobbed trying to regain some composure, 'I can't believe you'd make me do this against my will.'

'What you will do young lady, is go to your room and pack your bags for a trip to Medland. Young Darval Ellward has called a special meeting of the five houses. While there you will be betrothed to the young Lord Dresham. We'll leave in two days' time and you can prepare yourself by deciding that you want to marry Sorjohn Dresham!'

With that Maglen stormed out of the dining room and up to her suite. She rang for her maid and threw herself down on her bed sobbing her heart out. This morning she'd almost began enjoying life again, it lay in ruins.

Her maid entered and seeing her mistress on the bed shaking as she cried, ran to her to offer some comfort.

'Whatever is the trouble milady?' the maid asked as she sat on the edge of the bed and put her arm around Maglen's shoulders. Maglen immediately sat up and clasped her maid in a desperate embrace.

'Oh Celdra,' she wailed sobbing into the servant's neck, 'my father has made his mind up, he is determined that I will marry Sorjohn Dresham.'

'And you're still determined that you won't?' Celdra asked rhetorically. 'The other maids say he is quite good looking and acts the gentleman without any airs and graces.'

'Oh, he's handsome enough and I think he is quite a nice man,' Maglen replied, 'although I've not really got to know him that well. I just don't think of him in that way. It's not his fault and my parents say I can grow to love him, but I want to choose who I love. Do you think I'm being silly?' she asked.

'No milady,' Celdra replied, 'no one else can make your heart do as they wish. When it comes to it, no one can control their own heart when it comes to whom it will light upon.'

'Oh, thank you Celdra,' Maglen replied, giving her maid another hug, 'you always know just what to say. You are a good friend.'

'Well milady, you've always been very good to me and allowed me to speak my mind.'

'That's enough of this 'milady' business,' Maglen decided as she stood up, 'I've told you before to call me Madge when we're on our own. And I think it is more appropriate at this moment. As of now Maglen Launceston ceases to exist. I'm going to leave my father's house and disappear into the country where no one knows me. As of now, the only name I'll admit to is Madge.'

'But mil…, sorry Madge, you can't be serious!' Celdra exclaimed, 'you can't just go and leave all this behind!' and she waved a hand at the room and the luxury that surrounded her.

'Why not?' Maglen retorted, 'the country is full of people who live perfectly good lives there, why should I not do the same?'

'But mil…., Madge, you're a lady of one of the high families, you couldn't possibly live among the rough people of the lesser families.' Celdra told her desperately hoping to dissuade her mistress from doing anything silly.

'Celdra, I am not so stuck up that I can't give up this high-status life. I can live as other people do and I can work for my living.' But the look on the maid's face at this statement showed how much she didn't believe it to be so.

'Oh, all right,' Maglen conceded, 'I've got a lot to learn, but I will do it. I'll not stay here and be a slave to my father's will. Now help me pack a bag with the things I'll need on the road.'

Maglen was obviously determined and all Celdra could do was go along with this madcap plan. The maid was a sensible, level headed girl who had a lot of experience. Her parents had been farm workers and she had come to Launceston Hall as a young girl to learn to become a house maid. She had worked her way up from the kitchen to wait on the family before accepting Maglen's offer to become her personal maid. The two girls were of the same age and build and had formed a deep friendship, based on mutual trust and respect.

With Celdra's help Maglen was able to make a small pile of clothes that would be suitable. She really had very few things that could pass as normal attire among the farming community. They talked long into the night and Maglen learned a lot about things she had no knowledge of before. She knew about hiring fairs where itinerant skilled workers and general labourers could go to get hired for a season's work by farmers in need of their services. Women and girls went to get hired as field workers and this seemed to Maglen to be the best thing she should try for.

'But there are lots of skills you need to have before a farmer will consider taking you on,' Celdra tried to explain, she still hoped to dissuade her mistress from this rash plan.

'Such as?' Maglen asked quite undeterred.

'Well, mil. sorry Madge, do you know how to tie a 'stoop of hay?' Celdra asked and Maglen had to admit that she didn't. 'Well that's the most basic skill you'll have to have if you're doing any sort of field work.'

She went on to explain how, after the men had cut the corn with their scythes, the women followed on, gathering an armful and neatly tying it into bundles which they then stacked together awaiting collection by drays and a cart. Celdra grabbed some of the clothes that lay on the bed and rolled them into the size of a stoop. She then took a dressing gown cord and showed Maglen how to deftly tie the stoop together using the least length of cord. Maglen insisted of trying this new skill and quickly became adept at it.

'Each gatherer wears an apron with a large pocket in which the ball of twine is put with the end hanging out. Each woman has a knife which she sharpens every morning and that is her prize possession. If you intend to try for some field work, you'll need to get yourself a good blade.'

As they talked on, Maglen learned all about the rigours of root crop picking and the strictures surrounding dairy work. It gave her pause for thought and she did privately question the wisdom of what she had planned but the overriding dread she felt of entering into a forced marriage held her resolve together. Both moons were well past their zenith when the two young women went to their separate beds. Maglen decided to wrap herself in a blanket and sleep on the floor to get a feel of what it might be like out on the road.

She awoke as dawn was breaking, cold and uncomfortable, shivering in her thin night dress. She scrambled back into her bed and lay there shivering with the bedding pulled tightly around her until the shuddering subsided. This new life was going to take some getting used to!

The next day was a traumatic affair. Despite Maglen's discomfort during the night she was determined to embark on this mad scheme. She gave her father the impression that she would comply with his wishes, even assuring him that she had packed her bags; it made her smile to be telling the truth in essence, even though she had no intention of submitting to an arranged marriage. She began to think logically about the options open to her and while the long-term scheme was still a nebulous plan to support herself by being a farm labourer, she decided that she would start her life on the road in a slightly less drastic change to what she had known. She would start by going to visit Lord and Lady Norland in their castle. News of the refurbishments they were making to the crumbling edifice had reached Launceston and Maglen reasoned that a visit to pay her respects would not be out of order.

She would then leave Norland Castle, supposedly returning home but instead she would disappear into the country. She would head for Medland and then leave the capital and head for Upper Childe where Celdra had told her hiring fairs would be starting soon.

It was the middle of the night when Maglen made her way down the stairs and out of the rear of Launceston Hall. She had bid a tearful farewell to Celdra earlier in the evening and sent the maid to bed. If something went wrong and she was caught trying to make her escape, she didn't want the maid to be implicated.

She had made Celdra swear that she would not admit to helping her mistress in her escape. Maglen was worried that the girl, her friend, might lose her place and she deserved better than that.

She had found out when the Wagoner would be leaving Launceston town and was determined to be there in good time. She arrived at the wayside inn, called appropriately the 'Wait for the Wagon' on the outskirts of the town in plenty of time. She was dressed in one of Celdra's old travelling robes and wore a headscarf tied tightly around her head, hoping no one would recognise her. When the landlord opened his front door, he saw Maglen sitting on the bench where would be travellers waited for the wagon.

'Won't be long miss,' he called across to her, 'Jarge is just attending to his team, won't keep you waiting.'

Sure enough, within a few minutes the gate to the inn yard was swung open and a couple of sturdy drays pulled an already laden wagon out onto the road.

'Where you going to miss?' the wagoner asked.

'I'm going to Norland Castle,' Maglen replied, she didn't mind this part of her plan being known so close to home.

'Well I'm bound for Medland miss, but I can take you as far as Lindon Village, you should be able to get another ride from there. It'll take us a veld to get to Lindon but there's a lot of traffic heading up to Norland Castle now the new lord is putting things to rights,' Jarge told her. 'That'll be two slends,' he continued and when she looked somewhat aghast he added, 'but that includes accommodation and a breakfast for each of the five days.'

Maglen fumbled with her purse and pulled out a strand and offered that to the wagoner; she was not concerned at the cost, only that she had no small change.

'Ain't you got nothing smaller?' he asked in disgust and he dug his hand in his own money bag which hung from his belt. 'Well, I've got no change, so you'll have to wait for the money I owe you.'

They waited a few more minutes and two more travellers, a man and a woman, arrived and paid for carriage all the way to Medland. They told Maglen that they were heading for the hiring fairs at Upper Childe where they hoped to get places for the whole season. Jarge duly paid the three slends he owed her out of the others' fares.

It was a bit of a squeeze getting into the wagon to sit on the few seats that were available with the large sacks of goods that filled most of the wagon. The sacks were full of something soft for they made comfortable cushions and Maglen realised they were full of the wool that was one of Launceston's main exports. Maglen tried to sit quietly but the woman, who Maglen guessed must be at least thirty turns of age, was apparently determined to talk to her. The woman introduced herself as Joyanne and Maglen tried to answer her questions with non-committal grunts and nods of the head. The bumptious woman was well built without really being plump and had a weather-beaten face and gnarled hands that spoke of turns of hard work. She chatted away about inconsequential things and was obviously disappointed that she could not entice more conversation out of their travelling companion. In time she turned to use her male companion as her audience and Maglen was thankfully left to her own thoughts.

Chapter 8

As the day progressed Maglen was in turmoil and shuddered as she realised the enormity of the adventure on which she had embarked. Already her sensibilities had been rocked by the crudity of the life she had chosen. Gone were the niceties of polite society; in the world she had left, no one would have attempted to strike up a conversation in the way this woman had done. She felt very miserable and considered jumping off the wagon and running all the way back to Launceston Hall; she knew that would be the sensible thing to do but couldn't face the ignominy of returning in defeat. By now the household would be up and about their business. No doubt her absence would be known in the house. With a sudden pang she was sure that Crelin now knew she had gone; she could feel his anguish.

They travelled on and the sun burnt off the early morning mist leaving a very pleasant day. As they reached another village there were a few more travellers waiting for the wagon. The drays were changed and to avoid having to talk to the woman again, Maglen went and talked to the wagoner; she asked about the team of drays that were being led into the stables of the inn which they had reached.

'Are they not your drays? Are you leaving them here and what about these that are being harnessed in their place are these yours as well?' she asked.

'Ah well it's like this young lady,' the wagoner explained, hiding his surprise that anyone didn't know the way these things worked, 'I own a pair of drays, I bought them turns ago but I left them at the first inn that | reached on my first day as a wagoner. They became the property of the inn keeper, but he then gave me another pair in their place. I have to pay him a nominal sum for their feed and stabling, but I still have my two drays, you see. I might change teams four times a day, but I still own two drays.'

'Don't you sometimes get a worse pair than the ones you're giving the inn keeper?' Maglen asked.

'Quite often, these two here are not as good as the ones I started the day with,' he said as he connected the wagons harness to the drays' collars, 'the grey here is as lazy a kertle as I've ever met but she'll be someone else's problem this afternoon when we stop again. I sometimes get back the pair I started with, but the teams are always changing.' Maglen nodded, the system had obvious merits and appeared to work well.

'The only time I have trouble is when I have to do a long haul to some distant fifth where I can't change the team until I get back on the main routes. Then I have to stop and rest the animals, doubles the time it normally takes to cover the same distance.' the wagoner complained.

With more travellers fighting for the small amount of seating room available Maglen was able to get herself a ride up front with Jarge and her mood improved; she was not being crowded by the large bags that they carried, and she was certain they were making her itch. More importantly the woman who had joined the wagon right at the start of the day now had plenty of others to talk to. The sound of their raucous laughter made a back drop to the journey.

They travelled on through the southern Launceston land where the farms covered larger areas and the little pockets of habitation were further apart. Late in the afternoon they reached another wayside inn where Jarge announced they would be stopping for the night. Given her position up front Maglen was able to jump down and enter the inn courtyard ahead of the rest of the travellers. She was grateful of being able to get a drink at the pump in the centre of the yard.

'Thirsty after all your talking to the driver are we then my pretty miss?' Joyanne said with a sneer, adding to the others that had accompanied her into the yard, 'too stuck up to talk to the likes of me, that one. Travelled all the way from Launceston to where we picked up you nice people, without saying more than two words at a time. Well, each to their own, let's see what the bunk house is like this turn.' With that she led the way across the yard and into a solid looking building with a thatched roof. There were small windows let into the masonry walls all along the buildings length and in the centre of the roof a large chimney stack protruded and from this, two trails of smoke rose up into the evening sky.

With nothing else to do, Maglen picked up her bundle and followed the group into the bunk house building. This turned out to be a two-room barn of a place. The men turned right and the women to the left as they entered the building. Maglen found herself in a large room with two tier beds lining the walls all round. In the centre of the room was a large wooden table, built to withstand a lot of bad treatment, which judging by its condition, it had received. The five women ahead of her quickly claimed beds for themselves by throwing their bundles onto their chosen bunk.

The first in had claimed the beds nearest a fire which burned in a well blackened grate in the central wall. Maglen guessed correctly that the men's room would be a mirror image of the women's accommodation. She found herself forced to walk to the end of the room where and she was able to claim an empty berth near the far wall. Sitting on her bed she was at a loss to know what to do next; the snide remarks that Joyanne had made had hurt her deeply. She wasn't really trying to be aloof or superior she just had no idea how women of the class she was now trying to enter should behave. She longed to talk to someone but knew she couldn't risk getting to know anyone just yet, she was far too close to home.

Just then there was the clatter of kertle claw sets on the cobbles of the yard as several riders arrived at the inn. Several of the women leapt up and peered out of the grimy windows and Maglen did the same. In the courtyard several guardians were dismounting and tending to their kertles while one, presumably their leader marched straight into the inn. He returned and motioned two of his officers towards the bunkhouse. Maglen left the window and lay down on her bed, pulling the scant covers over her head. She did not wish to be found just yet and she guessed, correctly, that she was the subject of their search.

A guardian burst into the room, throwing aside the sacking drape that hung by the door to give the women some privacy. His arrival brought forth a few screams from the women who were in a state of undress as they changed out of the clothes they had travelled in.

'I'm sorry ladies,' he said as he backed towards the door and slid back behind the drape that shielded the door. 'We're looking for a high-born lady who we think might have travelled this way today' he called from behind the screen.

"Well that must be me;' someone replied and Maglen recognised the voice of the speaker as that of Joyanne, 'but is that any excuse for bursting into a female bedroom, unannounced?' she asked in a very affronted tone, but with a big grin to her female companions.

'I'm sorry madam,' the guardian replied, 'but the woman we are looking for has just passed her majority.'

'Young man! Are you daring to suggest that I am too old to be considered your quarry?' Joyanne replied in the same tone, skilfully hiding the smirk on her face.

'Madam, you're probably old enough to be my mother! Now please tell me, have you seen a young woman answering the description I have given you?' the exasperated guardian replied, it had been a long day since he and his men had been called to Launceston Hall.

'Young man, if you were my son you'd know not to burst into a lady's bedroom, uninvited.' Joyanne replied. This interchange had reduced the rest of the room to a fit of giggles and Maglen began to recover from the initial shock she had suffered when the guardian had burst in.

'Well we can't leave here until we've satisfied ourselves that the lady we're after is not here.' The guardian said in a resigned tone.

'Well some of us ladies have gone to bed,' Joyanne lied, 'So you'll have to wait until the morning before we can let you come in here.'

'Very well,' the guardian replied, he'd had enough for today, 'but we'll inspect you all in the morning.'

Inside the bunkhouse the occupants heard him walk away, his nailed boots rattling on the cobbles and there were several sighs of relief among the giggles from the women in the room.

'Oh, I hate them guardians!' one of the women swore under her breath. This seemed to be the general sentiment around the room which surprised Maglen. She had always thought of Fameral's law enforcers as honourable men who did a valuable job. As she lay under her bedclothes she was aware that someone had come and sat on the edge of her bed.

'Is there anything you'd like to say to me now, young lady?' Joyanne asked in a soft tone that was a revelation to Maglen. She sat up and turned to face the older woman.

'Thank you for not giving me away,' Maglen said, 'why didn't you do so, there might have been a reward?'

'Don't let anyone else hear you say that,' Joyanne whispered and then in a loud voice for all the room to hear added, 'come on girls, why don't most of you go and get your evening meal. Janteal, would you go and get me some food so that I and my friend here can eat in here.'

'I'll need some money,' the woman who Joyanne had spoken to replied. Joyanne started to reach into her purse but Maglen said she would pay for the food. She pulled her own purse up above the bed clothes, released the draw strings and extracted a couple of strands which she handed to the older woman.

'We only need food for the three of us,' Joyanne said handing the coins back to Maglen, 'haven't you got anything smaller?'

'Oh, I'm sorry,' Maglen apologised, 'I'm a bit new to this,' she added aware that she was dropping all her defences. She rummaged around in her purse again and found the three slends change from her mornings transaction with Jarge, which she handed over.

'That's better,' Joyanne said but then handed back one of the coins, 'you really do have a lot to learn about life at this end of the social scale.'

When Janteal had followed the other three women over to the inn's main building Joyanne turned back to face Maglen.

'Obviously you are the high born young lady for whom the guardians are looking. Young Lady Launceston would be my guess. But whatever brings you to this part of the land in this disguise?'

Maglen nodded an affirmation of her identity, 'I'm running away from my father,' she blurted out and dissolved into tears. Joyanne moved her position so that she could give her a hug. This gesture of support made Maglen collapse into a sobbing wreck. When the shaking spasm had died down Joyanne encouraged Maglen to tell her what had happened and, with her defences removed by this sudden display of affection the titled young woman related the whole sorry tale.

'Well I can't say I blame you,' Joyanne told her, 'I was never in that position, of course. My father would have struggled to find anyone to marry me off to. But I think I'd have done just the same as you have if he had.' This made Maglen chuckle which dragged her out of the despair which had overwhelmed her again.

By the time Janteal had returned with a tray of steaming dishes Maglen and Joyanne had formed a bond of trust which was a revelation to the young aristocrat.

'Janteal,' Joyanne told her friend, 'tomorrow we're going to get this young lady out of here and onto the wagon without the guardians realising that she is who they are looking for. Any ideas?'

The other woman sat and thought for a while as she ate the bowl of broth and chewed on the chunks of grain bread the inn had provided. 'We could always colour her hair with ashes from the fire and dull her skin colour with a solution of soot,' she pondered.

'That's a good idea,' Joyanne agreed, 'and if she wears a shawl tied tight about her head and stoops low they'll not get a good look at her face anyway.' Looking around the bunk room, Joyanne saw a pole leaning in the far corner. This she went and collected and gave it a thorough inspection. 'This gives me an idea,' she said.

She made Maglen stand up and stoop as if she had a back twisted with age and then hold out her hand. The pole had one end that had a large knobble on the end and this Joyanne put on the floor and held the other end so that the pole touched Maglen's out stretched hand. Joyanne marked the pole at this point and took out her knife and began cutting away at the wood. In a very short time she had separated the two halves and she offered the end with the knobble to Maglen who had caught on very quickly to what the older woman had in mind. Maglen took hold and used the newly formed walking stick to hobble around the room. Both Joyanne and Janteal applauded her efforts and Maglen was reduced to a fit of giggles. Joyanne then coloured and hardened the cut end in the fire and suggested that Maglen used the remnants of the butter supplied with their meal to rub all over the stick, especially the handle, to age it and make it look well worn. This done, Maglen had a perfectly normal and well used looking walking stick to finish her disguise.

The other two women then set about preparing the aging make up they had discussed, and they had a lot of fun applying it to the young noble woman. When the other women returned from the inn after their evening meal they were presented with a very frail looking travelling companion. They had all entered into the spirit of the subterfuge and Maglen was greatly relieved that despite all her efforts to conceal her identity, its revelation had caused no problems; in fact, it seemed to have made her some friends.

The next morning the women rose and went across to the inn for the breakfast which was part of the Wagoner's package deal. Jarge looked very hard at the frail old woman who passed him as he stood at the inn door but he kept his own council and the guardians were none the wiser. The leader of the guardian troop was determined to search for himself when his men assured him that their quarry was not in the inn or the bunkhouse.

'Well our information was obviously in error and we've wasted too much time here,' he said in disgust. He gave orders for his men to mount their kertles and the troop went galloping off down the road ahead of the wagon.

The wagon set off at its appointed hour and Maglen settled down to the life on the road. She was much more at peace with herself and with her companions although her face and hands were itching from the aging treatment they had received. The company on the wagon changed at each stop, some leaving and new travellers joining but Joyanne and her male companion were a constant. This gave Maglen someone to talk to and a protection against all the questions and prying eyes that seemed to be the nature of things at each stop they made. The search for a young lady of high breeding had caught the imagination of everyone who heard of her disappearance.

In a tavern several leagues away from where Maglen was travelling a meeting was taking place between the two eldest Lather siblings. They had worked out a time table which allowed them to work their ways around Northern Fameral meeting occasionally to correlate what they had found out and what they had achieved.

'I really think things are coming together sis,' Natheal said as he returned to their alcove table with another round of drinks, 'I'm getting lots of support for our ideas.'

'I'm not so sure we will be able to bring about a major change in Fameral politics,' Pardrea told him, 'there's still a lot of loyalty to the former House of Norland. The old Lord Gerandal Norland was well loved and respected and everyone is full of expectation of what the new Lord Norland is going to do. I've met a lot of resistance to our plans of forcing up the workers rates.'

'Well, I've been travelling all over Launceston and had a good reception everywhere I went.' Natheal countered.

'Well it's different in Norland where I have been. There's a new buzz going around now that this Jaxaal Norland has come into his own.' Pardrea replied. 'All the people are talking about the changes he is instigating. I think we'd be better off down south of the Childe Mountains in Swenland or Dresham where the ruling families are not so well respected.'

'Maybe you're right,' Natheal conceded, 'Old Galtaain Dresham is still well respected so perhaps we should aim our intention towards Swenland. Now that the old lord has been deposed there might be a chance for us while the new regent finds his feet.'

'Yeah, a blind man won't have such a good grip on things, so we might be able to stir-up some unrest when the harvest bathern really gets going.' Pardrea agreed.

'But until then,' Natheal decided in a tone that made this a firm decision, 'we'll head down towards High Tor Farm for the hiring fairs. Now that Uster Oostedd is away in Norland with the new Lord we may have more success in swaying the workers. I've been thinking about how we actually manage to get our point across. What we need is for you and some of your female friends to persuade the women to make the men follow my lead. You know the sort of thing, holding their children in groups until they agree. It's amazing what influence you can bring about with your knife against a child's throat,' he finished with malicious glee. Had anyone else witnessed this short conversation they might have been more than a little disturbed by the evil glint in Pardrea's eyes at her brother's words.

In his woodland home life for Bryland continued in a very pleasant manner. He had spent many hours, days even, studying the animals that shared his domain. He knew where the brocks lived in their fortress styled keep. These grey animals with their black and white faces were kings of their world and were scared of nothing. Bryland's appearance had obviously given them pause for thought but they soon worked out that he was no threat to them and they tolerated him. He respected this benevolence and didn't abuse their forbearance.

He taught himself about the woodland birds and realised that a pond on the other side of the hill behind his camp was the home of a breed of wild breesh hens. Their succulent flesh was a tasty treat and their eggs, which they seemed to lay all turn round, a delicacy to be enjoyed. He studied the night birds and saw the ones that could colour the night air with their long mournful hoots.

When some wool animals wondered into his valley, obviously some escapees from a distant farm, he was able to get himself a couple of fleeces that greatly improved his bedding; something he realised he would need when the weather turned really bitter. He saw the flock and when he approached them was challenged by the ram. The big male had gathered his own little flock and was determined to protect them, which he might have done but for Bryland's newly acquired stealth and his skill with the bow. His first attempts were not met with great success. The wool beast's, the sheep's fleece, had not been shorn for a turn or two and hung like a great shaggy defence against his arrows. Only by carefully shaping points on the ends and hardening them in a fire was he able to create the means of getting a shot to penetrate through into the sheep's body where it could bring the animal down and that was only possible at close range or with a shot that fell from high in the sky. Such sky shots were always a lucky strike, more often than not the shaft would bury itself harmlessly in the ground.

Rufran took to the new life very well, there was a good supply of excellent grazing all over the area and the gelding enjoyed being allowed to roam free. At first Bryland had tethered the kertle on increasingly longer cords but soon realised that he was probably not going to wonder off and get lost; he obviously enjoyed Bryland's company. Bryland decided to make the camp even more attractive to the dray by fully wind-proofing the walls to his stable and by using the last of his oiled cloth he was able to make it rain proof.

Rufran was a little disturbed by the Red Cannis when he appeared the first night he stayed in his new home but within a veld the two animals came to accept each other's presence. A few velds later the Red Cannis and his mate appeared with their latest litter of cubs and introduced them to Bryland and his dray. Rufran was intrigued by the cubs that showed no fear as they ran between his legs and sniffed at his claw sets. Bryland laughed as one cub stalked and then leapt on one of Rufran's front claws. The kertle hastily withdrew it and the cub made another attack on the claw in its new position. This then became a game and the other two cubs quickly followed their sibling, joining in the fun of the new game. This went on for a while until the female cannis decided it was time to take her family back to their den.

Bryland lay in his sleeping furs that night and chuckled at the memory of the cubs' game. His life was good, he decided, but deep down he knew he was basically very lonely. He missed the company of other people, his Alphen visits to Under Childe gave him some human interaction but it was fleeting and transitory.

More than that, he realised that he wanted some female company. Perhaps on his next visit he would seek out one of the bar or scullery maids and see if they would spend time with him. Ruefully he realised that only two or three batherns ago he might have been associating with high born ladies; as a senior member of one of the five ruling houses he was an eligible match for the highest born ladies. Now he would be grateful for the time of the lowest maids in the land.

Chapter 9

As Jarge had promised, five days after leaving Launceston the wagon pulled into Lindon Village and Maglen was forced to say goodbye to Joyanne and her companion. In all their conversations, Maglen had not found out what the relationship was between Joyanne and her male friend. With a giggle she realised that they were probably not related at all and it would be indelicate, to say the least, to press the matter. During their last conversation Joyanne had warned Maglen of the dangers in confiding her identity to the other workers she might meet on the road.

'There's one young woman who is trying to stir up trouble by getting the workers to 'gang together' as she puts it. Her name is Pardrea Lather and she and her brother Natheal are out to cause trouble. They've got this idea that if the workers get together they can force up their wages. They've got a real hatred for the ruling families and their fifth masters. If they find out who you are they'll hand you over to the guardians for certain. Unless, of course, they decided to hold you as a hostage demanding money from your family. I wouldn't put that passed them.'

'But why are they so against the ruling families?' Maglen asked.

'I heard that they ran afoul of Lord Swenland who threw them and their father off his land when they complained that he wasn't paying a living wage. Their father died that winter and they've never got over it.' Joyanne told her.

'Oh, that's awful,' Maglen replied, this side of Fameral politics was something totally unknown to her.

'Well all I'm saying is, if you meet up with either Natheal or Pardrea, don't let on who you are. They have a real hatred for the ruling classes,' Joyanne confided. She then went and re-boarded the wagon which was about to begin its last run of the day.

Maglen went and had a look around the village. She had been here before of course. The Launceston family caravan had stopped here overnight on its way to and from the last Fameral Challenge Meet. She made a point of avoiding the large inn in the village square where she and her family always stayed and went, instead, to a smaller establishment on the outskirts of the village on the Norland road.

Here she was able to get accommodation for the night. She was tempted to take an upstairs room when it was offered but opted instead for a bed space in the barn at the back of the stables. She was the only female staying in that part of the inn and was able to get a bucket of water from the pump and give herself an all over wash, her first since leaving home. She still couldn't wash her face or hair for fear of destroying her fragile disguise. This was a problem for her face itched abominably; she guessed it was the effects of the ashes and soot solution Janteal had concocted.

She ventured over to the main inn to get an evening meal and was very apologetic to the landlord when she was forced to offer him a whole strand; she had nothing smaller in her purse at that point. She was able to make it appear that it was the only coin she had in her possession and her apologies did the trick and the landlord accepted the large denomination coin, giving her enough smaller coins as change to last her at least until she reached Norland.

That night as she lay on her bed of straw wearing all her clothes to keep warm, she tried to send messages to Crelin. They had never been telepathic, but both had always sensed the other's emotions and she knew he was worried about her. She tried to assure him that she was alright, safe, warm and comfortable. The fact that the last was far from the truth she hoped would not disturb the message she wanted her brother to receive.

The next morning Feraard, Lord Launceston sat with his chamberlain studying the latest reports from the guardians who had been seeking his daughter. His hopes of finding Maglen quickly, as soon as he learned of her absconding, had faded with each passing day. His wife was pleading with him to redouble his efforts to find her, to double the already sizable reward which was on offer and to have every guardian in North West Fameral out scouring the country side. Instead the lord had decided to call off the hunt for her; firstly, because now a veld had passed hopes of finding her were fading and secondly, and selfishly, he was embarrassed by the fact that his daughter had run away because of him and his plans for her. The letter she had left on her dressing table had made her reasons for going quite clear.

Lady Launceston dissolved into tears when he told her of his decision to abandon the search. She was a little comforted by her son's assertion that his twin was all right and not in any danger. She had always known of the links that had existed between the brother and sister, their empathy had caused enough trouble when they were babies, but it had seemed a source of strength for them both as they got older. She was not at all happy about the ending of the search but was stoically resigned to it. Her husband reminded her of another meeting with the other lords that Darval Ellward had requested and made a big thing, for his wife's sake, of the chance this would give him of seeking out more information on his daughter.

The next morning Maglen was able to get passage on another wagon that was going all the way to Norland Castle. This one was carrying sawn timber from the woodlands that lay to the south west and this gave much more room for the human cargo. There were two other passengers waiting to board the wagon when Maglen came and paid the wagoner her fare. They told her that one of them was a mason and the other a skilled wood worker, both hoping to get employment at the castle where, it was rumoured that good wages and plenty of work were available. She felt a little more comfortable now that she had a disguise to hide behind. She had developed a high squeaky voice that she hoped, and Joyanne had confirmed, matched the frail old woman she was pretending to be.

The trip up to Norland Castle lasted another veld and Maglen was feeling fairly safe in her attempt to escape. The number of guardian patrols scouring the country side had subsided and she hoped that the pursuit had been called off, but she couldn't let her defences down too soon. She gleaned other bits of news from the inns where they made their overnight stops and from the few other passengers that joined the wagon as it progressed towards Norland.

When they crested the last rise before they reached Norland they were greeted by the magnificent edifice of the castle that lent the town a magnificent backdrop. It dominated the sky line with its imposing towers and cliff like walls. Norland town was impressive in its own way; much larger than Launceston and there seemed to be a lot more activity than in Maglen's home town. The wagon threaded its way through the streets to the town centre which was marked by a large square. Here all the other passengers alighted, thanking the wagoner for his skill in negotiating the roads they had travelled. The wagoner knew the two tradesmen wanted to actually go to the castle, but he expected Maglen to leave in the town. When she insisted that she also wanted to go to the castle itself, he agreed to take her but made it clear that he didn't think they'd be interested in hiring an old woman like her. Maglen was pleased that her disguise had apparently fooled him for their entire journey.

The evident hive of activity that she had first noticed as they approached the town was confirmed as they rode through it towards the castle. Everywhere work on the houses seemed to be taking place. Ladders were placed at so many of the buildings Maglen wondered if that was the way the people of Norland reached their upper floors until she saw that most had a man somewhere up their height, busily painting or rendering the walls. Walls were being repaired or painted; roofs were being tiled or slated and many lengths of guttering lay waiting to be put in place. Norland was a town repairing itself.

The activity was not just in the town. As they approached the edifice, Maglen could see that wooden scaffolding grew like ivy up the walls and a great deal of masonry work was taking place. A great deal had already been completed for great sections of the walls shone white in the afternoon sun where new stone work replaced lost or damaged sections. As the wagon rattled across the draw bridge Maglen saw that the moat had been drained and men looking like besmirched mud hoppers toiled waist deep in an evil smelling sludge. It appeared that they were attempting to reline the moat, presumably to make it watertight again. The wagon rolled under an imposing portcullis which hung ominously above the entrance. Great wooden doors were standing open just beyond the raised barrier and they led into a large open area within the castle itself. In the centre of this area stood a magnificent keep, itself as fortified as the outer castle walls.

The wagon stopped at a small kiosk like structure where a tired looking clerk sat with his quill and parchments. The clerk looked up and seeing the two men descending rose and spoke to them. They were soon directed to another part of the castle and the clerk turned his attention to Maglen.

'And what do want here old mother?' he asked.

'I would like to see Lady Janilla Norland,' Maglen told him, thankfully abandoning her squeaky voice. The unexpected rich tone of her natural voice seemed to surprise the clerk who stared at her in surprise.

'And just what would your business be with Lady Norland,' he asked. This was not going to be very easy, Maglen realised.

'It's a private matter,' was all Maglen could think to say.

'Well it might be private but unless I have a more convincing reason than that, here's where you'll be staying, until I have you thrown from the grounds,' the clerk sneered dismissively. Maglen was in despair, she was very tired; she'd been travelling for two velds and was exhausted.

'But it's important that I speak to her personally,' she wailed.

'Personally, is it!' the clerk continued in the same condescending tone, 'why should one of the highest ladies in the land wish to speak to the likes of you?'

'Because she knows me, we spoke together two batherns ago,' Maglen replied, totally at a loss to know how to deal with this officious little man.

'Well you'd better tell me your name and I'll send word up to her ladyship's apartments, when I can find time and we'll see if she wishes to continue her conversation with you.'

'I can't tell you my name, just tell her a friend would like to speak to her,' Maglen said, fighting back the tears in her frustration.

'Oh, you're a friend now,' the clerk sneered and Maglen looked up to the sky desperate to know what to do next. As her eyes strayed over the castle courtyard she saw an older man leave the keep and walk purposefully across the yard. It was a familiar face that she saw, and she called out to him.

'Chamberlain Draxen, one moment of your time if you please,' she called dropping instinctively into the high language. While the clerk did not understand the language reserved for only the highest members of Fameral society, he recognised it when he heard it and stared at her in astonishment.

Draxen stopped in his tracks; he was as surprised as was the clerk to hear his name and the high language called across the courtyard. He turned and stared at the old lady who stood with the yard clerk.

He immediately noticed that while obviously old and weather beaten she stood proud and erect and instinctively went to investigate. As he got up to this woman who had addressed him so strangely, he peered into her face.

'Chamberlain Draxen,' Maglen said dropping her bundle and grabbing his hand, 'it is imperative that I speak to Lady Janilla as soon as possible.'

Her desperation transmitted itself to Draxen and he stared even closer into her face.

'Lady.' he began as recognition flooded through him.

'Yes,' Maglen replied, cutting him off so that he didn't actually say her name.

'Well I'm just on my way to see Jaxaal now and I believe Janilla will be with him at this hour.' He told her and then reverting to common language he turned to the clerk and said, 'It's quite all right Jaldoon, I know this woman, she will be accepted into the family's quarters.'

Very good Chamberlain Draxen,' Jaldoon replied, 'as you say Sir. Sorry madam. Just doing my job Sir.'

'Quite so,' Draxen replied and turned and led Maglen across the courtyard and in through a very magnificently decorated doorway. As they passed it, Maglen noticed that for all its decorative qualities the door was solidly built and could be securely bolted from the inside. They climbed up two or three imposing stairways and finally reached a comfortably decorated room with rich carpets on the floor and tapestries hanging on every wall. Draxen paused for a few moments, apologising for the delay.

'I'm not as young as I was, and Castle Norland is built for fit young persons.' He smiled. He then led the way through to what was obviously a private drawing room.

As he entered he spoke in a low sonorous tone to get everyone's attention, 'If you'll forgive this intrusion everyone, there is a lady here who would like to speak to you.' and he stepped aside to reveal the diminutive figure of Maglen standing behind him. She stood looking at her feet holding her hands resting demurely on her stick in front of her. She might be of one of the five highest families in the land, but she suddenly felt as if she were in the presence of the highest group of nobles in all of Fameral as she did raise her eyes she saw Jaxaal and Janilla Norland sitting together on one couch and Lady Arianne Oostedd and Geldren Ellward on another opposite them. She then remembered that she had heard that as well as Janilla, Geldren was studying medicine and healing under Lady Arianne. Everyone in the room raised their heads and looked at the stranger standing before them. The dishevelled figure was a pitiful sight in a dress that was stained from two velds on the road and grey straggles of hair creeping out from under a shawl pulled tightly around her head.

It was Janilla who first had an inkling as to the identity of their visitor. She rose and went over to Maglen and stared into her face.

'It is!' she said triumphantly, 'Maglen Launceston what are you doing here in this state?

'Well I thought I'd come and see how your renovations were getting on,' Maglen lied.

'Oh, don't worry about why you're here,' Janilla said as she took Maglen by the arm and led her towards the fire, 'we got the news that you had left Launceston, although your father's message gave no reason. I wondered if you might find your way here and I can guess the cause. I think I was in a similar position three batherns ago and she gave Maglen's arm a comforting squeeze. This sign of support was too much and Maglen dissolved into tears as she sat on the sofa nearest the fire.

'Jaxaal,' Janilla called, 'can you ring for some kandrel and a few grain cakes might be in order. Jaxaal nodded and went over to the bell pull and summoned a maid. He then went over to Draxen who was hovering by the door.

'Well here's a fine situation that's presented itself!' he said in a soft tone for Draxen's ears only.

'Indeed, my lord,' Draxen replied equally quietly, 'we can't very well ignore a direct request for information from Lord Launceston when it has come knocking at our door.'

Jaxaal had made some shrewd assumptions when news of Maglen's disappearance had first arrived and her sudden arrival confirmed what he had deduced as to why.

'No, I feel duty bound to let Feraard know that his daughter is safe and well, but I'm loathed to be any part of facilitating an arranged marriage against the wish of those involved,' Jaxaal confided to his chamberlain.

'Well we needn't do anything for a day or two,' Draxen advised, 'she's obviously been travelling in disguise so hopefully she won't be traced here. It would be unthinkable to lie to your fellow lord but there is no reason for us to volunteer information unnecessarily.'

'I agree,' Jaxaal said with a wry grin and he went back to the sofa where Maglen was being comforted by the females. Arianne had sent for a bowl of warm water and some cloths and when they arrived she began cleaning the worst of the ashy grime from Maglen's face.

'This won't do at all,' Arianne announced as she inspected Maglen's skin closely, 'the ashes you used to dye your hair and face have burnt your skin. We'll need to get rid of every last trace of the horrid stuff and get some soothing oils onto the blisters. Hopefully you won't scar. We need to get you in an all over bath and out of these clothes, some of the ash remnants have got into the fibres and will only aggravate your skin if you wear them again.'

She then stood up and began issuing orders; Geldren was dispatched to Arianne's medical workroom to fetch various medicines, herbs and oils and with the help of two maids who had been summoned, Maglen was helped along various corridors and down some stairs to a very functional room. The first impression of Arianne's medical work room was of sparkling methodical cleanliness.

Maglen was relieved of her clothes and somewhat embarrassed, stood naked in the middle of the floor where a grating showed that water could be drained away. She was then subjected to a shower from several buckets of warm water that Geldren delighted in throwing over her and a copious supply of soap root enabled her to get rid of the last vestige of the ashes and soot.

As she sat using some very luxurious drying towels a maid arrived with a tray carrying a big pot of kandrel and several mugs. These were duly distributed and Maglen was encouraged to tell her story.

'Sounds as if your father is continuing with The House of Dresham to form links with a southern house where he failed when I refused to be betrothed to your brother at the Eve of Challenge Ball,' Janilla said and Maglen nodded her agreement.

'I've met Sorjohn Dresham of course,' Maglen said, 'but I don't really know him. Certainly not enough to know if I want to marry him.'

'Oh, he's quite nice,' Geldren interposed and then stopped and blushed as all eyes turned on her.

'What my cousins is hinting at,' Janilla said with a twinkle in her eye, 'is that Sorjohn Dresham is already spoken for and isn't available for the other half of an arranged marriage. Geldren here, and Sorjohn think they have kept their relationship a secret but we are all aware of what's going on between them,' she finished with a wave of her hand to the others in the room.'

'But,' Geldren began to protest but then realised it was pointless exercise and sat back down with an embarrassed grin.

Just then there was knock on the door and Jaxaal asked if the occupants were decent enough for two gentlemen to enter. When he and Draxen were seated with a mug of kandrel in their hands he asked Maglen to repeat her story and he then sat deep in thought. Janilla was a little concerned by her husband's reticence and asked what he was thinking about.

'You are not seriously considering sending Maglen back to her father!' she exclaimed in horror.

'If Maglen wishes to return to Launceston Hall, I'll gladly place a Norland coach, team and men at her disposal,' Jaxaal replied, 'but my guess is that is not what she wishes.'

Maglen vehemently affirmed that she did not wish to return home, her plan was to travel down to Medland and then go further.

'Please do not tell me, or Draxen, your plans,' Jaxaal told her, 'As Lord of one of The Five Houses I am duty bound to keep your father informed of what I know. Having said that, I will not help in any way towards putting you in a position where you will be forced to marry against your will. You are welcome to stay here at Norland Castle for as long as you wish. The more the merrier. As you can see I already have a wife, an aunt and a cousin to hen peck me mercilessly, another high-born female in my household will not signify!'

When the general protestations at this statement from his three female relations had died down Jaxaal went and knelt before Maglen taking her hands in his.

'Maglen you are welcome to stay here as long as you wish as our guest. In a couple of days, I must let your parents as well as your brother know that you are safe and well. But even then, I will not make you go anywhere you do not wish to go. In fact, I will soon have to leave for another meeting in Medland of the five Heads of Houses that Darval Ellward has called. When I meet with your father I will have to tell him I have seen you and reassure him you are well. Your mother is very worried about you, you know.'

Maglen stared into his eyes and then looked at Janilla and Arianne who smiled encouragingly back at her. It was all too much, and she dissolved into tears again.

'Right, that's enough,' Lady Arianne announced, 'come on girls,' she said addressing Geldren and Janilla, 'we've a patient's wounds to deal with. If you gentlemen will leave us, we'll attend to Maglen's burns.'

Chapter 10

Bryland made a decision, he would go into Under Childe two velds early; he needed some human company. He checked his stock of skins, only two were ready to be taken and sold and he only had another two waiting to be treated. Normally he would not travel all that distance without at least five good pelts, but the journey would be easier now he had Rufran to carry him and his stock. He decided to not take any skins to sell with him, that could wait a veld, he would just go anyway. He couldn't but ask himself if this was a sensible thing to be doing, but why not? He would feel better with the change of scene. It was a flimsy excuse really, he'd be going there in ten days, a couple of veld's time to compete in the Archer's competition but his need for social interaction was a powerful motivation.

As he rode into the inn yard at The Five Houses he was aware of a general air of bustle and activity. It seemed to be surrounding a large wagon that had obviously just arrived and from which a number of people were disgorging. As he stabled Rufran he picked up some of the conversations that were going on around the yard and deduced that the wagon was owned by a troop of travelling players. He was unable to get Rufran a stall on his own and the dray would have to share with a mare. The mare's owner was not too happy about this until he had established that Rufran had been gelded. It appeared that the travelling players would be putting on a show that night in the inn yard itself. This was more like it! With a greatly lightened spirit Bryland was delighted that he had decided to come into under Childe a veld early.

'I suppose you've come to see the shows at The Five Houses tonight?' the shoemaker said and was surprised when Bryland said that he hadn't but was looking forward to doing so.

'They always put on a good night,' the shoemaker told him when Bryland dropped in on him, 'very entertaining they are, and very informative. They usually have small plays to tell some of the latest news and I expect the goings on at the last Challenge will be one of the subjects.' This gave Bryland pause for thought but he reassured himself that any such playlet would probably focus on the love story between Jaxaal and Janilla.

Bryland bought himself a meal at the inn but was unable to get a bed for the night, all the rooms were full. It appeared that the ostler should not have allowed him to stable Rufran due to the influx of people to see the shows and Bryland was tempted to eat his meal and head back into the woods but his need for company prevailed and he decided he would have to share Rufran's sleeping space, it would be crowded in the stall with two kertles in there as well! He enjoyed the food and it was with tankard in hand that he headed out into the yard full of expectation. He managed to get a seat on a plank that had been put across two barrels, just one of many that now covered the inn yard. He was jostled good naturedly by a large woman who made him shift up so that she and her male companion could sit down.

The entertainment started when some musicians processed into the yard and made their way to the front of the audience where they took up positions in front of the large wagon which had been transformed into a stage. Bryland thought he recognised the tune as they processed around but couldn't put a name to it. His musing on the title was interrupted by a large man, the master of ceremonies who, dressed in a flamboyant costume, leapt onto the centre of the make shift stage and welcomed the audience. He then assured them that they were in for a night's entertainment, the like of which they had never seen before.

'Well, not since the last time we were here!' he said as an aside. This brought forth some general laughter and set the tone for the evening. He then went on to introduce the first act which turned out to be a male singer who led the audience in the choruses of some well know songs. The singer was followed by a juggler who amazed everyone with his skill. A young female acrobat then performed some impossible looking tricks to great applause. A comedian then had the audience in fits of laughter with a series of very short jokes and amusing anecdotes. This item was followed by a medley of tunes played by the musicians who had been sitting quietly enjoying the entertainment going on above them on the stage. The M/C then called a short interval which enabled everyone to replenish the contents of their tankards.

When the break was over the musicians again played some well-known tunes. During the break the stage had been redressed and as the audience took their seats they noticed that a large cloth or curtain on a long length of pole had been raised to hide what was on the stage. The musicians ended their medley and after a short break began a mournful tune that set the mood for what was to follow. The MC, now wearing a plain coat and a sombre expression on his face, then took the stage standing in front of the curtain.

'Ladies and gentlemen, we now bring you news of what happened in Medland at the last Challenge,' he intoned, and a cheer went up from all around the courtyard.

'Yes, you may well cheer, for as you all know, Jaxaal Norland won The Challenge and claimed as his prize the reinstatement of The House of Norland!' This was met with an even louder cheer and the stamping of feet on wooden floors and the cobble stones.

'Yes,' the MC shouted to make himself heard above the racket and waving his hands got the noise to decrease. 'Yes,' he continued, 'and we could present for you the clever way Lord Norland was able to arrange his marriage to the lovely Janilla Swenland.' This was met with suitable cheers and sighs of 'ahh.'

'But instead,' he said in a tone that hushed the crowd, 'we bring you a tale of lies and deceit, of treachery and malpractice that will make your blood boil. It is a tale of heroes,' and the cast-off stage cheered, 'and of evil villains,' and the cast led a round of hisses and boos. 'Ladies and gentlemen, we present for your delight and edification, "The Fall of Lord Neldon Swenland",' and he stepped sideways off the stage. The curtain pole was lowered to reveal a stable setting with a man kneeling reverently beside a clutch of kertle eggs. Bryland was suddenly struck with absolute terror as the MC's words sank in. This could be his worst nightmare.

'Lord Norland, Lord Norland,' the kneeling actor called, and another actor entered dressed in the red and yellow colours of the House of Swenland.

'Yes Bryland,' the new actor asked, 'what is it?'

'Master,' the kneeling actor replied, 'our top racing dam has laid her clutch at last and we may be able to pull of the swindle that I suggested to you.'

'But I want to win The Challenge without cheating,' the actor playing Neldon replied.

'Yes, I know my lord,' the actor playing Bryland said, 'but I cannot guarantee that our best kertle will win. If, as I have suggested, you use two kertles on the last three days of The Challenge then you can be sure of winning.

Bryland sat mortified, this was such a travesty of the truth; it was Neldon's plan to use two kertles and he, Bryland, had known nothing of it until after the event. The performance continued with the fiction being compounded, scene after scene. The whole story, as the actors were interpreting it, was played out and at every turn, Bryland was made to be the villain. The final enactment showed Neldon being led away by guardians in disgrace with the other actors, except the one playing Bryland who was nowhere to be seen, all standing around and bemoaning the fate of the wronged and duped Neldon Swenland. The enactment ended with the MC coming to the front and in a sonorous voice intoning the finale.

'And there, ladies and gentlemen, we see the downfall of a member of one of the highest houses in the land, laid low by the dastardly tricks and schemes of the real villain of the piece, Bryland Doltaary. And where is this evil man now, you might ask?' and here the MC lent forward to confide in his rapt audience, 'well, no one knows. After his despicable acts and treachery were revealed, Bryland Doltaary has simply disappeared. No one knows where he is, he has not been seen, and few would recognise him. He could be sitting in this very audience tonight! He could be sitting right next to you,' and he pointed all around the courtyard auditorium.' He stepped back behind the curtain which was then raised again, ending the show.

The audience sat mesmerised, Bryland with them. This was such a fantastic tale, brilliantly told if almost totally inaccurate. Bryland was tempted to stand up and defend himself; to tell what had really happened but he knew he could not. The whole courtyard was buzzing with the conversations that had sprung up following the end if the show.

Bryland managed to stop himself from running but as quickly as he could he left the courtyard and got himself into the stables. He went straight to Rufran's stall and disturbed the kertle's reverie by dragging his saddle off the rafters above the stall where it had been stored, and saddling the kertle. Rufran was delighted to see his master and gave welcoming snuffles as Bryland slipped his bridle over his head. As he led the him out of the stables he was able to speak to the ostler and asked him to tell the inn keeper that he would pay him what he owed when he came again. The courtyard was still thronged with people and there was just one subject of conversation the treachery of this Bryland Doltaary.

Bryland threaded his way through the crowd; luckily, he was not the only person leaving so he didn't feel so conspicuous but still he went in dread of someone recognising him. Despite his worst fears no one called out his name and he reached the road outside and was able to mount Rufran in relatively comfortable obscurity. He started off by letting Rufran amble at a gentle walk but as they approached the outskirts of the town he couldn't resist urging him into a trot which became a canter as they cleared the last of the houses. Luckily

Bryland was too much of a kertle master to give in to the temptation to go faster and dangerously gallop through the night and within a league or two he had reined Rufran back to a steady trot.

He travelled on; his mind racing over the dramatic misrepresentation of the truth that he had been forced to endure. He was still fuming when Bathos had joined his lover Alphos in the sky and the two moons cast their combined light on the road ahead. With this increased illumination he felt sufficiently confident in letting Rufran travel at a relatively easy, ground covering canter. In this way he was able to get back to his woodland hideout before the sun had chased the moons from the sky. Even though he was exhausted his first thought was for Rufran and he gave the kertle a thorough rub down and oiling before he put his kertle blanket on him and turned him loose in his stall.

As Bryland fell into his own bed his mind was still churning over and over the injustice that had been done to his name. He was aware that dawn had turned into early morning before he finally fell into fitful, dream ridden sleep.

Chapter 11

Maglen woke from the best sleep she had enjoyed for two velds. The treatment of her burns and the application of numb root had eased her soreness and the potion that Arianne had concocted for her to drink just before she went to bed had ensured she got the rest she needed. As she lay in a warm comfortable bed, drowsy in the morning light, she felt at peace with the world. Instinctively she knew that Crelin was also feeling a lot better. Leagues away in Launceston Hall her twin brother suddenly knew that his sister was alright, safe, warm and out of a stressful situation.

Maglen turned over but couldn't slip back into the dreams she had left. Her mind kept going over the options open to her. She could stay here at Norland Castle; Jaxaal and Janilla had made that very clear but she felt that would be an imposition. Her inclination was to continue on her mad cap flight away from her father's influence. If she could impose on the Norlands' generosity still further, she should be able to get herself down and south of the Childe Mountains and she felt she would feel safe there. She knew that the mountains were no real barrier; certainly not since reinstatement of The House of Norland. The Childe Cut was now seen as a valid and safe way to cross the barrier the Childes presented.

She had learnt a lot on her journeys so far and felt that she could face the world of the normal people of Fameral with some confidence. She knew that she would still stick out and be recognised as a member of one of the high families. Her fair hair, not to mention her almost white skin, marked her heritage and was difficult to disguise; this business with the ashes and the burns it had caused were proof of that. But if she could overcome that problem she knew she had the resolve to live the life of a common labourer. She still hoped to get work on the land and a hiring fair would be the best way of achieving that and she had heard that the best prospect for work and the best fairs were held south of the mountains.

Lady Arianne appeared sometime later with Geldren in tow; they were going to inspect and retreat her burns. Arianne's inspection showed a marked improvement, the soothing oils she had used had done their work. Geldren helped with the application of fresh oils and ointments and then sat companionably on Maglen's bed as the young Lady Launceston dressed herself in the clothes that Janilla had sent for her to choose from.

The two girls quickly established a friendship based on trust and Maglen felt happy in confiding her plans to Geldren. Although younger, Lady Ellward was interested in knowing what she could do to help and Maglen explained that she needed to be able to dress in clothes that would not reveal her true social standing.

'Well what you've got on now won't do at all,' Geldren said as she looked as Maglen twirled in front of a mirror. 'Janilla's dress fits you very well, you are both about the same size, especially here,' and she pointed to Maglen's breasts with a giggle, 'but it is far too good a quality for a simple farm girl.'

'Yes, that was one of the problems I had when I left Launceston,' Maglen confessed, 'I was wearing my maid's clothes but even they were obviously much better quality than the country girls would wear.'

'That settles it then,' Geldren said with glee, 'we'll just have to go shopping in the lower part of the town. We'll dress down so that we'll not be seen as high born, 'she said conspiratorially in a lowered tone, 'and get you fitted up with the right sort of clothes.'

The sheer excitement that the younger girl felt was infectious and Maglen found herself being drawn into Geldren's scheme with enthusiasm.

Later that day two females, dressed in all enveloping cloaks, even though it was a pleasant enough day without any real need for such heavy coverings, made their way back to Norland Castle from the town itself. They were laughing and joking with each other although they both laboured under heavy bundles. Once back inside the castle itself they both threw back the hoods of their cloaks to let the hot air that was trapped inside escape. Back in what had become Maglen's bedroom the two conspirators were finally able to relieve themselves of their heavy bundles and to take off their heavy cloaks.

'That went very well!' Geldren exclaimed with a laugh, 'I haven't had so much fun since we dressed Jaxaal up as an Ellward serf to get him inside the Swenland mansion in Medland.

'Is that when he found out why Neldon was lying about his injuries in his fight with Jaxaal?' Maglen asked.

'You're very well informed,' Janilla said as she entered the room, 'so come on show me what you've bought.'

'How do you know we've bought anything?' Maglen asked.

'Because I know my cousin,' Janilla replied with a grin, 'both Arianne and I knew something was going on the moment Geldren came and asked to be excused this morning's exercises in making infusions. So, what have you bought, I'm dying of curiosity.'

The two conspirators were then obliged to undo all their packages and Maglen was made to try on the various garments.

'We've got several petticoats and under skirts, the sort the field workers wear,' Geldren said, 'but we couldn't find any draws at all!'

'That's because the ordinary female field worker doesn't wear them.' Arianne said as she entered the room in search of her absconding pupils. When all three younger females had pulled faces at that she went on, 'you high born ladies have a lot to learn about the lower classes, or the lower classes have a lot to learn about how genteel folk behave.'

'That's why the comments about me being not who I was pretending to be started back in the inn bunkhouse,' Maglen said, some things dropping into place, 'I used the communal female wash room wearing just a bodice and my draws. I noticed that the others all kept at least one petticoat on.'

'Yes, a bit of a giveaway,' Arianne agreed.

'But how do they deal with, well, you know, those times?' Geldren queried.

'The same way you do,' Arianne told her, 'with absorbent pads and waist straps.'

The discussion then went back to the garments they had actually bought and Maglen was obliged to put on each one in turn and it was then discussed in detail. Suddenly Arianne was reduced to a fit of giggles.

'Do you remember Geldren?' she asked, 'this is just the sort of discussion we had back at Ellward House in Medland after your mother's shopping trip with you and Felda. Only then we were concerned that the garments bought might not be dressy enough for the Challenge social events. Now we're worried about the exact opposite!'

'Maglen insisted that we only bought the simplest clothes,' Geldren complained, 'we saw lots of lovely things, but she wouldn't entertain anything that had the slightest decoration on it. Not even blouses that had double stitched seams!'

'Well that makes sense,' Arianne agreed, 'double stitched seams and embroidered details are definitely only found on the better-quality clothes, not the sort of clothes that women that Maglen is hoping to pretend to be would be wearing.'

'That's as may be,' Geldren continued, 'but she wouldn't let me buy her more than two or three of anything.'

'But I explained that to you,' Maglen reminded her, 'I won't be travelling in a coach or on kertle-back. I'll have to wear or carry everything I own, that much I have learned already.'

'I take it then that you have decided to carry on with your disguised flight?' Arianne asked.

'I have no option,' Maglen replied, 'I will not submit to my father's demands and I won't subject Jaxaal and you Janilla, to the need to provide me with protection. I don't want to create more divisions in Fameral politics than there are already.'

'Well we can talk with Jaxaal and Draxen about that aspect,' Janilla told her, 'but I know we were serious when we made the offer of protection to you.'

'Bless you for that,' Maglen replied, 'but I think I've made up my mind. The one thing that Geldren didn't buy for me is a bag to keep my things in. The women that I met on the road all seemed to have bags made from rugs. At least that's what I think they were. They had wooden poles through loops both sides of the top and these could then be lashed together to keep the contents inside. They all had big wide straps which could be hung on the woman's shoulders to help carry the load.'

'I think I know what you mean,' Janilla said, 'I think I saw some of those in a store room at the back of the kitchen quarters.'

This led to a mad exodus from Maglen's bedroom as all four ladies ran down to the kitchen floor of the castle. If the sudden arrival of the senior female members of the house in the kitchen caused any consternation, the catering staff were good enough to not show it. Janilla led the way and soon all four were searching through the storerooms. Janilla was able, eventually, to find what she was after and half an hour later Maglen had packed her new 'second hand' bag with everything she now knew she would need for life on the road.

As the nobles sat down for their evening meal the preparations that had been made were discussed, argued and laughed over.

'Janilla tells me that you are determined to carry on with your disguised flight,' Jaxaal told Maglen as she sat next to him at the dining table.

'I know you have offered me protection, Lord Norland,' Maglen replied.

'Oh please, Maglen do call me Jaxaal,' he interrupted.

'Jaxaal,' Maglen corrected herself, 'but I do not wish to be the cause of any dispute between you and my father and you must agree, that is the only possible result if I remain here under your protection.'

'Perhaps, but are you are committing yourself to hardships no noble lady should endure,' he replied.

'If they are the hardships the common people have to face in their everyday lives then I'm sure I can tolerate them.' She said.

'Well I admire your resolve and I wish there was more I could do for you, but I am walking a difficult path. When you have gone I will have to let your father know that you were here and I when I meet up with him and the other lords. I'll need to be ready to tell him why I didn't keep you here or send you back to Launceston.'

'I am sorry I have put you in this position,' Maglen apologised.

'You have nothing for which to apologise,' Arianne assured her, 'but we do need to engineer things so that no blame can be attributed to Jaxaal, or to Janilla or myself for that matter. No blame can be allowed to be associated with either the house of Norland or of Ellward.'

'No, none of you can be seen to help Maglen in her flight,' Draxen contributed, 'what is needed is someone who has the influence to do what is necessary but is too young to be considered responsible,' and he looked at everyone around the table in turn, finishing with Geldren who he continued to look at intently.

Geldren suddenly realised that everyone was looking at her.

'Who me? What do you expect me to do?' Geldren asked.

'Well, let's see,' Arianne said with a studied expression that belied the mirth that rippled beneath the surface. 'I think I need to send you to Medland, Geldren, because,' she said, 'there are several important supplies that I need fetching from the medical shops there. You will need to go first thing in the morning to make sure you get what I need before the suppliers sell out, but you needn't hurry back once you've got them. You might want to take a trip south of the city for a day or two, I expect Jaxaal has some errands you could run for him to some of the Norland fifths down near Upper Childe.'

'Arianne!' Uster exclaimed, 'you can't be serious.' He knew this side of his wife's character and it always made him uncomfortable when it appeared.

Arianne was Jaxaal's aunt but had raised him as a son after his mother, her sister, had died; he knew her quirky sense of humour and quickly caught on to her drift.

'Yes, I'm sure I have letters and packages that need to be sent to the elders in Upper Childe,' he replied with a sardonic grin at Draxen. The chamberlain instantly knew that he was going to have to be creative and cobble together something to act as an excuse for Geldren's trip.

'But you can't send a young girl not yet past her majority on such an errand,' Uster complained.

'No, I suppose you are right,' Arianne said with a twinkle in her eye, she was warming to this little episode, 'Maglen, you haven't anything planned for the next few days, have you? Would you mind accompanying Geldren on her trip?' she asked.

'No, not at all,' Maglen replied, she had only just caught on to what was being proposed, 'Geldren and I are already friends and we can use a trip like this to get to know each other much better.'

Uster was still not happy at what was being planned. 'You can't be seriously considering sending two young females all that way on their own!' he exclaimed.

'But they won't be,' Jaxaal interposed, 'they will travel together and with a driver and footman to protect them. They will go in one of my light carriages and the Norland insignia on the doors will probably be protection enough.'

This seemed to settle the matter and the discussion around the table went on to consider all the ramifications that the planned trip would entail. It was Geldren who noticed that Maglen was sitting quietly in her seat dabbing tear away from her eyes. She got up and went around the table and put a comforting arm around her soon to be travelling companion.

'What's wrong Maglen?' she asked, 'do you not wish to make this trip with me? We can get you down to Upper Childe in little over a veld, if Jaxaal lets us use his best drays to pull the carriage.' She looked up at Jaxaal who, sitting next to Maglen, had heard Geldren's little speech and the lord nodded.

'No, it's not that, just the opposite in fact,' Maglen replied, 'you're all being so kind to me. This is just what a family meal should be like, with everyone talking about what is going on and everyone helping everyone else. Our family meals at Launceston Hall have been very strained affairs ever since my father got these marriage plans in his head.'

'Oh, you poor thing,' Geldren said and gave her new friend a hug and kiss on the cheek, 'but you needn't worry, we'll do all we can to help you.'

'Now,' Arianne said, 'we seem to have got things sorted out, you've got your clothes and a suitable bag to carry your things in, now I suggest you buy some dried food that is easy to carry when you get to Medland. Have you got enough money, we must make sure you've enough to be able to buy things you need in an emergency?' And she looked across at Jaxaal.

'Yes, I agree,' Jaxaal replied, 'how much do you think you'll need? Ten, twenty strands?'

'Oh, I couldn't,' Maglen protested, 'I already owe Geldren for all the clothes she bought this morning.'

'You don't owe me a stip,' Geldren replied still hugging her friend and stroking her hair, 'I enjoyed buying you those things and anyway,' and she paused before continuing, 'Arianne had given me the money to make sure we got what you needed.' Reality sank in and Maglen considered what she had left in her purse upstairs in her temporary room.

'I would appreciate being able to borrow some money,' she said, 'ten strands should be enough, but could it be in smaller denominations slends or stips preferably. I've discovered that having nothing but strands in one's purse marks you as being different from the country people.'

'I'm sure we can sort something out,' Draxen said and he pulled on the bell rope to get a footman's attention.

'But surely you were not crying because we're being kind to you?' Janilla asked.

'Oh no, not just that,' Maglen replied, 'I'm missing my brother and I know he's missing me and that makes me sad.'

'Would you like to write to him?' Janilla asked, 'I know how important these things can be. Both my brother and my sister write to me at least every other veld, even Neldon who's training with the guardians finds time to put quill to parchment. I'll make sure your brother gets it'

'Oh, would you? That would be a kindness,' Maglen replied and she cheered up immediately. She didn't say anything to the others but as she sat feeling a lot happier about her prospects she sensed that leagues away in Launceston Crelin was also feeling more cheerful.

Bryland got through the next few days by throwing himself into his work of preparing skins for market. He was deeply in shock, the revelation that he was thought of as the villain in the Neldon Swenland affair was a major blow to his self-esteem. He had always taken pride in his work as a kertle trainer and had revelled in his success. He hadn't let the fact that he had a lame left leg stop him doing anything he wanted to do. He limped when he walked and couldn't run facing straight forward but he had been able to see to the training of the kertles under his care. Now he had added his skill with the bow to his achievements but that, and the fact he could make a living hunting stags for their skins, stood for nothing against the condemnation of the world. His first thoughts were to run, to run to where no one had heard of him or what he was supposed to have done. Perhaps he could go north to the Ellward or Norland sea ports and take a ship to the northern lands.

'But how could I leave you my friend?' he asked the Red Cannis when it trotted into Bryland's camp for his evening meal, 'I've made friends and put down roots here and I'm not going to be forced to give them up against my will.' With this attitude in his mind he decided that he could risk one more trip into Under Childe for the next Archers'' competition. He'd sell his skins and if he won some prize money he would head off down to High Tor Farm where he had heard there was to be a hiring fair in a couple of velds. All assuming, of course, that he was not recognised as the villain portrayed in the strolling players show. It was a risk he was loathed to take, but knew he had to for his sanity's sake.

Chapter 12

It was barely dawn when Maglen opened her eyes and lay quietly in a comfortable bed. Strange how singularly comfortable a bed was when you first woke up and she was tempted to carry on dozing in the comfort for a while longer. But then reality thrust itself in upon her in the form of a chamber maid who entered her room with a mug of hot kandrel and a jug of hot water. She tried to roll over and ignore these blatant hints that she should stir herself, but it was too late, she was sufficiently awake to know that she needed to get up and get busy.

She rolled out of the bed and onto her feet, revelling in the deep carpet beside the bed. She thanked the maid who, having established there was nothing else she could do, left her to her ablutions. Maglen made the most of being able to wash in hot water without the encumbrance of clothes. She knew that when she was back on the road and staying in inn bunkhouses it was the practice to keep at least one layer of clothes on, even while trying to have an all over wash. When she had washed and dressed, she packed her bag using the leather thongs to tie the two rods that lined the top together. As she left the room she took a last look at high family living that she knew she was leaving behind, perhaps forever. This might have made her sad, but her spirits were high, and it was in a light mood that she made her way to the kitchen where she discovered that Geldren, dressed and ready to travel, had beaten her down to breakfast. The two girls sat together and made a big hole in the plate of hog meat slices that the cooks had freshly fried for them. Together with slices of flat bread washed down with copious mugs of kandrel they enjoyed a substantial breakfast.

A little while later they boarded one of Jaxaal's best light carriages; most of the family had gathered to see them off and were standing in their night clothes and dressing gowns, so early was the departure. Draxen came and handed Maglen a purse and a small package wrapped in cloth and tied with string.

'That purse has about five strands in small change,' he said, 'the other package contains a good quality knife that is very sharp, so be careful with it. A good knife is the one thing all farm workers have to have, or so I'm told'

'Thank you, Chamberlain Draxen, 'Maglen said to him, 'I don't know when I'll be able to repay you and the Norlands for this and all their kindness, but I will.'

'Nonsense young lady,' Draxen replied, 'now no more talk of repaying anything, these are gifts and you'll make an old man very unhappy if you mention them again!' To Draxen's great surprise Maglen then leant down from the carriage and grabbed him by the shoulders and kissed him on the cheek.

Amid shouts of goodbyes and good luck the carriage clattered out of the courtyard, across the draw bridge and down the road through the town, the dray kertle's claw sets clattering on the cobbles. Very soon they were out of the town and heading into the country side south of Castle Norland. In barely an hour they had covered more leagues than the wagons could manage in a half a day.

That night they stayed in an inn, Geldren insisting that they share a twin-bedded room in the inn itself.

'You'll have plenty of time to sleep in bunkhouses or stables before long, 'she told Maglen, 'but as for now, you are travelling as my maid and you'll share with me, understood?' Maglen could only agree with her with a giggle.

Janilla and Arianne had told Maglen that Geldren was the quieter, less forceful of the two Ellward sisters.

'Felda Ellward must be a force to be reckoned with,' Maglen thought to herself.

The coachman told them that they should reach Medland by lunch time the next day if they wished to make a similar early start in the morning and didn't mind travelling at the same speed. Despite the comfort of the Norland coach with its leaf spring suspension it had been a tiring day and both girls were happy to make an early night of it.

The Norland coach made good time and duly rolled into Medland at about mid-day on the morrow and made its way to the rear of the Norland Mansion. The Mulldays had been warned to expect guests and were delighted to greet the two noble ladies. Kremand was about to take their baggage up to the rooms that had been prepared when Geldren told them they would simply be changing the drays and getting on their way again. On the journey down, Maglen had said that she wanted to get as far as she could as quickly as possible and Geldren had understood her reasons.

Maglen seriously thought about going around the pentagon to the Launceston Mansion and raiding her rooms there for some of the things she kept in the capital. A moment's reflection made her realise that this would be a very foolish thing to do. For all she knew her father might have already travelled down to their Medland home apart from which there was nothing in her room which she could take that would blend in with the possessions that a country woman would have. They had a quick lunch, much to Jelanda Mullday's disappointment; the retainer's wife had hoped to be able to wait on them as befitted the daughter of one the foremost families and her friend but Geldren and Maglen were not to be deflected from their decision.

The coach left the city travelling through the Dreslah Park and Geldren told Maglen about the trip they had made there when Jaxaal first arrived in Medland. They rapidly left the city and its environs behind and headed south towards the Childe Mountains. That night they had reached the inn that marked the half way point between the city and the mountains and again got an early night's sleep. The landlord was not best pleased as he had expected good takings when he saw the House of Norland coach arrive. He was slightly assuaged by the copious food and drink that the driver and footman were able to put away.

The following mid-day the coach reached Upper Childe and the passengers disembarked. Maglen had decided that she would go on from here alone and on foot. Geldren was sad when Maglen told her of her decision but understood her reasoning. The inn was filling up with lots of migrant farm workers which reinforced Maglen's resolve to head for High Tor and the hiring fairs. The girls enjoyed a last lunch together in the room Geldren had hired; Maglen pointed out that she would probably be travelling with many of the workers who now thronged the bar and to be seen with a high-born lady who travelled in a Norland family carriage would not help her blend in.

At first Maglen suggested that Geldren eat alone in her room, but young Lady Ellward was having none of that.

'I've few enough friends and you are definitely one of my best friends now,' Geldren affirmed, 'I'll not see you eat down there with that lot when this is our last meal together.' During the lunch, over which they talked through Maglen's immediate plans, she decided that she would start using the name her brother called her when they were alone.

'I'll be known as Madge from herein forth,' she announced, 'Madge Falleen since I've fallen such a long way,' and she giggled.

'All right,' Geldren agreed, 'Madge Falleen it will be. At least we'll know who to ask for if we ever come looking for you.'

After their meal, Maglen sat brushing her long golden hair until it shone like brushed gold; she knew it would be the last chance she would get for who knew how long.

'That won't do at all!' Geldren told her, 'none of the people you'll be travelling with will have hair that well-groomed, or that clean come to think of it. We'll have to do something else.'

In the end they decided that Maglen should wash it again and then, while still wet, they wrapped it in a large scarf which they wound and tied into a ball which hung at the nape of her neck. With her smock hood raised up to the top of her head, the lustrous tresses were hidden out of sight.

'There, that's better Madge,' Geldren said triumphantly. Maglen was taken aback to hear that name used, it made her think of her twin and she knew he was anxious for her. She tried to send warm comforting thoughts to Crelin but wasn't sure if his mood was changing. They completed their preparations and Geldren then asked for more bread rolls to be sent up.

'But I can't eat another thing,' Madge told her, 'I'll burst!'

'They are not for now,' Geldren said, 'you may be grateful of them later today or tomorrow.'

Sometime later they made their separate ways out of the inn, Geldren in some state down the main stairs and out through the front door, Maglen/Madge was much more circumspect, slipping down the back stairs and out of the rear door into the courtyard. They met on the road a few yards down the road from the inn. They were both full of tears as they said their goodbyes and it was a feeling of loss that they saw each other go their separate ways: Geldren back to her luxury coach and her high-status life, Madge, on foot with her bag slung on her shoulders to a life of toil and drudgery.

An hour or two later, Madge became aware of how badly her boots fitted her; her right heel was very sore, and despite the season the heat of the wintry afternoon sun which still managed to be seen over the mountains ahead made her very uncomfortably hot. She couldn't stand the hood up over her head any longer and had slipped it down to rest on her shoulders. After a while Madge became aware of whispered comments as she passed slower walkers on the way up towards the Childe Cut. At first, she didn't pick up any of the words but as it became obvious that she was the focus of the remarks, she paid attention.

'Who does she think she's fooling, that golden hair's so long she's got it tied in a bun,' was one particular comment that made Madge turn and stare at the woman who had spoken.

'That fair skin's never seen the sun all day every day for a bathern,' and, 'have you seen her hands, they've never done a day's work in their life,' were the other most common comments she heard.

Madge was shocked that her attempts to hide her high-born origins had proved so ineffectual. She didn't know quite how to handle the situation and simply walked faster to get away from the perpetrators of the remarks. This was a mistake for she was not used to long walks carrying a heavy load: her back and legs ached; she was oozing sweat that added to her discomfort, her right heel was becoming unbearably painful and the disappointment that her attempts at disguise had failed just added to her despondency.

She walked on and was aware that people she had passed were now overtaking her. The comments didn't stop but now focussed on how unfit to the physical life she obviously was. It was a great relief when she got finally close enough to the mountain to be in its shadow. She stopped then at a small pond that formed where a stream run down into a hollow where it gently swirled around before exiting to continue its gentle path downhill. She sat and, taking off her boots and socks, bathed her aching feet.

'*Half a day's walking and I'm fit for nothing!*' she thought bitterly to herself as she felt the sting of the cold water on her feet. Her right heel was red raw, and she knew that if she carried on the way she was, it would start to bleed and there was a real risk of infection. She then remembered the small pot of salve that Lady Arianne had given her for her hands.

'Use this on your hands after you've washed them after you've finished working for the day,' Arianne had instructed, 'it contains some oils that will ease the pain and lessen the risk of infection should you get blisters and small cuts. There's a small amount of numb root in there to help with the pain relief. Madge decided that it would probably do her ankle no harm to have a small amount put on and she noticed an immediate improvement when the salve was applied. She decided to wrap a thin bandage around the ankle to protect the treated area and that helped a lot as she replaced her sock and boot. She ate one of the rolls that Geldren had thoughtfully supplied and this, washed down with a tankard of the fresh clean stream water, served as a reasonable meal. She allowed herself a brief rest after eating before packing everything away and hoisting her bag on to her shoulder, before continuing on up the path.

Very soon she came to what was the entrance to the Childe Cut and was aware that people seemed to be gathering around the entrance. Then she realised that the concentration was caused as people waited for their turn to enter the narrowing passage. As she slowly made her way in line she noticed that the whole area was decorated with the blue and green flags of The House of Norland. She'd heard rumours that before the restoration the Childe Cut was still very pro Norland. That was quite clear now.

Once she got inside the Cut itself, the speed at which she could walk, was obliged to walk, picked up as no one tried to squeeze into a narrowing gap. She was fascinated by the geological formation that was the Cut. She noticed that a feature in the wall on her right was mirrored by a corresponding one on the left hand one a few paces further on. This, she realised, was evidence that the Cut was formed by the mountains being ripped apart across their width by the movement of the ground itself. She had been taught about these things back in the school room at Launceston Hall when Crelin and she had been educated by their tutors. This made her think of Crelin and she immediately knew he was thinking of her at that moment. This made her sad but also gave her a warm hug of a feeling as they tried to comfort each other in their loneliness.

Sometime later she came to one of the natural fault areas in the Cut for which it was renowned. The debris from a rock fall had been cleared away and the area turned to a practical use. As she entered the cleared area she looked up and way above saw the sky, starkly bright against the gloom down at the bottom of the Cut. This area had been turned into a sort of cafe for there were tables and stools set about to serve the guests. Some were placed next to the stream that ran down the eastern wall of the Cut and had been steered into a decorative little run of waterfalls that filled the clearing with their musical burble. The cafe owners were busy serving pots of kandrel to travellers and Madge was tempted to indulge herself but decided against it. She reluctantly made herself carry on her weary way.

'See, I told you, too stuck up to sit and have a drink with the likes of us,' Madge heard from behind her as she stepped into the confines of the Cut again. She had no idea who had spoken the words, but she recognised the voice as someone who had made snide remarks earlier on the road.

She did stop a little further on where a slight bend created an alcove where she could sit beside the stream that flowed down the cut. She was tempted to bath her feet again but then realised that the stream was the only source of water to the cafe she had just passed and didn't think that would be appreciated. She could do without attracting anymore unwanted attention. She did get a drink of water, dipping her tankard in the water as it bubbled over the rocks. She resisted the temptation to eat another of her bread rolls and instead, picked up her bag and continued on her way.

It was quite late in the day when she passed the waterfall that fed the stream she had been walking beside all day. This marked the approximate centre of the Cut a fact that Madge was not aware of but might have been glad to know. She knew it was very dark down in this, the centre of the mountain, so much so that there were torches lit to illuminate the path at awkward places. Looking up she could see that the sky was getting darker and very soon it would be night.

Thankfully she came to yet another clearing and this had been converted into a bunkhouse system as well as a cafe. Madge decided that she would have to stay here and went to ask the price of a bed.

'Slend for a bunk space and another two for your breakfast,' the owner told her shortly in a take it or leave it manner. A shadow crossed Madge's face at this; it seemed a lot of money now she was getting her head round life at the low end of society.

'The hogs don't walk all the way here and fry themselves,' the owner said in response to her frown, 'and try as I might I can't get grain to grow on these rock walls.' He was obviously fed up with comments about his high prices and had long ago put together this sardonic riposte.

'Yes, of course,' Madge replied, 'it must be very hard to run a successful business in a place like this,' reinforcing her words with a smile that could melt the coldest heart.

'Well, yes, it's not easy,' the owner said, somewhat mollified. Madge agreed to take the accommodation but was a little surprised when the owner demanded payment in advance. She fumbled in her purse and handed over the coins, glad that she didn't have to ask for change. She then realised that she would have to buy an evening meal on top of the three slends she had already spent but was hungry enough not to care. Having made that decision she handed over the price of the meal and was soon tucking into a large bowl of delicious stew that was accompanied by fresh baked risen bread. In her reduced state this was a feast which she devoured with relish.

She began to feel a lot better and looked around her. The cafe was filling up as more travellers arrived. She began to nod an acknowledgement to the people who came and sat close to her, she was beginning to learn that the way to avoid undue attention was not to ignore everyone hoping they wouldn't notice her. She even passed a few words with a young woman, she guessed about her own age, who came and sat on the bench next to her. Thankfully all the travellers seemed as tired as she was as they soon began to make their way into the bunkroom area.

When Madge made her own way there she found that most of the bunks had already been claimed by others who, knowing how things worked had put their bundles onto a bunk.

'It's alright my dear,' the owner said, suddenly appearing at her side, 'I've already reserved you a good spot, here by the kitchen door,' and he pointed at a bunk that was, as he said, right next to the kitchen entrance.

Madge thanked him and gratefully put her bag on the bed. She sat down and gingerly removed her boots and socks. The bandaging on her right ankle appeared to have done the trick for the soreness was no worse than it had been earlier. She went and fetched a bowl of water and began bathing her feet to make sure they were clean. The young woman who had sat next to her at dinner came and sat next to her and asked if she was having trouble with blisters.

'Well my feet haven't blistered yet, but they feel as if they will soon,' Madge admitted.

'I used to have that problem, especially last turn when I started on the road,' the girl replied introducing herself as Braveen, 'the secret is to wear two pairs of socks if you have them. A tight pair next to your skin and a looser pair outside them. Then as you walk, if your feet move within your boot it's the socks that rub against each other, not your skin. It's that what causes the blisters.'

Madge thanked her and began rummaging in her bag for her spare pair of socks. Braveen was determined to chat to her new-found friend and Madge learned that, like her, she was heading towards High Tor and the hiring fairs.

'You may not get hired at High Tor itself at this time in the turn,' Braveen warned, 'I didn't last turn and had to go on down half way to Dresham Manor before I got my ribbon. It all depends on what the farmers are looking for and we are well into the dormant period.'

They chatted on and Madge learned yet more about the life into which she had launched herself. It was nice to have Braveen to talk to and Madge relaxed a lot as the two chatted. They were finally asked to stop talking and let the other women get some sleep and it was in a much happier frame of mind that Madge, wearing just her long shift petticoat and wrapped in her bed clothes, drifted off to sleep.

Chapter 13

Earlier that day at an inn in Upper Childe Pardrea Lather was waiting for her brother to arrive as they had arranged, but he was late. Pardrea was getting more and more anxious and with anxiety her temper was rising. They should have met together in the mid-afternoon but Natheal had not arrived at the agreed time. This meant that she would have to walk long into the night to get to the bunkhouse half way through the Childe Cut where she had planned to stop for the night and she hated walking carrying a flaming torch; the illumination was not good, and it made her arm ache.

If she didn't keep to her time table, she would not get to Under Childe in time to talk to as many of the women as she had planned. It was alright for Natheal, he was riding on kertle back while she was walking to blend in with the rest of the workers. They had a lot to discuss and Pardrea was worried; Natheal's long term plans were aimed at overthrowing the Fameral ruling families but things seemed to be slipping away from them.

The new Lord Norland had made an immediate impact on his lands and on the areas surrounding Norland. In general, the people were a lot happier than they had been a turn ago and the chance of instigating a revolution was slipping away. Natheal had been meeting with fellow conspirators who had been infiltrating groups down in Swenland.

You're quite right, sister dear,' Natheal had agreed with her as he finished the meal that he had ordered when he did finally arrive. He had sat and had his ear bent by his angry sibling as he ate, and he was sipping a mug of kandrel to finish his meal when she finally slowed her tirade enough for him to get a word in edgewise.

'I agree, we should have made a move before this new Lord Norland took his place, but we have missed that moment. It would probably have been too soon anyway. We need to stir up more dissent at hiring fairs and get the wage rates increased. That will weaken the farmers and land owners and make the workers look upon us as people they can trust and respect. Another turn and we'll be ready to move. Things might have been easier down in Swenland had the old Lord Swenland still ruled there. He was not liked very much, and a lot of people had reasons to hate him but the new regent, Darval Ellward has started well and the general feeling is to give him the chance to make things better.'

'So, what do we need to do now?' Pardrea asked.

'Just what we had intended all along; there's no need to change our plans. In fact, causing as much unrest as possible is even more important.'

'But if the workers are feeling more disposed to supporting the ruling families how are we going to make them stand up to them? Pardrea asked.

'Well, we need to bring as much pressure to bear on the workers as we can. I can persuade the men up to a point, but it would help if we can make their women put pressure on them as well and that dear sister is up to you.'

He then went on to explain what he was proposing. Pardrea was incredulous at first but warmed to the idea as her brother explained what he had in mind.

'The other thing we need to watch out for is people working for the guardians. The ruling families are beginning to suspect something is going on and they might be placing their spies in among the workers.'

'You really think the guardians would do that?' Pardrea asked sceptically.

'Oh, you'd better believe it little sister!' Natheal told her, 'they are becoming much more organised now there are five ruling families again.'

They talked on going over their plans until Pardrea realised that the daylight was failing, and she would have a long walk in the dark.

'Don't worry sister dear,' Natheal told her, 'I'll come with you and you can ride up behind me on my kertle. We can get you to the mid-cut bunkhouse before everyone has gone to bed.'

Bryland was pleased with the skins he had managed to get into a fit state to be sold. He now had five and was also planning to take four sides of stag meat with him to sell if he could. The need to get the skins meant that he had killed more meat than he could eat, even with the Red Cannis's help. He used the last of his supply of salt to preserve the meat that he had left over and hung it high in a tree wrapped in oil cloth so that it might survive without some unwanted scavengers getting it. As was his routine he made his camp tidy and as secure as he could. With the help of the spade that he had bought the last time he visited the smithy in Under Childe, he had dug himself a 'hidey hole' which he could seal with a woven lid that he covered with soil and leaves and into this he stored all the valuable things like his tools and his best clothes. He could no longer disguise the fact that someone lived in his little glade and could only reduce the visible signs as much as possible.

He saddled and loaded Rufran and having given the glade a last check over as he mounted; he rode off into the forest. He made good time and was able to get to Under Childe in time to visit the meat dealers before they put up their shutters for the night. He managed to sell all four sides of stags' meat to the second dealer he approached. Admittedly the price he got was well down on his expectations, but he felt better with some more weight to his money bag. His idea that he might head south and try to find work at a hiring fair now seemed more attractive. It had dawned on him that he might need to be able to rent a room in a town or village during the coldest weather and to do that he would need a great deal more money than he was making at the moment.

He was pleased that he had proved to himself that he could be self-sufficient during a part of the turn when the weather was reasonable, but he needed to think ahead. He needed to be able to live all turn round and that meant making enough during the ripening and harvesting batherns to live off during the dormant and planting ones. He wasn't sure he could do that as he was at the moment; he would have to think of improving his income in either money or provisions to provide for the lean times to come.

He decided to make his way to The Five Houses to get Rufran a stall for the two nights he intended to stay before he went to visit the leather dealer. The stable hands were welcoming but the landlord had not forgotten that he had left without paying for Rufran's stabling last veld end. Bryland reminded him that he hadn't actually left Rufran there all night, but the landlord was having none of that.

'You booked a stall and that stopped me renting it out to anyone else. The fact that you didn't use it is your problem, you still owe me the fee,' the landlord said with an air of finality. Bryland paid what he owed but it rankled when the landlord insisted that he pay for Rufran's stabling in advance.

'I take it that you've got yourself another champion for the archers' contest tomorrow night,' Bryland said, intentionally trying to gain some advantage over the landlord.

'Well I'm not saying that,' the landlord said, rapidly back stepping his position. In the end they agreed that Bryland need not pay for Rufran's stabling or for his own room until after the contest, but having made his point, he did pay the fee.

Bryland then made his way to the leather dealer's premises where he was warmly welcomed and encouraged to show the skins he had brought with him. They quickly agreed a fair price and Bryland was invited through to the rear of the leather dealer's domain to the little office where he kept a rather special bottle of distilled liquor with which they sealed their deal. Bryland became aware that the leather dealer was eager to get to know him better and become better acquainted and just at that moment Bry was feeling in need of some friends.

As the warming spirit flowed down Bryland felt himself relax and only then realised how tense he had been ever since he had entered the village. His worst fears that someone would recognise his true identity and make his presence known had not been fulfilled. The two men sat and made a good-sized dent in the bottle's contents and it was a very relaxed Bryland who made his uncertain way back to The Five Houses.

He enjoyed having a meal which he hadn't had to cook let alone hunt for himself and was sitting finishing off his sugared fruit dish when he tried to engage the serving wench in a conversation. She was pleasant enough but wouldn't be drawn into anything beyond a light banter. Bryland realised he was slurring his words and was probably making a fool of himself and very quickly wished he was somewhere else. He apologised and staggered upstairs where he threw himself onto his bed and fell into a fitful sleep.

He awoke with a sore head feeling very sorry for himself. The spirits he had drunk with the leather dealer followed by a fair amount of wine had given him an almighty hangover. He berated himself for not drinking copious amounts of water the night before and tried to make good the deficit from the water in his washstand jug. This he knew would not really have much effect for an hour or more and he gingerly made his way downstairs in search of some breakfast. The smoked hog's meat was more than he could face in his distraught state and he satisfied himself with a small amount of flat bread which did a lot to revive him, that and the jug of kandrel he managed to keep all to himself.

He made his way out of the inn and started to explore more of the village. It was really a small town but clung on to its village status. He felt a bit guilty that he wasn't doing anything more constructive but decided that he deserved a holiday. He had worked hard and while not full, his purse held a satisfying amount. He could afford himself the luxury of a day's idleness. He wandered through the streets and made sure that he had walked every byway in the village. Under

Childe was a pleasant enough place, the sort of place he could think about settling down and he began to day dream, pretending that he was actually looking for a house to buy and in which he could settle down.

This he knew was just a dream, but he indulged himself. It would be nice to be a man of property and to share it with a wife with whom he could raise a family. These thoughts blackened his mood as he was reminded how lonely he was. He didn't know any females to talk to really, let alone well enough to think about getting married. But he couldn't even think of forming a permanent relationship, his past was always there, lurking at the back of his mind. He was a disgraced and dishonoured man who could offer no woman a life of which to be proud.

He found a cafe and sat outside with a mug of kandrel deep in thought in his misery. He began to worry that just sitting there he might be recognised and his true identity revealed. He put his hand up to hide his face in a futile attempt to not be there. As he did so he felt the full beard that had grown up over the velds and now covered his face. This at least was some disguise, but he felt sure that anyone who used to know him would easily recognise him the moment they saw him. His reddish brown coloured hair not to mention his limp was a certain give away; he had been famous for his colouration back in the heady days at The House of Swenland. Perhaps he could do something about that, he would have to think about it.

Having finished his kandrel he wandered on and found his way back to the village centre where preparations for tonight's bow competition were being made. There were a few traders also setting up their stalls. He saw that the landlord of The Five Houses was busy creating a stall from which he would be able to sell ale to the crowd. Beyond this there was stall where kitchen fowl portions were being roasted on spits in front of a large travelling range. Bryland recognised the trader who was directing his staff as they finished the task of setting up the stall. It was Milden Northwood who Bryland felt sure was something to do with the Guardians. Bryland's first reaction was to turn and walk away, Milden, he knew had been at Medland during the Challenge in which Neldon Swenland had cheated, but the smell of the roasting fowl was overpowering.

Despite the risk of being recognised, he decided to take a chance and get some lunch. He pulled his hood up and tried to cover as much of his face as possible. He got out his purse and got the necessary money ready, he didn't want to have to stand and wait for change. He went to the stall and was able to get served by the junior member of Milden's staff. As he walked away he felt sure that he had got away without being recognised. He might have felt differently if he had seen how intently Milden Northwood stared after him as he retreated.

Chapter 14

Madge awoke from a comfortable dream aware that something was not right. She lay still and tried to identify the problem. Nothing, but no, there was a slight movement of her bedclothes. She lay still, absolutely frozen stiff with fright as the bedclothes were definitely lifted up off her right leg. She then felt a hand gently touch her right knee. She tried to control her breathing and not reveal that she was awake. The hand rested there for a while and then very slowly began to move up her thigh. It reached the spot where her petticoat was rankled up and deftly slipped beneath the fabric, maintaining contact with her skin.

Madge decided that things had gone quite far enough, no one had ever touched her there. She rolled slightly onto her right side so that, still feigning sleep, she could get her hand on the knife she had put under her pillow earlier. As she rolled the hand had stayed where it was which meant that now it was caressing the inside of her thigh. Madge was shocked to discover that being touched so intimately was actually a pleasurable experience; however, not knowing who was doing the touching was not and she brought her hand holding the knife down hard on her molester's arm.

There was a squeal of pain as the blade hit home and a clatter of a bedside stool as it was sent flying as Madge's assailant made a hasty retreat. Opening her eyes for the first time, Madge just saw the shape of a man's shadow disappearing into the entrance to the kitchen. Someone lit a candle and came to see what had caused the disturbance that had woken the whole bunkroom. In the candle light a trail of blood could be seen disappearing behind the kitchen door screen.

'One of them waiters got more than he bargained for,' the candle bearer said with a grin, 'I don't think you'll be bothered again tonight. But I'd keep that knife handy, just in case.' Madge realised that it was Braveen who came and sat down on her bed to put a comforting arm around her shoulders. When the shocked girl had stopped shaking with the fright, Braveen patted her on the shoulder and stood up. Madge lay in a state of shock, whimpering to herself; this world was a nasty, wicked place and she wished she was at home.

Away in Launceston, Crelin woke from a night mare where something wonderful had been happening but had suddenly turned into something awful. He lay in his bed, sweating with the fright of it and knew something was troubling his twin. He wished he was with her.

Madge was in a state of turmoil as she got up the next morning. She quickly washed and dressed trying to have as little interaction with the other women as possible. This was not easy as the rumpus in the night was the centre of everyone's attention. The blood spattered on the floor was a clear indication that something untoward had occurred. Madge had no certain proof who her molester might be although she had a very good idea. This was born out when the landlord appeared wearing a full sleeved shirt which he had tied tightly around the wrist and a clean pair of trousers. The amount of blood on the floor suggested that his clothes would have been well besmirched. There were a few ribald comments from some of the older women and some purposefully asked him to pass them things that entailed him using both arms; it was quite clear that he was favouring his left arm, the right tended to hang down by his side.

As she was clearing away her plates and utensils the landlord sidled up to her and grabbed her by the wrist so that he could whisper in her ear, 'you just be thankful that I'm a forgiving sort of man, young lady. Pull a trick like that again and I'll get the guardians onto you!'

'I'm sure the guardians would like to find out just how you got that wound on your right arm and why!' Madge replied staring the odious little man full in the face.' She then turned on her heel and picked up her already packed bag and stepped out of the cafe into the cut where she fell into step with the other travellers.

'That told him alright!' a woman said as she came and joined Madge, 'but you can't expect much else, travelling alone and with your clothes looking like a maid laid them out for you.'

'Do I know you?' Madge asked. She was sure that she recognised the woman from earlier on her travels.

'Aye we've met young miss. The last time I saw you, you were getting off the wagon at Linden Village,' the other woman said obviously with ruffled feathers, 'My names Pardrea, Pardrea Lather, everybody knows me.'

'I'm sorry I didn't recognise you straight away,' Madge told her, 'but what do you mean I can't expect much else?' Madge asked.

'Well my dear,' Pardrea replied lowering her voice so that only Madge could hear her, 'you are obviously not working class, your skins too pale and your hands look like they've never done a day's work in their life. Your hair is too long for a working woman. Oh, I know you've got it tied up in a bun but that's no good when you're working out in the fields.'

'But what were you saying about my clothes?' Madge asked.

'Well I couldn't help noticing that you were careful to brush the dust off your dress after you took it off last night, you were the only person who did that and then you carefully folded it along the seams so that the dress was not creased when you put it on this morning. You'd never see a working girl do that. Sleep in her clothes more like!'

'Is it that obvious?' Madge asked, shocked that she had given her breeding and background away so easily.

'Look dear, I've no idea why you're putting yourself in this position, but you'd be much better off getting back to where you belong.' Pardrea replied. She had decided that this obvious interloper could do with scaring off.

'I can't do that,' Madge replied shortly, 'I've nowhere to go.'

'Well I won't pry into your affairs,' Pardrea replied, 'but you need to find somewhere you can fit in better than you ever will here with the farm working community.'

'But why can't I fit in?' Madge pleaded, 'I'm willing to work and I don't want to do anybody any harm.'

'That's as may be,' Pardrea replied but you're trying to integrate into a tight knit community of workers who live a hard life and are very suspicious of anyone who doesn't belong. Look it's like this, the farmers who employ migrant workers tend to be hard task masters and they keep control of a truculent work force by punishing miscreants with harsh penalties and the last thing the workers need is to lose their place; they are hard enough to come by as it is. You've yet to find that out.'

'But why am I being treated the way I am,' Madge asked, 'I've tried so hard to fit in with everyone.'

'That's just it,' Pardrea replied, 'you've tried too hard. You can't change the way you look and the way you are, just like that. The working girls are suspicious of anyone slightly different. It's not unknown for the farmers to plant their own people in the hiring fairs to report on anyone trying to organise the workers into a resistance group.'

'But I've not been placed here, I'm just trying to get away from,' and Madge hesitated as she struggled to explain herself without giving away her identity, 'from where I came from.'

'I believe you,' Pardrea assured her, 'but you are going to be suspected of being a spy.' She had decided that a full-frontal attack, showing that she had seen through Madge's disguise might be just what was needed to get rid of this stranger.

'But why should anyone spy on the workers?' Madge queried

'Because if the workers get together at a hiring fair and all of them refuse the terms on offer then the farmers can't get the workers they need at the price they want to pay.'

'But what happens then?' Madge asked, totally confused.

'Well, then it costs the farmers, they have to pay the workers a fair wage. My brother, Natheal, has been working to get the workers to demand what is rightfully theirs'

But why should you, and all the others, be so rotten to me?'

'Because we, I, think you are here to find out who is organising the resistance and to then report it back to your family.'

'My family?' Madge asked in surprise.

'Well, you look as if you're the daughter of at least a Fifth Master, and you've no place here among the workers.'

'But I'm not,' Madge protested but then stopped saying anymore as she couldn't give her true identity away, that would be even worse.

They walked on in silence for a long time until other walkers came passed and effectively split them up. Madge was relieved to be on her own; she had a lot to think about. Things were a lot different out here in the world of the farm workers than what she had known in her secure home at Launceston Hall.

She was still deep in thought as she found a place to get a mug of kandrel to go with her remaining bread roll that provided her lunch. She was still in deep reverie all afternoon and it came as a surprise when all of a sudden, she had walked out of the Childe Cut and into the open country south of the mountains. She just went along with the flow of humanity and made her way towards the village she could see in the distance. This must be Under Childe. As they approached the outskirts of the village she could see that a series of marquees had been erected in the fields surrounding the village and wondered what their purpose might be.

'They are for the migrant workers to get a bed under cover,' Braveen told her as she caught up with her, 'the village will be full of people, it's Alphen-end tonight and they always have a bow competition in Under Childe. That attracts a lot of people any way and the sudden influx of workers on their way south means that there won't be a bed to be had in the village.'

The file of migrants wended its way down the slope towards the field where the marquees stood. The three large tents were pitched in a field a little lower than the road. Madge made her way towards the first one and queued to get inside but Pardrea came and stood right in front of her, blocking her passage.

'There's no spare beds for the likes of you,' she said staring hard into Madge's face, 'you'd better try one of the other tents.' Madge was so shocked at this rebuttal that she just stood and stared. When others arriving after her were allowed in she got the message. She was fuming with rage and tears were forming in her eyes as she went to the next marquee. The refusal was not quite as abrupt but equally as emphatic at the second tent's entrance. She climbed back up to the path and didn't even bother trying to get admittance to the last marquee. Instead she turned her face to the village and strode purposefully in that direction. Well if she couldn't sleep with the working women she would have to find a bed in the village.

The streets of Under Childe were a friendly, inviting place after the loneliness of the countryside and as dusk was falling the lights were being lit, giving a cosy feel to the cobbled streets. Madge's spirits rose as she made her way into the centre of the village and the smell of roasting kitchen fowl made her realise how hungry she was. The bread roll at lunch time had not been adequate to replace the energy she had expended getting here. She couldn't resist the temptation and went and bought a fowl quarter from the stall holder. He tried to get her in conversation, but Madge was not in the mood; she'd had so many rebuttals and put downs in the past two days she wasn't going to risk another. Milden looked intently at the young woman as she left his stall greedily biting into the succulent flesh of the fowl portion she had just bought from him. He was a trained observer and noted the fairly clean dress she wore but most of all he noticed the erect posture that was so different from the other women that jostled together in the street.

Madge made her way to a nearby inn and decided to see if it was possible to rent a room. The landlord laughed out loud.

'You'll be lucky at this time of day, young lady,' he scoffed, 'this is Alphen-end and there won't be a bed spare in the whole of the village.'

She went on and got much the same answer at the next two inns she tried. As she went into the courtyard of The Five Houses she didn't even bother to go and inquire in the inn itself. Instead she went straight into the stables and wandered down the aisle of stalls. Each one was occupied by kertles, drays, of every description. At the end she was about to turn and make her way back out it the yard when the kertle she was standing next to leant over and snuffled in her ear.

'Hello there, you're friendly,' she laughed as she reached out to stroke the animal. Rufran responded by nickering in reply and licking her hand. 'You just want someone to talk to don't you old fellow,' Madge said as she went close to put her arms around the kertle's neck. Rufran responded by put his head down to give Madge's shoulder a gentle affectionate squeeze.

Chapter 15

Bryland spent the rest of the day preparing for the bow competition and he went out of the village to a small glade where he could practice in peace. He was happy with the results of his training but, despite his aching head, made himself go through the routine that he had devised to test and practice every aspect of bowmanship. The sun was going down as he made his way back into the village.

The streets were noticeably fuller now with the crowds already making their way to the village centre for the competition. This was the busiest he could remember ever seeing Under Childe and realised that it was the influx of migrant workers on their way down south that had swelled the numbers. Well, with all these extra women around, perhaps there might be one who would spend time with him and it was in a more jovial mood that he made his way to The Five Houses.

He made his way into the main bar where it was almost impossible to hear yourself speak let alone find anywhere to sit down. He made his presence known to the landlord since he would be representing the inn in the competition later. The landlord told him to go around to the kitchen where the staff would make sure he got something to eat; it would be impossible to feed him here in the main bar. Bryland did as was suggested and came away from the kitchen with a tray piled high with food and a jug of ale. Looking for somewhere to eat his meal in peace he made for the stables; he could check on Rufran at the same time.

They could later never decide who was more surprised to see each other when Bryland entered Rufran's stall and saw Madge sitting on the manger chatting to the attentive kertle.

'Oh, I'm sorry,' Madge apologised, 'I'll get out of your way,' she said as she jumped down to the floor.

'No, don't leave on my account,' Bryland said immediately, the last thing he wanted was this attractive young woman to disappear. 'I don't think Rufran would appreciate your leaving,' he added to hide his impulsive reaction, 'he..he doesn't want you to stop rubbing his forehead like that.'

'Oh, Rufran, that's his name.' Madge said, 'I did wonder, I've been calling him 'kertle.' I think he has been trying to whisper his name to me, but it just came out as gurgles when he licked my ear.' She was pleased that she hadn't been hastily ejected from the stall and had been invited to stay. She took a surreptitious look at Rufran's owner and instantly decided that she liked the man; he had a handsome, it rugged, look about him but instinctively felt that he was some one she would like to get to know a bit better.

'I can see that you've been getting acquainted,' Bryland replied with a laugh, 'may I be permitted to know who has been keeping my kertle company and stopping him fretting while I've been away?' he asked as he took a good look at the young woman; he was rewarded with a wonderful smile and then a view of a very attractive profile as she turned back to look at the kertle. Few females of his acquaintance could claim such looks.

A shadow crossed Madge's face as she considered what to say but it was with a smile that she replied.

'Madge Falleen, at your service,' she said with a little curtsy, 'and may I know who Rufran's owner is?'

'Just call me Woodsman,' Bryland replied, annoyed with himself for not having prepared a more believable name, 'Bry Woodsman.'

'And what do you do Bry Woodsman?' Madge asked. She was a little concerned at the slight frown that seemed to cross his face and she hoped she hadn't asked the wrong thing, she didn't want to upset this nice looking, friendly man. The set of his face gave him the look of a man she felt she could trust and knew that she didn't want to do anything to upset him.

'I live in the woods and hunt wild stags for their meat and their hides when, I'm not here competing in archery competitions.'

'Archery competitions, what are they?' Madge asked.

'Some people have just started calling them archery competitions, and the competitors archers, they used to be called Bowmen' he told her, I think the new name comes about from the shape the bow makes when it is pulled back ready to fire the arrow.' Bry then went on to explain what a bow was, using his own as an example and to explain the complexities, such as they were, of the competitions.

'And are you a good bowman, er, archer?' she asked.

'I am one of this Inn's champions,' he replied with some pride, and I've yet to be beaten in these Alphen-end competitions.'

They chatted on until Bry remembered that he was getting very hungry and invited Madge to share his meal with him. They shared the copious amount of food and then managed to spend a couple of happy hours together talking as young people will when they are getting to know each other. The time passed quickly as they talked without either revealing anything of their personal histories. They were both aware that they each had things that they wished to keep to themselves and by tacit agreement neither probed or asked awkward questions.

The time came when Bry needed to make his way to the competition ground and Madge eagerly accepted his invitation to accompany him. They were both in high spirits as they walked and Madge accepted the offer to take Bry's arm. They happily made their way, arm in arm, through the crowds to the square and to the firing line.

The first-round competitions were announced and the first archers called to the mark and the competition began. Bry made his way to his allotted target and stood in line waiting for his turn. Madge manoeuvred herself so that she could get a good view of the proceedings, but this involved standing next to the one woman she would rather have avoided.

'Got yourself a boyfriend then I see,' Pardrea said in a sneering voice, 'perhaps he's not so choosey as to the company he keeps.'

'Look Pardrea,' Madge said as sharply as she could, 'I've done nothing to hurt you; I've gone out of my way to try and fit in. Now I've found someone to talk to who doesn't keep trying to put me down or make me feel small or out of place, why can't you just leave me alone.'

'Oh, I'm very sorry that I've upset your ladyship, I'm sure,' Pardrea replied, 'it's just that I'd have thought you would have learnt your lesson and would have gone back to your own kind.'

The people standing around them then hissed at them to be quiet and a hush descended over the village square. The first shots were taken, and cheers went up as some of the local heroes fired. Bryland's second shot hit the white centre spot and brought forth the loudest cheer so far and Madge felt a warm glow as her friend proved that his claims of his prowess to her earlier were the simple truth.

Bry was easily through to the final target and Madge felt a growing excitement as the tension mounted. The archers in the final were all experts and the competition was much closer than the earlier rounds. Bry took the lead with his second shot just nicking the outer edge of the white disc.

As he stood waiting while the other four archers tried to better his shot one of them, Straaka, turned to him and said, 'just like last time! I thought it might come down to a shoot off between you and me!' His next shot hit the white spot, giving him the lead.

Bry had three arrows left when all the others had failed to better Straaka's.

'Like I said, it's just you and me,' Straaka said with a big grin. Bryland's next two arrows were close and one did hit the white but not as near the centre as Straaka's had done.

Madge had cheered as loud as anyone when Bry had won his first-round target and willed him on in the final. His second shot had been fully in the white and he had been able to stand back and wait to see if anyone could better his shot. At first, she had not understood what was happening. Pardrea still stood beside her much to Madge's discomfort but the older woman did give her an understanding of what was happening. Madge was glad of the enlightenment.

'That young archer in the strange brown coloured cloak has got the best shot so far and if no one beats him, he'll not have to fire again but will win without having to use all his arrows.' Pardrea told her. 'But my money is on Straaka, that's the big man who's firing now,' Pardrea said, 'he won when we were here last turn.'

Straaka's last shot hit home well in the white forcing Bry to shoot again. Madge could hardly watch as he fired his next two arrows. One was close and the second hit in the white but didn't beat Straaka's best effort. Madge held her breath as Bry took his stance for his last shot of the competition. She had never seen anything so exciting; Launceston had nothing like these bows and she was fascinated by the whole event. As Bry lined up for his last shot he turned to face her and her heart leapt as he mouthed 'wish me luck.' She didn't know what to do and could only think to blow him a kiss. It was in that moment that she realised that her heart went with it.

Bry fired. It hit. He'd won, and the world erupted in applause, cheering and shouts.

'I take it you'll be giving the victor a special prize later,' Pardrea said with a sneer. Madge was shocked at the suggestion, shocked and hurt. She had been very lonely on the road and put up with a lot of abuse. Now she had found a friend and this hideous woman was trying to spoil even that for her. Pardrea saw the look in Madge's face and knew the younger woman was nearly in tears and couldn't resist the temptation to have another dig at this young madam.

'Oh, don't come the injured prude with me, young miss,' Pardrea said with real venom, in her voice

'I don't know who you are or why you're here, but I have my suspicions. The sooner you learn that we don't like hoity toity females coming into our world and snooping around.'

'But I'm not snooping,' Madge replied in desperate defence of herself.

'Now don't come that with me,' Pardrea said grabbing Madge by the arm as the younger woman tried to get away. Madge desperately wanted to get to speak to Bry, to congratulate him on his wonderful win and to get away from this odious woman. But Pardrea had her in a firm, painful grip and with her larger bulk and strength was able to pull Madge into an alley way at the side of the square.

'Look,' Pardrea said in a fierce, vicious voice, 'I don't know who you are, but my guess is that you're trying to infiltrate the workers to stop them getting their just rights from the hiring farmers. I think you are the daughter of some fifth master who has persuaded you to come down here and spy on what goes on. Well it hasn't worked my dear, never stood a chance of working, not with your pale complexion and your long flowing hair. Oh, I've saw you brushing it out when you thought no one was looking. Look, the best thing you can do is go home, back to your own kind and tell them that their schemes haven't worked, and they had better start paying the workers a better wage.'

'But I'm not here for that!' Madge whined.

'Stop trying to lie to me,' Pardrea said as she roughly pushed Madge away so hard the young woman lost her footing and fell into the mire that lined the edge of the alleyway.

Madge lay in the slime in the gutter for a while in a state of total shock; she was petrified that Pardrea was going to follow up her attack as she lay on the floor, but the larger woman had turned on her heel and left, confident that she had got her message across. Once she was sure she wasn't going to be attacked again if she moved Madge raised herself up and gingerly stood up. She knew her dress and cloak were covered in mud and that some had found its way onto her face. She crept to the end of the alleyway and peered out into the square. Pardrea was nowhere to be seen so she made her way as quickly as she could back to The Five Houses where she slipped into the courtyard and into the stables. She made her way down to Rufran's stall where the kertle greeted her joyfully sniffing and snuffling her a welcome.

Madge stood for a long time clinging onto the gelding's neck as her body shook with the spasm that racked her frame. After a while she calmed down and leant against the wall where she slowly slid to the ground. She sat there and pulled her hood up and over to completely cover her head. Hugging her knees, she crooned to herself in her despair and misery.

Chapter 16

'Becoming a bit of a habit!' the village mayor said with a grin as he handed the winner's purse to Bryland. From there, Bry had no option but to go for a celebratory drink since he was carried there by an army of well-wishers into the nearest inn. He kept looking around to see if he could see Madge but there was no sign of her. He tried to slip away from the celebrations but kept being pulled back. At last the celebrating party found themselves back at "The Five Houses where Straaka was 'in the chair' and insisted on buying Bry yet another brandy-wine. Eventually an hour or two later and considerably worse for wear he staggered out of the bar claiming he had to relieve himself, which was true. Having done so, he made his way out of the inn courtyard and back to the square where he had last seen Madge but there was no sign of her. He hunted around in desperation but everywhere he went there was no sign. He asked a few people if they had seen a slim, fair skinned woman but no one had or were too busy to pay attention.

 'Typical of my luck,' he thought to himself, 'I finally find a woman I like talking to and who seems to like my company and I go and loose her.' Dejectedly he made his way back to The Five Houses and entered the courtyard. He didn't want to go into the bar again; he'd already had far more than he wanted to drink and started for the back stairs up to his room. But then his inbuilt skill and thoroughness as a kertle master took over and he went to check on Rufran.

Bry didn't realise he was not alone as he began to give Rufran a steadying groom. Rufran didn't really need the attention but the oiling served to calm both man and kertle. As he worked his way down the animal's flank he began talking to him telling him how he had won the competition.

'I beat Straaka again in the final old son,' Bry told him, 'and Madge was there to see me. But I couldn't get to her after the competition finished and now I don't know where she has gone. I really wanted to talk to her but now I don't know if I'll ever see her again.'

'Oh, you'll get to see her again,' Madge said as he threw back her hood and stood up.

'Madge! You're here,' Bry exclaimed as he ducked under Rufran's neck and grabbed her in a hug. Madge was a little startled by the sudden display of relief and Bry felt her stiffen as he held her. He immediately let her go and took a step backwards. He then saw how besmirched her cloak and dress were.

'What on Alphos has happened to you?' he asked, full of concern at her dishevelled state.

'I ran into one of the women I met on the way here and she had a point to make,' Madge said stifling a sob that made her throat tighten. Bry sensed her disturbed state and could not stop himself reaching out to her again. This time she didn't stiffen but melted into his arms clinging on to the only solid thing she had been sure of in days. Their embrace seemed to last forever and would have done if each could have had their way. Bry held her tight and stoked her hair with his free hand, pulling her head into his neck and face. He made soothing sounds as he held and stroked her and couldn't resist kissing her hair as it pressed into his face. She sensed what he was doing and turned her head and tilted it up so that his lips found hers and Madge had her first real kiss.

They finally released each other and slightly embarrassed, they both turned their attention to finishing Rufran's oiling. The kertle seemed to sense the joyful spirits in the humans who were giving him this wonderful attention and he snickered his own pleasure.

'So where are you sleeping tonight?' Bry asked as he worked down Rufran's flank.

'I haven't been able to find anywhere; the whole village is awash with visiting people.' Madge replied.

'I thought they had erected marquees in the water meadows for the migrant workers,' Bry told her.

'Oh, they have, but it was made very clear to me that I wouldn't be welcome staying there,' Madge said with a gulp as she thought back to the trauma she had undergone trying to find a berth.

'Alright,' Bry said, 'look I know we've both got things in our past that we want to forget, but if you can tell me what's going on I may be able to help.'

It took a lot more coaxing bur slowly Bry managed to get Madge to tell him of all the troubles she had been through since her mad flight from Launceston had begun. They sat together in Rufran's stall leaning up against the end wall, side by side holding hands. She avoided giving away any specific details but Bry was able to get a good idea of what had gone on.

'I take it that you are not really a plant from some high ranking fifth family trying to get information about some kind of workers conspiracy?' Bry asked slipping into the high language. Madge was a little taken aback by Bry's use of the exclusive language but wanted to trust her new friend and after a moment's thought decided to give away a little of her past by answering in the same dialect.

'No Bry,' I am not a plant although, yes, I do speak the high language. Please don't ask me why.'

'Alright, so you are simply trying to get down south to the hiring fairs so that you can earn a living,' Bry asked rhetorically changing back to common.

'Yes, but I don't see how I can do that now,' Madge replied, 'my skin colour gives me away as not being working class and unless I can get a job I won't' be able to get weather beaten enough to fit in!' she sobbed in despair.

'So, you could do with getting your hair cut and darkening your skin,' Bry mused.

'The hair is easy,' Madge said, 'I could probably do that myself, but I can't make myself change complexion.'

'I may be able to help there,' Bry replied still thinking through the ideas that were starting to take shape. 'Look, I have a room booked here in the inn and you can sleep there,' he continued, 'but if you are really serious about changing your appearance I think I can do that.'

'You mean you could change my appearance so that I don't stick out like a sore thumb?' Madge asked incredulously.

'Yes, but you will have to be really committed to undergoing the change, there won't be any way to change back, well not straight away. The effects will wear off in two or three batherns.'

'Well that would be all right,' Madge replied, warming to the possibility, 'in a couple of batherns of working in the fields I'll fit in with no problem.'

'All right let's start with your hair,' Bry suggested and after a moment's hesitation Madge agreed; she had always had long hair, it was a sure sign of her high family status and losing it was crossing a one-way bridge. Bry looked around trying to find a small pair of shears, but there was nothing like that to be found. No doubt the stable hands did have such tools, but they obviously didn't leave them lying around here where members of the public or the inn customers could come and go. Finally, he went to Rufran's saddle bags and got out his own pair of good quality shears. They were larger than he would wish for the job in hand but they would have to do. He got Madge to let her hair hang loose and helped her brush it out. There was no disguising the high-born quality but what got Bry's senses reeling was the captivating smell. He couldn't resist kissing the top of her head as he finished the brushing out. Madge was startled at first when she felt his lips on her head but immediately realised that she liked the sensation. Bry would have been amazed if he had seen the smile that his attention had produced. He then gathered the hair together in as tight a bunch as he could achieve and held it like that by binding it with thongs.

'I'm trying to get as long as length as I can. You might be able to sell it to a wig maker and hair like this would command a good price.'

'Whatever you think,' Madge told him, she had already mentally handed her fate over to this strange but wonderful man. She knew that he too had secrets he was not going to reveal but the fact that he spoke the high language was evidence that he was a far more complex person than a simple woodsman who was good with the bow.

Bry began snipping away at the lustrous hair slowly working into the centre of the tress. It took a long time but finally he handed the now detached leather bound bunch to Madge who sat and turned it over in her hands. She couldn't stop the tears from streaming down her face; here was the embodiment of all that she had been which had been literally cut off.

'How do I look with short hair?' she asked still in a state of shock at the transformation they had wrought so quickly.

'Perhaps even more beautiful than you did before, it shows off that wonderful elegant neck line,' Bry said as he stroked his hand down the shortened locks and let it fall and rest on the pale skin of her neck.

'Do you really think I'm beautiful?' Madge asked in a small voice.

'I think you are the most gorgeous creature I've ever cut the hair off!' Bry told her and he kissed her on the top of the head again.

'Now shake your head to free the hair up a bit,' he requested, and Madge did as she was asked.

'It needs to be styled a little,' he told her, 'it looks as if an axe man has simply swung at it in one blow. He then began shaping the hair so that it looked as if it was meant to be the length it was; he rounded the outer parts making a good job of smoothing out the sharp edges.

When he was finally finished Madge jumped up determined to find something in which she could see her reflection. Eventually Bry took his large dagger out of his pack and polished the surface to give her a mirror of sorts.

'That's so different,' she said, turning her head this way and that to see the effect, 'and it feels so different, I've always had long hair, right from when I was a little girl. I never realised just how heavy it was.'

It was a short time later that she realised that she was itching, the styling that Bry had done had involved cutting off small bits of hair and it was these that now irritated Madge's skin right down her back.

'Don't worry about that,' Bry told her, 'you'll get an all over wash as soon as we can get to the leather works,' and he began to pack away the things he had used to groom her and Rufran. When he was ready they both pulled up their hoods and, arm in arm, slipped out of the stables and through the courtyard to the street outside the inn. There were still a great number of people milling about in the streets and the inns were obviously doing a fine trade in ale and strong wines judging by the drunken revellers that littered the street.

Bry was stone cold sober now and led the way through to the leather works, his presence ensuring that Madge had a trouble-free passage. She was suddenly revelling in having a protector, something she'd lacked ever since she had left Launceston. At the leather works Bry led the way around to the back and found the hidden key, glad that the leather master had shown where it was kept.

'I've got a good working relationship with the owner,' he explained, 'I sometimes arrive with my skins after he has closed for the night and he would rather that I get them safely in his sheds as soon as I arrive.'

They slipped into the yard and Bry relocked the gates and then led the way into the dying shed. Here he went straight away and lit two or three small lanterns that were dotted around the work area.'

'It's as dark as this during the day as well,' Bry explained, 'the leather master says that light can affect some of the dyes he uses.' He then checked the colouring vat where he had coloured his cloak and was delighted to find that it was newly filled. He touched the side of the vat and found that it was still warm. As Madge watched, totally bemused as he carefully filled three large buckets with water from the pump at the end of the room and placed them next to each other in the centre where a drain marked the lowest point of the floor.

Right,' he said with some trepidation, 'what I want you to do is take off all your clothes and then step into this vat'

'All my clothes!' Madge exclaimed in some alarm, 'you are joking!'

'I'm afraid I am not,' Bry said, he had known that this was going to be difficult for the young woman to comprehend, 'you need to get completely covered in this dye and to then step out of the vat. I'll rinse you off with the buckets of water and then you can dry yourself. I'm afraid there is only this old sacking to use as drying clothes but it's the best thing available.'

'But that means you'll see me completely naked!' Madge complained, 'my brother is the only male that has ever seen me naked, and the last time that happened is when we were four turns old.'

'I'm sorry my love,' Bry replied, 'if there was another way I'd suggest it, but I can't risk you rinsing yourself off completely, you might miss a bit and I'm not sure how damaging this dye will be if it is left on for a long time. If it's any consolation, you'll be seeing me naked as well because I'm going to go in the vat as soon as I've refilled the buckets with fresh water so that you can rinse me off. I could usefully change my appearance, especially if we are travelling south of here. I'm surprised I didn't think of doing this velds ago.'

'All right,' Madge agreed although she felt as if it was anything but alright and slowly began to remove her besmirched outer dress.

'I'll spare your blushes as much as I can by looking the other way while you undress,' Bry assured her.

'Well there's no point in that,' Madge replied, surprising herself, 'you're going to see me without my clothes on, you might as well see me in my under garments.'

'I'm getting undressed at the same time,' Bry said over his shoulder, 'I don't want to get my clothes unnecessarily wet when I throw the water over you.'

When he turned around he was astonished to see Madge completely naked and carefully folding her clothes on a bench to keep them off the floor which she correctly reasoned would soon be awash with water.

'Madge, you're beautiful!' Bry gasped and immediately berated himself. The last thing they needed was either of them to lose their detachment. Madge was equally impressed by what she saw and amazed that instead of shame or embarrassment she actually felt quite calm and self-assured standing there in all her glory. She couldn't help noticing that, for all his apparent detachment, Bry's body was reacting to the presence of hers.

Bry motioned her over to the tub where he had thoughtfully placed a small stool on which she could stand to get into the vat. She did so holding his proffered hand to steady herself and was relieved that the liquid was a pleasant comfortable temperature; it was a shame that it had such an awful smell. Standing up the liquid came up to her navel and at Bry's instruction she dipped herself down until her shoulders were covered. Then, as Bry had instructed her, she took a deep breath, held her nose closed with her fingers and dipped her head completely under the surface. Bry held her there for a count of ten and then as quickly as he could, helped her stand and then grabbed her around the waist and as she lifted her legs, swung her out of the vat and placed her on the ground.

Madge quickly rubbed her fingers all around her nose so that the places where her fingers had held it shut were treated to a coating of the dye. As soon as she had done this she felt the first bucket of icy water hit her as Bry poured it over her. She was glad when the third and last bucket had drained off and she could start drying herself on the coarse sacking. She was little shocked when Bry also started rubbing her down with sacking but was glad as the chaffing restored some warmth to her body, numbed by the icy pump water.

Bry then set about refilling the buckets from the pump ready for his own rinsing. Madge took great delight in carrying out his rinsing and made sure that every part of his anatomy was dealt with. She also relished helping him get dry, pummelling his firm body with the sacking.

To her amazement she was quite sad when the time came to get dressed again and very relieved that Bry had been as good as his word and had not taken advantage of the situation. As she sat in her under clothes dabbing at her muddy dress trying to get rid of the worst of the soiling she turned to Bry and asked him a question that had been floating at the back of her mind.

'Bry, what did you call me when you were explaining why I had to get completely undressed?' she asked.

'I called you Madge, didn't I?' he asked.

'No, you didn't,' Madge told him, 'you called me 'your love' do you do that to all the girls you're about to get out of their clothes?' she asked with an impish grin.

'Did I?' Bry replied, 'I wasn't aware of doing that. And I am not in the habit of getting young ladies out of their clothing!'

'If I thought you were I wouldn't have come here with you,' Madge assured him with a laugh. 'But do you?' she asked, 'love me, I mean.' Bry stopped what he was doing and came and stood in front of her and took her hands tenderly in his.

'As a matter of fact, I think I do love you although I didn't realise it until you said it. If that is a problem, then forget I said it and we'll mention it no more.'

'Oh, that's no problem,' Madge replied smiling into his troubled face, 'in fact it is a good thing because I think I'm in love with you, Bry Woodsman, or whatever your name really is.'

'My love, I can never tell you my real name,' Bry said with the pain of his situation swamping him again, 'can we just accept that we both have pasts we can't reveal and simply live for the future.'

'With all my heart,' Madge replied, relieved that she could also keep her secret, 'let's just get on with our new lives, in our new skins!'

They eventually made their way back to The Five Houses and slipped into the stables where Bry bedded Rufran down for the night. He also spread an extra layer of straw down beneath the manger.

'I'll be fine there for the night,' he said, 'now let's get you up to the room.'

'Oh, you won't be sleeping here,' Madge exclaimed surprising Bry and herself, 'if anyone sleeps here with Rufran, it will be me.'

'But I can't let you risk your virtue by sleeping here where any ruffian might stumble in upon you.' Bry replied in a tone that brooked no argument.

'But I'll not put you out of your own bedroom,' Madge protested, 'if you promise me that you will not harm my maiden status and the room is large enough, we'll share.'

Bry was not at all sure about this but agreed when he realised that Madge was not to be deflected.

They collected all their belongings that had been stashed in the stall and surreptitiously made their way up to Bry's room using the back stairs. Some late celebrations were still going on downstairs in the main bar and they made it into their room without being seen. Bry threw Madge's bag on the bed and his own on the chair against the rear wall.

'I'll be fine here,' he said as he arranged the cushions to serve as pillows.

'Enough of that nonsense,' Madge said, surprising herself again, as she came around the bed and grabbed him by the shoulders, 'I trust you to not take advantage of me and we'll share the bed, it's quite big enough!'

'But Madge, you can't do that,' Bry complained, 'as Madge Falleen it might be acceptable to throw away your reputation but we both know that that is not who you are. Can the lady I think you really are, consider spending the night with a man you hardly know?'

'Perhaps not,' Madge replied, 'but I'm no longer that person and anyway, only you and I will know. Now no more talk, I'm tired let's get to bed.'

'But Madge,' Bry continued to complain.

'Look Bry,' Madge replied, 'you've seen me naked, sleeping in the same room as me is just as bad and the fact that we do, or do not, share a bed makes no difference; now get into bed and give me another cuddle.'

Bry was as good as his word and while he did wrap his arm around her shoulders, he first wrapped a sheet around her and she slept and woke with her virtue otherwise intact. Sleeping with another person was a strange but comforting experience for each of them and they both felt that they had passed some fundamental landmark. Life would never be the same again.

Chapter 17

Crelin Launceston awoke the next morning knowing that something very dramatic had changed with his sister. He instinctively knew that she was no longer the little girl she might have been thought when she had run away from home, but he knew that nothing had really happened of which she was ashamed. He tried to reassure his mother, but Emileen Launceston was not to be moved out of her deep depression so easily. She was well aware of the links that existed between her twins and desperately wanted to believe Crelin when he told her that Maglen was fine and in good spirits.

It had been a traumatic time for Lady Launceston and she took a lot of the blame for Maglen's running away. She felt that her last discussion with her daughter had been what had pushed Maglen over the edge and made her run away from her home. She had spent long hours with her husband trying to get him to do more to find Maglen. Whatever he did or suggested doing she felt that she wanted more to be done.'

'Look Emileen, I've had messages sent to every guardian outpost this side of the Childe Mountains,' Lord Launceston had told his distraught wife, 'No one has seen hide nor hair of her since she left Castle Norland. We know she went there and Jaxaal and Janilla Norland did what they could for her, short of locking her up and sending her back here in chains. Is that what you would have wanted?'

'Oh, don't be ridiculous,' Emileen had snapped back, 'the Norlands were very kind to her and they let us know as soon as they could that she was well when she left them.'

'I'm not so sure that the Norlands have been as open with us as they might have been. I had reports from a wagoner that she might have reached Norland Castle a day or two earlier than they told us she did.'

'Then why didn't you press the matter with them?' Emileen asked clutching at whatever straw she could get hold of.

'Because for the good of our relations with someone who is probably the most powerful man in Fameral,' he snapped back, his wife had never really got a hold on the politics of the Island Nation.

'But why haven't you offered a reward for news of her? There should be posters up in every town and village in the land, and not just north of the Childe Mountains, for all we know she could easily have travelled through the Childe Cut.'

'What and let everyone know that our daughter has run away from home! Think it through woman. I have the good name and reputation of the House of Launceston to consider, something that thoughtless daughter of ours should have done!' Lord Launceston stormed.

'Your reputation you mean,' Emileen responded angrily, 'if you had put your family first before your political ambitions Maglen might still have been here, at home, safe with us. Is it really so all fired important to marry her off to that Sorjohn Dresham? Well, is it?'

'You don't understand these things woman,' Feraard threw back at her angrily over his shoulder as he stormed from the room ending the conversation with a slammed door.

There was still an air of frostiness between them as they and Crelin boarded their coach later that morning. They were on their way southeast to Medland and the meeting that Darval Ellward had called.

Madge awoke in a glorious haze of contentment, which was all the more marked because of the contrast it made to her life in the previous three velds. As she became aware of her surroundings she rolled on her back and reached out to touch Bry, but he wasn't there.

'Good morning sleepy head,' Bry said from the other side of the room where he was standing in his under garments by the window with a mirror propped up and attempting to shave. He had lathered himself as best he could with cold water and the poor-quality soap-root the inn supplied and was attempting to use his best knife as a razor. He wasn't being very successful.

'I thought you weren't going to shave off your beard,' Madge said as she swung her legs over the edge of the bed and sat up, 'you said it was a good disguise.

'It is and I'm not,' Bry replied, 'I'm simply trying to tidy up these odd hairs that are growing on my cheek bone.'

'But why now?' Madge asked, 'is it that important?'

'No, it's not important at all,' Bry replied, 'it's just that after last night's dyeing session my beard is that much more noticeable, and I hate the straggly look it's given me.'

'You're just as handsome as you were before your bath,' Madge said with a grin, 'now rinse your face and come and give me a good morning kiss. After I've had a turn with the mirror, I want to see what my skin colour is like now in the light of day.' Bry did stick his head in the water bowl and rinse off the suds and grabbing a towel mop his face dry before he took Madge's hands in his and kiss her fingers.

'That's not what I meant,' Madge complained and reached up and pulled his head down so that she could kiss him properly.

'Madge,' Bry said as he pulled back from her once she felt she had received the kiss she wanted and released him, 'there is nothing I would like to do than kiss you but we are not an old married couple and for the sake of my sanity I can't let us start behaving as we if we were. You don't realise how hard it was for me to not touch you last night.'

'No, bless you,' Madge replied, 'you were a perfect gentleman, other than the fact you were sharing a maiden's bed. You didn't even fondle my breasts!'

No and I won't,' Bryland told her, 'your brother wouldn't do that would he?'

'Well no, of course not,' she replied, somewhat shocked.

'Well we've got to behave as if we're brother and sister,' Bry told her, 'I've been thinking while you were still asleep. We both now have a very distinctive skin colour that matches each other very well. You're still paler than I am but at first glance anybody seeing us will put us down as brother and sister and I suggest that we use that to our advantage.'

With this Madge did what she had intended to do and used the mirror to look at herself as she stood by the window in the early morning light. She then carefully compared Bry's colouration and got him to stand next to her and studied them both in the mirror.

'You are right,' she said, 'our colour's the same and your beard hides your lower jaw. Our eye shape is not too dissimilar, we could pass as siblings.'

'Right, that's settled then,' Bry announced, 'and if memory serves me right a brother wouldn't fondle his sister's breasts, but he would tickle her!'

With this he proceeded to grab Madge round the waist and throw her on the bed and tickle her until she screamed in fearful delight. A knock on the wall from the next room and a bleary voice telling them that some people were still trying to sleep brought an end to their rough and tumble. With this rebuke they ceased their play fight and in a more sombre mood set about getting their morning started.

Bry finished dressing and put on his travelling cloak, much to Madge's surprise.

'Are you going somewhere without me?' she asked, suddenly scared that he was deserting her.

'No sister dear,' he replied with a smile and came and took her hands in his, 'I'll be with you always as long as you want me to be,' he said kissing her fingers; he had seen the flash of horror in her eyes as he had donned his outside clothes and correctly guessed her fears. He understood perfectly the fragile state her emotions were in.

'I'm simply going out to do a few things and to get us some food for breakfast. I don't want to be seen by too many people looking like this,' and he indicated his new skin colour, 'so if we eat something quickly here in our room we can get on our way and start our new life.'

'That sounds wonderful,' Madge replied although she still felt uneasy that he was leaving her in the room.

'Now you get yourself washed and dressed and I'll be back as quickly as I can,' Bry told her, 'Oh can you ride astride a kertle?' he asked.'

'Why yes, I can although I normally ride side-saddle at home,' Madge told him.

'I guessed as much,' Bry replied, storing away the fact that she was used to riding side saddle; that style tended to be only used by the highest ladies in the land.

'I think these peasant clothes I'm wearing,' and she pointed to the dress lying on the chair, waiting for her to put it on, 'are full enough for me to sit astride Rufran.'

'Right,' Bry said and disappeared out of the door and down the back stairs.

Madge was mystified by this conversation with Bry and thought about it as she washed and dressed. As she started to put on her dress she began to panic that perhaps Bry had changed his mind about throwing in his lot with her.

She needn't have worried for leaving her was the last thing on Bry's mind. In fact, he was using virtually all his money to buy a riding kertle for Madge to use on their journey south. He did manage to also get a couple of hot flat buns from Milden's stall as the trader was opening up for early business. Bry felt that he had been away for a long time and in fact Madge was getting a little concerned when he did manage to get back to her.

They sat in their bedroom eating the buns and drinking water from their overnight jug and planning their next move.

'I've no money left,' Bry explained, 'so what I suggest is that we go to my camp in the Misle Forest. I have one skin curing on a drying frame there and if I can get a few more I can probably get enough money by selling them to tide us over on the journey to the hiring fairs. It may delay our trip by a veld or two if you can put up with that, sister dear.'

'My dear brother,' Madge said with an impish grin, joining in the tone of the conversation, 'I am yours to command. Now that we've found each other, I don't mind where we go or what we do.'

'That's alright then,' Bry told her, 'but we will need to go south to find work. I can't make enough money from selling the odd stag skin to keep us both through the cold batherns.'

They made their way down to the stables where Rufran and the new kertle were tethered ready for their departure. Madge was delighted with her new mount and made a point of introducing herself to the young mare with several small biscuit treats.

'What's her name,' she asked.

'I'm afraid the trader didn't tell me that, you'll have to agree a name with her yourself,' Bry said with a smile.

As they rode out of the village Madge kept up a conversation with her new mount trying out various names, watching to see if any brought about a reaction. Bry sat watching the interaction of Madge and the kertle. He was fascinated by the way she took the business of naming the animal so seriously. It was difficult to realise that he had met Madge less than a day ago.

That he already loved her he had no doubt. It seemed incredible that this fabulous woman had crossed his path and had decided to cast her lot in with him. He was overcome with the responsibility he felt for her but at the back of his mind was the nagging reality of who he was. He longed to tell her about himself, to confess who he was and make a clean breast of things. But he knew he could never do that; he was a disgraced man without family or house ties. He knew Madge had turned her back on her former life, whatever that had been, but, even so, he could never be worthy of her.

For her part Madge was in raptures about the way her life had changed in just a few hours. This wonderful man had taken hold of her life and turned it completely around. She looked sideways at him as they progressed, amazed as how handsome he still looked now that he had a swarthy skin. Growing up in north Fameral she had not met many people from the deep south of the island continent but realised that his complexion now matched that of those from that area. With a jolt she realised that she too now had the same darker skin tone. She looked intently at her hands and the exposed parts of her wrists and arms, turning them over to see the effect the tanner's dye had made. She then turned back to look at Bry aware that her affection for him really was growing as their journey progressed.

She was well aware that buying her this kertle to ride, and the saddle and bridle, would have taken all the money he had won last night and yet, he had done so without a moment's hesitation. She really didn't care what the future held for her; instinctively she knew that if she could stay with him then she would be content. She suddenly felt a pang and knew that Crelin was thinking about her and worrying that she was turning her back on all she had been. She sat quiet for a while as they rode; could she really leave her high family life behind or would her heritage ensure that she could never throw off her origins. They rode on in silence.

'I think I'll call her Tilda,' Madge said a little while later, 'look at how her ears prick up when I say the name. I think she's telling me that she approves.'

'So be it then,' Bry replied with a laugh, 'just use it every time you speak to her and she knows that's what you are doing, and she'll soon accept it as your way of calling her.'

They made good time into the Misle Forest and reached Bry's encampment a little after mid-day.

Chapter 18

Rufran appeared to be as overjoyed as Bry was to be able to show a female partner around the camp site. Once the two kertles had been unsaddled the gelding led the way into the stable and even offered his new companion some of the hay that hung in a net up off the ground.

'They seemed to have hit it off all right,' Bry commented, relieved that the they hadn't taken a dislike to each other. He had been careful when he assessed the animals he had been offered at the traders stable; he had judged the newly named Tilda to be an honest animal with no vices or quirks of character and fairly docile. At that point he had no idea how good a rider Madge really was. As it happened she was obviously skilled in that respect and very at home with the handling of a new kertle.

Bry too was delighted to show Madge every feature of his home in the woods and she revelled in exploring the area. He got a fire going and soon they were able to sit and share a jug of kandrel.

'I'll have to get some more roasted kandrel beans next time we're in a village, my stock is running low,' Bry commented more as a thought to himself as anything.

'But I saw some kandrel bushes nearby,' Madge told him, 'if we collected some we could dry them and then roast them on a hot stone. I take it that you don't have a griddle in your stash of equipment.'

'No, I never thought of that when I left..,' and he just stopped himself from giving away his origins.

'Well we can still use a large flat stone that we can heat in the fire,' Madge said, 'I'll go and pick some beans when I've finished my drink. We can start them drying straight away.'

'You see Rufran!' Bry called across to his kertle, 'bring a woman into your life and they start domesticating you straight away.'

'Oh, that's nothing,' Madge replied with a laugh, 'if we were staying here any length of time I'd have tapestries on the walls and curtains at the windows.'

'But there are only wattle walls, an unthatched roof and no windows,' Bry complained.

'Well you'd better start getting your side of the bargain sorted out and finish them off, hadn't you!' she replied with a laugh.

'Rufran, I hope you can keep Tilda in better order than I'm managing with this one!' Bry said with a grin.

He did, in fact, set about making some improvements to the living accommodation by fetching more broom and dried ferns to make another bed area.

'You can stop that at once,' Madge said when she saw what he was doing, 'you slept with me last night and you'll do the same again tonight, and every night if I have my way.'

'But Madge,' Bry tried to reason with her, 'it's just not right. We're not married, and I've told you we never can be, I'm not the sort of person you'd want to marry anyway.'

'I'll be the judge of that unless you are married already?' Madge asked suddenly concerned that her rural idyll was about to get a harsh dose of reality.

'Alphos no! I'm not married,' Bry assured her, 'I've never even 'walked out' with a girl, and I've never had any attachment to any female. I think my lameness puts them off,' he said grinding to a halt at the mention of his handicap. He had always instinctively tried to ignore his impediment in the naive hope that others would ignore it as well.

'Your limp,' Madge asked in astonishment, 'do you really think that makes a difference to anyone?'

'Well it used to matter,' Bry replied, 'when I went to the village school I used to get teased and was made fun of all the time.'

'Well it makes no difference to me,' Madge affirmed, 'I'm not saying that I didn't notice straight away, of course I did, and having seen you naked I know how twisted your thigh is, I'm not blind, but that's your leg, not you!'

'Madge, you are more generous than most people I've met. When I was younger the girls all seemed to like the boys, who were good at kick-ball. I never was, so I got overlooked. The physical activities were always beyond me, so it has come as a surprise that I have skill with the bow. Not that it has helped with attracting females, until I met you.'

'But I liked you and we were talking before I knew you were an expert Archer,' Madge replied.

'But that doesn't change the fact that we should not behave in a way that would jeopardise your returning to your former life,' Bry told her as he came and stood in front of her with his hands on her shoulders.

'But that life has gone,' Madge replied with a sob but drawing on her resolve added, 'I can never return to it!'

'Are you sure of that?' Bry said, holding her chin and turning her head up so that he was looking straight in her eyes, 'circumstances may change, you may change; this rustic life out in the woods or labouring away as the lowest of the low farm worker might make you want to return to your former life. I don't know exactly what that was, Madge, but my guess is that you were at least the daughter of a house fifth or even higher born. Think it through Madge, you may want to return to that life; will you be able to do that if it becomes known that you've lived as a wife of a man you hardly know and who can never marry you.'

'But we'll be living as brother and sister and anyway, why can't you marry me, Bry,' Madge asked as the tears welled up and spilled from her eyes, 'I'll marry you. Why won't you commit yourself to me as I am committing myself to you? Is my possible past a problem?'

'Madge, there's nothing I would like more than to be married to you,' Bry said as he took her hands in his and kissed her finger tips,' you are the most beautiful, the most wonderful woman I have ever met, and it is tearing me apart but there are things in my past, things of which I have been accused, that cannot be ignored. In your former life if you knew what I am supposed to have done, you would run screaming back to your home, wherever that is, without a second glance. I am not the sort of person to whom you would really want to be married.'

'Well tell me what you are accused of,' Madge pleaded, 'I'll be the judge of whether I wished to be married to you.'

'I'm sorry, Madge,' Bry replied, 'I cannot do that. I can't risk seeing the condemnation in your eyes.'

'Then what you are accused of is true!' Madge said stepping back.

'No, it isn't,' Bry replied his own tears spilling down his cheeks, 'not in my heart. I did the things people are accusing me of, but I didn't know I was doing them. This doesn't make sense, but Madge, please believe me,' and he stepped forward and regained her hands in his, 'I was fooled into making it possible for someone else to do something totally reprehensible. I didn't realise until it was too late; I'm a gullible fool and it has ruined my life. Please believe me Madge, I'm not guilty of what I'm accused but I can't prove it. That's why I live here out in the woods with just Rufran and a red cannis family for company.'

'Well, you've got me and Tilda for company as well now,' Madge said, and she reached up and kissed him tenderly on the lips, 'come on show me more of my new home,' she said lightening the mood by dragging him after her as she skipped ahead of him.

Bry duly took her on a tour of the surrounding area. He showed her the parlip patch which he was already beginning to clear and propagate. From here he showed her where a side offshoot from the main stream fed into a flat marshy area.

'This will help get rid of our human waste,' he explained and when Madge seemed a bit nonplussed he gave her a brief introduction to the concept of natural sewage filtering.

He recovered the meat he had stored high in the branches of a tree and was pleased that his preserving methods had ensured it was virtually as fresh as the day he had hung it there. He then showed her where he had started to make an underground store for the non-perishable things that made for a more comfortable life.

As they sat finishing their stag meat dinners, washed down with one of the few flagons of wine that Bry was allowing them, Madge lay back and decided that she could easily get used to a life out here in the woods, as long as she could share it with Bry. At first, she didn't see him when the red cannis decided to come and visit. Bry got her attention and motioned her to be very quiet. She sat transfixed as the small animal made his way into the centre of the clearing and then sat down looking at Bry expectantly; he seemed to accept the presence of Madge as being normal. Bry tossed a couple of bones to the animal who gave a sharp bark which was the signal to his offspring who came scampering out of the undergrowth and began arguing over possession of the offerings.

Madge sat transfixed; she'd never seen anything like this. She knew her father and the other noble's sometimes hunted red cannis with packs of hounds, but she had never seen one this close or acting so tame. She collected together all the bones left over from her meal and began tossing them over to the young cubs who quickly caught on to the fact there was another source of supply.

'Here comes the dam,' Bry said in a whisper and nodded towards the far side of the clearing where the cub's mother was sticking her head out of the bushes. The animal then very slowly emerged and made her way towards the shelter where the rest of her family were busy with the meal and their games. She paused as she approached and sniffed the air. Everything was obviously to her satisfaction for she then continued and came and sat and then lay down at Madge's feet. Madge then carefully offered the dam the largest of the bones she had left. This was carefully taken, and the dam then set about cracking it to get to the marrow.

'I think I've just been adopted,' Madge said with tears of joy running down her face.

'She's never come that close before,' Bry told her, 'she usually keeps in the background and watches what's going on very carefully. It is usually her who decides when it is time for the family to go.'

But for now, the cannis seemed happy to be where they were. One cub obviously felt left out when all parents and his siblings all had bones, but he didn't. Much to Madge's surprise he then jumped on her lap and helped himself to the bone she still had in her hands. She expected him to jump off and run away with his spoils but instead he sat down on her lap and began attacking the bone with his little soft teeth.

'I've never seen that before!' Bry exclaimed in an astonished whisper. The cub continued his contented attack on the bone with play growls until one of his siblings, tiring of his own bone, decided to go and stalk Rufran's claw set as the kertle sat musing in his stall alongside Tilda. This was a great attraction to all his siblings who quickly joined in. The one on Madge's lap saw what was happening and decided to join in as well. He stood up but before leaping off her lap, turned and muzzled her hand giving it a thank you lick as he leapt after the others.

'I think that's a little cannis with a crush on you,' Bry said with a laugh as he stood and made a start on clearing away the meal. The young cannis were having a wonderful time stalking and then pouncing on Rufran's claw sets. Tilda was not at all sure if she liked the attention that she also got but Madge noticed that the kertle was careful when she put her feet down having raised them out of the way of an attacking cub that she didn't hurt one of the young animals. These games went on for a while until the dam cannis decided that it was time to go and with a yelp led the way back into the forest. All her offspring dutifully followed except the one that had befriended Madge; he came and brushed up against her legs before he too disappeared into the undergrowth.

'That was magical,' Madge gasped her eyes still full of tears of joy at the experience.

'I was hoping the male would show up, but I had no idea he would bring the whole of his family,' Bry told her, 'he usually drops by about this time when he can smell the fire and my cooking.'

The next day they set about working out their new life together although neither realised that that was what they were doing. Bry rose with the dawn and went and washed in the stream. By the time Madge stirred he had the fire rekindled and a jug of kandrel keeping hot beside it.

Madge also refreshed herself in the stream, delighted that she could do so; keeping clean, or not being able to, had been a trial on the road. After she had breakfasted as Bry had done on small flat bread cakes she set off to collect some more kandrel beans. Bry took Rufran and made his way out of the valley and across two hills to the place where he knew stags could be found at this time of day. He managed to get a fine stag quite quickly and, as he had brought Rufran with him, set about hunting a second. Rufran objected at first to have the freshly killed animal slung across his shoulders but finally took it in good part.

Bry's second hunt did not go so well, the disturbance to the herd of the first attack had scattered the animals and he had to resort to a subterfuge he had developed; he climbed up a tree to a fair height and then waited in ambush. Eventually he was successful and returned to the camp with both a stag and a hind carcass to deal with.

He was pleasantly surprised and relieved when Madge was quite ready to help with the skinning and cleaning of the carcasses. She had never done this sort of work before but knew roughly what was required. They hung the carcasses from branches on trees a little away from their 'house.' With their throats slit the animals slowly released their blood.

'We ought to catch that blood and make use of it,' Bry explained, 'but just now I have no means of dealing with it.'

The next operation was to skin the stag and Madge watched carefully as Bry began the process, mirroring his work on the stag with her own on the hind. As the sun was about to set they had two fine skins drying on the trees and enough meat to last them an alphen or two.

'With the other one I had already drying on its frame, that gives me three skins to trade in Under Childe,' Bry said with a satisfied stretch, 'we make a good team.'

'Of course, we do,' Madge said with a smile as she came and stood behind him and gave him a hug, 'marry me, please.'

'Madge, don't start that again,' Bry said with a sigh as he turned and returned her hug and added a kiss full on the lips, 'you know I can never marry you.'

'Yes, I know you told me that,' she replied sadly, 'but I'm going to keep asking. Now let's get some of this meat butchered and cooked, our dinner guests will be here soon I expect.'

The next morning Madge insisted on being shown how to use a bow and they had a lot of fun with her lesson.

'Look here young lady,' Bry said at one point, 'I'm standing behind you so that I can help you get your hands in the right place, not so you can turn and kiss me.'

'I appreciate your teaching me,' Madge replied, 'but I enjoy kissing you.'

'Yes, and I enjoy being kissed,' Bry replied, 'but it doesn't help with your training. Now pay attention or I'll slap your bottom till you do!'

'You're a mean, horrible brute,' Madge responded with a pout, 'and I hate you.'

'You said you loved me a moment ago,' Bry reminded her.

'That was then,' Madge told him, 'before you threatened physical violence.'

'Well you'd better behave yourself then,' Bry said shortly.

'Oh, you're worse than Crelin when he was showing me how to ride!' Madge replied without thinking. She immediately realised her mistake in mentioning her brother's name but, to her relief Bry made no mention of it.

The lessons did continue, and Madge proved a keen and able student. Before long she was sending arrows unerringly towards the targets they had set up.

'This bow's really too big and strong for you,' Bry told her, 'I made it to suit me. I'd better make one more suited to your strength and size.'

That afternoon he did start making Madge a bow tailored to her requirements from the timbers he had previously set aside to dry naturally. Two days later she was practicing with her own bow and the arrows that she had made with Bry's guidance, which better suited her arm length. Her skill with the weapon did improve rapidly but she soon acknowledged that she would never be as competent as Bry.

However, three days later it was with some pride and a great deal of surprise that she could make herself do it, that she shot, killed and brought home a wild breesh hen to add to their larder. Madge also applied herself to the job of cleaning the hides ready for their sale to the leather dealer in Under Childe. Under Bry's guidance she rapidly leaned how to scrape the inside of the skin to remove every last trace of muscle and fat.

Two velds after they left the village, Bry returned to Under Childe to sell the skins and to buy the things they agreed they needed for their travels. Madge felt very lonely as she watched him leave their camp to make his way to the village, but they had talked it through and agreed that it was just as well if she remained out of sight as much as possible. She got to thinking what might be happening out in the wider world and couldn't help wondering how her parents were and how they and Crelin were coping without her.

Chapter 19

Away in Medland, Maglen's father was meeting with the high officers of the guardians and receiving updates on their investigations into his daughter's disappearance. The leaders of the five houses were gathered together in the Fameral Family Council Meeting Room for yet another meeting that Darval Ellward had called.

'My lords,' Darval began, 'I am grateful that you have all been able to spare the time to come here; there is a grave matter that I feel we need to discuss. I have been approached on a number of occasions by a man called Natheal Lather. I don't know if any of you have met this individual?' he asked.

'Natheal Lather,' Lord Dresham replied, 'a young firebrand with ideas well above his station?'

'That sounds like the same man,' Darval replied.

'Nasty piece of work,' Lord Dresham continued, 'came and demanded an interview with me last turn. Seems he has ideas about getting better wages for the itinerant farm workers.'

'That's what he talked to me about,' Darval told his fellow lords, 'went as far as threatening me that he'd get all the migrant workers to refuse to work for the House of Swenland unless we offered significantly more money to them. As you are probably well aware there is no way I can harvest my grain crops without a significant amount of help from migrant workers.'

'He threatened me with getting my own house fifth workers to stop their labours unless I paid more.' Lord Dresham replied, 'I told him to go and get lost and the devil had the effrontery to threaten me with violence!'

'What, he threatened your lordship's person!' Lord Launceston exclaimed in alarm.

'Not me directly,' Lord Dresham assured his fellow lords, 'but he made it clear that he has a number of pike-men armed and ready to follow his orders.'

'Pike-men!' Lord Ellward said rising from the chair where he sat slumped, 'where did he get them from.'

'They are probably the unaffiliated men left over from the dissolution who have not yet been assumed by a house or who don't wish to be assumed,' Jaxaal said as much thinking to himself as speaking to his fellow lords, 'I wondered if there would be any repercussions after the display of strengths that went on at the last Challenge meet.'

'You mean these are all former Norland men he's gathered together?' Darval asked, 'that doesn't seem likely. They would be the first to try and return to their former homes and positions.'

'I agree,' Jaxaal confirmed, 'I think it is more likely that these are the lower skilled men from all five houses who would find it difficult to win back places having left their homes to gather behind the house banners during the unrest at the last Challenge meet.'

'I think you are right, Jaxaal,' Lord Launceston agreed

'Just how much money was this Natheal Lather asking for?' Jaxaal asked and was astonished at the figures that he was quoted.

'But that would make the harvesting of the grain totally uneconomical,' Jaxaal replied, shocked by the figures.

'Exactly what I told him last turn,' Lord Dresham agreed, 'he went away and started trouble up in the north of my lands at Vale Farm. It wasn't one of my fifths, as your lordships know I only have five fifths and my forebears didn't want their lands running over with nobles, but Vale Farm has always looked to the House of Dresham and old Jedraah Balental has been a good friend. Well this Natheal Lather stirred up trouble when Jedraah was trying to hire in the workers he needed, and the poor man could not get enough reapers without paying twice the going rate. Jedraah got his crops harvested but it cost him so much he had to sell the farm. As it happens I stepped in and bought it off him and he now farms it as a tenant. At a very small rent, I might add. So, in reality Natheal Lather stole the cost of that harvest from me!'

'This is terrible,' Lord Ellward said and he slumped back in his chair. Darval was more than a little concerned at the condition of his father. Parina whispered to him that his father was looking very pale as he sat drooping in his chair. Darval knew that this was far more than just a reaction to the news of workers unrest, disturbing as that might be. He wished his aunt Arianne was here to look at her brother.

'Is this really such a major problem?' Lord Launceston asked, 'surely the machinations of just one man cannot cause us any real problems, can they?' he asked in a slightly derisory tone.

'I think the problems are very real,' Lord Dresham replied, 'it was just one farm last turn, but I've had word that he has a growing following. He has a sister who it appears is as nasty an individual as her brother and she is making a thing of getting the women workers to support the men in their outlandish claims.'

'It's difficult to know just what we can do,' Jaxaal mused, 'we need more information on this Natheal Lather and the armed men he has at his command. We need to find out just what his plans are. It is just possible that his ambitions go far beyond just raising the workers' wages. It can't have escaped your lordships notice that we five family heads rule by grace and favour, by the goodwill of the people. Yes, they are beholding to us for their livelihoods, but it is only by good management that we keep that goodwill. If someone with a grievance, real or imagined, decided to challenge us and was able to generate support we might be hard pressed to keep our positions.'

They all agreed with this and a message was sent requesting the senior guardian officers to attend them. The senior officers duly arrived and took their places at the chairs in the centre of the semi-circle of desks. Jaxaal smiled inwardly to himself remembering the first time he had been in this room. That had been during the last Challenge when he was summoned by their lordships after the attacks on him. Now he was one of the five ruling lords.

The senior guardian officers were charged to have their men find out as much as they could about this Natheal Lather and to report back in a veld's time. As they were dismissed, Feraard Launceston followed them out to the ante-chamber where he asked if there had been any news of his daughter since he last spoke to them. He was brought up to date of probable sightings in Upper and possibly Under Childe which he was assured would be followed up with all the resources they could provide. This had to satisfy the Lord who returned to the meeting room in a sombre mood.

Bry returned to their home in the forest the following afternoon and was very pleased with himself. He had got a good price for the skins although it had taken him a long while to convince the leather master that it really was him, so effective a disguise the staining of his skin proved to be. He apologised for making so free with the tannery's resources, but the older man just laughed.

Bry had purchased all the items that he and Madge had agreed they needed for their journey. He had also managed to get a repaired second-hand griddle from the smithy in Under Childe to aid in the roasting of kandrel beans.

Madge had then proudly served him with a mug of kandrel made from the beans she had dried and then roasted on a hot stone.

'This griddle will make things a lot easier,' she had congratulated him.

'There is one other thing I have got you, my love,' Bry told her and he went and got another smaller package out of his saddle bag.

'What's this?' Madge asked excitedly as she eagerly unwrapped the package. The slithery nature of the contents at first made her flinch in horror but Bry simply laughed.

'There's no reason to be scared of your own hair!' he told her. Madge then picked up the fallen tresses and realised that it was a wig made from the hair they had cut off as part of her transformation.

'But why?' she asked somewhat perplexed.

'My love, there may come a time when you will want to resume your former identity and your own hair, reaching down to the middle of your back will help with that,' Bry told her.

'But when did you get this made?' she asked.

'It was only just being finished when I went back there this morning,' he explained, 'I took all that lovely hair of yours to a wig maker on the morning that we left Under Childe, just before I went to buy Tilda.'

'That's why you took so long!' Madge exclaimed, 'but I've left that person behind me,' she added, tears filling her eyes.

'Madge, we don't know what the future holds,' Bry said as he took her in his arms, 'there may come a time when you will need and want to be that person again. It will take turns for your hair to grow to that length again and what hair you've got left now is died a much darker colour and all that's got to grow out again.'

'But it must have cost a fortune to have made,' Madge complained, 'I can never repay you.'

'Don't be a silly breesh hen Madge,' Bry told her, 'It was only the labour it cost us, remember it was your hair they were working with.'

With that Madge insisted on trying on the wig and was delighted at how well the base to which the hair was attached fitted her head and she spent some time looking at her old self in the polished dagger that served as her mirror until Bry gave her his last gift from his shopping trip, a polished plate that gave a much better image.

They spent the rest of that day preparing for their imminent departure. This involved making a lot of hard decisions as to what they could take with them and what would have to be left behind.

Bry had to enlarge his underground store to accommodate everything that they decided they could not take with them. He wasn't at all sure if he would ever be back this way; if it were down to him alone then he was pretty sure he would but suddenly there was another force in his life and he knew that where Madge wanted to go, he would follow, even if it was him that led the way!

Once they had completed these preparations they thoroughly enjoyed another large meal that evening and were able to feed their cannis friends as they finished half of one of their carcasses. They both intuitively realised that they were ending a significant part of their relationship.

'Well, if we had got married instead of getting ourselves dyed,' Bry announced, raising his tankard of wine in a toast, 'this would be the end of our 'Primary Alphen' and the start of our 'First Turn' together. So, here's to us.'

'To us!' Madge echoed, 'I suppose we had better get our minds around the fact that, to the rest of the world, from now on we are brother and sister.'

'Yes, that's right,' Bry agreed, 'you'd better tell me how brothers behave towards their sisters; I'm an only child so I don't know about these things.'

'Well just remember that as the female, sisters are always right!' and she ducked as Bry threw a cloth at her.

It was early the next morning when they finally mounted their kertles and with a last look back, left their little glade. Bry's eyes were moist but Madge's were streaming tears as they finally turned their back on their little idyll. Madge realised that this had probably been the happiest few velds of her life and she was very quiet as they made their way to head deeper into the Misle Forest.

'What do you call this place, our home?' Madge asked as they turned to look back as they left the glade.

'I haven't actually given it a name,' Bry replied although he too felt that it should be called something significant. 'What about, Cannis Glade?' he suggested.

'Cannis Glade,' Madge said turning the name over in her mind, 'yes, that will do very well. Let's hope our little friends keep it well guarded for us until our return.'

'We may not be back this way again,' Bry told her, 'we don't know what the future holds for us.'

'No, we don't,' Madge agreed, 'but we can promise ourselves that we will always have this wonderful place in our hearts. If you won't marry me Bry, promise me that if things don't work out for us on the road that we'll return here.'

'Of course, my love,' he replied even though he thought the chance of their being able to do so was unlikely.

Bry was confident of their route through the forest to High Tor although he had never been that way before.

'This track leads all the way through the forest,' he told Madge, 'and will emerge very close to High Tor Farm. We should be there in a velds or so.'

'Bry, I'm worried,' Madge confessed as they made their first overnight stop, 'what if we can't get hired together and we have to take work at different farms. I don't think I could cope being on my own now.'

'No, I don't want to do that either my love,' Bry told her, 'but remember that is actually what we had both planned before we met.'

'Yes, I know that,' Madge agreed, 'but we have met and that has changed everything. Please, promise me that you won't abandon me now we have found each other,' she begged.

'No, my love,' Bry promised her, 'I couldn't cope with that either.'

They both felt the need for physical comfort and simply made up a single bed so that they could sleep in each other's arms that night. Madge was now totally confident that Bry would not abuse his promise to respect her maiden status and revelled in the experience of falling asleep with his breath on her cheek.

They then quickly fell into the routine of rising early and after a brief breakfast making a start on their days travel. They would stop for lunch wherever they could find suitable grazing for Rufran and Tilda. They would then continue till late afternoon when they would find somewhere where they could spend the night. This was invariably sufficiently off the track to be undetectable from fellow travellers. Bry had made yet more use of oiled cloth to provide them with a waterproof roof to the lean-to shelters that he created each night or simply draped it over a cord to provide a waterproof shelter.

Having taught herself how to roast kandrel beans on a flat rock heated in the fire, Madge was able to develop the idea to make small flat bread cakes each evening which lasted them the whole of the next day. Both Rufran and Tilda enjoyed small bits of this flat bread as their treats and the four made a good team. For the most part they had the forest to themselves but occasionally they would catch up with and share the track with other travellers.

Madge was a little concerned when sometimes they would be passed by black cloaked guardians; she had a dread that despite their darkened skin disguise she would be recognised and dragged off, back to Launceston Hall, but her camouflage seemed to be working very well. About four days into their journey they caught up with a group of workers walking their weary way and Madge realised that the group contained some people she had met before. As they passed the walkers she slowed Tilda as she drew alongside one younger woman and purposefully struck up a conversation. Braveen was a little taken aback to be addressed as she walked; she'd been lost in her own thoughts as she trudged along.

'How far have you come?' Madge asked in a friendly sort of way as she dismounted and walked beside the other woman.

'All the way from the north of Medland,' Braveen replied, a little bemused at being singled out by this previously mounted woman.

'Oh, I hope you don't mind me talking to you as you walk,' Madge said, sensing the others surprise, 'it's just that I wanted to give my kertle a rest and I'd rather do that when I can talk to someone,' Madge improvised.

'Not at all,' Braveen replied with a smile, 'walking can be a lonely occupation even in a big group like this.'

'So, you've walked all the way from Medland, that's a lot of leagues.' Madge commented, hoping to draw more out of her former friend.

'Oh no, not all the way,' Braveen told her, 'North of the Childe Mountains there are good wagon services and you can travel quite cheaply, if you don't mind the hard seats and the slow progress. I managed to pick up a few velds work in Under Childe but when that ended I've had to walk from there. There are wagoners who ply the routes south of the mountains but none that come through the Misle Forest which is the direct route from Under Childe to High Tor Farm, where we're all headed,' and she indicated her fellow walkers.

'My brother and I are headed that way as well,' Madge told her, 'we hope to find work there or at one of the other hiring fairs.'

'Well, the fair at High Tor is a good one,' Braveen l told her, 'as well as the farm itself there will be owners from a few other places. If you can't get hired there, then you can always try Vale Farm further south. That used to be a good place to work but they went broke after the troubles last turn so I don't know if they will be hiring now. Failing that you can travel still further south to Dresham Town where there are lots of farms affiliated to the House of Dresham. That's where I hope to get work this turn,' Braveen said with a sigh and a faraway look, 'the weather's so much warmer down in the south. You can sleep out in the fields without even a thin blanket and never feel cold.'

'Yes, that sounds good,' Madge replied, storing what she had learnt away for future use.

'But you must come from the south,' Janteal said staring deeply at Madge's complexion, 'I just love the dusky look you southerners all have.'

They talked some more until Bry, who had also dismounted to give Rufran a rest, suggested that they remount and get on their way. Bidding her friend farewell Madge leapt up on Tilda and the two kertles and their riders trotted on their way.

'That surprised me,' Bry commented once they were well ahead of the walkers, 'I didn't expect you to strike up a conversation like that.'

'I surprised myself,' Madge confessed, 'but what was really surprising is the fact that Braveen didn't recognise me. I met her in the Childe Cut,' Madge told him, 'we spent some time together, she was very helpful when I needed a friend. But the important thing is, she didn't recognise me! That means this skin colour and short hair you've given me is really working. I feel so much better.'

Her lightened spirits were infectious, and they travelled on in a bright mood for a few more days.

A veld later they had left the forest and travelled up a gentle slope before they got their first sighting of High Tor Farm. It was imposing at every level; the farm buildings were numerous and well laid out and the House itself was of substantial proportions. The farm was built on the crest of a gentle rise and as they approached they could see a neat and orderly village laid out in an attractive vale beyond. Both Madge and Bry could see that this was a well-cared for and well-maintained establishment, quite befitting the home of the now Lord Norland.

That Jaxaal had been raised here in secret seemed improbable until it was realised just how far from the main centres of Fameral society High Tor was located. Their first instincts were to go straight to the farm but in time, they independently remembered that that was not their place in society anymore and they turned towards the village. There they discovered that they had arrived in the middle of this round of hiring fairs and the village green had been given over to the process. A large notice told them that the next fair would be held the next day and was being run by the farmers from the south west of

High Tor. They made their way to the village inn where a bunk house was doing good trade, judging by the number of people milling around outside. Down on the pasture below the inn a marquee had been set up to cater for the overflow of humanity.

Here they were able to get a couple of bed spaces, but only by posing as a married couple. The weary steward who was in charge of the marquee had jumped to the assumption that they were a married couple and despite Bry's misgivings, they made no attempt to correct the misconception. The married quarters were sited at the rear of the tent and this suited Madge and Bry very well because they found that they could tether Rufran and Tilda just outside at the rear where temporary stabling had been provided and there was a flap in the tent wall, giving them access to their kertles.

'Well so much for posing as brother and sister,' Bry said in a resigned undertone when they were alone.

'Well, we don't have to pretend to be a married couple,' Madge said with her impish grin returning, 'we could always get married at the civic building I saw at the far end of the village.'

'Madge!' Bry exclaimed, 'please don't start all that again.'

'Oh, come on Bry,' Madge pleaded, 'please marry me, or at least explain to me why you can't.'

'Madge,' Bry replied, 'I've told you before, I can do neither of those things.' That seemed to settle things again although Madge was very quiet for a while.

They made the best of the circumstances in the marquee and found that it would serve their purposes very well. There were modesty curtains hanging from ropes strung across the tent to give each couple some privacy although they did nothing to cut down on the noise level. The area next to Bry and Madge's space was occupied by a family, a couple and three young children who were making most of the noise that pervaded the area. Bry had gone off to see what farms were advertising as hiring on the morrow so Madge was left on her own. She was removing her travelling dress when she discovered two pairs of dark brown eyes staring at her round the intervening curtain wall.

Chapter 20

'Come away from there you two, 'a woman's voice called, 'leave the poor people alone. They don't want you spying on them.'

'Oh, I don't mind,' Madge said, surprising herself. A few velds ago she would have been very disturbed by this invasion of her privacy, especially as she was in a slight state of undress. But now, after the horrors of the bunkhouses toilet facilities and the intimacy she had developed with Bry, this was nothing to even notice or at which to react. The children's' mother then appeared and herded them back into their own space.

'I am sorry about that; I'll try and keep them where they belong,' the woman apologised.

'Oh, I don't mind,' Madge assured her, 'My husband and I have been travelling alone for a long time, it's nice to have some company,' she continued, revelling in being able to refer to Bry as her husband.

'Well, I'd stay and chat, we've been travelling alone too,' the woman replied, 'but the baby needs feeding.'

'Well bring the baby here; if you wish to, I'd love to have a chat.' Madge told her. This was a totally new experience for the young noble woman. She knew from her earlier experiences in the bunkhouses that the travelling women were much more relaxed about such things as breast feeding and other bodily functions and expected to pass the time of day with other people.

'Well if you don't mind,' Madge's new friend replied, 'I'd like that.' Shendaar Brinkle, as the woman introduced herself, appeared to be just two or three turns older than Madge who was impressed at the cleanliness of the mother's clothes and those of her children. She and her husband had been working as migrant workers for three turns, she told Madge.

Her two older children took their mother's invitation as applying to them as well and followed her into Madge and Bry's bedroom. The eldest, the boy sat happily at his mother's feet playing with a toy kertle woven out of basket withies. His younger sister, after a little hesitation, climbed on the bed next to Madge and then proceeded to sit on her lap.

'It was ever so romantic really, the way we met.' Shendaar remembered. 'It was here, at High Tor. We were both looking for work as singles and had seen each other in the crowd of people. I thought Brindle Brinkle was the most handsome man I had ever seen and apparently, he liked the look of me as well. Well to cut a long tale short, we were both hired by the same farmer and even sat together on the cart on our way to the farm. I found out later that Brindle bribed the farmer to take us both and pushed another man out of his seat so that we would be sitting together. I was only half a bathern past my majority and this handsome man came into my life and took it over. We were married at the end of that Harvest bathern and have been on the road ever since.'

'You've always been travelling?' Madge asked in amazement, 'and you've raised three wonderful children.' She said as she idly stroked the well brushed hair of the toddler on her lap.

'Well I've never been scared of hard work,' Shendaar replied, 'get that from my mother. Brindle works so hard to provide for us that we've never been short of money for food or clothes for the children.'

'Do you work now?' Madge asked, 'I mean with a nursing child?'

'Oh yes, although I admit it's not been easy,' Shendaar replied. 'We had a good turn last turn, made more money than we ever have before, although I'm not happy about how it happened.'

'What do you mean?' Madge asked, anxious to learn as much as she could about her new life.

'Well we went to the fair at Vale Farm, not that it was really a fair as such. It was just the one farm looking for workers but there was this man, Natheal Lather, who went around everyone who turned up looking for work, telling them that if they followed his lead they would be much better off. Brindle and I weren't that interested, but he had a lot of armed men supporting him and they were very threatening to us when we told him that we just wanted to get some work.'

'What happened?' Madge asked, intrigued.

'Well, this Natheal Lather insisted that we refuse to accept the positions the farmer was offering at the rates he was quoting until he had negotiated a better deal.'

'And did you do that?'

'To our shame, yes, we did,' Shendaar replied lowering her voice to just a whisper.

'Natheal has a sister called Pardrea, she's far worse than he is if the truth be told. She came around all the women and threatened violence if we and our men didn't do what her brother told us to do. It was awful, but we needed the work. We only had the two older ones then, although this one was on his way. I couldn't work because I was near my time, so Brindle decided that we would stay and take the work when we were allowed to. We got a much higher rate for his labour; the best we've ever earned but it turns out it was too much for the farmer to stand. We heard later that he had to sell the farm to cover his debts after he had to borrow money to pay the rates the Lather twins forced him to give us.'

'They're twins, are they?' Madge asked, 'I've met this Pardrea but not her brother.'

'Well we felt awful when we heard what had happened,' Shendaar went on, 'but it was too late to do anything about it. That poor farmer, he's a kind soul in his way, was always giving the children fruit from his trees and always treated us very fair. Anyway, Natheal Lather turned up here two days ago and has been trying to get support for his ideas; he wants to try the same thing here. Tells us it's all in our interest and that it's our duty as working men and women to 'gang together' or 'unite' as he puts it. Very good with words is Natheal Lather, can turn a phrase round and make it mean something quite different. Brindle challenged him about Vale Farm, but he simply said it was the farmer's fault that he had gone broke and he should have managed his affairs better.'

The baby fed and changed, fell into a peaceful sleep and Shendaar put him to sleep in the travelling cot in their bedroom before returning to carry on the conversation with Madge. The two women developed a friendship based on the mutual respect they felt for the other. Madge had to improvise some of the background that she let slip.

Fortunately, she and Bry had talked through what they would say if asked about their past. Since people's natural skin colour seemed to darken the further south they lived they had agreed that they would say they came from a small village way south of Swenland Grange quite near the southern coastline. Madge had never actually been that far south and Bry only once or twice, but he had given Madge a feel of what the countryside was like. They had even created a layout of their home village in their imagination and played games as they had travelled describing parts of their fictitious home to each other.

Luckily Shendaar was very happy to lead the conversation and Madge felt that she acquitted her part quite well. They were sharing a joke and tears were streaming down both their faces as they were joined by Bry who had found out all he needed to get ready for the next day's fair. Shendaar's husband Brindle arrived shortly after and appeared to be a little unsettled. Despite this he was introduced to Bry and Madge and seemed pleased that Shendaar had made a friend.

'That man and his sister are here again and causing trouble already!' Brindle exclaimed as he threw his pack on his bed and sat down. Shendaar bustled around and quickly handed her husband and Bry a mug of kandrel each.

The four then set about organising to get their evening meals; it turned out that both couples intended to buy a meal from one of the hot food stalls set up on the village green by some switched on villagers and it was agreed that Bry and Brindle would get the food while the women would prepare a place where they could eat it together. Madge pulled back the curtain that separated their sleeping quarters and the opened space provided a comfortable dining area. Admittedly they could only sit on their beds and had to use the benches their spaces had been allocated as tables, but it worked well. Madge was again impressed at how well the two small children behaved, the boy making sure his sister had everything she needed. The meal went well, assisted by the sharing of Bry's last flagon of wine. As they sat back after the meal sharing yet another jug of kandrel they began talking about the upcoming fair.

'That Natheal Lather has called a meeting for tonight on the village green,' Brindle reported, 'and the way he's talking he expects everyone to be there, if you know what I mean.'

'You mean he's threatening violence if people don't turn up,' Bry commented, 'I saw him roughing up a couple of young men when I was over the other side of the village.'

'But how can one man do such things?' Madge asked.

'Oh, it's not just him on his own,' Brindle told her, 'he's got a right load of tough-nuts to back him up. They are armed with pikes, a lot of them. I think they follow him because they don't stand much chance of good work on their own. They can get much better pay with him than they could ever get on their own merit, most of them would struggle to find a place without him. They're not the brightest of beings.'

'Do you know what the meeting's about?' Bry asked.

'No, but I can guess,' Brindle replied, 'he'll be wanting to organise everyone into agreeing to only accept work when he has negotiated the rates.

It was agreed that the two men would go to this meeting to find out what was being said while Shendaar and Madge would stay to look after the children. As the men prepared to leave, Bry went and got his bow from Rufran's saddle and armed himself with a few arrows. In answer to Bindle's raised eyebrows Bry told him that he didn't want to cause trouble, just be ready if it arose.

'I take it that you're proficient with that toy?' Brindle questioned him.

'Oh yes,' Bry replied, 'and while it is only used as a toy in competitions it can be a useful weapon. I've been hunting wild stags for their skins these past two batherns. I'll try and keep it concealed but I'll feel much better if I have it to hand should things turn nasty. I don't like the sound of men ganging together to cause trouble.'

On the village green there was quite a lot of people all milling around. The back drop to the green was marked by a couple of wagons piled high with straw bales which, with another two empty wagons pulled up in front of them formed a framed stage. Bry's first worried thoughts were that there would be another re-enactment of the fallacious story of how he was made the villain of the piece in Neldon Swenland's attempts to cheat and win the last Challenge. But then sanity won through over Bry's paranoia and he realised that the wagons had been placed there ready for the hiring fair the next day.

The crowd quickly swelled until Bry guessed that all the men who would attend the fair were standing on the green. There was a slight stir as a group of men, some carrying blazing torches and some armed with pikes marched into the area, forcing a way through the crowd. They processed round until they came to the wagons where a few mounted the stage. In the centre was a dark-haired man dressed in dark coloured tunic and matching britches. He wore a bright red neckerchief that made a sharp contrast with his dark beard and white shirt that he wore but the most striking thing about the man was his bright shining, night black eyes.

'That's Natheal Lather, 'Brindle told Bry although he had already guessed. He was an imposing sort of man, an impression that was only accentuated by the entourage of big burly men he had around him and the flickering light from the torches some held aloft.

'He knows how to get attention, that's for sure!' Bry admitted in some awe at the theatrical scene as it unfolded. Just then there was another stir as another man took the stage and called out in a clear sure voice.

'Natheal Lather,' The man called.

'That's Rennald Brackenstedd,' Brindle told Bry, 'he runs High Tor Farm now that Uster Oostedd is away in Norland with the new Lord Norland.'

'What do you want Brackenstedd?' Natheal asked, 'you can't stop us having a quiet friendly meeting.'

'I know that Natheal,' the farmer replied, 'I'm not here to stop your meeting, I'll be interested to hear what you have to say. It's just that I want to make sure that this meeting is peaceful. I don't want you or your bully boys throwing your weight around and threatening these good people who, as we all know, have turned up here to get work.'

'Well it's to help them get work that I'm here too,' Natheal said with a sneer threading its way through his voice.

'Good, I'm glad to hear it,' Rennald replied, obviously totally unmoved by the others supercilious attitude, 'just make sure that this meeting stays peaceful and while you are at it, make sure your men with the torches don't set the bales behind you alight.'

Natheal then said something to those within ear shot which brought a round of laughter and guffaws. Later they found out that under his breath and so only those next to him could hear Natheal had said, 'we'll burn them quick enough if we don't get what want!'

Rennald Brackenstedd had then left them to their own devices and Natheal had taken the centre stage and addressed the crowd. He thanked them for coming and attending his little informal gathering.

'You mean we had a choice?' a man standing close to Bry and Brindle called out.

'Friends,' Natheal replied in an oily voice, 'no one has made anyone do anything they didn't want to.'

'Tell that to your thugs who threatened to smash the bones in my hands with their clubs if I didn't come.' The same man replied but quickly ducked down out of sight. There were general murmurings of agreement from all over the green.

'My friends,' Natheal called out, determined to get the attention back to him, 'I'm sorry if the intentions of my comrades have been misconstrued. Let me assure you they were simply trying to impress on you all how important it is that we all gang together, to unite, in our common aims of getting the best terms we can for our labour. Working together we can make the farmers pay us the proper rate for the job instead of the pittance they usually try and get us to accept.'

There were murmurings among the crowd at this and Bry realised that, for all the apparent viciousness of Lather and his team, there were genuine grievances that rang a chord with the crowd. Natheal then went on to explain how, in the morning, when the farmers were shouting the rates they would pay, no one was to take up the offer by stepping up and taking the ribbons that the farmer offered unless he or his 'team' as he called them, had agreed that the rates were fair.

'That's what he did at Vale Farm last turn.' Brindle told Bry, 'made the workers wait until the farmer had doubled his opening offer.'

'Why did the farmer offer more than he could afford?' Bry asked not really understanding how these things worked.'

'Because at that time he had crops that were dying in the fields and if he couldn't get the reapers in there within a day or two the whole harvest would have been lost.' Brindle replied.

Just then there was a disturbance as a man in the front of the crowd leapt up on the stage and ran towards Natheal and threw a punch which nearly found its mark. It missed as Natheal leapt backwards and the punch thrower, now off balance went crashing into the bale wall at the back of the stage. Two of Natheal's henchmen then grabbed his would-be assailant and held him, pinning his arms at his sides.

'Don't listen to him,' the man called out, 'he'll destroy your way of making a living. I should know, I've lost mine because of him. Some of you know me; I was charge hand at Vale Farm till last harvest bathern. I worked for Jedraah Balental, and a good boss he was too, till this scoundrel came with his thugs and ruined the poor man.

Any further words that the former charge hand might have said were cut off as Natheal punched him hard in the stomach. The man would have collapsed into a writhing heap on the stage if Natheal's thugs had not held him up. The poor man struggled to stand up and brace himself, he knew what was coming.

Natheal was winding himself up to throw another punch at his captive victim when an arrow thumped into the bale wall and quivered there, the feathered flights waving just before his face.

'If you hit him again,' a voice from the back of the crowd called out, 'the next one will take your eye out!'

Chapter 21

Brindle realised, with some surprise and a little shock that it was Bry who had fired the arrow and who had called out and now stood with another notched on his bowstring.

Natheal recovered his shock and motioned to his henchmen to go and find the man who had fired the arrow. In the confusion that followed several things happened at once; the former charge hand was released and slumped to the floor and as everyone turned to see who had fired the arrow Brindle grabbed the bow from Bry's hand and quickly disappeared into the growing dusk at the side of the green away from the stage. Another man grabbed the other arrows that Bry had secreted in his jerkin and he too disappeared into the dusk. As Natheal's thugs arrived at where they thought the Archer must have been they were met with a chorus of denials as to where he was. They searched high and low and frisked a few people; Bry included, but could not find any evidence as to the Archer or his whereabouts.

Having met with no success Natheal's acolytes made their reluctant way back towards the stage area. In the confusion and the brief respite it provided, the charge hand had slipped from the stage and was now safely hidden in some bushes off to one side where he was being violently sick. Natheal then tried to regain some form of control over the crowd but the moment was lost, and the people began to leave the area. There were lots of mutterings about what had happened, and opinions were evenly split between those who thought Natheal was a man worth listening to and following and those who saw him simply as a violent thug determined to force his will on others.

Bry made his way back to the married quarters' marquee and wended his way around to the back to his allocated space. Madge was sitting there, obviously in some state of distress and anxiety as was Shendaar. Madge was holding the little girl while her brother was kneeling on the bed with his arms around his mother's neck, trying to comfort her.

'Bry! What happened?' Madge asked as he entered the from the rear entrance.

'There was some bother on the green and I couldn't stand by and let Natheal and his thugs beat up an innocent man.

'Brindle explained what had happened when he came back with your bow,' Madge told him, 'do you think that will be the end of it?' she asked.

'I very much doubt it,' Bry replied as he came and sat down beside her on the bed and accepted a mug of kandrel that Shendaar handed him, 'what happened to my bow?' he asked, looking around the bedroom area.

'It's safely hidden in Rufran and Tilda's stall along with mine and the rest of the arrows. We put it there under their straw when Brindle came back with it and told us what had happened. That was a bit rash, wasn't it?' Madge asked, 'making yourself conspicuous like that, I mean?'

'I suppose it was,' Bry admitted but I'd had the feeling there was going to be trouble and couldn't help getting an arrow notched on my bowstring, just in case. Well when Natheal hit the poor defenceless man I didn't really think about anything else and fired to make him stop.'

'Could you really have hit him in the eye as you threatened to do with your next shot?' Brindle asked as he came and joined them.

'Oh, he could,' Madge told him, 'he's an expert with the bow, and he's quite famous up in Under Childe.'

'Will other people know you; will they be able to point you out if Natheal and his men start asking questions?' Brindle asked, thinking through what might happen next.

'I doubt it, Bry replied, 'I don't look anything like the man people saw win the last competition there.

This raised the married couple's eyebrows and Madge felt obliged to explain that they had both changed their appearance before making this trip. She offered no explanation as to why or how they had done this and, led by Shendaar both she and Brindle were good enough not to press the matter.

'You may have changed your appearance,' Brindle said, 'but you can't change the fact that you are lame. I hope you don't mind me mentioning it. I wouldn't normally.'

'I don't mind at all,' Bry assured him, 'it's not something I can hide away and pretend doesn't exist. I wish more people would accept it as something that is there and might as well be acknowledged rather than pointedly ignored. But you are right, someone will have noticed and if Natheal comes looking for the mysterious Archer, he might have been told about me and know to look for someone with a gammy leg.'

'Well there's no need for you to show yourself any more than is necessary,' Brindle replied, 'you wait here with the girls and I'll go and see what's happening on the village green.

'Do you have to go?' Shendaar asked, 'Natheal's sister was here and making herself very unpleasant,' she told her husband.

'What happened?' Bry and Brindle asked in unison.

'Well soon after you left, Pardrea arrived and called all the women into the centre of the marquee and started holding forth how we had all better make our husbands do as her brother told them or she would come and punish us. She threatened the children' Shendaar said and collapsed back on the bed in a quivering heap.

'Yes, she even came and grabbed this little one's hand and dragged her into the centre of the area,' Madge told them, indicating the tearful toddler in her arms.

'What happened then?' Brindle asked, bristling at the thought of his child being threatened.

'Well, Madge was wonderful,' Shendaar said, 'Pardrea was yelling that if we didn't do as she told us everyone would suffer, and she held little Twillen up in the air by her arm to make her point. The poor child was crying and then Madge marched straight up to Pardrea and slapped her hard across the face and caught Twillen as the evil woman dropped her. Madge then calmly turned and carried Twillen back to me. You should have seen her Brindle, it was amazing!'

'What did Pardrea do then?' Bry asked.

'Well, Madge had hit her so hard she fell back on her backside and sprawled on the floor. I bet she'll have a right royal bruise on that cheek. Then some of her acolytes came to help her up and some started to come after Madge, but a couple of the other women stood up and barred their way so then they all left. There were a whole lot of rude comments shouted after them as they left the tent. It was wonderful; I never thought anyone would stand up to Pardrea let alone all the women turning against her and her gang.'

'Are you alright?' Bry asked turning to Madge.

'Actually, I'm a lot better than I was,' Madge replied, this coming as a surprise to her as well as to Bry, 'I owed that woman something and I think she got it. She was the one who dumped me in the gutter in Under Childe the night we.' and she stopped abruptly, realising she was about to say, 'the night we met.'

'You know her?' Shendaar asked in surprise.

'Well, let's just say we have met in the past and neither of us like the other very much,' Madge replied.

'Well you've done nothing to further your friendship with her,' Bry commented with a wry grin, 'at least I remained hidden when I fired that arrow. We will have to be careful; she may come looking for you tomorrow.'

'Let her!' Madge retorted, much to everyone's surprise, 'I grew up wrestling with my brother and he's bigger than she is. I could take her!'

'You sound like a boasting barroom brawler!' Bry said with a chuckle as he came and gave her a cuddle which of course involved also embracing Twillen who Madge was still holding. The toddler was delighted at this extra attention and turned her head, so she could give Bry a kiss on the cheek. This produced a fit of giggles as she got tickled by his beard.

'Well it sounds as if the wee one hasn't suffered too badly,' a large woman said as she came and stood in the makeshift doorway.

They all looked at her and Madge realised that it was Joyanne, the woman who had befriended her on the road from Launceston. She was a little concerned that the large woman would recognise her and reveal that they had met when Madge was travelling alone. However, it was Shendaar who recognised Joyanne as one of the women who had blocked Pardrea's path when the slapped woman had made to pursue Madge.

'Ah, I think we owe you our thanks,' Shendaar said as she rose to welcome the new comer, 'do please do come in.'

'May we both come and join you?' Joyanne asked as she took a step into the foursome's area.

'Yes, please do,' Shendaar replied as she stood up, 'can I offer you a mug of kandrel?'

Joyanne accepted the invitation by crossing over to the bed where Shendaar had just risen and sat down. She was followed in to the area by a slightly smaller woman who Madge immediately recognised as Janteal who jostled her large friend up the bed to give herself somewhere to sit. Madge was momentarily alarmed that she would be unmasked but neither of the newcomers seemed to have recognised her.

'We just came to tell you that the rest of the women have agreed that we'll keep an eye out for Pardrea and her gang in case they decided to come back to continue where they left off,' Joyanne told

Madge. 'That was a very brave thing you did, by the way, there's a lot of women who were delighted to see that evil woman get what she deserved. The only worry is that Pardrea is not the sort to let you get away with pulling that trick.'

'What do you think she'll do?' Bry asked; suddenly concerned for the woman he loved.

'There's no telling,' Joyanne replied, 'but you'd better believe that she, or her brother, will do something. Don't worry about tonight, I've arranged for a rota of women to keep an eye on you and the children.

The conversation then moved onto other things and, as ever, the children were the centre of attention. Shendaar then decided that it was the children's bed time at which Jallden complained that being the eldest he should go to bed after his younger sister. Bry solved that problem by asking Jallden if he would help him bed the animals down for the night, to which the young lad readily agreed.

Bry went and attended to the kertles, giving each a full grooming and oiling. He gave a running commentary of what he was doing and why he was doing it to the lad who stood nervously in the doorway.

'Don't be shy lad,' Bry called, 'come and say hello to our kertles; they'd like a bit of company.' The boy slowly crept into the stall area and tentatively made his way to where Bry was oiling Tilda's head.

Rufran became aware that they had company and put his head down to sniff the newcomer, which caused the boy some concern and he backed away from the inquiring nose.

'Oh, don't be scared of Rufran,' Bry told him, 'he won't hurt you, he's just saying hello. Look, you see that bag hanging up there, reach in and get a couple of the small biscuits in there and give him one. He'll like that.'

The boy did as he was told and took great delight in having his hand licked by the enormous kertle. He then had to get another biscuit and give Tilda a treat as well. With the ice broken, the lad became much more relaxed and asked if he could help and Bry was only too pleased to show the boy how to clean and oil the kertles' claw sets. As they worked, Bry explained everything about how the kertle's claw sets worked to give the drays a good grip on the ground when they were pulling heavy loads. He went on to explain how racing kertles were bred so that their claw sets were slightly longer giving them more speed when running flat out. Bry wasn't sure how much the boy was taking in or understanding but the lad had a sure touch with the kertles which he had noticed before in the young stable lads who were destined to become good kertle handlers.

'Thank you for not talking down to him,' Brindle said as he entered the temporary stall, 'so many people only use baby talk with him and he's an intelligent little boy who understands a lot more of what's going on around him than people give him credit for.'

'He's a good lad, is Jallden' Bry agreed, 'I don't know if he has done this before, but he's picked up the technique straight away.'

'He may be good with kertles, but his mother wants him to get washed and ready for bed.' Brindle said as he picked up the young lad.

'How old are you, Jallden?' Bry asked as his father swung the boy on his back.

'I'll be four turns old at the end of the next bathern, 'Jallden replied as he waved farewell to Bry and both kertles.

Bry carried on and was finishing the kertle's grooming when Brindle returned.

'This is some nasty business going on with this Natheal Lather and his sister.' He said as he came and sat on a bale of straw to watch as Bry put away all his gear.

'You're a skilled kertle manager,' Brindle said as matter of fact rather than a question.

'Yes, I know my way around a kertle and a stable,' Bry admitted, hoping the conversation would not go much further in that direction.

'Are you looking for work in that line?' Brindle asked.

'I suppose so,' Bry replied although he hadn't really given the matter much serious thought; he would take any work he could get. A lot depended on what Madge could get. He told Brindle this, hoping he wasn't giving away too much of the tenuous links that bound him and Madge.

'Well if you want work as a kertle handler,' Brindle told him, 'you should carry a bridle over your shoulder when you line up at the fair and if you and Madge want work at the same farm you should stand together and hold hands. That's the accepted way to indicate that you are married and wish to be hired by the same farmer. That may not happen, of course,' Brindle told him; he was feeling his way in this conversation but his suspicions that Bry was new to hiring fairs was being confirmed by every question and reply that the swarthy man gave.

Bry thanked him for these insights and they talked on. Both sincerely wished that all four of them would find work together; friendships such as they had quickly forged were few and far between on in the world of the itinerant worker.

Back in the main marquee Shendaar was dealing with her son's washing and getting him to bed which gave Joyanne a chance to have a very quiet chat with Madge.

'I see you managed to make a more permanent change to your skin colour than the soot and ash we used on the road from Launceston,' Joyanne said with a knowing look.

'You. You recognise me?' Madge whispered, shocked that her disguise had been seen through so easily.

'Oh, don't fret yourself, your secret's safe with me and Janteal,' Joyanne assured her with a friendly hand on Madge's shoulder, 'remember, I got a good look at you when we were daubing you all over with that gunk Janteal managed to concoct in the bunkhouse. You've done a good job and I wouldn't have recognised you but for the way you stood-up to Pardrea made me think of a young lady I met a few velds ago. That and the fact that your hair is starting to grow out, your roots are beginning to come through light blond again.'

Madge put her hand up to her head instinctively and shot a worried glance around the room but Shendaar was dealing with her offspring and paid no attention.

'Now, now, there's no need to worry,' Joyanne assured her again, 'your secret is safe with us and if you want to continue staying in hiding that's up to you, milady.'

'You know who I really am?' Madge asked in fright.

'I worked that out when the Guardians arrived that night at the Inn on the road from Launceston,' Joyanne confided, 'I see you have picked up a travelling companion since we last met.'

'Yes, I have, but he doesn't know who I really am, please don't tell him!' Madge pleaded.

'Like I said,' Joyanne assured her yet again, 'you secret is safe with us. I wish you well. How are you finding life on the road?'

'Very hard,' Madge admitted, 'although we've only just started looking for work.'

Chapter 22

News of the meeting at High Tor Farm hiring fair was sent by signal messages the next morning by undercover guardians who had been in the crowd, posing as migrant workers. The messages, flashed from reflecting mirrors from hilltop to hilltop, were received by the senior officers away in Medland with some consternation. The news then quickly found its way to the five lords who had reconvened to discuss the possible threats that might be appearing.

'I'm tempted to let things ride for the moment,' Lord Launceston told his fellow lords, 'we shouldn't be seen to be enforcing our will by arresting this Natheal Lather. That would only cause more unrest and give these discontents some martyr's banner to follow behind.'

'It's easy for you to say, 'do nothing,' Lord Dresham replied, but it's mine and the Swenland farms that are being threatened, and, may I remind your lordships, if we southern families have a bad harvest the whole of Femeral will suffer.'

'Quite so,' Jaxaal affirmed, 'we are all endangered by this and we must all react together to deal with the threat. I don't like the idea of meeting force with force, but it is an option we should not deny ourselves. As it happens as soon as I was installed as Lord Norland some former retainers came and asked if they could have their previous jobs back as house guards.'

'You mean you have your own army!' Lord Dresham exclaimed in some alarm.

'Hardly,' Jaxaal reassured him, 'it's only about twenty or so pike-men who like to march up and down the castle battlements with their pikes and shields, pretending they are defending us against some imaginary foe. There's no way you could call them an army although they might have a role to play if the reports we've received are accurate.'

Lord Ellward then admitted that he too, had a small detachment of men who carried out similar duties at Ellward Abbey. Lord Dresham then, after some consideration, revealed that he too had a few men who trained with pikes, shields and staffs, 'it would not hurt to have them ready to help if the need arises,' he agreed.

It was then agreed that messages would be sent, and these small armed contingents would make all haste to attend their lordships in Medland prior to being sent south of the Childe Mountains.

As the meeting disintegrated into smaller discussions to sort out the practicalities, Lord Launceston came across to speak to Lord Dresham.

'I suppose I have some young men who train every veld to keep fit, or so they say. I actually think it is more to impress the young woman than for their health,' Lord Launceston confided with a knowing grin.

'So, you have troops as well,' Lord Dresham replied with a wry smile, 'I only have a few trained men but I'm sure there are more who would leap at the chance to get out of working in the fields for a veld or two. I think I'll send word to Sorjohn to collect as many as can sensibly be spared.'

These extra men would be sent direct to High Tor Village. Before the meeting broke up the discussion got around to the knotty problem of who should be in overall command of the Fameral Army as they had started to call it. Lord Launceston suggested that the rather ancient guardian Commodore Mustoove might be the best person but Lord Dresham pointed out that he really was too old and too set in his ways to take on the task. Jaxaal was all for giving the job to Commander Northwood but before he could press that point of view, at Darval's suggestion that Jaxaal himself should be appointed as Supreme Commander was agreed upon. Jaxaal himself was not sure if he really was the right person but the confidence the other nobles placed in him convinced him to accept the position.

At that moment down at High Tor Farm the next hiring fair was beginning. The normal process where farmers would walk around, listening to the workers who stood in rows around the village green calling out their skills before making offers of work had begun but had been quickly stopped. The farmers were quickly surrounded by Lather's armed henchmen and made to stand on the stage that had been set up and instead call out the rates of pay that they were offering. This was a total change to the way most fairs were conducted and caused a lot of confusion.

When the farmers and workers understood what the pike-men wanted the 'fair' began and several farmers mounted the stage and tried to get the numbers of men they required but were largely unsuccessful in getting men to take their ribbons.

'If you take a farmer's ribbon,' Brindle told Bry and Madge as they stood right at the back of the crowd, 'it means you have accepted the terms he has offered for the period he has offered. It is a sign that you have got work; it's called being ribboned. Once you've taken a ribbon that signifies a binding contract between you both, but be careful, some farmers will offer you good food and good pay and promise that they will never make you work before sunrise or after sunset. Then when you get to the farm you'll find that means that you must start at sunrise and can't finish until sunset, which isn't what the farmer implied. If you argue the point they'll remind you of their exact words and you can't deny that they offered you anything else. It's that sort of sharp practice that gives men like Lather a lot of support.'

'Sounds like there's a lot of good and bad on both sides,' Bry replied.

The 'fair' continued but it was quickly obvious that Lather and his men were not going to allow anyone to be ribboned unless they, the 'union,' had agreed the rates. Confusion abounded, and several workers walked away from the village square muttering that they would try elsewhere or return when things had changed or 'got back to normal.' Natheal Lather quickly realised that he was losing control of the situation and started to force the ribboning of workers to the few farmers who were deemed to have increased their rates to an acceptable level. This was a slow process and the confusion was made worse as the workers milled around trying to get close enough to farmers to hear what they were offering. Madge and Bry tried to stand in line with the centre of the square so that they could keep an eye on what was going on all around them. As they were jostled by other workers who were following the loudest shouts of rates and conditions Brindle suggested they move their position, he told the dusky pair, 'I saw Rennald Brackenstedd, the High Tor Farmer talking to some workers earlier. I think he is attempting to get workers in the normal way. He's a good master, probably the best. Why don't you two come with us?' he asked.

Bry and Madge looked at each other and it was obvious that they both wished the same thing, so they immediately followed on after their new friends. The four of them reached the far side of the square where the road up to High Tor Farm began and found that hidden behind the wall there was a small gathering of people talking with Rennald Brackenstedd.

'Leave this to me,' Brindle said as he went up to the farmer and introduced himself. He was obviously recognised as Rennald Brackenstedd greeted him warmly. The two men spent a few moments in discussion and it was clear that Brindle was negotiating not only for himself and Shendaar but Bry and Madge as well. Both men looked over to where Bry and Madge stood and beckoned them over to join in the discussion.

'I gather that you are a kertle master,' Rennald said, looking directly at Bry, 'what experience have you had. Bry gave a brief synopsis of his experience and qualifications, including the selective breeding of kertles without actually saying where he had gained that it or that his main expertise lay with racers.

'Well we have need of experience in our stables now that Uster Oostedd has moved with the new Lord Norland up to Norland Castle,' Rennald told him. 'You won't be in charge of course but I'm sure we have need of your skills,' and he handed Bry a ribbon in the green and blue colours of High Tor Farm which signified that it was a Norland House Fifth and that Bry was now a temporary employee of the fifth.

Bry was thrilled to be given this job; Uster Oostedd was legendry among kertle breeders throughout Fameral and it would be an honour to work in the stables he had created. But Bry's pleasure was tempered by the fact that nothing had been said about Madge. He held up his hand which still clasped hers in his, the signal that they were a couple and asked, 'do you have a ribboned place for my wife?'

'Ah yes,' Rennald replied and a frown crossed his brow, 'you have clearly indicated that you are a couple and I suppose I must offer work to you both,' and he turned to Madge who he scrutinised carefully.

'What skills do you have, my dear/' he asked.

'I can turn my hand to anything,' Madge replied, she had been thinking through what she would say when asked. 'I can work in the kitchen or wait in the house and even turn my hand to needlework, if that is required. I can work in the fields and of course I am experienced in helping my husband with his duties with the kertles. I can also do a little book-keeping if required.'

'Book-keeping eh? Well I'm sure that we will have need of your services,' Rennald replied, 'Brindle here has made it clear that he and his wife would prefer to be employed where you two have been placed.' He handed Madge a ribbon as well and then turned looking for someone.

'Welcome to High Tor Farm. Now if I can get my son's eye, he can show you where to take your things.'

At this point a well set young man came over and was introduced as Rydall Brackenstedd, the farmer's son.

'Since there are the four of them,' Rennald told him, 'they can share part of Parlip Cottage.'

'Parlip Cottage?' Brindle asked, 'that sounds very grand, if a bit rustic.'

'Oh, don't be fooled by the agricultural sounding name,' Rydall said with a grin, 'it's actually the best house on the farm, apart from High Tor itself. It was my parent's house until Uster and Lady Arianne moved away with Jaxaal when he became Lord Norland.'

'Do you have things you want to bring with you?' Rydall asked as he started leading the four up the lane away from the village centre where the fair was still in full swing.

'Yes, our children are with the child minder back in the marquee,' Brindle told him, 'and our friends here have two kertles stabled there as well.'

'Right we'll go there and collect them first,' Rydall replied, and he led the way up a side lane and around the outskirts of the village to the field where the marquee had been erected.

'I think this is the best way to go,' he explained, 'it avoids the village centre.'

'You obviously know every nook and cranny of this place,' Brindle commented as Rydall led the way through a gap in a hedge and along a wall where there was a path well hidden from view by some heavy vegetation.

'Oh yes,' Rydall grinned, 'Jaxaal and I used to use this route when we were sneaking into the village to go to the back of the inn.

They reached the field where the marquee stood and quickly collected all their belongings which they loaded onto Rufran and Tilda. Jallden was upset that he wasn't allowed to ride on Rufran's back but Bry explained that he was already a carrying a heavy load; Bry's pack and half his parents' paraphernalia. Both Madge and Bry noticed that he accepted this with a good grace and didn't throw a tantrum. As a reward Bry hoisted the young lad up onto his shoulders where he rode in some pride.

'I can see that the four of you are good friends, it will be good to have Parlip Cottage occupied again,' Rydall said as they made their way up to High Tor Farm itself.

'So, you knew Lord Norland when he was just Jaxaal Oostedd?' Shendaar asked, 'is he as handsome as they say he is?'

'Well I'm no judge, of course,' Rydall replied, 'but I would say he is a very fine-looking man. I've known him all my life, we grew up together here on the farm and I was his best man, his groom attendant, when he and Janilla got married.'

'Oh, it's so romantic,' Shendaar said with a sigh, 'to win the Challenge and then ask for the hand of the girl you love.'

Madge was very quiet for a moment, "I remember Rydall from the weddings,' she thought, 'he doesn't recognise me, or he hasn't let on, if he does. I'll just have to play it by ear, but I think my secret identity is safe.'

'Yes, I suppose it is,' Rydal told Shendaar although that only happened after he had got the House of Norland reinstated.'

'Did you have no idea that he was the late Lord Norland's son?' Madge asked.

'No, none at all,' Rydall replied, 'we knew that Lady Arianne was the sister of the late Lady Norland although that connection was played down and never mentioned, but it never dawned on any of us just who Jaxaal's parents were. Even he didn't know, he grew up thinking he was Uster's blood nephew, not Lady Arianne's. I knew, although it was supposed to be a secret, that Jaxaal had been taught the high language; he would swear at me at times using it when no one else was around.'

'You really knew him well then,' Brindle commented.

'Yes, I suppose I knew him better than anyone outside his family; we used to practise sword fighting together.' Rydall replied, 'I made both the swords that we used when Uster was training him.'

'So, you're a smith?' Bry queried.

'No not yet, although I've been training here under old Jassoon for the past three turns. I'm going off to Cordale Complex to train as a smith under the masters there in a velds time, or at least I'm hoping to be accepted as an apprentice.'

As Rydall was explaining his future plans the party arrived at High Tor Farm itself and he led the way through the well kempt farm yard to the cottages that surrounded the north and eastern sides of the inner farm complex.

'That's the smith's house where old Jassoon lives,' Rydall said as he pointed out one of the cottages, 'if I can be accredited as a smith and earn my belt, I'm hoping that I will live there when old Jassoon retires. And this is Parlip Cottage where I used to live, before father's promotion to Quintrall when we moved into High Tor House itself.'

He led the way into the cottage through the well cared for front garden and into the building. The first sensation the newcomers encountered was the smell of new paint work.

'Yes, I'm sorry about the smell,' Rydall apologised, 'we thought the old place needed freshening up a bit and it has been completely refurbished. My mother has enjoyed herself choosing knew curtains and carpets. The whole party then also had great fun exploring the house. Finally, Rydall left them to settle in and suggested they might like to visit the High Tor kitchen to make the catering arrangements.

All six of the new occupants had fun exploring their new, if temporary, home. Shendaar and Madge quickly assessed the layout of the upstairs rooms and made decisions as to who would sleep in which room. Jallden was a little disappointed that he would not have a room to himself but would still share with his sister even though there were rooms to spare.

'I don't want him getting used to things he may not have in the future,' Shendaar explained to Madge when she questioned Shendaar's reasoning. 'We may not be here all that long, although this is a wonderful house.'

'It is,' Madge agreed, 'I think Bry and I could be very happy in a house like this,' and to her own surprise she really meant it. She had grown up in one of the largest houses in the land with all the benefits that wealth provided. This might have made the accommodation that Parlip Cottage provided seem very limited but her recent history made her appreciate the space it offered as absolute luxury. They eventually found the men who were exploring the out buildings where they had bedded Rufran and Tilda down in a dry and draught proof stable and were checking through the barns and store rooms at the rear of the cottage.

'I think that Parlip Cottage is bigger than some Fifth Masters houses elsewhere,' Brindle commented when the women finally found them, 'I think we've fallen on our feet here alright.'

'That's all down to the fact that the farmer remembers you and your skills,' Bry told him.

'That, and the way you two impressed him, that was a large part of it,' Brindle countered, 'I agree with Madge, Shendaar and I would be very happy if this were our permanent home.'

The two women then made a visit to the kitchens in High Tor House and came away with sufficient basic supplies to start off their larder and the makings of a few main meals and breakfasts.

Chapter 23

The lightened mood among the new occupants of Parlip Cottage were echoed in two of the noble houses at opposite ends of the continent; messages had arrived at both Dresham and Launceston and the eldest sons of both houses were coming to terms with the instructions their fathers had sent from Medland.

Crelin Launceston was ecstatic at the chance of doing a real job and had called his squires together to give them instructions to go and get all the men who trained in the square to report to the Hall. His changed mood sent a powerful message to his twin and Madge was immediately aware of the difference in her brother's frame of mind. She had no idea of the cause only that he was pleased and had a sense of purpose; she didn't know why but instinctively felt that he would be coming closer to where she was and that thought thrilled her.

Sorjohn Dresham was similarly enthused by the instructions he had received from his father to collect all the available able-bodied men and to march them north-west, all the way up to High Tor Farm

Meanwhile, back at High Tor farm, as the new occupants were being installed into Parlip Cottage, down in the village things were going from bad to worse for the Lather twins. The story of how each had been faced down by the mysterious Archer and the dark-skinned woman had become common knowledge. The mystique and aura that they had previously enjoyed were destroyed and that meant that they were being looked upon by many with some ridicule. The visiting farmers who had come to High Tor to hire workers suddenly found that they could return to the normal hiring process without Natheal Lather wading in and disrupting things until he got his way.

This was a new experience for the firebrand and one he did not enjoy. As he stood talking with some of his henchmen and his sister, he decided that they could make no further progress here but would move on to the next fair. He assembled his men and made them line up, the pike-men in the lead and the others in three ranks behind them. He then gave them the order and the party moved off. Pardrea had organised the women who were attached to the men in the group into three ranks as well and they followed on. To all intents and purposes anyone who saw them go felt they were watching a small army and their camp followers beginning a campaign march.

Pardrea had acquired a kertle to ride and having got the women into order, she rode ahead to catch up with her brother. Both were in a foul mood and tried to blame the other for the debacle the High Tor Fair had become.

'You shouldn't have been put off by someone firing an arrow into bales behind you!' Pardrea fumed, 'they're only toys after all.'

'You weren't there so you don't know.' Natheal retorted, 'that arrow hit that bale with quite a force and whoever fired it threatened to take my eye out with his next shot.'

'But the arrows aren't pointed; they're rounded to make a mark on the targets in the Archery Competitions.' Pardrea snapped back, 'unless it actually hit your eye all it would do is leave a bruise.'

'What, like the one on your face, sister dear?' Natheal asked with a sneer, 'I hear that that small dark woman stopped you in your tracks and you did nothing to retaliate.'

'That's only because she had some friends who stopped me getting to her. I went back there this morning, but she was nowhere to be found.'

As the party in Parlip Cottage were finishing a late midday meal, Rennald Brackenstedd came to finalise the basis of their various jobs. Brindle and the two women were told to report to the farmyard early the next morning where they would be assessed and have work assigned to them. He then had a long discussion with Bry about his previous experience. Bry again explained that he was a kertle handler, had controlled the breeding programme at a large estate, without mentioning which one, and had trained as an animal healer so that he could treat any sick or injured kertle in his care.

To Bry's joy he was then allocated to work in the stables with a special responsibility for the kertle breeding facility. Rennald made no secret that he was eventually looking for someone to become the charge-hand to oversee the whole kertle operation.

'We have a full breeding programme under way and with Uster Oostedd's transferring up to Castle Norland I need someone to take charge so that everything continues as it should.' Rennald told Bry. 'If you make a success and show some aptitude, I may well I may invite you to apply for the position full time. That would mean that you could be assumed to the High Tor Fifth of the House of Norland if you so wish.'

Bry was very grateful for the opportunity. Since that was the position he had held at the House of Swenland he was well aware of the chance he was being offered. He couldn't help the wry smile that came unbidden at the irony of the situation; all his working life he had been in awe of the reputation of Uster Oostedd and now here he was, about to take over the great man's stables and stud.

'Is it normal for itinerant workers to be housed in accommodation like this?' Bry asked Brindle when he had a moment alone with him.

'Well it's not unheard of but it is very unusual,' Brindle conceded, 'Workers are usually housed in large bunk houses, sometimes they are no more than converted barns, waiting for the next harvest to be brought in. The field workers sometimes find themselves reaping a harvest and then having to give up their sleeping quarters to store it.'

'So, we're really lucky to have this house,' Bry decided.

'We are indeed, but I expect that we'll be sharing it with quite a few others before long.' Brindle told him.

The household did expand during the late afternoon when several other ribboned workers, including Joyanne and Janteal, were billeted to the cottage. There's a rumpus going on at the hiring down in the village,' Joyanne told the assembled workers as they crowded into the kitchen and shared a few jugs of kandrel.

'Those Lather twins were in a right strop and started holding workers hostage demanding that the mystery Archer who fired at Natheal last night and you missy,' she said looking at Madge, 'were brought before them to answer for your so-called crimes.'

'What happened?' Bry asked, full of concern for the people put in danger.

'Well they threatened a lot and did a lot of shouting, but we told them that the people they wanted had fled in the night and that seemed to pacify them. They then tried to take control of the hiring but by then the crowd weren't having any more of their nonsense. I think the way you put Pardrea in her place last night,' She said turning back to Madge, 'had a deep effect on everyone. Suddenly the Lathers didn't seem so formidable. In the end they let their hostages go and they and their men have left to go south.'

'That's when a proper hiring fair took place and we were ribboned to work here at High Tor Farm,' Janteal said, joining in the conversation.

'Be warned young missy,' Joyanne said to Madge, 'Pardrea was in vile mood this morning; she had a dark, blue bruise on her face when she appeared, trying to find you. She came with a couple of those pike-men right into the married quarters and demanded that you were handed over to them.'

'What happened then?' Madge asked concerned that her actions had caused someone else to get hurt.

'Well she hunted through the whole tent and even went through the stabling area at the back. She was cursing and swearing but finally accepted that you weren't there and stormed off in a huff.'

'That Natheal then made a speech in the main village square,' Janteal said, taking up the story, 'his men made everyone go and listen. He's got some weird ideas about overthrowing the ruling houses so that everyone gets a 'fair deal' as he puts it. He then made everyone chant, 'Fair Deal,' over and over again. Then he left saying he was going to spread the word down south and we should all remember what he had said and should demand better wages.'

'Do you think you should get better wages?' Bry asked. Janteal seemed a little confused by the question and looked desperately around the room for support.

'Well, we could all do with more money in our purses,' Joyanne said, helping her friend out, 'but when it comes to it, I've clothes to wear, food to eat, somewhere to sleep and enough for a glass of wine occasionally. What more does a woman like me need?' This brought a round of nods and words of agreement from everyone in the room.

Just then Christash Brackenstedd, Rennald's wife arrived with a couple of kitchen maids who were carrying a tray bearing a roast hoglet. This steaming dish was placed in the centre of the table and Christash explained that this was a welcoming gift for the newly ribboned workers.

'You won't get this every day, or even every alphen,' she said with a smile, 'but it was a tradition Lady Arianne introduced and now I am the Quintrell, I intend to carry it on.'

It was in a greatly lightened mood that the company sat down to enjoy the feast that the wild boar represented. The relief that the stress of the past two days was over was palpable and spirits rose, helped with a few bottles of High Tor Fruit Beer.

The next two velds passed in a pleasant camaraderie that the courteous but firm and fair way that Rennald managed his Fifth instilled in all who worked for him. There was a small party held in High Tor House itself to say goodbye to Rydall Brackenstedd who was leaving to go Cordale Complex to begin his training to become a master smith.

Bry was sorry to see the young man go; they had struck up a friendship in the short time they had known each other. Two days after taking up his duties Bry had found a mare that had got a twisted claw set which needed training back into the correct alignment. This required the making of a special metal shoe that would pull the two halves of the claw set straight. He went to see Old Jassoon, the High Tor smith, to see about getting the shoe made but was directed straight to Rydall.

Rydall had quickly assessed the situation and as they discussed the requirements, each young man had got the measure of the other; both liked what they saw. The fact that Bry was also a skilled Archer came out as the two men chatted and Rydall asked for a demonstration. It so happened that this occurred just as most of the workers were taking their mid-morning break and a makeshift target was set up in the farm yard. Both Bry and Madge were asked to show their prowess and Madge ran Bry a close second in their mini competition.

Several others asked to have a try with varying degrees of success and it was quickly realised that both Bry and Madge were very skilled. Rydall asked to look at the arrows and immediately understood the reason for the twist that had been given to the flights. This understanding gave Bry an insight into Rydall's perceptive abilities, so he was delighted when the trainee smith asked if he could try to make some arrow heads.

It was later that same day when Rydall appeared carrying the arrows he had borrowed, each now fitted with a lethal point on the end. Bry tried these arrows out and was delighted at the effect that the heavier weight at the tip had on the arrows accuracy. He was also astonished at the destructive power of the new projectile. The simple wooden target they had set up in the morning was soon reduced to a splintered wreck as both Bry and Madge experimented with the new invention.

Commander Northwood, who had arrived with a contingent of guardians, also asked Rydall and the other smiths if they could modify the metal heads that were fitted to the men's pikes making them sharp at the points and down the edges. This he thought might have lot of benefit if some of his ideas were adopted.

Rydall did leave on his journey to Cordale Complex and that evening Rennald came to talk to Bry and Brindle, Madge and Shendaar as they were sitting sharing the inevitable jug of kandrel.

'My son thinks he has gone to Cordale to be assessed to see if he can become an apprentice,' Rennald explained, 'but in fact, I'm assured by old Jassoon, the smith here who has trained him, that he will be made a smith immediately. He will earn 'his belt' as they call it.'

'Well that's good news,' Bry commented, 'I know he has a lot of skill from the way he made that correction shoe for the mare with the twisted claw set.'

'Well, yes, it is good news,' Rennald agreed, 'but it does raise a slight problem. We, that's Christash, I and Old Jassoon have been invited to go to Cordale to witness his accreditation. We really want to go, we know the boy has worked really hard this past three turns and we would like to be there when he receives his belt.'

'Well what's stopping you?' Bry asked.

'Well it's like this,' Rennald began and then took a deep breath. 'I have a charge-hand foreman, Simtraain, but the dear old fellow has only risen to that position because he has outlived everyone else. He's as much a part of High Tor as the house and buildings themselves. He was a bit miffed when I was appointed Fifth Master ahead of him when Uster moved away so I made him foreman to placate the old boy. But the simple fact is he isn't really capable of looking after the farm while I'm away and it would be cruel to put him in that position.'

The others sat and looked at Rennald in astonishment, the drift of this conversation was obvious and Bry was more than a little concerned at the implications.

'What I am thinking, what I am asking, is would you be prepared to take on the responsibility for the management of High Tor for a brief period Bry, while I and my family, are away? It is especially important just now as we have herd that there are a lot of men being sent here from all over Fameral, I gather that the ruling lords are taking the potential threat posed by the Lather twins very seriously. That's why I need someone with a cool head and experience in charge here at High Tor for the next three or four velds.'

Bry's fear were realised and he desperately searched for a way out. The last thing he needed was to be put in a high visibility position while he was trying to melt away into Femeral society.

'But surely you have other permanent staff, better suited to taking on High Tor?' he asked almost beseechingly.

'Well, yes of course I do have a full complement of staff, but to be honest with Rydall, Christash and myself here all the time there has been no need to train anyone else. You must remember; I've only taken on the Fifthship since Uster Oostedd left what, three batherns ago. I haven't had the need to think about a possible replacement. Look Bry, I'm well aware that you are a very capable young man. You've shown that time and again during the two velds you've been here. Don't think I'm not aware of the subtle but significant changes you've made in the working practices in the stables. I'd let things slip a bit there; it's not my area of expertise but I'm quite sure Uster himself would approve if he came here now and saw what you have achieved in so short a space of time and I am also aware of how competent your wife is, she has already made a difference with the paperwork required to run this place.

'But there's more to managing a Fifth than just good husbandry and book-keeping'!' Bry complained.

'Such as what?' Madge asked. She could see that Bry was desperately trying to avoid having this responsibility placed upon him and she instinctively didn't want him to do that. She was very proud of her partner and was delighted that a capable and successful man like Rennald had seen Bry's qualities so quickly.

'Well, there's all the money and wages to be dealt with, for a start,' Bry countered and then, desperately trying to find justification for his reticence'

'Well I can help with that aspect of it,' Madge replied and everyone in the room sat and stared at her in astonishment. She realised immediately that she had made a mistake and frantically tried to justify her statement. 'Before I met Bry I was lucky enough to receive a good education,' she explained, hoping that would suffice.

'But it involves recording all the workers hours and then working out their wages, and that must be done every veld,' Rennald explained.

'Yes, I know,' Madge replied, bitterly regretting having started this conversation. She knew she should have taken Bry's lead and kept her head down but, having started, she felt she had no option but to give some explanation. 'I was taught basic arithmetic along with my brother,' she said, 'but it comes from a time in my life I want to forget, so please don't ask me about it.' This had the desired effect from Madge's point of view and the others didn't press her for more details. It was agreed that she would spend time in the morning with Rennald to learn what was involved and it was tacitly accepted that would serve as an opportunity to prove she could do what would be required.

Bry then realised that without actually having accepted Rennald's offer he had agreed to become the temporary manager of High Tor Farm. He sat in something of a daze for some time after Rennald had left; while the others chatted on about the way things had turned around in such a short space of time. It had been decided that they would celebrate by demolishing the last of Bry's leather flagons of wine.

The next couple of days passed in a haze of getting to grips with their new responsibilities. Despite their own reservations Rennald seemed to have complete faith in their abilities and didn't hesitate to place his trust in them.

'One thing you need to be aware of is that we usually offer free board and lodgings to any companies of guardians, who pass through, and we now have the added factor of the men who are being sent here,' Rennald told them during a break in one of the training sessions he was giving Bry and Madge. 'The guardians never showed themselves, or rather tried not to, when Jaxaal was living here so as not to draw attention to the place but they kept a close eye on the farm and the surrounding area. Jaxaal didn't know who he was but the authorities did.'

'Doesn't that cost the farm a lot?' Bry asked, 'I mean housing and food for a company of guardians won't come cheaply.'

'Yes, it does cost the farm quite a lot,' Rennald agreed, 'but you must remember that this is now a House of Norland Fifth and as such we have a duty to contribute to the central government. This is just one way we do that.'

It was still with some misgivings the following day that Bry saw the Brackenstedd family party mount their carriage and head away towards the Misle Forest on their way to the Childe Cut but Madge came and took his arm in hers and gave it a squeeze. She understood that he felt very nervous about the responsibility thrust upon him.

Despite his misgivings things worked well for him as the farm workers accepted the new arrangements as if nothing had changed. Brindle proved to be very knowledgeable about the agricultural side of the farming business. They were getting well into the Ripening Bathern which meant a special demand for good husbandry and he was instrumental in getting this aspect sorted out and organised. The only down side of that was the attitude of old Simtraain, the former charge hand. He had accepted Rennald's decision to appoint Bry as temporary manager but, deep down he bitterly objected to being usurped. Thankfully this displayed itself merely as his muttering to himself under his breath. Madge noticed this and made a point of placating the old boy by asking him his advice on a myriad of things. This eased his hurt feelings and the good food that Shendaar insisted that he try every time he came near the kitchen did a lot to bring him around to accepting the new managers of High Tor. The process was completed by Twillen Brinkle, Shendaar's young daughter who was fascinated by the old man's beard and insisted that he pick her up every time he appeared so that she could run her hands through it and pull at the curly growth.

Chapter 24

Away in Medland the Five Lords were completing their deliberations. They had been kept abreast of the developing situation down in High Tor by the reports from under-cover guardians who were mingling with the itinerant workers.

'The situation has reached intolerable proportions!' Jaxaal fumed, 'we cannot allow things to go any further. Armed men rampaging around High Tor Village is not to be allowed to continue.'

'I agree,' Lord Ellward replied on behalf of himself and the three other lords, 'my pike-men militia have arrived from Ellward Abbey and with Lord Norland's men who arrived yesterday, we now have a significant force of trained men at our disposal. I suggest we make full use of them.'

'Yes, we can despatch them straight away down to High Tor,' Jaxaal agreed, 'I have been talking with the Head Guardians and the Medland City Elders and all together we can muster over one hundred armed and trained men if we include the Guardian Militia. I suggest that they are all placed under the command of the Guardians, after all they are the only trained and disciplined force we have.'

This was duly agreed, and orders were drawn up, signed and issued. Later that day amid lots of cheers and shouts of encouragement Fameral's first diminutive army began the march south of the capital. Hardly anyone in the crowds that watched them leave had any idea what it was all about, but many enjoyed the spectacle and the festival spirit the colourful display they provided. The various divisions within the ranks were denoted by the different colours that the men wore: blue and green of Norland, the maroon and blue of Ellward and the orange of the Medland troops. Despite the rainbow of colours that they wore, every man had the same cap badge depicting the five-pointed elongated Femeral star. They made a memorable display as they marched through the streets of Medland out to Dreslah Park and off into the southern part of the country. Slightly less romantic were the disparate collection of wagons that followed on behind them carrying all the food and equipment that the makeshift army needed. Jaxaal was all for going with the troops. 'After all,' as he explained to his peers, 'Until a few batherns ago, High Tor was the only home I knew.'

'But we've just had word that this Natheal Lather and his men have left High Tor and were last seen on the road south west of there, heading for Swenmore Village' Lord Darval Ellward told him, 'that's my territory now that I'm regent of Swenland. I'm heading straight home as fast as I can get there to be with Parina and Joqtal.'

'Yes, I can understand that,' Jaxaal told him, 'how is that nephew of mine doing?'

'Oh, he's dancing Parina, Felda and the nursery staff around like you wouldn't believe,' Darval replied, 'the poor little lad has just started teething, or so I'm told.'

'Well give them all our love,' Jaxaal replied, 'will you have time to visit us at Norland Mansion. I know Janilla and Aunt Arianne would love to see you.'

'I'm not sure,' Darval replied, considering the matter, 'I want to spend some time at the Ellward Mansion with my parents before I head off south again, I don't think my father is very well.'

'You really are amazing, you know Darval,' Jaxaal told him, 'I thought he was looking a bit pale and he seems very tired but how you picked that up when you are completely blind I'll never understand.

'Give Aunt Arianne my love,' Darval said as he was about to leave, 'and my regards to Uster.'

'I will do that,' Jaxaal assured him, 'we will be heading south west ourselves tomorrow. Rydall, my best man, is going to be made a master smith at Cordale Complex in a veld's time and I'm hoping to be there for the ceremony.

Life at High Tor Farm continued much as it had before, as far as the farm workers and the villagers were concerned. The village square and the emotions of the villagers were put to rights after the disturbance caused by the arrival of the Lather twins. It became common knowledge that the new temporary manager at High Tor was the one that had fired the arrow that had thrown Natheal off balance and his wife was the one that had slapped Pardrea down and put her in her place. All in all, the spirits of the whole community rose in the aftermath as the harvest bathern approached.

Bry's concerns that he didn't really know all that much about the agricultural side of the farm, he was a kertle master after all, were allayed as Brindle turned out to be a mine of information and quickly slipped into the role of foreman with that responsibility.

They were soon both working at full stretch, Bry overseeing the care and preparation of the dray kertles that were required to pull the wagon full of seeds and tubers that were being planted and Brindle taking charge of the work groups who were actually doing the planting.

Old Simtraain started with a very negative attitude to the new manager but rapidly warmed to his new boss as he was included in a lot of the decision making and his opinions as well as his intimate knowledge of the farm were clearly respected. Shendaar was delighted to find that she was expected to take charge of the domestic arrangements within High Tor Farm. She was an expert caterer and was able to organise the kitchen staff without upsetting them. In fact, her three children did a lot to charm all of the staff. On the whole life was pretty good for the four friends and that friendship could only deepen.

Their little idyll was rudely interrupted two velds later when news arrived that the whole of the small Famerian army were about to arrive at the village. None of the villagers let alone the occupants, old and new, at the farm knew anything about the Famerian Army. Luckily a senior guardian officer with a small group of men arrived ahead of the main body of troops explaining the circumstances and made the arrangements for the billeting of the men.

'It seems our 'friends' Natheal and Pardrea have stepped things up a lot since they left here,' Bry told the company at dinner that night. 'They have abandoned their attempts at influencing the wage rates at hiring fairs and are attempting to overthrow the rule of the five houses.' This was met with gasps of astonishment.

'Well, they haven't completely abandoned their interference at hiring fairs,' the guardian officer, who had been invited to dine with them, commented, 'what they are doing is using force to make the workers refuse the rates the farmers are offering and then claiming that it is the farmers fault. This Natheal then makes speeches denouncing the farmers and the five families and calls for support to overthrow what he calls this evil system of government. I'm told that he is very clever at manipulating the crowds he draws and uses his own supporters who he plants in the mob to generate cheers at everything he says. He is gaining a lot of support and people are flocking to his banner. It doesn't help that we've just come through a comparatively rough period and people are feeling hard pressed and unsure of the future.'

The next day, on Bry's orders, two marquees, normally used to house migrant workers at hiring fairs were erected in the low meadow below the village which caused quite a stir. He had to make an announcement as several villagers were worried that there was to be another fair and they didn't like the idea of Natheal Lather and his men taking charge of their village again.

'It is just because of the troubles we experienced at the last hiring fair that these soldiers are coming,'

Bry said in a loud voice to make himself heard, 'they will only stay a short while before moving on. They are on their way to Swenmore Village where the Lather twins have taken their followers. Rest assured, these soldiers are our friends and will sort out the problems so that we never have to suffer the troubles that we had at the last hiring fair, again.

'Only a short while?' Bry was asked to confirm by one of the village girls. 'There won't be time to get to know any of them properly,' she complained when Bry repeated what he had told the crowd. She then blushed as she realised what she had said and ran off in a fit of embarrassed giggles.

The troops did start to arrive the next morning and it was not lost on Bry and Brindle that the soldiers tried to march smartly and to keep in step as they entered the village. They had travelled through the Childe Cut as had the smaller of their wagons. Sadly, the larger vehicles had been forced to travel over the Childe pass as they were too big for the narrowest parts of the cut and would not catch up with them for a veld or more.

Later that afternoon another group were seen approaching from the south east and the guardian commander told Bry that this was the men from Dresham. There was a marked difference in the way this new troop entered the village. The notion of marching in step and in keeping in straight columns was obviously a foreign concept to them. They shambled into the village centre and some started to wander off in search of food water and their billets but were rudely called back and ordered to line up by the enraged commander.

'I have never seen such a despicable display!' he roared, 'you are a ramshackle, disorderly humiliation to the colours and cap badge you wear. Call your selves soldiers? You are a disgrace.'

'Sir!' the young man who had ridden at the head of the arriving men called out. 'My men have just marched two hundred leagues in what is probably record time to get here to do their bit for Fameral. They are neither soldiers nor trained guardian officers; they are men of the House of Dresham, loyal to their house and their country.

They are here at their Lords request and as such are worthy of the respect they are due. If they are untrained and ill-disciplined it is because they have received neither; that's why they are here to get that education and to serve their country as best they can.

'And who the Alphos are you?' the enraged commander roared.

'Sir, I am Lord Sorjohn Dresham of the House of Dresham and you I take it are Commodore Mustoove to whom I was told to report, which I now do.'

The commander was somewhat taken aback by this confident young man. He was not used to being talked back to in this manner but immediately recognised that the young lord had made a good point; he had jumped to a conclusion he had no right to make and immediately back stepped his position. He invited the young lord to accompany him to a meeting of the senior officers.

'Thank you, Commander,' Sorjohn replied, 'but I'd rather see to the needs of my men first. They really are exhausted after their race to get here on time.'

'Quite so,' the commander agreed and looked around, searching for someone in the throng in the village square, 'Ah Sergeant!' he called to a black cloaked guardian, 'please attend to this officer and help him get his men fed and billeted in one of the marquees and then show the officer up to High Tor Farm.'

As the sergeant led the young lord and his men down to the low meadow Sorjohn asked him a few questions. 'Are you in charge of basic training or raw recruits, Sergeant?'

'Not specifically, Sir, but I can arrange for that to be done,' the guardian replied.

'Well in that case, if it doesn't interfere with your other duties, could you arrange for my men to receive some basic drill training? I think they would also benefit from an understanding of what they should be doing if it comes to a battle, so would I for that matter.'

'Well sir, some battle exercises have already been planned for tomorrow for all the troops,' the sergeant replied, 'that's so everyone gets an idea of what they should do when the time comes. The most important thing is for them to understand how orders are given in battle and what they are to do when given the different orders. May I ask what arms your men have brought with them?'

'Very few, if any,' Sorjohn replied, 'I think one or two have ancient swords and a few more have daggers but really, they are just ordinary civilians who have volunteered to do their bit for their country.'

'Right Sir, I understand the situation,' the Sergeant told him with a smile, 'I'll get these men of yours fed and quartered and the see about arming them. The first thing will be to get them to obey the marching orders and to know what each one means and why they need to follow them implicitly.'

By then they and the men had reached the marquee in the low meadow where the men were told to pick a bed space and put down their packs.

'I'll leave you now men,' Sorjohn announced in a clear voice, 'This guardian sergeant will see to your needs and then give you some basic training. You've all done very well to get here as quickly as you have; now your lives as Famerian soldiers can start. Do what this sergeant tells you and obey any order you are given by any guardian officer and I'll see you later.'

As he was about to leave the marquee his men all stood and gave a cheer. 'Thank you for all you've done for us,' one of them called after him as he left the tent.

'Who was that?' one of the Medland soldiers who was resting on his cot asked.

'That was Lord Sorjohn Dresham,' he was told, 'and a better man never lived.'.

'But he looks just a boy!' the old soldier replied.

'Aye, he's barely passed his majority, but he's got a good head on him has that one and he made sure he looked after us on the road here. Came on kertle back but barely rode it at all; walked here the same as the rest of us he did, not many lords would do that.'

'Nor many officers!' the soldier replied with a wry grin.

'And he paid for our meals on the road here, he did, and made sure that we all had a glass of ale every night!' the Dresham man confirmed, 'he's a good man.'

Chapter 25

As the Dresham men were settling in to their new life another young lord was leading the volunteers from his house. Crelin Launceston was enjoying the experience as much as Sorjohn Dresham had done. At last he'd been given a real job to do, one with responsibilities and the edge that he could fail just added to the experience.

Over and above this but a secret he kept to himself was the certainty with which he felt he was getting closer to his sister. He had missed her terribly and the conviction that they were getting closer together worked wonders to lighten his spirits. He had led the volunteers from Launceston all the way to Medland where they had spent a day recovering from their journey. He had then received instructions that he should follow the main force that had left a veld before and head for High Tor Farm.

His men had been grateful of the break in Medland and weren't so pleased that after only one day's rest they should be asked to take to the road again. Crelin did his best to lighten their spirits and led them in singing some songs that seemed to fit the rhythm of their marching feet.

Inevitably the songs degenerated into bawdy chants and rude parodies of well know airs and ballads. In his protected high family upbringing Crelin had been shielded from this part of Fameral culture and it came as quite an eye-opener to the young lord. However, he quickly caught on to the camaraderie that singing these songs engendered and joined in with a will. They had made the walls of the Childe Cut reverberate as they sang their way through the narrow gorge.

Away in High Tor Madge, was filled with a wonderful sense that Crelin was in good spirits and that he was getting closer. She knew that men from Launceston were on their way and expected to arrive at any time in the next day or two. At first, she had been filled with dread that her father would be leading the men from his house but this feeling that she was picking up from Crelin made her sure that the elder Lord Launceston was not approaching.

Time moved on and it was late in the day towards the end of the veld that the whole village became aware that yet more troops were approaching. The raucous singing of the Launceston men was heard long before the leading rider and the front ranks of the troops appeared over the hill. As they marched down into the village Crelin made sure that the song they were singing was a clean one.

The whole village seemed to turn out to welcome the new arrivals who made a fair show of halting and standing to attention. Commodore Mustoove came forward and introduced himself to the mounted man at their head, as did Bry. Bry was getting used to his role as host of this growing army. He was somewhat surprised that Madge did not come and stand at his side as he welcomed the arrivals, she had done so on all the previous occasions, but she was nowhere to be seen.

She had intended to be with Bry but in the last few moments, as the approaching troops reached the village outskirts her courage failed her, and she fled to hide beside some of the cottages around the village square. From here she watched as the troops were dismissed and sent to their quarters. She was thrilled to see Crelin but a little taken aback at the assured maturity he displayed. She saw Bry make an obvious invitation to the leader of the new troops to accompany him and lead the way up to High Tor House. Keeping to the shadows and the side roads, Madge followed on and crept around to the rear of the buildings that made up the house. As she had guessed Crelin's first concern was for his kertle and he had been shown where to stable the gelding.

As she crept up to the rear of the stall Madge heard Crelin tell the person with him that he would groom his kertle and see to his feed before joining the party in the main house. He then obviously set about this task and Madge heard the other person walk away across the court yard.

'Well old son,' Crelin said to his kertle as he took off its saddle and harness, 'so this is the famous High Tor Farm! I never thought I'd get to see the place where Jaxaal Norland grew up.'

'No, neither did I,' Madge said as she stepped into the stall entrance, 'and now I'm its temporary mistress.'

Crelin instantly recognised that voice but as he spun round his hopes of seeing his sister were dashed as he beheld a dusky skinned short haired woman. In his disappointment he just stood and stared at the new arrival silhouetted by the light streaming in through the doorway behind her.

'I know I've changed my appearance, but I thought my own twin would recognise his sister,' she said, her voice cracking with emotion. The static tableau lasted for a few heartbeats before recognition flooded Crelin's senses and he leapt into Madge's embrace. They clung desperately to each other for what seemed and age.

'Madge is that really you?' Crelin asked, tears of joy streaming down his face as he stroked his sisters head and neck.

'Yes, it's me my darling brother. I sensed that you were getting closer and I've been on edge all day as that feeling grew.'

'I've had the same feelings,' Crelin said, 'But what are you doing here?' he asked, 'what happened to you.

'Look Crelin,' Madge said in the high language and clinging to him tightly before pushing him away so that she could look into his eyes, 'there's so much to tell you and there just isn't the time right now. Look, I'm running High Tor along with a man I'm pretending to be married to, we're not married, and I am still a maid, but everyone here believes that Bry Woodsman and I are man and wife. Oh, I so want you to meet him, but he mustn't know you are my brother. Do you understand?'

'No sister dear, I do not understand at all, but if you say you are all right then that's good enough for me. I take it you want me to go along with this subterfuge?'

'Would you do that for me?' Madge asked.

'Well since you've asked, and I've found you again, of course I'll play your games, haven't I always?'

'Yes, you have Crelin dear. Now we had better get into the house, just remember you don't know me and we've never met.'

'All right sister dear, you always did lead the way so nothing's changed accept your appearance. How did you do that by the way?'

'I'll explain everything when we get a chance to talk.' Madge said as she turned towards the stable door, intending to make a belated appearance at the dinner table. Then a sudden thought hit her, she spun round and pushed Crelin who was following her, back into his kertle's stall. 'Father isn't on his way here, is he?' she asked in panic.

'No, he's not coming here, but by now he'll be on his way with mother to attend the bow competition in Swenmore that's being held in honour of Lord Neldon Swenland's ascension to rule of The House of Swenland,' Crelin told her, 'father came back to Launceston Hall from the Lords' meeting in Medland and told us about the developments down in Cordale Complex and he started issuing orders that ended up with me leading the Launceston men here.

'So, my little brother has at last been given some responsibility to act on his own initiative,' Madge said giving him another hug.

'Well, father appears to have mellowed in the past few velds,' Crelin observed and then pushing his sister back a little he was able to look down at her, 'and less of the 'little brother' you barely come up to my nose.'

'That's as may be, but remember I was born first so I'm older than you and I always will be.' Madge said with an air of finality as she led the way to the main house.

The meeting that afternoon included all the senior officers and was held in High Tor Farm itself and as acting hosts Bry and Madge were included. With so much guardian activity in the house and village they were being kept very well informed of everything that was going on in other parts of the continent. The happenings at Cordale

Complex and the trouble caused by the Red Cannis renegades who had terrorised that area of Fameral began to filter through.

Madge thoroughly enjoyed the interaction that occurred between Bry and her brother and was delighted that Crelin went along with the subterfuge asking Bry about how he began the temporary management of High Tor Farm. The discussion finally centred on the training of the men under their command and the objectives that the ruling council had decided upon. It was obvious that some major shifts were taking place in Famerian history when the news that Lord Roaken Ellward had suffered a seizure and was bedridden and barely able to communicate filtered through to the Farm.

The implications of this development did not become clear for a few days. After a veld spent training the newly recruited soldiers and carrying out field exercises where the whole army went through the motions of attacking supposedly defended positions, the fledgling army was considered ready to move out.

A major tactical development came when Commander Northwood devised a different method for the men to use when they actually engaged the enemy. He called for every man to have his shield modified so that there was a rounded slot cut in the right-hand side of his shield. This he instructed the smiths who carried out the work had to be large enough for a pike shaft to pass through easily.

He then had the pike heads modified along the lines that he had discussed with Rydall before he left for Cordale, so that as well as a sharp point, they had sharpened edges down the sides. These reasons for these modifications were not apparent until he introduced a new way for the pike men to arrange themselves as they prepared to engage the enemy. The advantage this new technique gave them was such an improvement that the men were enthusiastic about their chances of success and couldn't wait to get to grips with the rebels.

Eventually the orders arrived and Commodore Mustoove mounted his kertle and led the Army out of the village and down the road to Swenmore the next day. It took a whole veld for the village to return to something approaching normality. More than one of the village girls regretted to see the soldiers leave and the dismantling of the marquees was watched with a sadness and a few tears in more than one pair of eyes.

Madge had finally managed to get some time alone with her brother and had told him all that had happened to her since she left home. She finally got around to telling him how she had changed her skin and hair colour. She did so with some trepidation and couldn't help giggling self-consciously as she had admitted that Bry had dunked her naked into the dying vat.

'You mean that this Bry, to whom you are pretending to be married, got you to strip naked and jump in a vat of dye!' Crelin exclaimed, 'what were you thinking?'

'Well it wasn't like that,' Madge tried to explain, desperately trying to keep a straight face. She did manage to get herself under control and went on to explain, 'he was naked too.' But this, of course, only made things appear even worse and they both dissolved into a fit of giggles.

'Madge, what has happened to you? The sister I knew would never have done the things you seem to have done?' Crelin wondered in awe, 'you were always so refined, so proper.'

'Well, I left that little girl on the road somewhere between Launceston and Under Childe. I've learnt a lot since we last met. But tell me about things at home,' Madge implored, 'how is mother, how has she taken my disappearance?'

'Not well, I'm afraid,' Crelin said instantly becoming serious; his sister was about to get a harsh dose of reality. 'Mother has suffered greatly, I'm afraid. I think it has unhinged her mind a little. She has taken to locking herself in her work room, supposedly working on the new tapestries for the west wing, although no one has seen a stitch. For a bathern she ranted and rage at father, never satisfied that he was doing enough to find you. After that she seemed to draw in on herself. Now she wanders around the house murmuring to herself. She's had your room locked shut apart from when she goes in there to air the room and remake the bed, which she does every day or so.'

'Oh Crelin!' Madge exclaimed as the tears streamed down her face and she crumpled in a heap against her brother's chest, 'what have I done. I never meant to hurt mother. It was just father that I was angry with.'

'Well, I'm sorry to tell you so bluntly,' Crelin apologised, 'but there's no point in my trying to soften the news, you always know when I'm lying or trying to cover things up.'

'How's father taking my disappearance?' Madge asked as she snuffled into Crelin's shirt and jerkin.

'I'm afraid he's taken it very badly although he tries not to admit it,' he told her, 'he gets very angry at times and swears he will disown you if you ever show your face again. That sends mother into another of her distraught states which makes father even angrier. I dared to suggest that you might already be married a few alphens ago; I think I must have picked up your emotions when you and Bry got together. That caused all sorts of rows.

Father stormed that you'd have married a commoner and to have done it just for spite. Mother then got angry with him saying that it might be better if you had married someone not of the five houses at least that would stop this silliness of marriages arranged for political ends. I think some of the things I'd let slip about what I was picking up from you had given mother the idea that you wanted to marry a commoner.'

'She might be right there,' Madge confirmed.

'Anyway,' Crelin continued, 'they rowed about it for velds. In the end, to placate mother, father agreed that he would not make you marry a noble and mother made him promise that. Then I told them I thought you were already married and in all but reality I find that you are! Well that was the worst thing I could have done; mother went off in a screaming rage. She was so angry that she would have missed your wedding and not had any part of it. It was totally irrational of course, but that is the way mother is at the moment. To be honest I think she is going a little insane.'

'Oh, what have I done!' Madge wailed, 'I love Bry, but if I marry him now I'll break mothers heart. If I don't marry him, or he won't marry me I really will be seen as a fallen woman, I don't know how long we can go on pretending to be married while we are not. Crelin you have no idea how hard it is to share a bed with someone and not be intimate with them.'

They sat cuddling each other for a while until Crelin decided to change the subject.

'Tell me about these Lather twins, the ones that have caused all the problems this army has been created to solve.'

'Well, I don't know much about Natheal Lather,' Madge told him, 'it's his sister Pardrea I've had most contact with,' and she went on to tell Crelin of all that had occurred between the two girls.

'So, you slapped her across the face and knocked her down!' Crelin said in wonder at his transformed sister. They talked on about the impending war with Lather's rebels and the changes that the uprising might cause to the whole of Fameral. Despite these distractions Madge was very quiet for a few days as she came to terms with the trauma she had caused to those she loved.

Chapter 26

Once the Army had gone and the village had been put back to rights, Bry took control of the workload and good progress was made with preparing for the harvest. A little while later he felt that they had recovered most of the progress that had been lost while the soldiers had taken over the village. He was glad of this when word arrived that the Brackenstedd party were expected to arrive home within a couple of days.

Both Bry and Madge were nervous when they saw the carriages bearing the returning family approaching the village; they had done everything they could to make sure the house and farm were in as good condition as when the Brackenstedds had left.

Rennald and Christash alighted from the first coach and made a point of saying hello to their staff who had lined up in the courtyard. As he greeted old Simtraain, Rennald asked how the old man had got along with Bry; he had felt guilty about how he had usurped the old retainer, but his fears were soon allayed.

'Oh, that young man has done wonders, Sir,' Simtraain assured him, 'I couldn't have done better me-self, Sir. I gave him a lot of advice of course but he handled the upheaval the arrival of all them soldiers very well.'

'Yes, I was warned that we had played host to the new Fameral army and I can see that the low meadow has been well used. No doubt the pasture will recover.'

Madge was keen to show Christash that her home was just as she had left it but was surprised when the Quintrell stopped her heading towards the house.

'Ah, but first there is someone you need to meet,' Christash said, 'there have been a lot of changes in the Brackenstedd household since we left here an alphen ago. May I introduce you to my new daughter-in-law,' and she turned towards the second coach where two young couples were alighting. Both Bry and Madge noticed immediately that Rydall was firmly holding the hand of a beautiful young woman with stunning auburn hair. This young lady was eagerly looking all around her and had the biggest smile imaginable on her face.

That Rydall and Shanda, as she was introduced, were very much in love was evident from the way they held each other's hands and talked to each other. The party made their way into the house and enjoyed a sociable meal in the main dining room. During this meal the all events at Cordale Complex were revealed and the story of how Rydall and Shanda had got together related. The other couple were introduced as Jeldraan and Lucindra and that Jeldraan was to be the new smith at High Tor. Bry looked at Rydall with a quizzical expression since when Rydall had left for Cordale the smithy at High Tor had been the height of his ambition.

'A lot has changed in a very short space of time,' Rennald told the assembly and then went on to explain that he was now to move up to Castle Norland and take charge of all the Norland farms.

'My son, Rydall here, has now been appointed as Quintrall of the new High Tor Fifth of the House of Norland,' Rennald announced with pride.

'That means that you are now Quintrell, milady,' Madge said to Shanda as they were dealing with the aftermath of the meal and she dropped a curtsy.

'Oh don't,' Shanda said with some embarrassment, 'I'm not sure if I'm going to get used to being a noble woman. Three velds ago I was a simple country girl with a crush on a house guest who had come to stay. My only dream then was to be a smith's wife.'

'Oh, I'm sure you will do very well,' Madge told her, 'you have the style and grace of a noble woman.'

'As do you,' Shanda replied, 'I noticed how straight and erect you naturally stand.'

Life at High Tor got back to something of normality and Bry was pleased to explain to the new Quintrall all that he had done in the stables as well as the rest of the farm. Rydall was still fascinated by the bows that Bry and Madge possessed and asked if he could try them. Very soon Bry had made him a bow which he practiced with as often as his duties allowed. Jeldraan and several others, including Brindle and Shendaar were also intrigued by the bows and the competitions that quickly took place. Rydall set about ways of making arrows and arrow heads, apologising to Jeldraan for taking over the new smith's domain.

'Oh, don't apologise,' Jeldraan had said, 'it's an honour to work alongside the best smith in all of Fameral. And, anyway, I'm as interested as you are in these new toys.'

'Ah, I think we will find that these are soon to be considered as anything but toys,' Rydall had replied. The new Quintrall did neglect his duties for a few days while he developed a jig that aided in the fletching of the arrows. This simply allowed the flights to be stuck onto the end of the arrow shafts using a machine to correctly align them so that they imposed a rotating motion to the arrows as they flew, just as Bry had developed back in his woodland glade. Bry was delighted at this development and with the lathes that Rydall then set up to turn and cut the arrows to length, they very quickly made a significant quantity of good quality arrows with metal tips. Unlike the competition arrows, these could punch holes in wooden planks and even pierce thin bight metal plate.

Rennald and Christash Brackenstedd had duly left to take up their new lives in Norland and as the new Quintrall, Rydall revelled in attending to the minutia that running a large farm required. Shanda came to terms with being the first lady of a fifth, subtly guided by Madge whose earlier life had equipped her for just such a role.

Bry was thoroughly enjoying the demands of overseeing the stable and stud at High Tor and rapidly lost the sense of awe that had initially overwhelmed him that he was working where the legendary Uster Oostedd had ruled supreme.

A veld later it was with mixed emotions they received the official announcement and invitation to compete in a Archery Competition that was to be held at Swenmore village arrived. The competition was being held, the message read, to celebrate the return of Lord Neldon Swenland to the leadership of his house. The news that Neldon had completed his guardian training had travelled with the returning Brackenstedds. Added to this was the news that the sudden illness of Lord Ellward had necessitated that Darval Ellward should return from his regency of Swenland to take over the management of his homeland. This in turn had made it necessary for the newly pardoned, and newly married, Lord Neldon Swenland to return to the House of Swenland as its ruler.

Rydall was delighted and started to make plans for a significant party from High Tor to attend. He naturally assumed that Bry and Madge would go and represent the Fifth in the competition, but his invitation did not receive immediate acceptance from Bry. The last thing he wanted was to venture that close to Swenland itself. He was so well known there that he could easily be recognised despite the disguise his change of skin colour provided.

'But why do you not want to go to Swenmore?' Madge asked him when he told her he didn't want to make the trip. Bry found himself in a quandary at this. He felt that he couldn't reveal the real reason without risking the love and respect that Madge held for him and to lose that was the worst thing he could imagine.

'But we always planned to go further south if we didn't find work here in the north,' Madge reminded him.

'Yes, I know that,' Bry agreed, 'but that was when I thought we would be heading towards Dresham. Going to Swenmore is a completely different matter.'

'But why?' Madge pleaded, 'I just don't understand.' She desperately wanted to head in that direction as that was where Crelin had led his militia. But she was only too aware that both she and Bry still had secrets that they had not revealed to each other and she assumed that this was part of Bry's past he wanted to leave buried so she didn't press the matter.

Not so almost everyone else at High Tor who might be involved in the trip to Swenmore. They were all excited at the prospect of the impending celebrations and the fact that they had a proven champion Archer in Bry was just adding to the anticipation. Rydall was somewhat taken aback when Bry told him that he didn't want to make the trip. Bry tried to claim pressure of work as the reason for his reticence bur Rydall assured him that representing the High Tor Fifth would take precedence.

In fact, Bry would have loved to take part in another competition and the value of the prize money on offer was a great lure, even though his desperate need for money had reduced with his position at High Tor. Slowly his resolve was worn down by the pressures that were brought to bear. In the end it was Madge who swung the balance.

'Look Bry, we both know that we both have things in our past that we want to forget or keep hidden but, remember you have changed your appearance. If you make a point of wearing your cloak with the hood up the chances are no one will recognise you anyway,' she said as she came and gave him a cuddle. With this impetus, Bry climbed down and agreed to compete in the Swenmore competition.

It took a couple of days to make the arrangements so that the High Tor party could make the trip to Swenmore. At Bry's suggestion, Rydall asked Brindle if he would remain at the farm and take charge of things while he was away. Brindle was only too glad to accept this assignment, especially as Rydall tied it in with an offer of a permanent senior position for him and Shendaar at High Tor.

Rydall insisted that everyone at High Tor who had become a Archer should make the trip and compete in the competition at

Swenmore. This seemed a bit excessive to some and it meant that several large wagons were needed to be brought into the High Tor courtyard as the party assembled to begin the journey. Bry decided to make the journey on Rufran and to everyone's surprise Madge decided that she would ride Tilda.

In fact, Madge actually split the journey by alternating between riding Tilda and riding in the family carriage so that she could spend time with Shanda, with whom she had made a firm friendship. Both women revelled in looking at the countryside as they travelled south west; it was so different from the lush greenness of the continent north of the Childe Mountains. There were small villages and hamlets that they passed through but these were few and far between, unlike the more populous north.

The plants that grew here were those that thrived in drier, warmer conditions and they both noticed a steady rise in the temperature the more south they travelled necessitating the shedding of thick woollen outer clothing.

'I wonder how much hotter it gets down in the very south,' Madge mused as she looked out of the coach window.

'But you're from the south, I thought,' Shanda replied, 'surely you know what it is like.'

'Oh, yes, of course,' Madge answered, berating herself for her lapse in concentration, 'what I meant is, I wonder how hot it is down there at this moment.' She hoped she had covered her slip but saw the flicker of Shanda's questioning eyebrow.

'It gets so warm down there that some of the farm workers sleep outside, lying on the ground without any bedding at all,' she added, remembering her conversation with Braveen. She hoped that throwing in this detail that she had picked up from her earlier travels would cover her mistake and stop Shanda's questioning her true origins.

Chapter 27

Down in the wide-open spaces a couple of velds travel below Swenmore where the grain fields stretched for more leagues than the eye could see, Natheal Lather was gathering his own army together. He and his sister and all their acolytes had travelled down from High Tor and had achieved a lot more success at the hiring fair in Swenmore. At first the town welcomed them; the sudden influx of people suggested that the local tradesmen would do some good business, but that euphoria was short lived. The rebels actually had very little money, and several became violent when they were refused credit by the trades people. Natheal Lather received a sharp lesson on the high cost of maintaining an army in the field.

Following the visit by a deputation of the town elders, Natheal decided that they would travel further south in search of new recruits and other places to plunder. In general, Natheal had picked his location very well, by luck if not by judgement. There were small villages and hamlets scattered throughout the area, providing homes for the workers tied to the land. Due to the distances involved the guardian presence in the area was somewhat marginal and since the former Lord Swenland had paid the minimum he could to provide such cover the area was known for a lawless outlook. This encouraged the lower elements of society to migrate there and these dregs of humanity provided a ready source of men for Natheal's army. Word quickly spread and many flocked to the black and white zigzag banners that Natheal adopted as his emblem. A few disgruntled workers drifted over the Childe mountains from the northern houses but more came from the east from the Dresham lands. The greater part, however were from Swenland and they had the least distance to travel.

Natheal had no real plan as to what to do with his new rebel army. He had been forced to act sooner than he had originally planned by the growing strength in the houses under their new Lords. Now that he had started the rising he couldn't stop it, so he found himself with a growing force eager and keen to do his bidding. He desperately sought some cause to fight for, some objective that would justify the army's existence. Finally, he decided to return and 'capture' the town of Swenmore and then hold it against the ruling families. That at least would give him a base and be a good focal point for new recruits.

He began to think through the likely outcome of his actions so far and decided that he needed to weld the motley crew he had assembled into a coherent force. He began to appoint sub commanders and allocate groups of men to each one. This established a chain of command that had been lacking. This came none too soon; there were definite indications that the gathering might degenerate into a ramshackle orgy of drinking and fighting amongst themselves.

Natheal's most useful lieutenant proved to be Jorgraan Nefarald, a former guardian officer, dismissed from the force for drunken brawling. He, at least, was aware of the need for discipline and was able to give the rebel army a code of behaviour that went someway to holding them together. They began exercises, marching in line abreast as if storming an enemy position and practicing basic pike drill so that most of the men could wield the otherwise cumbersome weapons.

While the rebels did not have the efficient methods of sending messages that the guardians had, Jorgraan was able to get information illicitly from the system by 'reading' the flashed messages that were sent by the guardians. By this method he learnt of developments elsewhere and so Natheal knew that a government army had been formed and had already left High Tor Village and was heading towards Swenmore. This annoyed the rebel leader who wrongly assumed that the government men were aware of his plans to capture the town. He rapidly issued orders that the rebel army should begin the two-veld march back towards Swenmore and the factors were thus put in place for the first battle in the Fameral civil war.

The party from High Tor arrived at Swenmore having made very good time on the journey. They pulled into the town to discover that the Fameral Army was firmly ensconced in the area. Again, the marquees that were usually only used during hiring fairs had been erected and now served as barracks for the troops. For a large part, the officers and senior members of the force had found billets in inns in the town and it took a while for the senior members of the High Tor party to find accommodation.

As they searched around the various options Bry and Madge made the tacit decision that they would not stay in any of the inns. It was expected that members of all the ruling families except the Ellwards would be arriving for the next day's Archers" competition and that was a prospect that filled them both with dread.

Towards the north-west part of the town they found a small inn, barely more than a bar, which did have some stabling at the back. Having talked to the landlord they looked around the stable they saw a small hay loft and realised that it would provide them with adequate and private sleeping accommodation. They were used to effectively camping in Cannis Glade, their little woodland home, so this would be comparative luxury.

They agreed a price with the landlord who was delighted to be making money out of otherwise dead space. Having bedded their kertles down they went to explore the rest of the town. They inevitably found their way to the village centre which was marked by a square bordered by rows of shops. They found a stall selling hot food and indulged themselves in portions of roast kitchen fowl. As they sat on a bench they saw that a stage was being created at one corner of the square. A fellow customer of the food stall told them that a show was to be put on that night by a company of travelling players. Bry was suddenly filled with a terrible foreboding. His fears were compounded when he recognised some of the people setting up the stage as members of the company which had put on the play he had seen in under Childe that had named him as the villain of the Neldon Swenland deception.

'I don't want to stay and see this show,' Bry told Madge who was immediately upset.

'But why?' she asked, 'I love these travelling shows, they are always good fun and the plays that they end with are a good way of keeping up with the latest news.'

'But I think I've seen this one,' Bry replied lamely.

'But you haven't seen one during the two or more batherns while we've been together, and they are bound to have changed the final play,' Madge pleaded, 'I do so want to see the show, it will be fun.'

Bry was not convinced but in the end, he gave in and agreed that they would return for the show that evening. They worked their way back to their lodgings, checked on their animals and taking their bows and training arrows, went in search of somewhere they could practice for the next day's contest. They found themselves in a small flat meadow which was surrounded by trees. At first, they thought they had the area to themselves but then realised that there was another Archer down the far end of the clearing. He had set up a basic target and was collecting arrows that he had already fired in preparation for another session.

Bry recognised the Archer and in a delighted voice called out, 'hey, Straaka, can we join you?'

The large Archer looked up and saw the swarthy couple approaching from the direction of the town.

'And just who might you be?' Straaka asked as the pair got closer.

'Why, don't you recognise the man who always beats you in the Under Childe competitions?' Bry asked.

The large Archer finished collecting his fired arrows and came and stared at the pair. They were both swarthy skinned, like people from the deep south of the continent but these two didn't have the black hair that the southerners usually did, theirs was mid brownish, like their skin.

'Straaka, it's me, Bry Woodsman,' Bry said as he clasped the big man's hands.

'Bry, is that really you?' he asked and peered deeply at Bry's face, 'what have you done to yourself, caught too much sun?'

'Straaka, it's a long story which I'll tell you later, but for now, I take it you are practicing for tomorrow's competition, may my partner and I join you?'

'I see things have changed for you since we last met,' Straaka replied as he looked at Bry's very attractive companion. Bry introduced Madge to his old friend and the three of them then spent the whole afternoon talking and practicing for the next day's competition.

Eventually they made their way back to the town where Bry and Madge went and stowed their bows in the stable loft at the inn where they were lodging and then headed into the centre. They bought a meal from yet another wayside vender where they met up again with Straaka. The two men still had a lot to catch-up on and were deep in conversation when Madge announced that she was going for a walk around the town and would meet them in the square before the evenings show started.

She wandered off in the direction she had seen a coach disappearing as they had been buying their evening meal. She searched each inn, checking in the courtyard of each one searching for the coach she had seen. She made a point of keeping her hood well up to hide her face as much as possible, it was just possible she would run into her parents; Crelin had told her that they were expected to arrive for this celebration of Lord Neldon Swenland's ascension as ruler of his house. She had to reach the largest inn in the town centre before she found what she was looking for; there in the courtyard of the inn was a very fine coach bearing the insignia of the House of Norland.

She slipped into the inn via the courtyard door and found her way to the bar and asked if the Norland party could be sent a message.

'Lord Norland and his party are currently dinning in my best parlour,' the landlord told her, 'and what would the noblest family in the land want with a message from the likes of you?' he asked with a sneer.

'Just tell them that Madge Falleen would like to speak to them.' Madge replied standing erect and as tall as she could.

'Now why should I go and disturb them at their meal?' he asked again.

'Because they will be very annoyed if they don't get that message,' Made replied staring the man full in the face.

'Well, I'll see to it when I'm free,' he replied and began to serve another customer.

'That had better be now my good man,' Madge said in a strident voice as she slapped the flat of her hand on the counter causing everyone in the bar to look in their direction.

'Oh, all right, young lady,' the landlord replied surprised at the authoritative tone that this strange woman had suddenly used, 'I'll go and ask them now. Don't worry Jarge,' he said to the customer he had begun to serve, 'this won't take long, then I'll throw this woman out and get you your ale.'

He disappeared though to the side of the bar, wiping his hands on his apron before tentatively knocking on a door. There was a lot of talking going on inside the room, so his first knock was not heard for as well as the Norlands and Geldren Ellward, Rydall and Shanda Brackenstedd were catching up on what had happened since they all last met. The landlords knock was finally heard, and he was asked to enter.

'I'm very sorry to disturb your lordship, Sir,' he apologised to Jaxaal, 'but there is a Madge Falleen in the bar who would like to be allowed to see you. Shall I send her away, Sir?'

'Madge Falleen?' Jaxaal queried, 'do we know a Madge Falleen?' he asked his companions.

'Well the only Madge I know is Madge Woodsman,' Shanda said, 'she and her husband have been in charge of High Tor while Rydall's parents were away.'

Janilla sat and frowned and shook her head, 'it's not a name I'm familiar with,' she said.

'But I am!' Geldren exclaimed, 'its Maglen!'

'Maglen?' Janilla and Jaxaal asked incredulously.

'Yes,' Geldren said excitedly, 'we agreed that she would change her name to Madge Falleen when we parted at Upper Childe.'

'In that case, yes, please show her in,' Janilla told the landlord, 'and please bring another flagon of wine and another glass.'

Duly chastened, the landlord disappeared and a few moments later the door opened and Madge stepped into the room. Geldren was about to run up to give her long lost friend a hug but then she saw this short haired, dusky stranger and stopped in her tracks.

'I, I'm sorry to disturb you at your dinner,' Madge managed to say, she was surprised at her own emotional state at this reunion and momentarily feared that they would not recognise her. But she need not have worried for Janilla came around the table and stood in front of Madge, putting her hands on the dusky woman's shoulders. She stared deeply into Madge's face and then put her hand up to the others chin to tilt her head up slightly.

'Well, you've done a good job of disguising yourself this time,' Janilla congratulated her before taking Madge in her arms in a warm embrace, 'I wouldn't have recognised you without Geldren having said you'd changed your name.'

At this point the landlord returned with the extra glass and the requested flagon of wine. When he saw the little scene in the middle of the room he apologised to Madge.

'I'm sorry miss, I didn't realise you actually knew the nobles.'

'That's quite alright, Landlord,' Jaxaal told him, 'just keep our guest's arrival a secret, will you?'

'Very good Milord, just as you say Sir. I didn't mean no harm miss,' and he hastily made an exit.

'I take it you are still wishing to keep your true identity a secret?' Jaxaal asked.

'Yes, I am,' Madge assured him, 'I still don't want to be forced to marry someone my father has chosen for me. I know who I want to marry, although I can't persuade him to do that.'

'I'm intrigued,' Janilla replied as she led Madge to the table and settled her into a chair. She then sat beside her and took a hand in hers. Geldren then pulled her own chair around so that it was on Madge's other side and sat taking her other arm in a warm embrace.

'Geldren!' Madge exclaimed, 'I didn't expect to see you here. I heard about your father's illness. I thought you'd be back home in Ellward.'

'I was,' Geldren told her, 'but father's condition has stabilised as Aunt Arianne puts it, and there's nothing I can usefully do there. Father is not at all well,' she said with a sob, 'but he's in the best possible hands,' she said, pulling herself together. 'We talked through what this business with Natheal Lather and what it might mean. Aunt Arianne decided that if it really does come to a battle there will be people injured and Janilla and I will be needed here to help deal with them.'

'But this is the Madge Woodsman I was telling you about!' Shanda said as she came out of the corner where she and Rydall were sitting.

'Ah!' Jaxaal said, 'is this situation going to cause you problems?' he asked Madge.

On her part, Madge was momentarily flummoxed at the presence of the new Quintrall and Quintrell of High Tor, but she recovered her composure and turned to them.

'You are about to find out who I really am,' Madge told them, 'can I ask that everything you hear in this room you keep a secret; it would cause a lot of problems if the information became common knowledge.'

'Yes, of course,' Rydall assured her, 'but just who are you?'

'I am not Madge Woodsman, as you have just discovered, 'Madge told them, 'as my friends here are aware, 'and she acknowledged the three nobles, 'I am actually Lady Maglen Launceston of the House of

Launceston. I have left my former home to escape the plans of my father to force me to marry someone he has chosen for me.'

'There, I told you she carried herself like a noble woman,' Shanda told Rydall.

'Right,' Janilla said, 'now tell us all that has happened to you since we last met and more about this mysterious stranger that you want to marry.'

'Well, that's just it,' Madge began, 'he is mysterious. He calls himself Bry Woodsman, but I know that isn't his real name. He's good looking in a rough cast sort of way. He has a lame left leg and is very good with kertles. He's also an expert Archer and is here to represent High Tor in the competition tomorrow.'

'Look, why don't you start at the point where you left Geldren at Upper Childe and tell us everything that has happened,' Jaxaal urged her and she began to recount her recent history. The five sat in astonishment as Madge explained how she had travelled through the Childe Cut and reached Under Childe in a wretched state. She recounted her earlier dealings with Pardrea Lather and how hurt and humiliated, she had hidden in a kertle stall.

'And then, as I was talking to this friendly kertle, this wonderful man limped into the stall and into my life.'

'But when, and how, did you change your skin colour?' Geldren asked, 'and how far down does that lovely dusky colour go?'

'All the way,' Madge replied turning to her young friend with a giggle. She then went on to explain how Bry had persuaded her that the only way she could effectively fit in with the working people was to lose her fair skin and long blond hair.

'So that wonderful waist length hair is lying in some tanners-yard waste bin in Under Childe?' Janilla asked aghast.

'Oh no,' Madge assured her, 'without my knowing, Bry took it to a wig maker and had it made into a wig which I've still got at the bottom of my saddle-bag.'

'How long after we last saw each other did you dye your hair,' Geldren asked, 'I can see the roots are growing back to your normal blond colour.'

'Well, that was only two or three days later. That's when I got dyed all over, my hair included. Bry dunked me in a vat of tanner's leather dye,' Madge told them.

'But that must have made a mess of your clothes!' Geldren exclaimed.

'Well, it would have done if I'd been wearing them,' Madge agreed.

'You were naked!' Janilla asked with an embarrassed giggle.

'Yes, but so was Bry,' Madge defended herself forgetting her previous experience that this made it sound even worse. 'Look, you had better know, Bry and I have been living as man and wife as far as anyone else knows. We are not married, he won't marry me for some reason, but he has been a perfect gentleman, apart from the fact we share a bed. I am still a maiden and he has never even touched me in any intimate way,' and she looked at each of them to impress on them that she was telling the truth.

'I'm looking forward to meeting this Bry Woodsman,' Janilla decided, 'now; tell us the rest of what has happened to you and what brings you here.

Madge continued recounting her history as they demolished the flagon of wine and another was sent for.

Chapter 28

'So, you've become an expert with this bow toy?' Jaxaal asked.

'Well, yes I suppose I am pretty good,' Madge admitted, 'although I'm not really an expert, not like Bry or some of the other Archers you'll see tomorrow.'

'Don't you believe her!' Rydall contributed from his corner, 'she is a master with a bow. I'll allow that Bry is perhaps slightly better, but she ran him a close second in the demonstration that they put on for us at High Tor. That's why they are representing my Fifth at the competition. And don't discount these bows as toys Jaxaal. I made a few metal arrow heads and they can punch holes in wooden boards and metal plates. We could have done with them when we faced the Red Cannis and they may have a part to play in dealing with Natheal Lather and his rebels.'

'But you say that the arrows the Archers will be using in the competition will be the blunt rounded ended ones. They won't do much damage, will they?' Jaxaal asked.

'Well, I wouldn't wish to be hit with one, that's for sure,' Rydall replied, 'they'd leave a nasty bruise at the very least, but I've developed the way to make arrows with metal tips and I brought a supply with me from High Tor.'

'You brought some?' Madge and Jaxaal asked in astonishment.

'Well, yes I did,' Rydall replied, 'as soon as I saw Bry and Madge firing them I realised that they would make effective weapons and set about jigging up the smithy in High Tor to produce a good quantity. I had all the suitable shoots from the coppiced trees around the farm harvested and set about making arrows by the dozen. Jeldraan, Old Jassoon and I were up most of the two nights before we left, making them. I have a wagon back at the inn where we a staying with over a thousand. I suggest you recruit as many Archers as you can, Jaxaal. I think your little army is going to need all the help it can get.'

'That's true,' Jaxaal replied, 'you all may as well know, I've just heard that at best, our Fameral army is going to be outnumbered at least five to one. Natheal Lather has managed to get a lot of support and they are on the move and heading this way.'

'Oh Jaxaal,' Janilla exclaimed, 'are we going to get defeated in this war that nobody wants?'

'To be honest, my love, I don't know. We've done all that we can to prepare ourselves, but we are going to be hard pressed. I've had the guardians find out as much as they can about this Natheal Lather and I think he's an inspired leader of men. We'll find out how good he is as a military tactician in a few days' time.'

'But what about you, Lady Maglen Launceston,' Jaxaal asked, turning to Madge, 'what about you? What does the future hold for you? You really have turned your back on the world of Fameral high society.'

'Yes, I know, Jaxaal,' she replied with a sob as the enormity of her situation sank home, 'I can never be accepted back into 'polite society' and, if my secret identity is revealed, I will probably lose the friendships I have made since I left Launceston.'

'Well, I will always be your friend,' Geldren said as she again grabbed Madge's arm and gave it a hug.

'I'm sure we will all still be your friends,' Janilla told her, 'although it may make things a little difficult should your true identity become common knowledge.'

'Well, I'll just have to keep an appointment with that dye vat every turn,' Madge said with a grin, 'as long as Bry will stand by me I'll be content. I just wish he'd marry me. Then I'd be prepared to face the world.'

They talked on for a while and Madge heard that her parents were expected to arrive in Swenmore the next morning as were Lord and Lady Dresham. Madge was just about to leave to join up with Bry so that they could go to see the show.

'Oh Jaxaal, can we all go and see this show?' Janilla asked, 'it's simply ages since the travelling players visited Norland.

'Yes,' he replied with a smile, 'I think we could all do with some entertainment.'

As they all stood up and were about to leave when there was a knock on the door and Lord and Lady Swenland were announced. Madge was a little surprised that Shanda immediately leapt forward and embraced Lady Swenland, greeting her as a long-lost friend.

'But we are the best of friends,' Shanda explained, 'Festera and I grew up together in Cordale Complex. Now I'm a Quintrell and she has become Lady Swenland.'

'I'm delighted to meet you Lady Swenland,' Madge said. Shanda then went through the explanation of just who Madge really was, swearing her friend to secrecy. Jaxaal was soon in deep conversation with his brother-in-law.

'So, you've arrived with nearly fifty kertle riders?' Jaxaal asked in astonishment.

'Yes,' Neldon confirmed as Janilla came across and hugged her brother, 'we've been practicing with small pikes, which we call lances, I think we might have a part to play in the forth coming battle.'

The two men began to talk through the implications until Janilla called a stop, 'we have to get along to the village square if we want to see this show they're putting on.'

'Yes, we must get there,' Neldon agreed, 'I've promised Festera we would see the show and I want to see it for myself. I've heard reports about it.'

The whole party then made their way to the village centre letting Madge go on ahead. She hunted around for a while trying to find Bry. Finally, she heard him calling her from the centre of the square where he and Straaka had commandeered a bench. She worked her way through the crowds that were pressing into the limited space and was eventually able to join the men. They made space for her on the bench and she nestled in between them. Any hopes that Bry might have had that they would keep the bench to just the three of them were dashed as more and more people squeezed into the square forcing those already there to squash up together.

Bry was a little disturbed when the group of nobles arrived and were shown to a raised stand at one side of the stage. As he recognised Neldon he ducked down and would only sit up once he had pulled his hood up over his head. Madge saw this and was puzzled by his behaviour, but further considerations were cut short as the musicians began to play a tune that Bry recognised. With a sinking feeling he realised that this was indeed the same travelling company that had put on the show in Under Childe. He was a little comforted when he realised that with Neldon in the audience; they were unlikely to put on the play that told the story of the last Challenge with him there.

The master of ceremonies still wearing the same flamboyant costume leapt onto the stage and called to get everyone's attention. His opening patter was just the same but obviously fresh to most of his audience for the laughter echoed around the square and set the right atmosphere. The programme was much the same as when Bry had seen it before. When the interval arrived, there was no possibility that they could go and refresh their tankards so great was the crush of people; instead they just sat and talked. As she looked around Madge saw Janilla looking at her. The noble woman was looking intently at Madge's companions and then raised her eyebrows in a question.

Madge understood the question and answered it by turning and hugging Bry, giving him a kiss on the cheek. When Madge looked up again she saw that Janilla was deep in conversation with her brother. It was not lost on her that Neldon took a surreptitious glance in their direction and the said something to his sister. Further contemplation of what might be being discussed was cut short by the starting of the second half of the show.

This started, as it had done before, with the master of ceremonies taking the stage with his hands raised to quieten the audience and a sombre expression on his face. He then took up a place in front of a make shift curtain and face the audience.

'Ladies and gentlemen, we now bring you news of what happened in Medland at the last Challenge,' he intoned, and a cheer went up from all around the courtyard.

'Yes, you may well cheer, for as we all know, Jaxaal Norland,' and he duly bowed towards where the nobles were sitting, 'won The Challenge and claimed as his prize the reinstatement of The House of Norland!' This was met with an even louder cheer and the stamping of feet on wooden floors and the cobble stones.

'Yes,' the MC shouted to make himself heard above the racket and waving his hands got the noise to decrease. 'Yes,' he continued, 'and we could present for you the clever way Lord Norland was able to arrange his marriage to the lovely Lady Janilla Swenland.' This was again met with suitable cheers and the predictable sighs of 'Ahh.'

Bry sat in absolute shock, his worst nightmare was about to be re-enacted and he started to rise. Madge sensed his tension and knew he was about to try to leave but held tightly onto his arm.

'But instead,' the MC said in a loud attention-grabbing voice from the stage 'at Lord Neldon Swenland's expressed wish, we bring you a tale of lies and deceit, of treachery and malpractice that will make your blood boil. It is a tale of heroes,' and the cast off-stage cheered, 'and of evil villains,' and the cast led a round of hisses and boos.

'Look Madge,' Bry pleaded, 'I really do have to go, I can't stay and watch this!'

'Nonsense,' she replied, 'it's only a play and I love watching these plays. Just sit through this for me and then we'll go.' This did little to placate Bry's terror but without making a scene, since Madge still had him in a vice like grip, he had to give in to her. The matter was decided by the number of hisses they got from their neighbours telling them to be quiet.

'Ladies and gentlemen,' the master of ceremonies continued, 'I would like to point out that, as I have intimated, Lord Swenland himself has requested that we present for your delight and edification, "The Fall of Lord Neldon Swenland",' and he stepped sideways off the stage. As Bry had seen before the curtain pole was lowered to reveal a stable setting with a man kneeling reverently beside a clutch of kertle eggs. The play continued as it had before with each scene making Bryland Doltaary out as the evil villain of the piece. It was with a considerable amount of shock that Madge put together the different parts of the puzzle and that full realization came to her.

As the play drew towards its final climax and ending, as before the MC came forward to the edge of the stage and began his final address. 'And there, ladies and gentlemen, we see the downfall of a member of one of the highest houses in the land,' and he turned and bowed towards the seat where Neldon was sitting, 'laid low by the dastardly tricks and schemes of the real villain of the piece, Bryland Doltaary.'

Bry sat huddled in his seat with his hood pulled up over his head. Madge could feel him shaking and deeply regretted that she had made him stay and suffer this presentation.

'And where is this evil man now, you might ask?' the MC continued, leaning forward to confide in his rapt audience, 'well no one knows. After his despicable acts and treachery were revealed,

Bryland Doltaary has simply disappeared. No one knows where he is, he has not been seen, and few would recognise him. He could be sitting in this very audience tonight! He could be sitting right next to you,'

At that point a voice rang out from the side of the stage. 'Enough!' Lord Neldon shouted as he leapt across, onto the stage. 'This travesty must stop now and never be repeated!'

The shocked MC recoiled from this sudden onslaught; he was not used to being interrupted at this stage of the presentation. He usually had the audience in the palm of his hands at this point and could milk the situation and suggest that they show their appreciation by contributing generously when the collecting bowls came around.

'I have never seen such a despicable distortion of the facts,' Neldon raged. He then took the centre of the stage and turned to address the audience while the MC sidled away to the side of the stage. Their play instead of pleasing had obviously upset one of the highest nobles in the land where the exact opposite had been the intention.

'As some of you will know,' Neldon said in a loud voice that reached every corner of the town square, 'I am Lord Neldon Swenland. I have just assumed the rule of The House of Swenland having served a term of training as a guardian. That was deemed by the ruling Lords to be a fitting punishment for my transgressions at the last Challenge. I am not proud of what I did but I have served my punishment and have been returned to my former position.'

This was met with cheers from all around the square since this was a Swenland town.

'But I tell you now,' Neldon continued, 'the blame for the deception I attempted rests with me alone. At no time did anyone else have anything to do with the plot. Bryland Doltaary has been portrayed as the villain of the piece but in fact he was a faithful member of my house who loyally and honourably did everything that was asked of him. At no time did he plan any part of the deception. In fact, I don't think he had any idea that the ploy of using two kertles was being considered. It is true that he has disappeared since the Challenge and I would dearly like to find him again and restore him to the high position within my house that he deserves. I hereby announce that I will give a reward of 50 strands to anyone who enables me to apologise to my old friend and restore him to his rightful position.'

This produced a marked reaction in the crowd; 50 strands were an enormous sum to most people and showed the importance that Lord Swenland placed on finding his old friend. Bry sat rigid in his seat, his worst nightmares had come back to haunt him; he sensed that Madge must have made the connection and now knew that he was in fact Bryland Doltaary.

Madge did in fact know who Bry was; she had suspected the truth for some time during the play and Bry's reaction had only confirmed what she had deduced. His skill with kertles was a clear indication of his past experience and the fact that his claim that he had been wrongly accused of things he hadn't done had just been vindicated. Bry's reaction was the final confirmation that Madge needed; she decided to act.

Neldon also knew that his old friend was in the audience; Janilla had recognised Madge's companion when she had pointed him out and she had told her brother. That recognition had not been instant as Bryland had managed to change his appearance so significantly but Janilla remembered him from her days at Swenland Grange. He had been the stable lad who had the job of bringing out her and her sister's riding kertles. He was a good-looking man with a pronounced limp who had always been kind to poor Parina. That limp and his skill with kertles had rung bells with her when Madge had talked about her mystery man. With those clues the sight of Bryland's profile as he sat next to Madge, silhouetted against the lights behind him, had confirmed the identification. She had then whispered her findings to Neldon who then had also recognised the dusky man as he sat in the audience.

'My Lord Swenland,' Madge called in a loud clear voice as she stood up, 'I can help you in your search for your friend. He's here, now beside me,' and she dragged Bry to his feet, virtually lifting the reluctant man.

An audible gasp ran around the audience and everyone turned to stare at the swarthy couple. With Madge and Straaka taking his arms Bryland was propelled through the throng of people who magically cleared a path for them. When they reached the stage Straaka bodily lifted his smaller companion onto the platform where Bryland regained his feet to be warmly embraced by Lord Neldon. A great cheer went up and everyone was calling, shouting and gathering around to share in the celebrations at the reunion. In the melee, Madge managed to slip away and disappear down a side street. Bryland was then re-united with Janilla who hugged the former Swenland man and told him how glad she was that he had been found. She kept looking, hoping to see Madge and include her in the reunion but she was nowhere to be seen.

In fact, Madge was running down a street with tears pouring down her face. The comfortable world she had managed to build had just collapsed around her and she had pulled it down herself. Now she was sure she had alienated the man she loved by giving him away. Now he would never want to marry her, and she wasn't at all sure if she wanted to get married anyway; she couldn't face the horror of hurting her mother more than she had done already.

She made her way back to the little inn where they had stabled their kertles. She checked on both Rufran and Tilda and attended to their feeds and bedded them down for the night. She then climbed up to the hay loft and simply slumped down and curled up in her sleeping roll and tried to cry herself to sleep. The tears came easily but sleep didn't; she had been so happy as her life with Bry had developed. She had always sensed that he was an honourable man and now that his origins had been revealed she knew that her trust in him had not been misplaced. How ironic that he was now to be returned to his high-status place in the house of Swenland which a suitable match would be perhaps for a daughter of one of the five houses. But that elevation was the very reason why she could not now marry him. He would be a high-ranking member of one of the Five Houses; Neldon might even make him a noble and as such he would be among the highest in the land. Had he remained as Bry Woodsman she could have married him, happy that her real identity could remain hidden but as the wife of Bryland Doltaary, especially Lord Doltaary as he might become, she would be sure to be recognised. Janilla had warned her against re-visiting the dying vat; the long-term effects could be dangerous, and her hair was already growing out. She lay huddled in her sleeping roll, a miserable scrap of humanity who wished she were someone else and a long way away.

It was a long time later that she heard someone moving around down in the stall below and Rufran's welcoming snickers. She knew it must be Bry and braced herself for his reaction to her betrayal of him. He obviously satisfied himself that the kertles wanted for nothing for she heard him slap them both affectionately as was his way when he left them and start to climb the ladder up to the loft where she lay.

'Madge is that you?' he asked the relief in his voice was palpable, 'I thought I'd lost you when you disappeared like that. I couldn't see you once Neldon stopped greeting me like a long-lost brother and it's taken me this long to get away and to come and find you.' He stopped as he sensed her distraught state and came and knelt beside her shaking form, putting a comforting arm around her shoulder.

'Madge whatever is wrong?' he asked as he stroked her hair, 'thanks to you everything is all right now. I've been returned to my former position; the world now knows that I was not guilty of the things of which I had been accused and Neldon has made me a House Quintrall.'

'I'm very glad for you Bry, er Bryland. It's what you deserve. I'm sure you'll be very happy back in The House of Swenland where you belong.'

'What do you mean I will?' Bry asked, 'We will more like. Now we can be married. I'm a man of high standing and we can afford to live very comfortably.'

'Yes, you can,' Madge replied, 'but now we can never be married. When you were simply Bry Woodsman we could have lived happily as man and wife in our little glade with our Cannis friends but as a high noble, well known and visible for all of Fameral society to see, I can never marry you.'

'But why not?' Bry asked in desperation, he was at a total loss to understand what was happening, why the woman he loved and who had plagued him for batherns to marry her was suddenly saying that she couldn't.

'Because of who I was,' Madge replied, the tears streaming down her face, 'of who I am.'

'You mean a Quintrall of the House of Swenland is not a fitting match for Lady Maglen Launceston of The House of Launceston?'

'You. You know who I am!' Madge asked in astonishment.

'Madge, Maglen, I recognised you immediately when I found you in Rufran's stall back in Under Childe. Remember, I was in Medland for the Challenge and even attended the Eve of Challenge Ball at the Ellward's mansion. And, anyway', Janilla told both Neldon and myself who you were when she came and congratulated me on being returned to The House of Swenland.'

'I don't remember you being at the Eve of Challenge Ball,' Madge replied.

'I was there but I kept in the background. It was watching you dance when I think I fell in love with you. I don't dance because of my leg and I had a feeling that something was about to happen. As it turned out, I was right. I refused to follow Lord Swenland into the courtyard where he attacked Jaxaal and that put me in his bad books.'

'But all the time we've lived together you never said anything.' Madge replied.

'Well I reasoned that you would tell me if you wanted me to know. You didn't, and I was delighted. It meant you might stay with a poor woodsman in his lowly little hovel in the woods. Had you decided to return to your former life, as a dishonoured man, I could never go with you. But as I've just told you, Neldon has invested me as Quintrall and as such we can be married.'

'No, we can't,' Madge replied, the tears again streaming down her face, 'I have hurt my parents very badly, especially my mother. I can't suddenly reappear in Fameral society as your wife without causing her untold pain.'

'But as I interpreted what I heard,' Bry replied, 'you ran away from home so that you couldn't be forced into a marriage you didn't want.'

'That's true,' Madge told him, 'but when I talked to my brother at High Tor, he revealed just what pain and suffering I had caused her. It would be callous to suddenly reappear as if I didn't care what she has been through,' and she dissolved into yet more tears that racked her body.

Bry laid her down and snuggled in beside her and cuddled her as she finally fell into a fitful sleep. They both knew that this might be the last time they could share a bed together like this.

Chapter 29

The morning of the Swenmore Archer's Competition dawned fine and clear and after an early breakfast the nobles and all the senior officers and those in charge of significant portions of the Fameral army assembled, at Jaxaal's request in the courtyard of the main inn. Jaxaal then explained what he intended to do as supreme commander. Milden Northwood had arrived at the town as dawn broke bringing with him as many guardian officers as could be released from their normal duties. The increase this made to the overall numbers was pitifully small but Jaxaal was delighted; it meant that his army would have a good number of trained men who could pass messages between the various troops as they scattered over the battle field. The experience he had gained during the episode with the Red Cannis told him that such communications would be critical, especially if he was to adopt the tactics he was mulling over.

During the meeting he explained what he had in mind and then sent the bulk of the officers back to their commands to oversee the final days training. He had received word via the guardian scouts out in the field that the rebel army was approaching from the south west and would arrive at a point ten leagues from Swenmore during the night or early the next day.

'Right,' he announced, 'I want the senior officers, that's you Commanders Mustoove and Northwood, Lords Neldon Swenland, Sorjohn Dresham, Crelin Launceston and Quintrall Bryland Doltaary to come with me on a trip to reconnoitre the land to the south west of here. We're going to pick the spot we want to fight; I'm not leaving that up to the whim of Natheal Lather.'

At Milden's insistence they took a small detachment of mounted guardians as a protective escort and made their way out of the town. It caused a bit of a stir and quite a lot of interest when Sarina, Jaxaal's racing kertle was led out for the lord to mount.

'I'm astonished you've brought the best racing kertle in the land on this jaunt!' Neldon expressed his surprise.

'Ah well, I took her all the way from Norland to Cordale Complex to give her the exercise she's been lacking while I've been involved in Fameral business. Since we came straight here it makes sense to keep up the work-outs so that she gets fit enough for the next Challenge. If I really am serious about defending my title she will need some more specialised training. Will you be entering the Challenge?'

'No Jaxaal,' Neldon replied, 'I made a decision while I was training as a guardian that I would never race again. Mind you, that doesn't mean that the House of Swenland won't be competing and now that I have my kertle-master restored to his rightful position you had better be ready for some real competition.'

Shortly after the army leaders had departed, Madge arrived at the largest inn in the town and tentatively scratched on Janilla's door. Lady Norland and her cousin Lady Geldren Ellward had been busy preparing their supplies of bandages and antiseptic ointments in preparation for what they feared may happen the next day. They greeted Madge and Janilla held her in a warm embraced and desperately asked her for forgiveness apologising for her indiscretion the previous evening.

'I'm so sorry that I gave Bry's identity away to Neldon last night,' Janilla apologised, 'but I thought it might help once I'd realised just who your partner was.'

'I thought I was the one who gave him away!' Madge exclaimed.

'Well, yes, you told the whole crowd who Bryland was,' Janilla conceded but Neldon only jumped on that stage because he already knew he was in the audience. When you pointed him out to me I had a good look and that simply confirmed his identity. I'd had a shrewd idea of who your mysterious man was from your description: good with kertles and a lame left leg. Remember I know Bryland Doltaary very well; he was among the top stable hands at Swenland Grange. You had already told me that he had changed his skin colour the same way you had, so I knew to make allowances for that.'

'So Neldon knew he was there when he made his little speech exonerating him?' Madge asked.

'Yes, I thought that if Bryland was returned to his position it would make it easier for you to come out of hiding,' Janilla explained.

'But Janilla!' Madge wailed as she crumpled in a heap, 'it hasn't helped at all. I have hurt my parents, my mother, so much I can never come back into society and now Bry has become a noble he and I can never be together. He's now a part of the society that I've left and into which I can never be accepted back.'

'But I don't understand why you can't resume your former place,' Janilla said, somewhat bemused.

'Oh Janilla, you are generous to a fault but think it through! I have been living as Bry's wife for nearly three batherns. I know that nothing untoward has happened, I am still a maid and Bry hasn't even touched my naked body. I know that, but no one else does; all the world knows is that we share a bed and he has seen me naked every time I've bathed in the stream at Cannis Glade.'

'You say, 'all the world,' but just who does know those details?' Janilla asked.

'Well, no one, I suppose,' Madge conceded, 'but everyone who stayed in the married tent at the High Tor hiring fair knows we shared married quarters.'

'So just a few workers,' Geldren said as she joined the conversation, 'look, if we changed your appearance back to what it used to be when you were Maglen Launceston you could resume your former place in society.'

'But how can that be?' Madge asked incredulously, she desperately wanted to find a way out of her dilemma and was willing to clutch at straws.

'You say you have a wig made from your hair before it was dyed?' Geldren asked.

'Yes, it's in my saddle bag back at the small inn where we are staying,' Madge told her.

'Right you go and fetch it,' Geldren ordered as she stood up, taking command of the situation, 'Janilla and I will start preparing some face creams that will restore your natural fair complexion.

Half an hour later Maglen Launceston was looking at her reflection in a large mirror, astonished at the transformation a lightened skin and her own long blond hair had made to her appearance.

'That ointment will easily wipe off so be careful not to rub your face or the back of your hands,' Geldren told her.

'This is wonderful, but I can't go out like this,' Madge complained, 'I may be recognised for who I really am.'

'Well there are a lot of things happening at the moment,' Janilla told her, 'this awful war has turned the world upside down, as if things weren't changing enough already. Ostensibly, we're only here to attend this Archery Competition to celebrate my brother's ascension to his place as Lord Swenland. It has just coincided with the trouble this Natheal Lather has stirred up.'

A few hours after the Fameral Army leaders had left Swenmore a very imposing carriage bearing the Launceston Crest arrived in the square and Lord and Lady Launceston looked around and obviously made a choice and instructed the driver to take them to the largest inn they could see. The landlord was a little flustered by their arrival, he already had Lord and Lady Norland staying in his best rooms and he would have to do some swift reorganising if these newly arrived nobles were not to be turned away.

The Launceston's arrival had not gone unnoticed up in the main guest room where the three young noble women were finishing Madge's transformation back into Maglen. They heard the crunch of metal rimmed wheels on the gravel outside and all three peeped out of the window.

'Right, you two stay here,' Janilla told them, 'I'm going to have a word with your parents Maglen.'

'Oh no, Janilla please don't,' Madge pleaded, 'my father will force me into a marriage I couldn't bear!'

'In that case I'll see if I can have a quiet word with your mother.' Janilla assured her and she hastily left the other two noble women in the bedroom.

'It's funny that you are determined to not marry Sorjohn Dresham,' Geldren said as she packed away the creams and colouring agents they had used to achieve Madge's transformation, 'I was able to have a long talk with him last night after he returned from training his men. I think he is very nice; I wouldn't mind marrying him in a turn's time when I reach my majority,' she added with an embarrassed smile.

'Yes, I believe he is a nice man,' Madge agreed, 'and I had heard that you have a fondness for him; given time I might have grown to like him, but I will not be forced into an arranged marriage just to suit my father.'

Janilla made her way downstairs but kept herself in the shadows as the landlord bustled around attending to the immediate needs of the Launceston party. When they were shown into a small snug bar where they could be served privately she waited until the landlord had left them before going and scratching on the door. She didn't wait for an answer but let herself in and immediately apologised for the intrusion.

'Just what do you mean by barging in here unannounced?' Lord Launceston challenged her.

'Oh Feraard!' Lady Emileen Launceston admonished her husband, 'that's no way to greet Lady Norland who I'm sure needs no formal announcement to be able to come and speak to us.'

'Well, yes,' The lord replied, duly reprimanded, 'I am sorry to be so rude. We've had a long hard journey and I'm very tired, we both are. Now what do you want?' he asked.

'Feraard that will do!' Emileen Launceston continued in her previous tone, then, in a softer voice she smiled and asked, 'Lady Norland, can I offer you a cup of kandrel?' and she reached for the jug the landlord had supplied.

'No, thank you Lady Launceston,' Janilla replied, 'I came to talk to you about your daughter.'

'We don't have a daughter!' Feraard snapped back at her as he turned his back on the ladies, then, in a softer but still bitter voice he added, 'we did have one, but she has disowned us and is now dead to us.'

Emileen let out a sob and looked imploringly at Janilla, 'do you have news of Maglen?' she asked beseechingly.'

'If you do, we don't want to hear it,' Feraard snapped, still with his back to them.

Janilla summed up the situation, it was one she was all too familiar with; her father had flown into these dreadful silent rages and she knew better than to push the fuming lord.

'In that case I'll leave you to recover from your journey in peace,' she replied and stared intently at Emileen Launceston and with a toss of her head towards the door invited the distraught mother to follow her as she left the room. She closed the door behind her and heard Emileen berating her husband for his rudeness. A few moments later the door opened, and Lady Launceston flew out of the room desperately seeking where Janilla had gone. She saw the younger woman standing on the stairs where she turned and climbed them up to the next floor. Emileen hastily followed trying to not look as if she was in an undignified rush. As she reached the first floor landing she found Janilla waiting for her. Janilla put her finger to her lips and led her along the landing to a window seat that looked out onto the town centre.

'Lady Norland, do you have news of Maglen? Have you seen her since she left Castle Norland over a bathern ago?'

'Lady Launceston, please call me Janilla and yes I have seen Maglen,' Janilla said taking the other's hands in hers.

'Then she is still alive! Oh, thank Alphos. Is she all right? She's not been hurt has she?' the distraught mother asked in voice she could barely control.

'Yes, she is well physically, a little sun tanned perhaps but well in body.' Janilla assured her, 'but she is very upset that she has caused you so much pain and anguish.'

'Oh, the silly girl'' Emileen exclaimed, 'I don't care what she has done, as long as she's all right. Where is she, can I see her?'

'Well I think we can arrange that, as long as you promise me you won't start shouting and screaming at her for running away from her home.'

'I won't lose my temper, if that's what you mean. I just want to hold her and hug her. I've missed her so much.'

'That's what I thought,' Janilla said as she stood up still holding Emileen's hands, 'come with me and she led the way to the doorway just a few paces back down the landing where she scratched lightly on the door before opening it. She stepped inside and drew the bemused mother behind her. 'Maglen,' she said, please forgive me but there is someone here who really wants to see you.'

The room was very bright with bright midday sun pouring in through the window and after the gloom in the corridor it took Lady Launceston a moment or two to focus on the person she most wanted to see.

'Mother!' Madge exclaimed as she saw who Janilla had brought with her.

'M..Maglen!' Emileen stuttered, 'you've cut your hair!'

The tableau lasted several seconds before mother and daughter rushed into each other's arms where they embraced each other fervently.

'Oh, my silly girl,' Emileen cried as the tears of joy rolled down her face and soaked into her daughter's hair, 'where have you been. I've been so worried even though Crelin kept telling me you were all right.'

'Mother I'm fine,' Madge assured her, 'I'm just so sorry I've caused you all this pain and hurt. I never meant to upset you; it's just that I couldn't face being forced into an arranged marriage. I still don't.'

'What Maglen is trying to say,' Janilla interrupted, 'is that she has had a lot of time to think and she may be able to cope with a marriage that pleases both you and Lord Launceston.' Both mother and daughter stared at her.

'I think I may be able to make a suggestion to Lord Launceston that will gain his approval,' Janilla continued, determined to maintain the initiative now that she had got this far. 'I intend to speak to my brother, Lord Swenland, I believe that he has needs that correspond to your husband's. Geldren and I will leave you here with your daughter and return downstairs and see if we can get him to agree to meet with Neldon when he gets back this evening.' With that the two healers left the mother and daughter to enjoy their reunion.

Chapter 30

The Fameral Army leaders travelled along a well-worn track that Neldon explained was one of the main communication links for his Swenland homeland. 'None of the paved roads you have up north,' he explained as he led the way and tried to remember the lay of the land that stretched ahead of them. Jaxaal explained how he wanted the battle to progress and Neldon thought there may be a suitable spot a little way ahead of where they had reached at mid-morning.

When they did reach the place Neldon had in mind Jaxaal sat and thought about it and then asked Bryland to come and assess the shallow valley they had reached.

'I have no knowledge of these bows of yours,' Jaxaal explained, 'if we could get the enemy onto that valley floor, how close would your Archers need to be to be able to hit them?'

'But I haven't got any Archers,' Bryland complained, 'there's only Madge, Straaka and me!'

'Oh Bryland!' Jaxaal laughed, 'I'm told that there are over fifty Archers entered for tonight's competition and others arriving all the time. This celebration tournament in honour of my brother in law's ascension has created a lot of interest. I didn't realise just how popular these Archery Competitions had become down here in the south. With your help I'm hoping to persuade a lot of the Archers to join our little army.'

'But we haven't got enough arrows to carry out a meaningful attack.' Bryland pointed out.

'Well thanks to Rydall we do have a significant number,' Jaxaal assured him, 'so will you and your Archers be able to shoot the enemy if we can get them down on the valley floor?'

'Well, we could land arrows among them from here,' Bryland replied and he reached behind him and got his bow ready to fire, 'but we wouldn't have much control on their accuracy. Watch this shot, I'll try to get it close to that small bush on its own in the centre of the field.'

He notched an arrow and drew back and let fly, aiming high in the sky. Most of the watchers lost sight of the shaft as it streaked into the air but Bryland was used to having to watch the flight of his arrows and saw it bury itself in the soft ground a good twenty strides short of the bush and as much to one side where the wind had taken it.

'Well, there's your answer,' Bryland announced, 'we would need to be at least a good fifty paces closer to be able to pick our targets.'

'Right, you mean on that slight ridge half way down this slope?' Jaxaal asked and received a nodded agreement.

Jaxaal had a good look around the area at the top of the rise where they were standing and called Milden over to him. He was aware that the guardian had been away on the nearby hill top and had received some messages from his officers who were scouting ahead.

'Commander Milden,' he called, and the guardian officer came over to where Jaxaal was sitting on Sarina's back, 'do you have any news of the rebel forces?' he asked.

'Yes Milord,' Milden replied, 'I have literally just received news that the main rebel force is about thirty leagues away and heading up the road towards us. They should get here just before dark tomorrow.

'Excellent!' Jaxaal exclaimed. 'In that case Commander, I would like you to arrange for some of your men to stay here tonight. I want you to spread your men out and to build lots of small camp fires all along this ridge. If the enemy have spies in this area I want them to think that the whole of our army is encamped up here so that they are forced to take up a position on that hill opposite us.'

'Is that wise Milord?' Milden asked, 'you'll be giving the best defensible position to the enemy.'

'That's the whole point,' Jaxaal replied, 'I'm offering an option they will be pleased to take and think it will be an advantage. It may prove to be just that for them or it may, as I hope, be their downfall. The battle the day after tomorrow will tell. We are going to go back to Swenmore now, but we and the rest of the army will leave there tomorrow morning and be back here before sunset. Keep me informed if there are any changes in what we think is going to happen, I don't want the enemy arriving sooner than us.'

The rest of the leadership of the Fameral army made their way back to Swenmore and arrived just as the sun was beginning its final descent towards early evening. There was an air of excitement in the town; everyone knew that the nobles and senior officers had been out to where everyone expected a battle to take place. There was also a lot of activity in the town square where the stage from the previous evening's performance had been cleared and five Archer targets were being set up. The air of expectancy had also been heightened by the arrival of the noble families from Launceston and Dresham, the latter arriving with a fair-sized company of Archers to compete in the evening's competition.

Thirty leagues south west of Swenmore the rebel army were making their slow progress up towards the area Jaxaal had chosen for the battle. News of the gathering Fameral army had reached Natheal as his band had travelled down to the towns and villages of north east Swenland where they had been recruiting men to their cause. He was greatly encouraged by the way his rhetoric had won over so many to march behind their black and white zigzag banner. He had admitted to Pardrea that he didn't really have any specific goals for his rebel army to achieve. His long-term aim had been to overthrow the ruling families and let the people rule themselves, but he had thought no further than the overthrow of the five houses.

His plans to force the farmers to pay higher wages had met with immediate approval with the lower members of society. He was now becoming aware that his initial success was based purely on their greed and the apparent chance to get something for nothing. He had played on the discontent that had been rife among the workers in the outer regions of the former Lord Swenland's realm and been able to get almost as much support from Lord Dresham's outlying districts. In some respects, he regretted not sticking with the original ploy of simply disrupting the hiring fairs, but the new Lord Norland had managed to win back the hearts of a great number of his those living in his main recruiting area. The hiring fairs had become more difficult to manipulate, even with Pardrea putting pressure on the women. The debacle at High Tor had been the last straw and had forced him into instigating this rebel rising far sooner than would have wished.

But it had gone far better than he had dared hope; giving the rebels a banner to follow had been a master stroke. It had given them an identity that they obviously needed. There was an enthusiasm and drive that carried all before it. Deep down he knew he was having trouble controlling the rabble elements in his makeshift army. At the last village his intention had been to approach the village elders to negotiate food and shelter for his army, but he had lost control of his men very rapidly. The pillage and destruction of the homes and livelihoods of honest workers that had taken place before he could resume control had been devastating. He had needed to establish his dominance over his men and the corpses of the worst offenders now hung from the gibbets that he had ordered erected in the village square. He needed this forthcoming battle to focus his men's minds.

The reports that reached him kept him informed of the progress of the Fameral army that Jaxaal Norland was leading against him. He knew he had several times more men than Lord Norland and decided to turn his army around and march to face the oncoming government troops. He had no knowledge of warfare, few Famerians did, but felt sure that he needed to get his men into a position of strength and to then stand and let the smaller numbers of Jaxaal's army expend themselves against his pike wall. What exercises his lieutenant Jorgraan had been able to get the men to carry out had concentrated on getting them to form an impenetrable wall of pikemen; it was his army's only strength.

They marched on up the road towards Swenmore, leaving the ruins of Thrack village in their wake. Natheal had given up trying to get the men to march in three ranks and in step so it was a ramshackle horde that moved along. The rebel army travelled slowly but steadily and made camp some fifteen leagues from where Natheal hoped to deploy his army to face the Famerian Government Army.

Chapter 31

Night fell on the town of Swenmore where an air of excited expectation could almost be tasted. Everyone knew that tomorrow or the next day there would be a battle and if that wasn't enough, tonight there was to be a big Archery Competition. The excitement was contagious as word spread that a great number of expert Archers had arrived from Dresham and several wily entrepreneurs had started offering odds on the possible outcome. When Bry and the other nobles arrived back in the town there was a lot of money changing hands and Bry paused as he made his way through the throng in the town square to look at the odds being offered. He was surprised to find that he was being rated among the top ten along with Straaka. There were a couple of other names he recognised from the Under Childe competitions, but the rest were unknown to him although some were attracting a lot of money and were obviously well know down here in the south-west.

Having assessed the situation in the square he went as quickly as he could to the little inn where they had their lodgings; he was desperate to make sure that Madge was there and that she was all right. He knew that his sudden elevation had upset her although he couldn't see why; as a Quintrall of a main house he was a fitting match for her. Perhaps she didn't see him in that light, perhaps she didn't really love him, although, deep down he couldn't accept that. Their time together in Cannis Glade had welded a bond that he knew would last as long as he breathed.

It was with some relief that he discovered her in the stable, stripped to the waist and drying herself on some sacking having obviously having had a thorough wash. He startled her, and she grabbed the makeshift towel around her to protect her modesty until she realised who it was that had disturbed her ablutions.

'Oh Bry!' she exclaimed as she threw herself at him, dropping the towel and revealing her body, naked to the waist, 'I was beginning to worry that something had happened. I was scared that you had run into the rebels and were lying injured in some ditch along the road.'

'No, you silly breesh hen, I'm well, we're all well and a lot happier now we know the lay of the land where the battle is going to be fought.'

'There will definitely be a battle then?' Madge asked as she pulled up her dress and re-buttoned it.

'Probably the day after tomorrow now, I don't see how it can be avoided,' Bry replied, 'although Jaxaal has said that he will send messages to Natheal Lather asking for a meeting in the morning before things go any further to try and avert a fight. We don't hold out much hope, the rebels are going to be in a strong position when it comes to facing up to them. Jaxaal has some plan but at the moment he's allowed Natheal the most defensible location for his men which means the Fameral army will have to attack uphill against far superior numbers.'

'Are a lot of people going to get hurt or killed?' Madge asked, all the more aware of the implications that a battle held.

'We don't know,' Bry told her, 'no one is still alive from the last time there was a full pitched battle on Fameral soil.

'Oh Alphos! You might get killed or injured,' Madge wailed, and she clung to him.

'I don't think I'll get anywhere near their troops,' Bry reassured her, Jaxaal says I'll be in command of the Archers and well behind our forward troops. I don't know how many Archers there will be. Jaxaal is going to recruit as many volunteers as he can at tonight's competition. He wants me there so the Archers will recognise their commander. I don't know how many there will be; pitifully small numbers I guess.'

'In that case I'll be there as well,' Madge told him, she knew this would be a bone of contention.

'Oh, do be serious,' Bry retorted, 'there's no way I'll countenance you putting yourself at risk on the battle field.'

'I'll be at no more risk than you will, and you needn't think I could possibly stay here while you go off, maybe never to return. Anyway, I think Lady Norland and Geldren Ellward will be there. They have been preparing lots of dressings and antiseptic salves and pain killing potions and other equipment in case they are called upon to treat the wounded.'

'You been to see them, I take it,' Bry replied.

'Yes, I have,' Madge told him her eyes bright and shining and grateful to change the subject, 'My parents have arrived, and I've seen my mother. We were able to spend some time together. Oh Bry, she's forgiven me for running away from home!'

She then went on to relate all that had happened since he had left her that morning. How Janilla and Geldren had changed her appearance with coloured creams that she had only just washed off and how she had worn her wig so that the only difference her mother had perceived was that she had appeared to have shortened her hair by a hands length.

'And your father, what was his reaction?' Bry asked.

'He doesn't know that I've been found,' Madge replied in a small voice, 'he's completely disowned me.'

'Would it help if I went to him and asked for your hand in marriage?' Bry offered.

'I don't know,' Madge replied as she stared at her man in astonishment, 'would you really do that. Would you actually go and face him, just for me?'

'Why not?' Bry asked in reply, 'he may be a ruling lord, but I am now a noble as well. 'In fact, I think I'd better sort out just what I want to do now in my own mind,' he said with a grin as he climbed up to the loft to get a change of clothes ready for the Archery Competition.

'After all,' he told Madge as she too changed into the skirt and blouse that she preferred to wear when using her bow, 'as a lord I may not wish to be associated with a common field worker like you.'

'But I'm not a field worker!' Madge protested, joining in the lightened mood with some relish.

'Ah, but you wanted to be. It is only meeting me that has saved you from that ignominy!'

'Oh, you are an infuriating man!' Madge berated him as she beat him playfully on the chest with her clenched fists before he took her in his arms and kissed her long and hard. They fell back on the hay that made up their bed and lay there in each other's arms for a long time until they heard the first bugle call that announced that Archers wishing to compete in the competition should assemble in the square.

The whole town seemed to be full of bustle and noise as they made their way to the centre. Feeling expansive, Bry purchased some roast kitchen fowl portions from a stall outside one of the inns and they ate them as they made their way to the square. The transformation was almost magical with the abundance of brightly burning torches and lanterns that illuminated the square as if it were day. They made their way to the competition official who sat at a table taking the names of the contestants as they arrived and told them which of the five targets they had been allotted.

As they expected, Madge, Bry and Straaka were all at different targets and would only compete against each other if they reached the final. They bade each other good luck as they went to their allotted places and as she waited for the proceedings to begin Madge made a point of selecting her five best arrows and arranging them in order with the best one in the centre and the next best two in fourth and fifth place. Bry and she had worked out this strategy back in Cannis Glade, reasoning that that order gave them the best options to adjust to the conditions of the actual competition they were in. She sat quietly on her allotted bench and breathed deeply letting her shoulders sag and relax as she breathed out. Bry had told her that this was the best way to relax both body and mind.

Her attempts to relax her mind were somewhat thwarted as she saw the nobles arrive and take their seats in the elevated stand. She was delighted to see that her mother appeared to be in very good spirits but dismayed at the scowl her father seemed to have imprinted on his face. Her mother was sitting next to Janilla beside who was an empty chair, of Jaxaal there was no sign. Geldren Ellward was sitting next in line and chatting to Quintrell Brackenstedd who sat delightedly holding her husband's hand. Next came Lord and Lady Dresham who were talking to Neldon and Festera Swenland. Her brother Crelin and the Dresham children, Sorjohn and Katrina were sitting in the row behind their parents and it was with a pang that Madge realised that in other circumstances that is where she would have been sitting.

'Well perhaps I'll be Quintrell Doltaary if Alphos wills it,' She said to herself, 'and I'll take my place again amongst the nobles.'

Further contemplation was cut short as the official in charge of the competition stood up and called for attention, so Madge didn't see Janilla finally catch sight of her and turn to Lady Launceston.

'There she is,' Janilla told Lady Emileen, 'sitting on the fourth bench along. The dark-skinned girl with brown hair.'

'But that can't possibly be my little Maglen!' Emileen exclaimed, what has she done to herself?'

'Well I did tell you she had disguised herself,' Janilla reminded her, 'that skin colour will fade in a bathern or two and her hair is already growing back to her usual blond colouring.'

'Well, I wouldn't have recognised her if you hadn't pointed her out,' Emileen replied, 'no wonder she has remained hidden all these alphens. So that skin colour I saw this afternoon was simply make-up you had applied. I thought she looked a little pasty-faced.'

'Oh, don't blame me,' Janilla said with a giggle, 'That was Geldren Ellward's doing; I merely helped mixing up the colours.'

'And a very good job you did as well, the two of you,' Emileen replied, giving Geldren an approving nod.

'So that hair was just a wig!' Emileen exclaimed, 'putting things together, no wonder it was so much shorter than it used to be. Well, at least is still reaches her shoulder blades, which is quite acceptable.'

Further whispered conversation was cut short as the official completed his welcoming address and an explanation of the rules for this competition.

'But before the competition actually starts,' the official intoned, 'Lord Norland, the leader of our Fameral Army wishes to say a few words.' This was greeted by a tremendous cheer that made the buildings rattle; as many of the army as could do so had crammed themselves into the square and there was not a single empty standing space anywhere. When he could quieten the crowd down and make himself heard Jaxaal welcomed them all there.

'I'm sorry that it has become necessary for Famerians to take up arms against other Famerians but with Alphos's help we will prevail. We will be heavily outnumbered, but we are trained and if every man remembers what he has been taught and obeys the commands of his officers we are a match for any force this Natheal Lather can put against us.' This was greeted by a few cheers which swelled until the crowd were chanting 'Norland, Norland.' This shook Jaxaal. The last time he had heard chanting like that was just before he ascended to the rule of his house and it had been a chilling experience. He quickly called for quiet again and reminded his audience that this was a 'Famerian' cause and that should be their chant.

'But while we are smaller in numbers we have more advantages other than our better training.' Jaxaal told them, 'we have cavalry, kertle mounted lancers who will drive most standing troops before them and, I am hoping, a new weapon that will prove useful. The very bows that you men, and women, lining up to compete in tonight's competition are about to use. The arrows that you are using tonight are made, I know, for their accuracy but we have a new type of arrow that can be used in battle. Thanks to our smiths we have a good supply of metal tipped arrows and if you Archers will enlist in the Famerian Army you may prove the decisive factor. Any man, or women, who does so enlist will be paid the same as the regular soldiers, a slend a veld, with all your food and accommodation, such as it is, provided. This invitation is not limited to just those competing tonight but to anyone who has a bow and is willing to march tomorrow morning. Well, what do you say?' Jaxaal called raising both arms in the air. This was greeted with another plaster shaking cheer which degenerated into the new chant of 'Fameral, Fameral.'

'Well that went down as well as I hoped it would,' Jaxaal said as he took his place amongst the nobles to watch the competition, 'we'll just have to see how many Archers take up the challenge in the morning.

Some distance southwest of the hill where the expected battle would take place Natheal's men were also making a great deal of noise as they made the most of the ale and food they had plundered from the villages they had ransacked that day.

'Ah well,' their leader said to himself, 'they may as well enjoy themselves. Who knows what the day after tomorrow might bring.'

Pardrea came and sought him out; she had been travelling with the rest of the women in what passed as their baggage train.

'So, brother dear, are we all set for a glorious victory in two days' time?' she asked, helping herself to a flagon of wine from the store set aside for the commander of the rebels and dropping down beside him.

'Well, who knows,' Natheal replied, 'we should prevail. The reports I've received suggest that we outnumber them by probably five to one and I hope to have a hill to defend. It will be difficult for them to dislodge us from it.'

'Do you know who is leading them?' Pardrea asked.

''I'm not absolutely sure,' Natheal replied, 'the reports I received to start with suggested that it was Guardian Commodore Mustoove who Jorgraan told me was a crusty old stick-in-the-mud officer of the old school. He said we'd have no problem predicting what the old fool would do but the latest news is that Jaxaal Norland has taken charge of what they are calling 'The Fameral Army'.'

'Is that a problem?' Pardrea asked.'

'I've really no idea,' Natheal confessed as he stood up and began to pace up and down, 'He is an unknown quantity. He suddenly appeared at the last Challenge when he won and got the House of Norland reinstated. He's made a success of managing the Norland properties by all accounts. That's one reason we're here, now. If Norland had been as mismanaged as the Swenland lands used to be, we might have had more success with disrupting their hiring fairs. Not that Swenland is the easy pickings it used to be. This Darval

Ellward who was appointed as regent has made some big changes. This war has become inevitable.'

'We are going to win though, aren't we?' Pardrea asked again. Natheal realised that his sister was becoming very nervous about the forthcoming conflict and tried to reassure her.

'We are certain to win,' he boasted, 'and you and I will be eating at the best restaurants in Medland in a couple of velds.'

Chapter 32

The Archery Competition Official finally managed to get control of the crowd in Swenmore town centre and as the last chants of 'Fameral, Fameral' died away the first five Archers took their places. The other Archers in Madge's group decided to be courteous and let her shoot first. She prepared her bow and notched an arrow, taking long slow breaths to steady her nerves. As Bry had trained her to do, she took careful aim, concentrating on where she wanted the arrow to hit the target. She took a deep breath and held it waiting for what breeze there was to die down. She released the arrow and watched with satisfaction as it struck the target just nicking the white centre circle. A gasp came from most of the other competitors in her group who were suddenly wondering why they had been so generous towards her. The round of applause that her shot generated drew the attention of everyone around her and she heard Bry's voice congratulating her.

As for Bry, he was having trouble controlling his emotions; so much had happened in such a short space of time. The last time he had competed in a bow competition he had been just Bry Woodsman, virtually a tramp living from hand to mouth and desperate to win the competition to get the money bag he badly needed. Now he was Quintrall Doltaary of the House of Swenland and potentially a rich man. On top of that, against all the odds he had the love of the most wonderful woman he had ever met. It took a lot of self-control to calm himself down and steady his breathing and heartbeat. He had watched Madge take her first shot, willing her to do well. He saw her go through the ritual they had developed to steady themselves before firing and his heart had leapt for joy as her first shot in real competition had hit the white centre circle on her target. Now it was his turn and he took the same care in preparing to fire. His arrow flew straight and true and hit the target a fingerbreadth away from the white centre bringing forth a great cheer and few shouts which revealed that the callers knew him for the champion of Under Childe, despite his changed appearance.

There were over sixty competitors and it took a while for the twelve or so Archers at each target to take their turns. Because of the congestion, each target area had to be cleared of the arrows that had made their mark and bounced to the ground after each round. Both Bry and Madge had agreed to make sure that they retrieved their own arrows after each shot to protect the secret way their shafts were fledged. The twisted feathering that gave their arrows the rotation in flight was a secret Bry wanted to keep to himself, for a while at least. Tomorrow most of these Archers would be using the arrows that Rydall had made on his 'arrow jig' and they all had the twisted flights.

The competition continued into the second and then third rounds. As she had already hit the whiter disc on her target Madge could sit back and relax watching the other competitors take their turns. She saw Bry hit the black part of the target just outside the white circle with his second shot and as far as she could tell no one on his target had done better. A great shout went up as a Archer at the target three along from Madge's hit the white circle fairly in the centre and she saw Straaka raise his bow a loft and shake it in triumph.

To Madge's joy, Bry's third shot hit the white circle almost exactly in the centre; it was almost certain that he would not be beaten and would be in the final.

At the target immediately to her left Madge kept an eye on a Archer dressed in the colours of The House of Dresham who she saw was taking the same care to prepare himself for each shot as Bry had taught her to do. Sure enough, he was obviously an expert and his third shot hit the white disc on his target. No one else on that target had got anywhere near the centre. The Archers on Madge's target were faring little better that the Dresham Archer's competitors and she wasn't called upon to fire again.

'Would you believe it!' one of her competitors complained, 'we let her go first, she gets a lucky shot to just nick the white and she goes through to the final.' Madge was incensed.

'You don't have to fire again, Miss,' the judge at her target told her, 'but you have four arrows left; do you wish to try and better your first shot?'

'Yes, I'm sure I can do better than that,' she replied glaring at the Archer who had derided her. She took careful aim, relaxed her breathing and concentrated on the white disc. Her arrow flew straight but dipped at the last moment, hitting the target a fingers breadth below the white disc. A gasp came from the competitors behind her.

'That's the next best shot on this target,' the judge told her, 'the only one better than that was your first arrow.' Madge tried to not to smirk as she selected her best arrow and prepared to fire again. The whole town square went quiet as she prepared herself; the competitions at the other targets had all completed and she was the last Archer standing in the firing pit. Madge was unaware of any of this, her training and practice had taken over and she took as much care with this shot as she had the first two. She allowed herself to adjust the point at which she was aiming to be the top of the white disc; she wanted to compensate more for the distance than she had previously done. The arrow arched across the space between her and the target and hit the white disc fully in the centre.

There was an explosion of noise as the whole square erupted in a cheer and shout that matched any that had gone before; the crowd loved it. There was the prospect of a thrilling final to come. Away in the noble's stand Janilla was sitting with Jaxaal and Geldren and next to Lady Launceston who was in an elevated emotional state. This had been the day she had dreamed of for alphens; her daughter had been restored to her and she had held her and kissed her. The fact that Maglen had then insisted that she had things to do and must leave her mother for a while had come as a disappointment but her discussions with Janilla, Lady Norland, had reassured her. She was at a loss to know how to proceed with her husband who seemed to be working himself into a position of intractability against his runaway daughter. Janilla had promised that she would see what could be done. Not that Emileen Launceston held out much hope, she knew her husband very well; she had suffered his moods and rages all their married life.

'Well what do you think of your daughter now?' Janilla asked in a whisper to Lady Launceston.

'I think that the little girl who ran away from home has become a very competent self-assured young woman!' Emileen exclaimed in shocked delight and stood up and waved at her daughter.

Madge couldn't resist a triumphant look at the Archer she had beaten and who had made disparaging remarks. She then turned to look at the nobles after she had exchanged blown kisses of congratulation with Bry and was astonished to see her mother waving excitedly at her. She gave a little wave in return and set about moving her bow and equipment to the new shooting pit that was being set up for the final. She missed her father saying something to her mother.

'Do you know that southern woman?' Lord Launceston asked surprised that his wife should put on such a display.

'Well, I met her this afternoon when I was looking around the town,' Emileen improvised, she never told me she was skilled Archer and competing tonight.'

'Well sit down, woman,' the lord snapped, 'you're making a spectacle of yourself.'

The final was to be shot over a greater distance than the first elimination round and it took a while for the officials to set up the new target and make sure the press of people did not impinge on the firing area, so great was the interest to see the action.

'Did I see you wave to your mother?' Bry asked as they met in the rear of the shooting pit where the final competitors were given a bit of space to prepare themselves.

'Yes, I think Janilla must have told her who I was despite my disguise. As I told you, I met her this afternoon while you were away on the trip to the battlefield,' Madge replied.

'I take it your wig did come in useful after all.' Bry grinned, 'does that mean you are reconciled with your parents?' he asked, hopefully.

'No, I'm afraid it doesn't,' she replied, 'my father doesn't know who I am or that I'm here and he has disowned me,' she finished with a sob.

Bry put his hand on her shoulder, desperately wanting to give her a hug but knowing that would be out of place at that moment. They both turned and congratulated Straaka who had won his heat and was literally giving another Archer a pat on the back.

'Ah we three meet again,' the big man said as they joined him, 'This is Thrackeen,' he told them indicating the Archer dressed in The House of Dresham colours, 'He's beaten me almost as often as you have Bry. But he's a good man, despite that.'

'Ah, you're the new Quintrall of The House of Swenland,' Thrackeen said as he clasped Bry's hand, 'will you be leading this new Archer army?'

'Lord Norland has asked me to do that, Yes,' Bry replied, 'and this is my partner Madge,' he added including Madge in to the conversation. He had been sorely tempted to introduce her as his wife but was able to restrain himself in time, they could do without that complication just at this moment. They all acknowledged that they needed to sit or stand quietly and compose themselves for the competition still ahead of them.

A hush fell over the square as the competition official stood and signalled for quiet. When the hubbub had virtually disappeared, he announced the names of the five finalists and it was with some horror that Madge realised that she had called herself 'Madge Woodsman,' the name she had been using for so long. To her relief Bry was introduced before her using his real name, Bryland Doltaary. Again, out of courtesy, the four men decided that Madge should fire first, and she felt nervous as she took her stance. Now every eye was upon her and she prepared herself, carefully selecting her third best arrow.

The target was now a good half as much again away as the first-round ones had been and it seemed very small across the other side of the square. The greater distance was emphasised by the darker area half way between the shooting pit and the target; all the torches that lit the square had been moved to illuminate the two places leaving a gap in the middle. As she had been taught she again took her stance, breathed steadily and calmly before holding her breath and taking aim. Her arrow streaked across the square, seemingly disappearing as it left the lighted shooting pit only to reappear as it struck the target. It was a good shot, hitting the black area a hands breadth below and to the right of the white disc. A great cheer went up from the crowd; the final had got off to a great start and the excitement was mounting.

The other Archer and then Thrackeen then took their turns both hitting the target but no closer than Madge had done. Straaka was next to fire and his shot seemed to equal Madge's but high and to the right. Bry was the last to fire and he went through the same ingrained ritual that he had taught Madge. His arrow streaked away and hit the target directly below the white disc. This gave the officials a problem as they had three arrows of equal merit and they couldn't say which of them was the best and which Archer need not fire in the next round unless beaten.

By nodded agreement the three of them decided to all fire again. This decision was announced to another great cheer but a few groans from those in the audience who had placed bets on who would lead after the first round. All five Archers then fired again but none of them were able to better any of the three better shots fired in the first round. Then Thrackeen appeared to take the lead with an arrow that almost touched the white spot. The other Archer's shot actually missed the target and his arrow thudded into the straw bale wall placed behind the target. Madge said she would fire next which again was just a ploy to control her nerves.

She had been watching the other's arrows carefully and realised that they all veered slightly right at the last moment and she looked away into the gloom. Sure enough, she saw what the cause of this divergence might be. The target area used for the final target was marked by a road that crossed the square at the far end. This road passed through the line of houses and a wind was blowing through that gap. She saw a piece of straw blow right across in front of the target, proving the point.

She fired her third shot and this time allowed for the extra wind that was blowing down there Her arrow flew straight and true and hit the white disc just off the very centre, putting her in the lead. Her success was met with a tremendous cheer by the crowd who were loving the changing fortunes happening before them.

Sensing the crowds growing fervour the chief official announced that they would now operate the 'worst first' rule. Madge turned to Bry and Straaka asking what that meant.

'Well, as you know,' Bry told her, 'when one Archer is clearly in the lead, as you are now, the others take it in turn to fire their remaining arrows until one of them makes a better shot and becomes the leader. Under the 'worst first' rule the Archer with the worst shot is the next to fire and he, or she, will keep firing until they beat the next worst Archer, or they use all five of their arrows.'

'It gives a more entertaining spectacle for the audience,' Straaka added, 'but it means that we have to line up, worst to best.' The official then took charge and asked the five Archers to sit in the order that their success dictated. The first Archer then took his fourth and then his fifth shot without bettering his previous best effort and was thus eliminated. His disappointment was assuaged by the size of the money bag he was handed for reaching the final.

Thrackeen then took the firing position and was able to beat Straaka's best shot with his last arrow. This meant that he was placed third and that Straaka had to fire again. With his last arrow Straaka beat both Bry and Madge's best shots moving him into the lead. Bry was then next in line and his first shot hit the white disc almost in the centre; it was going to be almost impossible to beat him. Madge felt suddenly very nervous as she took her position to fire her fourth arrow. Her ingrained routine stood her in good stead but her next shot was a little rushed and hit the target close to but just off the white disc. She drew herself together and she made her nerves take a back seat, taking her time to study the target, picturing just where she wanted her arrow to land. The shot flew straight and true through the cool night air and her allowance for the crosswind was perfect.

A tremendous cheer went up as her arrow struck home and many, including Bry and Straaka thought she must have beaten them but the scoring officials took a long time checking the measurements of the marks that Bry and her best arrows had made. Eventually they made their decision and made a performance of announcing the results.

Usually the results of Archery Competitions were obvious, but this had been a much higher quality competition and as such had got the closer finish that it deserved. The chief official took great pleasure in the 'theatre' he was creating and called for silence. He didn't get complete silence but did manage to get the crowd to quieten enough for his voice to be heard.

'My Lords, Ladies and gentlemen,' he declared in what he felt was suitably sonorous tone, 'I can now announce the results of this celebration Archer's Competition. We are fortunate to have the heads of four of the ruling houses here with us tonight.' This was greeted by a great patriotic cheer from all round the square.

'I am delighted to announce that Lords Swenland, Norland and Launceston have agreed to do us the honour of presenting the prizes to the first, second and third prize winners.' This too met with cheers so that Lord Launceston, who was about to decline the offer to participate felt obliged to do so.

Jaxaal was asked if he would give the third prize winner his money bag, which he did with great pleasure and as Straaka received his money bag cries of 'Norland, Norland,' rang out around the square. Jaxaal was a little taken aback by this. This whole competition was intended to celebrate Lord Neldon Swenland's elevation to ruler of his house, but Jaxaal accepted it in good faith; it was a measure of the patriotism that pervaded the town.

As Lord Launceston was asked to come and present the second prize to the runner up who was announced as 'Madge Woodsman' the whole square erupted in a celebration of the implied announcement that Bry had won the competition. Madge was so delighted, secretly she dreaded the idea that she might have beaten him, her relief flowed through her; he deserved to be the winner. She grabbed him in a full embrace and kissed him full on the lips; she didn't care that her parents were standing just behind them, she was so proud of the man she loved.

As she did this she missed the little scene that played out behind her; her mother had taken her husband's arm and stopped him stepping forward so that she could whisper in his ear.

'Be nice to her,' she said with a sudden rush of blood to the head, 'after all, she is your daughter!'. The emotion on the moment had overridden her common sense although deep down she reasoned that Lord Launceston would not make a scene here in public and she so desperately wanted her daughter back in her family where she belonged. Even with that in her mind she was aware that she may have already lost Maglen, her little girl, to the separation that adulthood would bring; the embrace and kiss she saw Maglen give this Bryland Doltaary spoke volumes of the changes she had undergone.

Chapter 33

Lord Launceston was, for once in his life, totally dumbfounded and lost for words; Emileen's little speech was still reverberating around his head and he stared hard at the dusky woman who was now standing waiting to receive her prize. He stepped forward and took the money bag from the official and held it out to Madge who came forward, curtsied and accepted the bag, momentarily holding her father's hand. Over his shoulder she saw her mother standing with tears running down her smiling face.

Madge took the bag and then leant up and whispered, 'thank you, papa D,' the name she had always called him when she was a little girl, still in the nursery. The Lord just stood and stared, totally lost for words. In that instance he did recognise his daughter and in a display of emotion he rarely used took her in a full embrace and hugged her.

The presentation of the first prize then took place, Neldon handing his Quintrall the large bag that held his winnings. He then turned to Lord Launceston who was still holding his daughters hand.

'Lord Launceston,' Neldon said as he turned to face the northern noble, 'may I introduce an old friend and my new House Quintrall, Bryland Doltaary.'

Bry stepped forward and took the offered lord's hand in the accepted hand clasp appropriate to the greeting of two nobles.

'Congratulations, young man,' Lord Launceston said, 'that was a fine display you and your fellow Archers put on, I've never seen the like. I gather that you will be leading this new Archer army that Lord Norland has called for.'

'I have that honour,' Bry replied, 'we hope to play a significant part in the forthcoming battle.'

'I should add,' Neldon interjected, 'that Bryland is named as Quintrall but will need to be married to assume that place.' He then turned to Madge and taking a large bag from his other pocket, 'I believe I owe you this for returning my Quintrall to me,' he told her with a big smile on his face as he handed the bag to her. Madge nearly dropped the heavy bag; it obviously contained the fifty strands he had promised to anyone who found Bry.

'I think we need to get away from these celebrations,' Jaxaal said as he indicated the festivities that had broken out all around the square, 'there are still some things that we need to discuss before tomorrow and I feel that this might also be the time to sort out some other matters.' It was not lost on Madge that Janilla, who was standing on the fringe of the group, gave a smiling nod to her husband and then a big grin to her. Madge knew her well enough to realise that Janilla had been up to something behind the scenes and that was confirmed as Lady Norland took Emileen Launceston's arm and guided her through the throng.

To Madge's amazement, her father kept her hand in his as they too made their way in their Ladyship's wake. With Bry walking on her other side she was in a total emotional daze as they reached the largest inn and went through to the large dining room which had been set aside for them.

'I thought you had disowned me after I ran away,' Madge whispered to her father as they sat down at the well laid table.

'I had, you little minx,' he replied with a rueful smile, 'and I never intended to speak to you again but when your mother told me just who had done so well in the competition and you called me 'Papa D', the way you used to, well, I knew I had my little Maggie back.'

Madge couldn't stop the tears streaming down her face and she leant over and kissed her father tenderly on the cheek and gripped his arm in a firm, relieved grasp. Bry was amazed at the transformation in the woman he loved; he knew how scared she had been of her father's reaction. This closeness was a revelation.

'Lord Launceston,' Jaxaal said as he came and sat on the Lords other side, 'I feel we need to sort out a few things and while this may not be the best place, it is certainly the best time. I am well aware of the significance in your reunion with Maglen and as you know I am conscious of the reasons for her previous disappearance. I think you are also aware that situations in other houses now need resolving.'

Lord Launceston sat a little bemused; this was not at all what he expected.

'Your house still needs to establish firm trading links with one of the southern houses to give you access to the supply of-good grain that you need, and you need to develop a good outlet for your wool. Am I right?' Jaxaal asked.

'Well, yes that has always been the need of us northern houses,' Lord Launceston replied, 'as you well know.'

'Quite so,' Jaxaal agreed, 'I am fortunate in that I am married to a daughter of The House of Swenland and have those ties to cement the relationship between our houses. I make no secret that I am also negotiating trade agreements with The House of Dresham,' and he nodded at Lord and Lady Dresham who were engrossed in the meal that had been serve.

'May I suggest that you could now establish the links you require with a southern house by allowing your daughter to marry a senior member of the House of Swenland.'

'Why do I feel that I am now being manoeuvred into a position I was trying to achieve for myself a couple of Batherns ago,' Lord Launceston said with a wry smile, 'admittedly that was with the House of Dresham.'

'Ah,' Janilla said as she joined her husband for the meal, 'that was an option that was never going to be open to you,' and she looked across the room to another table where Crelin and Geldren were sitting with Katrina and ,Sorjohn Dresham. It was lost on no one that Geldren had moved her chair very close to Sorjohn's and apparently presuming they were unobserved, was holding Sorjohn's hand under the table.

'I need to have a quiet word with my cousin as to what is and what is not the right way to go about courting the man you've set your heart on,' Janilla whispered with a giggle.

Neldon then joined the group at their table and Janilla, with a malicious glint in her eye set about questioning her brother on what he, as Lord of the House of Swenland would want in the way of links with the House of Launceston. The conversation went on in a very stilted way for some time until Lord Launceston decided that enough was enough.

'All right, all of you,' he announced in a very stern voice but with a big grin on his face, 'I can see where this is going, let's cut to the quick. I've made a mistake in these matters in the past; I'll not do so again. Maglen,' he said as he turned to his daughter whose hand he still held, 'would you be prepared to marry Quintrall Doltaary of the House of Swenland to please me?'

Madge looked at her father and then at Bry, who sat opposite her and with tears filling her eyes said in a clear voice that the whole room could hear, 'No father, I will not marry Bryland Doltaary to please you, but I will marry him if that is what he wants.'

'It had better be,' Janilla retorted, 'if my cousin Felda was here she'd say, 'you had better do so, or she'd kick your ankles,' but since she is away in Ellward I'll kick you both, hard, if you don't!'

'It would appear Madge darling,' Bry said as he stood and reached across and took her free hand, 'that we have no option!'

'At last!' Janilla exclaimed, 'you've made the right choice, all of you,' she said to her brother and Lord Launceston and the happy couple who had moved around to the end of the table and were embracing each other.

'When will the marriage be?' Lady Launceston asked suddenly panicking that that Launceston Hall was in no fit state for a big social event. People looked at each other somewhat nonplussed; these sudden events had taken everyone's breath away.

'Now, tonight!' Madge announced, 'there will be a battle the day after tomorrow and I'm not letting Bry, er, Bryland,' she corrected herself, 'go into that without having married me first. We will be marching away tomorrow morning so there won't be time then.' This was met with astonished gasps around the room, but Madge was not to be deflected.

'All we need is the town clerk to come and make the official record of the union and any of you noble lords can officiate,' she said and stared down everyone in the room daring them to argue. Her mother did start to complain that these things should be done with time and care in their planning.

'Yes, I know mother,' Madge said as she went and hugged her parent, 'in normal circumstances, I would agree with you, but these are anything but normal circumstances.'

Discussions then hastily took place and all sorts of solution to the myriad of problems that presented themselves were considered. It was as if everyone in the room took ownership of the impending wedding and arrangements were made to get Madge redressed in a suitable gown and for her bride's attendants. Madge asked Geldren, Janilla and Katrinna to fulfil those roles and Bry turned to Neldon to be his groom attendant. The party then split into groups with Madge and the younger noble ladies disappearing to Janilla's apartments to see what they could rustle up in the way of a bridal gown and bridesmaid's' dresses while Bry and the young male nobles went to Neldon's room.

Ladies Launceston and Dresham then set about organising the celebration catering with the landlord. The poor man was already overstretched as he was playing host to several of the country's ruling families as well as the tremendous influx of customers that the arrival of the Fameral Army had entailed. Despite the already heavy demands on his supplies he did promise that he would put on a buffet supper despite the short notice.

It was almost an afterthought that Lord Launceston remembered that the town clerk needed to be dragged out of his home and asked to attend the nobles to officiate and deal with the legal requirements. In a surprisingly short space of time all the component parts were assembled, and the wedding could actually take place. Neither Bry or Madge could quite believe the speed with which their lives hand turned around and it hit them both as they stood together in front of the town clerk and Lord Dresham who had agreed to officiate. Surrounded by nearly all the nobles in the land Madge and Bry became Lord Bryland and Lady Maglen Doltaary, Quintrall and Quintrell of The House of Swenland.

It was Emileen Launceston who thought to ask Madge where they newlyweds would be spending their wedding night.

'Oh, I hadn't thought about that,' Madge told her, 'I suppose we'll have to go back to our little inn on the outskirts of the town where we've been staying.'

'But surely, can't we find you a room somewhere more fitting,' Emileen complained.

'Possibly,' Madge replied, 'but we have our kertles that will need attending to, we will need them tomorrow.'

'What do you mean 'you will need the tomorrow;' you don't intend to go and be part of this awful war do you?'

'Mother, Fameral needs all the men, especially Archers, it can get,' Madge replied defiantly.

'Men, yes,' Emileen pleaded, 'but not women! You've no place in the middle of a battle.'

'Mother, I proved tonight that I'm one of the best Archers in the country, Fameral needs me,' Madge told her brooking no denial.'

'I can see that there is to be no arguing with you,' Emileen conceded. She was secretly delighted at the self-assured young women her daughter had become and decided to raise another matter that had crossed her mind from something that Janilla let drop. In a whisper meant only for her daughter's ears she broached the subject. 'Maglen, I know you are now a respectable married woman but just how have you been living you and Bryland? You obviously have had a very close relationship.'

'Yes, we have,' Madge admitted, 'but I promise you, I am going to my marriage bed as a maid, but I won't get up as one,' and she blushed deeply.

As they made their way back to their humble sleeping place Bry and Madge clung closely to each other as much as because of the crush of people that thronged the streets as the emotions that were flowing over them. Despite the passions that they had bottled up for so long they made a point of tending to Rufran and Tilda's needs before they climbed up to their straw strewn marriage bedroom.

Madge again woke in a glorious haze of contentment and had the same emotions she had experienced the morning after she and Bry had spent their first night together but now she felt fulfilled and totally satisfied physically and mentally. Bry had proved to be a gentle and sympathetic lover but who matched her own desire and appetite for bodily satisfaction. As she started to drift towards consciousness in the early dawn she was aware that, as usual he was lying snuggled up to her back with his arm across her shoulder. The difference was that for the first time they were both completely naked. She realised that his arm was where it had been every night for the past two batherns and she moved it so that his hand naturally fell across her breast. She was rewarded by Bryland, though still asleep, gently caressing the soft roundness. Contented she drifted back to sleep.

Later that same morning, several leagues further south of Swenmore Natheal finally managed to get the rabble army to resume their march but knew he had to keep them going through the heat of the day. It took all his ability as a leader to get the response he needed and to keep them travelling so that they would keep their rendezvous with destiny on the morrow.

Chapter 34

Madge and Bry both awoke an hour or so later when one of the kertles snorted at something and they became aware of movement out in the inn yard. They both jumped out of bed and set about starting the day; they knew it would be a long and busy one. Once they had washed and dressed they realised that they did not have to dash off immediately and Madge decided that she was now able to treat them both to a breakfast in the inn. The landlord was delighted to welcome the winners of the previous evening's competition. He was almost beside himself when Madge revealed their new titles and she had to insist that he didn't keep referring to them as Lord and Lady Doltaary. The landlord took this as a great honour and was sorry to see them packing up all their belongings as they prepared to leave to join the departing army.

'Don't worry,' Bry told him, 'we'll be sure to visit you again if we're back this way. I won't forget your generosity to us when we were in desperate need of accommodation,' Bry told him as he paid their dues and included a large tip.

The Fameral army began to assemble in the town square which had miraculously been cleared after the previous evening's competition. As Madge and Bry entered they were immediately aware of where the Archers were gathering as Straaka stood on a large cart and was calling all Archers to him. The cart was one of two that Rydall had brought from High Tor which were crammed with his new mass-produced arrows. As Bry and Madge arrived and dismounted a young boy ran up and nervously told Bry that Lord Norland would like him to attend him in the centre of the square.

Jaxaal was giving his last instructions to his section leaders on how he wanted the army to travel. Basically, the main force would march in two groups with the Archers in between them. The baggage train would follow with the mounted lancers behind them. He reasoned that if trouble arose on the journey the untrained Archers and the civilians in the baggage wagons would be protected. The lancers would guard the rear and, due to the speed of their mounts, be able to deploy quickly should the need arise elsewhere in the column. Jaxaal was sure that there was no risk of ambush along the way; the intelligence from the trained guardians assured him the rebels were all together and approaching the area he had chosen for the battle.

They made good time on the journey.

It was the start of the harvest bathern season and the days could be mild; this was one of those. Their officers encouraged their men to sing as they marched, and this lightened the mood and the journey. At Jaxaal's insistence they made regular stops so that the men could get a break for personal needs and some light refreshment. This improved the men's conditions and helped with the general disposition of the troops. In this way they made good time and by mid-afternoon they were able to reach the ridge where Jaxaal had planned for them to spend the night and to make their stand.

The men were ordered to make camp and get themselves bedded down for the night and the number of campfires along the ridge made a clear signal of where they were.

As the dusk was falling the rebel army was approaching the area that Natheal had noted on their journey south. He knew they were on the south side of a suitable hill which his army could defend; he was thankful that they had reached it before they made camp for the night. Many of his men desperately wanted to stop long before they reached Natheal's goal but by force of his character he made them carry on until the sun had set.

As his men slumped to the ground, Natheal climbed up the hill with his second in command and as they crested the rise they saw a ring of camp fires on the ridge the other side of the shallow valley before them.

'There!' Natheal said in triumph, turning to Jorgraan, 'we've managed to get the better place to make a stand. Jaxaal Norland will have to fight hard to dislodge us from this hill and his little army will die trying. Get the men bedded down where they are so the enemy over there cannot see our camp fires, but I want men posted up here to keep an eye on the enemy camp. If they move, I want to know about it.'

As he returned to the impromptu camp was a little disconcerted that the men still seemed to have ample supplies of ale and wine and they were obviously going to make the most of them.

'*Who can blame them,*' Natheal thought, '*who knows how many won't be drinking anything tomorrow night!*'

Pardrea again came and sought out her sibling. 'Are we ready for this fight?' she asked.

'As ready as we can be,' Natheal replied, 'if we're not, it's too late now.'

'Should we try and talk to this Jaxaal Norland and see if we can get sensible terms?' she suggested.

'What!' Natheal shouted 'surrender! Are you mad woman? We outnumber them at least five to one.'

'No, not surrender,' Pardrea snapped back, 'but just because we outnumber them perhaps we can get them to, well, just go away. I don't suppose they want anyone to get hurt any more than we do.'

'That's just the point, you stupid woman,' Natheal retorted, 'we've got to destroy this government army so that there is no further resistance. If we let any of them escape, we'll never know when they are going to attack us as we march on Medland to claim our rightful place.

'So, tomorrow is a fight to the death?'

'Their death, yes,' Natheal assured her and he opened another flagon of wine.

As the night came on Commander Northwood sought out Jaxaal Norland having made yet another round of his observers and received their reports.

'What's the news Milden?' Jaxaal asked as the senior Guardian officer dismounted and entered the leader's tent.

'As good as we had hoped, Jaxaal,' Milden replied, having first established that they were on their own. He was proud that Jaxaal insisted that they be on first name terms, but it was a privilege he was careful not to abuse. 'The last reports suggest they are bedding down on the other side of the hill.'

'Good,' Jaxaal replied offering a jug of kandrel to the Commander to help himself, 'things are knitting into place quite nicely.'

'If you can call giving the enemy the best position,' Milden replied. He still didn't understand Jaxaal's reasoning and the Lord went through how he intended the battle to progress.

'Well it's a good plan, if it works and the enemy are obliging enough to react the way you want them to,' Milden commented.

'If they don't or if the plan doesn't have the effect I want I've a few fall-back positions in reserve. Neldon's lancers are an unknown factor that could prove very effective. I wouldn't want to face a man on a charging kertle who's holding a sharp pole at my chest! But I think the real hope lies with the Archers.'

'You think those toys can really do some damage?' Milden asked.

'Yes, they can be very impressive in the right hands.'

Just then a guardian officer arrived and handed Milden a short message. He looked at the parchment and smiled.

'This confirms that the rebels have made camp the other side of the hill,' he reported.

'Excellent,' Jaxaal replied, 'now get your men well rested and keep a watch out, I don't want to be surprised by a sneak attack under cover of darkness.'

'Very good my Lord,' Milden replied returning to the formal form of address while his junior was present, 'I don't think there's much risk of that, the report says that they are exhausted and are simply collapsing where they stand.'

Jaxaal was amazed at the information the guardians were able to collect; he could only wonder at the skill and expertise a trained guardian possessed. He had a little insight into their rigorous training from the odd comments his brother in law had let slip about his time as a guardian.

Chapter 35

The morning of the battle dawned cold and damp; a thin mist covered the ground shielding everything in the valley from view. Jaxaal was up early and having washed and dressed as best he could he snatched a quick breakfast eating flat bread and smoked hog's meat slices crouching by a campfire. There were the sounds of activity all around as the camp stirred and men prepared themselves, trying to get some warmth back in bodies chilled by the night in the open.

Madge and Bry had fared better than most; they were used to sleeping 'rough.' They had spent the worse time of the turn in Cannis Glade and their bodies were attuned to effectively camping in the open. Apart from which, they had spent their second night as husband and wife snuggled together in warm sleeping furs lying next to Rufran's body. The kertle had provided some warmth and a useful windbreak.

Jaxaal went and tended to Sarina who had fared very well in a thick kertle shroud. She was delighted to see her master and squealed when he appeared to groom and saddle her. As soon as she was ready Jaxaal leapt on her back and they trotted back up the hill behind their camp. He started the journey in a chill mist that shrouded everything, but they quickly climbed above the thin fog and were met by a dazzling sunlight that rebounded off the feathery whiteness. Jaxaal's first instinct was to look over to the hill where the rebels were expected to take their stand and sure enough he could see the hilltop was now being covered by a coating of men wearing the beige, smock coloured tunics that the rebels had adopted as their uniform.

He immediately returned down the hill and sought out Milden who was in his command tent and receiving verbal reports from guardian officers.

'Ah Milden, have you heard about the enemy's disposition?' he asked.

'Yes, my Lord,' Milden replied, tacitly acknowledging the presence of some of his junior officers, 'they have taken the bait you left for them and are occupying the hilltop as we speak.'

'Yes, I've just been up into the clear air to see them for myself. So far, so good. How quickly can we get our men in battle formation?' he asked.

'Very quickly My Lord,' Milden replied, 'I'll have the bugler sound the appropriate call straight away.'

He issued some rapid orders to a guardian standing waiting for just such instructions who disappeared out of the tent. A few moments a bugle sounded a particular series of notes and after a suitable pause, repeated them.

Away on the hilltop opposite the bugle call was heard and received with mixed understanding. Natheal and Pardrea had risen early and were pacing around on the very summit of the hill.

'There, they're only just waking up,' Pardrea crowed, 'I told you we should have attacked as soon as it was possible to see the ground at our feet. It could have all been over by now!'

'But it does mean we are more prepared than they are,' Natheal told her, 'if they are only just waking up.'

'I fear not, Sir and Miss,' Jorgraan told them. His memory of the meaning of guardian bugle calls had not diminished even though he had been drummed out of the service several turns before.

'That is the call to form into battle formation. I fear they are ahead of us in terms of the readiness of their troops.'

'But there are only a few men wandering about over there!' Pardrea pointed out indicating the gentle slope that rose out of the mist down in the valley.

Jorgraan looked across where she was pointing, shielding his eyes against the bright spring sun that was shining in their faces.

'I'm afraid they are just a few look-outs who are no doubt relaying our every move to their commanders.'

A cold chill ran down Natheal's back as he realised the organisation and training his cobbled together army were facing.

'But we still out-number them five-to-one,' he said trying to recover some cheer from the situation.

Away on the ridge the scene was still shrouded in mist as the divisions of The Fameral Government Army lined up. The government men began to feel the warmth of the sun breaking through and as it began to win against the night mist, they were able to see the hill opposite. When it had disappeared enough for the tops of the bushes on the valley floor to be seen, Jaxaal called Commander Northwood to him.

'Milden I'm going to go and see if I can talk to this Natheal Lather, under a flag of truce. Are you prepared to accompany me?'

Of course, my Lord,' the Guardian replied, 'I'll get a white flag pinned to a staff and join you, I assume we'll be mounted.'

Milden did as he had promised and asked Bry and Madge to arm themselves with their bows and to secret themselves in the bushes at the bottom of the slope they were on.

'Don't do anything unless these rebels don't honour the white flag but I'll feel more comfortable if I know Lord Norland isn't going into this parley totally unprotected,' he told them. The newlyweds then took their bows and a supply of tipped arrows down to the bottom of the hill. They were able to get themselves hidden before the mists cleared enough to reveal their progress.

Jaxaal mounted Sarina and he and Milden trotted down the hill and onto the valley floor. This development caused a lot of comment in the rebel ranks and there were more than a few cat calls. When Jaxaal reached the centre of the valley he stopped and called out in a voice loud enough for everyone in both armies to hear him.

'Natheal Lather, I am Jaxaal Norland,' he called, 'I would have a word with you.'

This caused even more comments and a ripple of whispered conversations ran around the rebel army. The two government men waited patiently which proved too much for the highly-strung Sarina. The racer was uncomfortable not being able to see her feet and she kept jerking and starting at unseen and imaginary dangers in the mist at her ankles. Milden's mount was a sturdy dray and not given to such nervous tension. Unlike Sarina he had been out on early morning manoeuvres with the guardians on exercises so often that the phenomenon of ground mist was a familiar experience.

They waited for what seemed quite a while before Natheal appeared standing on a small knoll that protruded from the rebel held hill some way above the two mounted men.

'What do you want Norland,' he shouted down making it sound like a sneer, 'have you come to surrender?'

'Far from it,' Jaxaal replied, 'I've come to offer you terms. If you and your men will lay down your arms and walk away from here in peace, no further action will be taken.'

'You can't be serious!' Natheal called and there were shouts and jeers of derision from the men around him, 'we out number you at least five to one. Now if your men lay down their arms we will let them go.'

'Yes, you out number us,' Jaxaal called in reply, 'but we are trained and well-armed and have the law on our side. If you insist on fighting us, you and your men are committing treason against the lawful government of this nation. Most of you will die and those that don't will be tried in the courts for your crime of treason.'

'Your words don't frighten us,' Natheal taunted but deep down he knew that Jaxaal's words would have made a deep impression on most of his men who had only joined his army on the hope of easy pickings and a good life without having to work for it.

'Very well,' Jaxaal replied, I shall return to my army. Within the hour we will proceed to remove you from the hill you occupy and deal with you as the law demands.' With that he turned Sarina and he and Milden galloped from the field and climbed up to the ridge where his army waited, now in clear view of the enemy.

Once Jaxaal was back at his command post he satisfied himself that all the government men were ready and stood in his stirrups with his sword raised above his head. As he did so the sun that had been steadily rising appeared above the tree line away to his left bathing him and his army in bright spring sunshine. He swirled his shining sword above his head a couple of times and then pointed it ahead of him at the enemy. Immediately a bugle sounded, and the men lifted their shields and prepared to advance. The orders were shouted and with the Norland Division in the centre the infantry section of the army advanced.

Rydall had told Jaxaal about the impression that the Red Cannis brigands had made when they entered Cordale Complex and the lord been very impressed by it. The steady deliberate march, punctuated with the rhythmic thump as they had struck their pikes on the road had made a lasting impression on all who heard it. Jaxaal had adopted this for his own army although the way of producing the sound had to be changed, the soft turf over which the army marched would muffle any strike made with the pike ends. Instead they had trained to clash their shields and their pike shafts together on every fourth step.

This produced an eerie and ominous accompaniment to their approach. The effect was heightened by the tight formation that the government troops maintained as they approached. They reached the valley floor and began the approach across the level surface where the last of the morning mist was swirling around their feet and then disappearing. When they had lined up on the ridge they had assumed positions that were spaced around the arch of the semi-circular valley. Now as they approached the hill where the rebels stood awaiting them the five divisions were drawn together. The men facing them sensed that when they got to them there would be no gaps in the line. This was a menacing factor which simply added to the fear that slowly grew among the rebels.

Natheal sensed the rising panic among his men, he felt it himself, and realised he needed to do something and quickly. He leapt to his feet.

'Men,' he called straining to make himself heard above the almost overwhelming onslaught to the mind and ears that the approaching troops were creating, 'we know they can march in pretty lines. We'll soon see if they can die in them as well.'

This didn't immediately generate the reaction he had hoped, just a few cheers, so he looked at the acolytes standing behind him and fervently waved his hands at them. Fortunately, one realised his leader's desperation and began to chant, 'Lather, Lather.' This was quickly picked up those around him and did spread, eventually, to most of the rebel troops.

This did nothing to deter the advancing government troops who started the climb up the slope of the rebel's hill without slowing their progress. They just kept coming. When they were close enough that their pike heads were almost touching the rebel shields the order, 'Halt,' was called and they stopped. It had been Commander Milden Northwood who had developed the strategy that the troops were about to employ. He had realised that they needed to do more than simply walk up to their opponents and thrust their pikes at their shield wall, they needed an advantage.

The first order was then followed by, 'prepare to engage,' and several things happened at the same time. The first rank raised their pikes above their heads and levelled them at head height. At the same time the second rank lowered their pikes to the right of the men in front of them and notched them in the slots that had been cut in the side of the shields. They then pushed their pikes forward so that they protruded well beyond the shields. The third rank took a step back and then lowered the points of their pikes until the almost touched the ground and moved them forward until they were level with the bottom of the front row's shields.

When this arrangement had been achieved the order, 'advance,' was shouted and the whole army took a step forward. They took another pace and many of the protruding pikes touched the enemy shields. This was the signal for the second rank to pull back their pikes and then ram them forward, hoping to find a gap in the enemy shield wall. At the same time the front-rank soldiers could pick their targets and thrust their pikes forward at the exposed heads of the enemy. While the front two ranks were thus employed the third rank thrust their sharpened pikes forward at mid-calf height causing a lot of injuries and, more importantly, a lot of panic as the enemy front rank found themselves attacked at three levels. In most cases they tried to step back out of the way of the onslaught but couldn't because of the crush of men behind them; their superior numbers were actually proving a disadvantage.

The 'hand-to-hand' conflict lasted for a count of perhaps twenty or so before the order to retreat was given. The government's third rank, rapidly withdrew their pikes and then turned and ran back down the hill. Once they had removed themselves, the second rank also withdrew their pikes from protruding through the front rank's shields and once free, they too turned and ran after the third rank. The front rank then stepped backwards in line and in step so that their shield wall was maintained intact and their pikes were still held menacingly towards the enemy ranks.

For the most part the rebels could not follow their retreating enemy because so many of them were nursing wounds, quite a few to the legs of the front rank. Quite a number were dead or severely wounded and lay where they had fallen. They were also under orders from their leader to stay in their formation on the top of their hill. The rebel ranks behind them saw the government troops retreating and began shouting and jeering.

Once the retreating front rank commanders were sure they were not going to be followed they issued orders to their men and they too turned and followed their compatriots to the valley floor where to the rebel's surprise, they turned and reformed their lines. Once all three ranks were back in formation they ominously just stood in silence that seemed almost louder than the rebels' shouts. They then began the rhythmic beating of their pikes against their shields and the sinister sound soon silenced the rebels. Another shouted order started the tight formations to again advance up the hill.

'Here they come again!' several of the rebels shouted, some in terror. Relentlessly the formations approached, and the mesmerising sound of the beats just added to the fear the approach engendered which was heightened by the fact that now the rebels knew what to expect. The attack followed the same pattern as the first although the actual hand to hand conflict appeared to go on a lot longer. To the rebel front ranks the attack seemed to last a life time; for many it was the end of it.

Away on the hill side opposite Jaxaal and his senior officers watched with grim satisfaction as the tactics they had devised and the training they had made their men undertake bore the fruits of success. At several points along its length the government army was making slow but definite inroads into the rebel ranks. Jaxaal had been alive to the possibility that his smaller force might easily be outflanked and had given orders for Nelden's lancers to be ready to attack and stop any such move that the rebels might make.

The rebels were suffering terribly in terms of losses and their dead and wounded lay strewn along the line they had tried to hold. The government army's tactics had limited their causalities dramatically but there were some. Where possible the wounded men were passed back to the rear of the attacking ranks and several were carried on make shift stretchers made out of broken pike shafts. A cry went up from the watchers on the hillside opposite the battle as a man in the Dresham black and white colours was seen to lead the attack on their section of the enemy lines and receive a pike shaft wound to the stomach. Janilla and Geldren watched anxiously as the wounded were brought down the rebel's hill and across the valley and up to the medical centre they had established based on the wagon they had equipped.

Janilla saw that Geldren was in a bit of a state as she prepared bandages and antiseptic washes.

'My dear,' Janilla asked, 'what's wrong?'

'This is a terrible thing, this battle,' Geldren wailed, letting her tense emotions break.

'Yes, I know,' Janilla told her as she gave her young cousin a hug, 'but we knew it would be. We are healers and our job is to tend to the men we can help and ease the suffering of those we can't.'

'But I think Sorjohn has just been hurt if not killed,' Geldren wailed , the tears streaming down her face, 'he was the man leading that second Dresham attack.'

'The one who got injured?' Janilla asked and both women stopped their preparations and looked at the scene laid out below them.

'There he is,' Janilla pointed out as a stretcher was seen leaving the valley floor and being carried up towards them; it's occupant wearing the black and white chequered livery of the House of Dresham. What Geldren saw was the red blotch that was spreading across his lower abdomen.

'I know you both have a fondness for each other,' Janilla said with her arms around the younger woman's shoulders, 'has it gone beyond that?'

'We have an understanding,' Geldren confessed, 'the night before we left Swenmore, Sorjohn and I were able to spend some time together, while everyone was celebrating Madge and Bry's wedding. We got very intimate.'

'You don't mean?' Janilla asked, letting the question hang in the air.

'Oh no!' Geldren exclaimed, 'although we did kiss and cuddle a lot once we were alone. No, I mean we've made promises to each other. We want to be married as soon as I've reached my majority next turn.'

'Oh, my dear, I am delighted for you,' Janilla told her, 'although I am not surprised. I think I am picking up some of Aunt Arianne's abilities to detect that sort of thing going on.'

'But now he has been injured and may be dead or dying for all I know,' Geldren wailed, collapsing in a heap.

'Well we will know as soon as he is brought here to us,' Janilla told her, realising that a business-like efficiency would be the best way to get Geldren thinking and acting like the healer she needed to be. The first few causalities arrived at their temporary medical centre calling for their attention and their expertise kicked in so they missed seeing the way the battle proceeded.

Jaxaal gave the orders and the second wave of attacks was called off.

'Commander Milden, do you think the next attack will be the one to attempt our planned rout or should we make one more serious attack before we try it?'

'I think it may be time, My Lord. After all, if they don't take the bait the first time we can reform the attacks and try again.'

'I agree,' Jaxaal told him and began issuing orders. The prearranged signals were sent and Neldon's brigade of lancers split into two groups and stealthily positioned themselves at either extreme of the battlefield. Jaxaal was able to speak directly to Bry as he was in the centre of his brigade of Archers and placed just below Jaxaal's command post. Bry passed on the orders to his men and the Archers spread themselves along the curved ridge that ran around the slope they occupied.

As the section that Madge was leading arrived at their allotted position a young Archer asked her a question.

'Excuse me Marm, but I've never fired at a target more than fifty paces away, I don't know how to aim at anything as far as the bottom of that hill opposite.'

'Well, just keep an eye on me,' Madge told him, 'your bow looks to be about the same power as mine, watch the angle I hold my bow and try to match it.' All the Archers began to prepare their bows and arrange their supply of tipped arrows by sticking them in the turf at their feet where they could easily get at them in the heat of battle.

When he was satisfied that all was in place for the next phase of the battle, Jaxaal gave the order for the pike-men to attack again. The five sections again reformed their clinically exact alignments and again began the intimidating sound barrage as they moved forward. Up on the hill the rebels were resigned to the onslaught that they knew was coming their way.

'Our front ranks are standing on the dead and wounded,' Jorgraan told his commander in chief.

'Well tell them to push their bodies out in front of the lines,' Natheal told him, at a loss to know how to deal with the tactics the government troops were employing. He was beginning to think that Pardrea's idea of simply attacking on a broad front might be the best option. This standing and letting the enemy come and decimate their front ranks was much costlier in terms of men and of moral than he had expected. He was wavering and knew that that was not the way of a good or successful army commander.

The government troops were relentless in their approach and seemed not at all inconvenienced by the bodies strewn in their way. They reached the rebels line and engaged it as before but with perhaps even more venom. The rebel lines gave way and retreated slightly but eventually held as the press of men behind them prevented any further retreat.

This impasse seemed to last forever and might have done but for a shrill warbling whistle that rang out. The noise confused the rebels, they had no idea what it signified but the government troops did, they turned and ran. They ran for all they were worth back down the hill they had already climbed three times and across the valley and into the bushes at the foot of the opposite hill. Even the front rank ran and they too kept running, not stopping where they had on the previous two occasions to reform their attack formations.

The rebels suddenly found that they were no longer being pushed back and fell forward over the dead at their feet. The release of pressure meant that the men behind the front ranks were able to take a step forward. This became two and then three and then, as cries of, 'they are running,' rang out became a charge down the hill in pursuit of the fleeing government men.

Bry was waiting for this charge and held his nerve until most of the rebel force were actually on the level floor of the valley. He then ordered 'Fire,' and all the Archers let loose their arrows. As arranged they all immediately reloaded and fired again while their first arrows were still in the air. They repeated this firing five or six times at the approaching hordes.

Chapter 36

On top of his hill Natheal was at first beside himself with rage that his orders to stand firm had been ignored but then he too got caught by the euphoria that the apparent capitulation of the enemy produced and mounting his kertle, he drew his sword and waving it over his head, led the men who remained on the hill top in a charge after their compatriots.

The effect of the arrow barrage was devastating, the rebels were taken completely by surprise and at first didn't realise what was happening; men were falling all around them and for the most part they didn't see the incoming projectiles. But the charge didn't stop completely as it crossed the valley floor Bry realised that they were getting close to the men who were hiding in the bushes at the foot of their hill. He ordered the Archers to pick their targets which changed their method of attack; instead of simply letting off a barrage all at once, each man fired on his own initiative at specific targets.

This had the immediate effect of singling out the leading attackers who fell with arrows in their chests and midriffs. Up on her ridge Madge was not comfortable at this development although she had known it would come. Firing blindly up in the air there was no responsibility, well, little, for where the arrow landed; now she had to take full blame of where her arrows went and who they hit. She wouldn't shirk from the duty this imposed; the battle had become almost personal. During the initial attacks it had been a distant thing happening to others away on the hill opposite, now she was directly involved. Even more harrowing was the prospect that if they failed to stop the onslaught she and her fellow Archers could be directly attacked.

She made herself select a target and purposefully aimed at the man's upper leg. She repeated this tactic and several men went down. She braced herself as she realised the agony her arrows had inflicted. But the dread of what might happen if they were not stopped hardened her resolve. Later she would recall and for turns be haunted by flash backs of her victims suffering, but for now, there was work to be done.

The Archer proved to be as devastatingly effective as Jaxaal had believed they would be; the experience of the apprentice smiths with their blow pipes against the Red Cannis had given him an insight and sown a seed that had now born fruit. It was time to see if the other new development could play a significant part in the battle. Jaxaal gave the pre-arrange signal and Neldon's lancers made their move, galloping out of their places of concealment and charging up and around the rebels' hill. As the two mounted groups joined up on the far side of the hill they turned and climbed to the top bursting over the summit and appearing to those on the far side of the valley. The sight of the armed men on kertle back proved as big a deterrent as Neldon had promised they would be and the rebels who had remained on the hill now desperately joined the charge down to the valley floor.

The advance of the rebels across the valley was halted and they now crouched down and those who had them hid behind their shields as the deadly arrows continued to rain down on them. The government pike-men who had apparently fled in terror now emerged from concealment in the bushes and formed a ring of shields around the rebels cowering on the valley floor. Natheal reached the bulk of his men and tried to rally them into some kind of formation; he still hadn't realised or accepted that the battle was effectively over.

Jaxaal saw him and called to Bry who was positioned in the centre of his ring of Archers, 'Bry see if you can wound Lather, but I want him alive.'

Bry waved an acknowledgement and notched yet another arrow onto his bowstring. He took careful aim and fired, hitting his target in the upper thigh. Natheal at first just stared at the shaft that had suddenly appeared sticking out of his leg but then grabbed his leg around the arrow as the pain shot through him. He leant forward unable to control his body position and slowly fell to the ground, writhing in agony.

Madge had also seen Natheal go down and looked for his sister. She finally picked her out, some way away still trying to rally support by waving her sword manically above her head. Suddenly Madge was refilled with her hatred for the woman and, with an icy calm, notched another arrow and took careful aim at her previous tormentor. The arrow flew straight and true and hit Pardrea in the upper thigh. Madge watched as the stricken woman sank to the ground. The fall of their leader and his sister had not gone unnoticed by a lot of the rebel troops and shouts of 'it's all over!' and 'we surrender,' rang out.

Without waiting for Jaxaal's order, which the leader was about to issue, Bry called a ceasefire. The arrow bombardment ended and most of the Archers came forward to the edge of their ridge with arrows notched on their strings, alive for any untoward hostile activity amongst the rebels.

Jaxaal then spurred Sarina to the edge of the ridge from which they had watched the battle unfold and stood in his stirrups and called in a loud clear voice. 'Men of the rebel army, you are now defeated. Lay down your arms and surrender to my wishes and you will not die here on this bloody field. Resist and you will be shot and left here to die in agony.' He didn't realise at the time that the Archers had used up virtually all their arrows; most stood with their last shaft notched on their bowstrings.

Jaxaal made a memorable picture at that moment and turns later the minstrels would conjure up that image as they related the end of the Lather uprising.

There were enough men writhing on the floor to strike a chilling terror into everyone who heard Jaxaal's words.

'What's going to happen to us?' a rebel voice asked.

'Yeah, if we surrender, will you let us leave here and go home, like you said earlier?' another called.

'Oh no!' Jaxaal called, the anger evident in his voice, 'that was before any Famerian blood had been spilled. Now you will all face the justice of the Famerian courts in Medland where you will be taken. For now, those of you that can, stand up and leave all your weapons on the ground and put your hands behind your heads. You will be bound and tied together ready for the march north.'

Jaxaal looked across to where Milden Northwood sat on his kertle surveying the human desolation spread out on the valley floor.

'Commander Northwood, I hesitate to put yet more burdens on you and you guardians but how can we extricate these wretches from this place and stop them just running off?'

'Well, My Lord, it will take virtually the whole of our army to guard them on the road from here to Medland. We've reduced their numbers by a significant proportion but they still out number us by several to one.'

'Can it be done?' Jaxaal asked, 'Do we need to hold trials here to sort out the leaders and let the others go?' Jaxaal asked, once Milden had got close enough for them to have a quiet word without shouting to each other.

'Holding field trials might create more problems than it would solve,' Milden concluded, rapidly thinking through what the essentials were, 'I'm afraid you cannot stand down your army at this point, if that is what you were hoping.'

'Right,' Jaxaal decided, 'can I leave you to organise the guarding of the prisoners and the deployment of our troops now we seem to have won the battle.'

Receiving Milford's rueful agreement Jaxaal headed Sarina up the hill towards the medical encampment that his wife and cousin had established. The medical centre was overflowing with activity as wounded men were being brought in or dragging themselves there. Janilla and Geldren were not alone, thankfully, they had enlisted the help of as many women as they could back in Swenmore and these recruits were busily cleaning and dressing wounds. These helpers included Katrinna Dresham, Festera Swenland and Shanda Brackenstedd; the young noble women had leapt at the chance of doing something to help. The older Nobel Ladies, Lady Dresham and Lady Launceston had declined to accompany the army in that role but were busily preparing for the influx of wounded men that Janilla had correctly surmised would descend on Swenmore when the battle was over. Janilla and Geldren were acting as senior medical staff and their training under Lady Arianne was standing them in good stead. They moved methodically through the line of wounded men assessing the needs of each one and issuing instructions to the attendants.

When Sorjohn Dresham was brought in both Katrinna and Geldren went to attend to him. He was conscious but in a lot of pain. With tears in her eyes, Geldren poured out a dose of a numb-root based potion and got him to drink it. This immediately eased his suffering a great deal although he was obviously still in pain. Gently the two noble women removed his outer garments and inspected the wound in his side. Both girls were shaking as they began to clean the injury and Janilla came and told them both to go and deal with other patients, they were both too emotionally involved with Sorjohn to make rational and clear decisions, she told them. She then inspected the wound and told the Lord that he was extremely lucky.

'That pike head has punctured your stomach wall and torn it along a bit but has not actually hit any internal organs. It appears to have torn or cut the stomach wall for some distance around your side. Did you turn to your right as the pike hit you?'

Sorjohn nodded. 'You may think I'm lucky,' he winced, 'but my side is telling me something else.'

'Oh, that will be hurting you a lot, I appreciate that, and the worse news is that it will take a long time for that wound to heal. We need to clean it thoroughly and then stitch it up. You will need to have a lot of careful nursing and there is a high risk of infection. That is more dangerous than the actual wound.'

'Is there any good news?' Sorjohn asked with a wry grin, despite the pain he was in.

'Well I imagine that my cousin is going to make sure you are going to get the best care it is possible to give you.'

'Oh, you will,' Geldren said as she ran and embraced the young lord.   .

'So that's how things lie is it?' Katrinna said with a secret smile at Janilla, 'I wondered where my brother had disappeared to, the night before we left Swenmore. I did notice that Lady Geldren was also missing at the same time.'

'I think they are very well suited,' Janilla said as she went and extricated the invalid from her cousin's embrace.

'Now we need to sedate the poor man, so I can clean that wound inside and out and then practice my needle work on him. I hope I brought enough thread and a big enough needle.' She said with a wicked wink at Katrinna.

Lady Katrinna Dresham was duly impressed at the business-like way Janilla set about operating on her brother. He was given another dose of numb-root potion and this seemed to put him to sleep while he was treated. The work in the medical centre seemed to go for a long time and Janilla looked out of the tent only to see that the queue of patients waiting treatment stretched down the hill and on to the valley floor. She wiped her brow on her sleeve, gritted her teeth and carried on. Once Sorjohn had been sewn up he had been put to recover in the back of the wagon and Geldren had torn herself away from him and threw herself into the endless work of administering first aid to the wounded.

Katrinna quickly learnt what the trained women were doing and made herself as useful as she could. Working beside Geldren she had an opportunity to study the woman that had captured her brother's affection. She liked what she saw, and a mutual respect grew between the pair. Geldren was well aware that many women would have shrunk from the gory and intimate jobs they were called upon to do but Katrinna braced herself and simply got on with what was required.

Jaxaal returned carrying a jug of kandrel and made his wife and cousin take a break from their ministrations. He sat with Janilla to make sure she did actually get a rest and stopped her simply taking a mouthful of the hot beverage and carrying on.

'Oh, Jaxaal this war business is awful, I never imagined it would be this bad,' Janilla told him with a sob.

'Me neither,' Jaxaal replied, putting a comforting arm around her shoulder, 'I tried to picture what it was going to be like, but I came nowhere near. The minstrels' songs tell of the glories of war. I've not seen any today. I've seen some very brave men and others who didn't know they were brave doing some very courageous things. But the truth is War is a terrible gory travesty, I hope I never have to go to lead men into battle again. That field down there is strewn with dead and dying men who just a few hours ago had dreams of some glorious future, all they have found is pain and suffering.' He shifted his position and pointed to the hillside opposite.

'I walked that hill a short while ago, there are men with some terrible wounds lying there with their guts hanging out.'

'Are there any still living injured men down are there?' Janilla ask as she started to rise, 'I can't sit here and let injured men suffer in pain.'

'No,' Jaxaal told her as he pulled back down on the seat, 'I had all those still alive brought here. That's where the main pike injuries occurred. The amazing thing is virtually all the dead are rebels; the government army seem to have lost very few men. The training the guardians made the troops under go has paid real dividends. As I walked across that hill I found a rebel soldier going around, inspecting the dead and wounded. He was in a terrible state and kept pleading to Alphos for forgiveness; he was seeking out those of his compatriots that were mortally wounded and putting them out of their misery. He saw me and fell to his knees, offered me his sword and asked me to execute him as he had committed murder.'

'What did you do,' Janilla asked.

'I took his sword and broke it on the ground then told him he had done his best for his comrades and to go and join the rest of the surrendered men. Poor fellow, he may never recover from the horrors he's seen today.'

'Will you, my love?' Janilla asked as she stroked his matted hair out of his eyes

'Who knows, I hope never to see a hillside so covered in blood again. Look you can see a dark band of discoloured grass running around the hill where the rebels made their stand. We might have even won just using our trained pike-men, but the Archers were the deciding factor. All the bodies on the valley floor have arrow wounds.

The two sat there comforting each other for a while until the pressure of things they both had to do called them both away.

By mid-afternoon the medical team were still facing an enormous workload when the Lather twins were brought in within a few minutes of each other.

Natheal was mouthing off at everyone: the government troops for injuring him, his own men for letting him down and the medical staff for letting him suffer. Janilla immediately made him drink a draft that effectively knocked him out.

'That's better!' she said and then explained to Katrinna that she shouldn't have administered the drug without due cause but decided that the stress he was causing to all around him was justification enough. His sister was less noisy but even more bitter in her condemnation of everyone around her.

Madge and Bry both arrived a short while later although independently, wanting to know the condition of the one target they knew they could identify.

Geldren did the initial assessment of Pardrea's condition and decided that the arrow head in her thigh needed to be removed as soon as possible. She offered the rebel a draft that would dull the pain sufficiently for the wound to be attended to, but it was rejected with a sneer.

'As you wish,' Geldren told her, 'but I won't treat you without you having had either a pain killer or you being held down by some strong men. It's your choice.'

'And just who are you anyway?' Pardrea snapped back.

'I am Lady Geldren Ellward of the House of Ellward,' Geldren told her, 'and I don't care if you live or die but die is certainly what you will do if that arrow doesn't come out and soon.'

'Do you need some help Lady Geldren?' Madge asked as she came and stood on the other side Pardrea's bed.

'You, Madge Falleen!' Pardrea exclaimed in disgust as she saw who it was who had joined them.

'Ah, thank you Lady Maglen,' Geldren answered, 'yes I may need you to hold her down while I twist this arrow head out of her leg.'

'Lady Maglen! Then I was right, you had been planted in amongst the workers back at Under Childe,' Pardrea claimed in triumph despite her pain.

'That's where you are wrong,' Madge told her, 'when we met back on the road from Upper Childe I was simply a lonely girl on her way to the hiring fairs south of the Childe Mountains, in desperate need of a friend and the means to make a living. Instead I met you and ended up abused, mistrusted and in the gutter in Under Childe. Yes, Lady Geldren I will be delighted to help you restrain this one.'

'So just who are you, were you?' Pardrea asked suddenly mollified and using a much quieter voice.

'I was Lady Maglen Launceston of the House of Launceston,' Madge told her, also dropping her voice so only Pardrea and Geldren could hear her, 'I had run away from my home and family to avoid a forced marriage. I am now Lady Maglen Doltaary, Quintrell of The House of Swenland.'

'Well now we have all been introduced,' Geldren interjected, can we get on and deal with this patient's injury. Ideally I need to know if this arrow head has barbs or has a straight point.'

'Well that's easy,' Madge told them, 'I only ever used straight pointed arrows. I thought the barbed ones might not fly so straight.'

'You shot me!' Pardrea exclaimed her eyes flashing with venom.

'Be thankful I relented and aimed for your legs and not your heart, which was my first choice of target' Madge told her, 'so you can pull that out without doing any further damage, Geldren.'

'Well we had better break the shaft and get her clothes off her,' Geldren decided.

'Oh no, that won't be necessary,' Madge retorted, 'I'll pull it out as it is, there's no point in breaking a perfectly good arrow.'

'Not without giving her some painkilling drugs,' Geldren insisted.

'Oh, don't bother,' Pardrea snapped back, bravado taking over from common sense, 'I can take it.'

'Are you sure?' Madge asked, impressed by the rebel's bravery.

'Yes, do it,' Pardrea hissed through gritted teeth. As she took hold of the arrow shaft Madge quailed at the thought of what she was about to inflict.

'Go on do it,' Pardrea pleaded, 'it's got to come out and I'd rather you did it quickly than someone else do it slowly. Madge realised that Pardrea was serious and with no further ado, grabbed the arrow shaft and pulled it straight out. Pardrea screamed at the sudden pain and grabbed Madge in a tight embrace as the pain shook through her. Madge clung onto her in return and comforted her as the spasms subsided. Geldren then did get Pardrea to drink a potion which eased her into a sleep.

Bry was an interested bystander as Janilla dealt with Natheal's wound. Unlike Madge, he had used a barbed arrow when he fired at the rebel leader and this gave Janilla a quandary to solve. Having established what she was dealing with, she had to decide whether to cut it out or push it through. She asked Bry how long the shaft would be so that she could determine how deep the head was in Natheal's leg. The answer made her realise that the best solution was to push it through. She paled at the thought of having to do this. Bry understood her reticence and offered to provide the force if she would tell him what she wanted him to do.

Janilla inspected the wound again and satisfied herself that no major ligaments or veins were in the arrow heads path. She then raised Natheal's knee so that the arrow had a clear path out and braced herself, holding the leg firm. She nodded at Bry who also put his arm around Natheal's leg to give himself some purchase and pushed hard and surely so that the arrow head came cleanly through the skin of the leg on the other side. Bry then use a pair of snips, usually used on metal to cut off the tail part of the arrow. He then grabbed the protruding barbed head and pulled what was left of the shaft through. Natheal was unconscious as this was done but his body did react to the pain it had suffered, and he moaned before relaxing back on the cot where he lay. Janilla then set about cleaning both entry and exit wounds and decided that both needed her needle work to close the gaping holes in the skin.

They worked on all through the afternoon, both Bry and Madge staying to help as best they could. An hour or two after he arrived

Bry was called away to take part in the meeting Jaxaal had called to arrange what they were going to do next. After a lot of discussions where all the options were explored they finally agreed that all the rebels would be tied together with knotted ropes so that they could walk in three columns. This would allow the smaller government force to march on both sides of the prisoners to prevent any chance of escape.

Commander Northwood and his guardian officers took charge of the process, the rest of the army providing the manpower. It was late afternoon as the army and their prisoners began the slow march back to Swenmore and Milden Northwood was busy sending message ahead of them to get things prepared for their arrival. This mainly meant the provision of food and shelter for which hiring fair marquees would have to suffice. The returning column reached the town in the afternoon of the following day and the town's folk had made hurried preparations for the victorious armies return.

The town dignitaries were somewhat bemused by the lack of enthusiasm to celebrate the triumph the victors had won but the need to guard their prisoners was an impediment to any festivity. The real reason was the horror of warfare had come as a major shock to everyone who had participated. There had not been a battle on Fameral soil in living memory; the horror of this one would be remembered for generations.

It took several velds for the prisoners to be escorted all the way to Medland where they were incarcerated in a disused warehouse that had been quickly converted into a secure prison.

The five ruling lords then found themselves forced to sit in judgement as the highest legislature in the land. They quickly decided that they would impose a punishment of forced labour on most of the rebels. This solved the problem of finding sufficient labour to finish the harvesting that had to be done, (and also avoided having to pay to house and feed the prisoners at government expense.)

Since Natheal Lather had stripped many farms and farming communities of their able-bodied men to fill his rebel army the arable farmers were desperate for manpower to complete the planting that was required. In most cases this meant that the men worked at what they normally did without pay. Lords Launceston and Dresham chuckled that it was fitting punishment for those who had started all the trouble over pay rates.

It was Jaxaal who pointed out that depriving the men of their livelihood at a time when many of them needed to earn the money to carry them through the non-productive batherns would be simply creating more resentment that could overspill into more trouble in the future.

'Natheal Lather rose to power because some greedy farmers forced wages down below the level that enabled the common workers to live. We mustn't make the same mistakes again. I know it is tempting to punish the rebels as hard as we can, but I think we need to think through the consequences of our decisions before we enforce them. I know some of you would like to see Lather and his sister hung for their crimes but think about it my lords. Creating a couple of martyrs is not going to help us heal the wounds that have rent this nation. We might well let it be known that hanging them is an option we are actively considering but then appear to be magnanimous and commute their sentence to life imprisonment.

The house where my father was incarcerated all those turns might be adapted for that purpose.'

The lords saw the wisdom of Jaxaal's thinking and agreed to the proposals. It was Darval Ellward who suggested that the farmers might be required to pay the conscripted labour a basic wage for their work and this was readily agreed. In a surprisingly short space of time the legal requirements were handled, and the makeshift prison emptied as the inmates were marched off to the places they were going to work out their sentence. For the most part they were happy with this believing that they had got away lightly. Natheal and Pardrea Lather were duly chastened by the prospect of a public hanging and accepted their life imprisonment as a better option.

Jorgraan, the former guardian officer who had thrown his lot in with Lather was also condemned to life imprisonment and secretly felt greatly relieved at that sentence; it was he who had actually carried out Natheal's orders to hang the ring leaders who had instigated the looting of the villages south west of Swenmore. There were a few of the rebels who were identified as having played a major role in the uprising and they were tried, found guilty and sentenced to a prison terms ranging from one to three turns.

Jorgraan did, however, put his intimate knowledge of Guardian procedures to his own use and was able to escape when he was left guarded by a young trainee. The repercussions for that trainee and his immediate superior were duly severe but for Jorgraan it meant he was able to simply disappear into the lower sections of Fameral society where he put his undoubted talents to various nefarious uses.

Chapter 37

A veld and a half after the battle Bry and Madge along with Rydall and Shanda managed to return to High Tor, the Doltarrys to collect the possession they had left there and the Brackenstedds to resume their ownership of the Fifth. Word of all the happenings had been sent to High Tor and the Brinkles had become aware of the change in status of their formal friends. The first meeting when the travelling party arrive at the farm was more than a little strained.

As Madge dismounted from Tilda she looked around and was able to hand the reins to a stable lad who had appeared to deal with the kertles. She then saw Brindle and Shendaar coming out of the Main House and started up the path to greet her old friends. Madge was a little taken aback by the way Shendaar was looking at her feet and holding on tightly to Twillen's hand. Before she reached them, the pair stopped and Shendaar dropped a curtsy and whispered something to her young daughter who then also made a fair attempt at a bob. Madge was tempted to laugh until she saw the apprehensive look on Shendaar's face.

'Hello, you two,' Madge said to them.

'Hello Madge,' Twillen replied with a small smile.

'Twillen!' Shendaar exclaimed, 'I told you that if you speak at all you are to call her Milady.'

'No, she isn't,' Madge replied and immediately stepped forward and scooped up the young girl as she had often done before and set her to ride on her hip, 'when we are in company you may, perhaps, call me 'milady' but when we are alone I shall be very upset if you call me anything but 'Madge.' Madge then turned to the young girl's mother and said, 'Shendaar, that goes for you to. You are one of my best friends. You and Brindle were both there for me at an important time in my life and the friendship we shared then I hope will continue.

'Is your name really Maglen, I mean Lady Maglen?' Twillen asked, embolden by the way Madge had lifted her up and was holding her in a comforting cuddle.

'Yes, it is,' Madge told the young girl as she buried her nose in the young girl's curls, 'but I may well be Lady Maglen Doltaary or Quintrell Doltaary to the rest of the world but to you I am, and always will be Madge. I will be honoured if you decide to call me Aunty Madge.'

'And I am still Bry, but I'd like you both to call me Uncle Bry,' Bry said as he joined his wife before stooping down and swinging Jallden Brinkle up onto his shoulders where the young lad gave a whoop of delight. 'We are both very grateful for the friendship you two shared with us when we were simple travellers on the road.' Bry told Brindle and Shendaar, 'but now our fortunes have changed for the better as far as I am concerned, yours have as well. I think you are both very well set here at High Tor with the Brackenstedds in charge but if for any reason you want to find a position at some other fifth then you will always have one with us, wherever we decide to be based.

It was over an alphen after the battle that Lady Launceston got her wish that they held a ball at Launceston Hall to celebrate the marriage of Madge and Bry. It was slightly subdued affair: people were still in a state of shock after the civil war that had shaken the whole of Fameral, but every house family was there. Madge was still dusky skinned, but the colour was beginning to fade, and her hair was now definitely two toned as the brown grew out. To please her father, she wore her wig at the ball and lightened her skin colour, although not totally returning it to her former colouration; she had grown to like the face that stared at her out of her mirror.

Sorjohn Dresham attended the ball although he was confined to a wheeled chair, on Lady Arianne's orders; Geldren Ellward made sure that he obeyed her instructions and was beginning to rule the southern lord with a firm but sure hand. Close observers recognised that there was a lot of fun about the couple's relationship and Sorjohn was in no way allowing himself to be henpecked. He had been moved, gingerly from Swenmore up to hospital in Medland and had progressed well enough to be released to convalesce at Norland Castle, once he was passed the danger of infection setting in.

Since her brother was there, Katrinna Dresham used that as an excuse to go and keep him company; in fact, she had an interest in studying under Lady Arianne and had joined her growing college of noble students.

As Bry and Madge were recovering from the stress of their wedding ball they started discussing where they would now live. Bry was now a Quintrall of The House of Swenland and as such had duties down at Swenland Grange. He also had a position to fulfil at High Tor Farm, taking charge of the stud and stables there if he so wished. Immediately after the ball Uster Oostedd had requested a meeting and explained that he was now very busy establishing a kertle breeding programme at Castle Norland and would like to explore the possibility of merging the programmes of the three studs; Norland, Swenland and High Tor to get the best possible results from the available kertle breeding pool.

'I think you are going to be a very busy man,' Madge told Bry, 'and we're going to spend a lot of time travelling. I'm sure that Rufran and Tilda will enjoy being so much with us, but we may decide to do most of our travelling by coach.'

'Well, that's a nice idea,' Bry agreed, 'but coaches and the kertles and men they entail to run them cost a lot of money.'

'Oh, don't be silly Bry,' Madge laughed, 'you are now a very wealthy man and, I might point out, you are married to a very wealthy woman; I have my own private fortune my father has just informed me. I came into it on our marriage.'

'But I can't live off you!' Bry exclaimed.

'As I said,' Madge retorted, 'you won't have to, you effectively own two fifths. And any way, if you get short of cash you can always enter a few Archery Competitions! I intend to,' she added with a laugh.

'But just where shall we live, you and I?' he asked, 'we need to make some decisions.'

'Well we will have to have accommodation at High Tor Farm and at Swenland Grange,' Madge replied, 'and I've told my parents that I want my suite here at Launceston Hall kept for us. But our home, our real home where you and I can disappear and forget the world will have to be Cannis Glade in the Misle Forest.'

'That's just what I was hoping you would say,' he replied, 'but I suggest that we up-grade the accommodation and actually build a single storey building that will merge into the woodland.'

'Oh yes!' Madge exclaimed delightedly, and they spent the next few hours going over what would suit them both. They ended with a copious number of plans sketched on parchment and a joyous sense that life was just going to get better.

THE END, so far.

Bob Hambleton

"Sarina's" saga will continue with "Sarina's Season."

About the Author

Bob Hambleton is a writer of unusual novels and short stories. He draws on a vast range of experience gained through an eventful life to colour and populate his writing.

Bob started his working life with a five-year craft apprenticeship in scientific instrument making. He was then recruited into the method study department which led to a series of appointments in project and production management. He gained a post graduate degree in Management Science at Cranfield University.

Working for part of the Mars Group he won a major national award and his paper on this work was awarded the Operational Research Society President's medal as the best paper of the year. This in turn led to his gaining a position as the manager of the UK Management Science group with the Digital Equipment Corporation computer company.

Throughout this time, he also developed his interest in folk music becoming a (fairly) well-known singer-songwriter as well as an organiser of folk music events.

His life took a twist when he was diagnosed with multiple sclerosis. He took early retirement on health grounds and developed his creative side through his writing, and his lifelong love of folk music. He had the honour, as a musician with Dorset Triumph Folk Dancers, of representing the UK in both World and European Folklore festivals.

He now lives happily in Scotland with his second wife and is dedicating his time to writing 'The Sarina' series and other novels as well as a number of short stories. His writing objective is to create the sort of novels and stories that he likes to read in the hope that others will as well.